NOBLE NORFLEET

BOOKS BY

REYNOLDS PRICE

NOBLE NORFLEET 2002

FEASTING THE HEART 2000

A PERFECT FRIEND 2000

LETTER TO A MAN IN THE FIRE 1999

LEARNING A TRADE 1998

ROXANNA SLADE 1998

THE COLLECTED POEMS 1997

THREE GOSPELS 1996

THE PROMISE OF REST 1995

A WHOLE NEW LIFE 1994

THE COLLECTED STORIES 1993

FULL MOON 1993

BLUE CALHOUN 1992

THE FORESEEABLE FUTURE 1991

NEW MUSIC 1990

THE USE OF FIRE 1990

THE TONGUES OF ANGELS 1990

CLEAR PICTURES 1989

GOOD HEARTS 1988

A COMMON ROOM 1987

THE LAWS OF ICE 1986

KATE VAIDEN 1986

PRIVATE CONTENTMENT 1984

VITAL PROVISIONS 1982

THE SOURCE OF LIGHT 1981

A PALPABLE GOD 1978

EARLY DARK 1977

THE SURFACE OF EARTH 1975

THINGS THEMSELVES 1972

PERMANENT ERRORS 1970

LOVE AND WORK 1968

A GENEROUS MAN 1966

THE NAMES AND FACES OF HEROES 1963

A LONG AND HAPPY LIFE 1962

REYNOLDS PRICE

NOBLE NORFLEET

SCRIBNER

NEW YORK LONDON TORONTO SYDNEY SINGAPORE

SCRIBNER
1230 Avenue of the Americas
New York, NY 10020

This book is a work of fiction. Names, characters, places, and incidents either are products of the author's imagination or are used fictitiously. Any resemblance to actual events or locales or persons, living or dead, is entirely coincidental.

First Scribner trade paperback edition 2003

SCRIBNER and design are trademarks of Macmillan Library Reference USA, Inc., used under license by Simon & Schuster, the publisher of this work.

For information about special discounts for bulk purchases, please contact Simon & Schuster Special Sales:
1-800-456-6798 or business@simonandschuster.com

Set in Electra

Manufactured in the United States of America

1 3 5 7 9 10 8 6 4 2

The Library of Congress has cataloged the hardcover edition as follows:
Price, Reynolds.
Noble Norfleet / Reynolds Price.
p. cm.
I. Title.
PS3566.R54 N64 2002
813'.54—dc21 2002022327

ISBN 0-7432-0417-4
0-7432-0418-2 (Pbk)

FOR

SUSAN MOLDOW

NOBLE NORFLEET

ONE

The first time I ever made real love with another human being, I thought I'd die. I didn't feel guilty, just smothered in pleasure. That same night my family vanished from the face of the Earth so far as I knew. I was seventeen years old. I'd got home late, well after midnight. I still believe the three of them were safe at that hour. I stopped at their doors the way I'd done for years; and I thought I heard them all breathing steadily, asleep. The way I felt, it was all I could do not to wake somebody up and spread the joy that was still high in me. But of course I couldn't tell what I'd done, where I'd been or least of all who I'd been with. So I went to my own bed and finally slept sometime before dawn. The last time I looked at my clock, it was past two in the morning.

Church bells woke me—it was nearly eleven—and at first the room around me felt normal. It was not much bigger than a piano crate, but it had thick walls and a door I could lock. I lay on my back with my hands down beside me, and for several sweet minutes I let my mind rerun last night and its big surprise. I'd known for five years that I had a working body, but except with myself I'd never tried to prove it. Well, it was proven now beyond any doubt. And I felt justified in what I'd done. I'd hurt nobody, least of all God (for whatever reason I was sure of that, and I still don't doubt it). And I'd pleased two sane souls, her and me.

But once I'd got to the end of my rerun, the stillness bore in on me from all sides. The house was too quiet. A slow chill crawled up my legs and back. I pulled on my underpants and walked to the door. There were no sounds from the hall or any other room. At normal volume I said "Anybody?"

Nobody said a word, not a creak or a laugh. For reasons I'll explain, our house almost never went completely quiet.

So I turned left and went to the next room—the last one on the hall, which was our only bath. It was cleaner than usual. Even the towels were neatly folded. I went ahead and took a long shower that soon had me ignoring my feeling that the house was empty. That round of pleasure lasted so long I expected Mother to burst in and tell me I'd have to pay the water bill if I didn't quit. She was normally generous, but occasionally she'd have sudden outbursts of frugal fears—we'd be in the poorhouse by sundown if such-and-such form of waste didn't cease. Anyhow I quit and dried myself, walked to my room and laid out a set of clean clothes. Before I dressed I even stopped in front of the mirror. It had been a wedding present to my mother and father and had hung in their room till Dad left us hanging. Literally the next day Mother told me to move it to my room. It had such good memories for her she couldn't stand to see it, but she couldn't bear to give it away. Somebody might crack it. Even that early, Mother was thinking how mirrors had memories that could be released to walk round the house and cause real pleasure or actual damage.

Till then I'd never paid much attention to how I looked. I thought I was average. People didn't run from me nor flock to me either, not in droves anyhow. But this Sunday morning I had to admit I looked a lot stronger in muscle and bone than ever before. And my face and thick black hair were improving, almost as I stood there. When I put on my pants, I realized I was moving like a china doll. I'd been so happy in my fine skin these past twelve hours, I was scared of breaking. Then a harder chill hit me, and I shook like a beat dog.

I said it out loud—"They're surely at church"—but I knew my mother hadn't been to church since Dad walked off. My brother and sister were good-hearted heathens. By then I was starting to feel a real dread. Something was wrong. Had I somehow caused it? I already knew I'd had more pleasure in the past few hours than Mother had known in her whole life.

My brother and sister were a lot less lucky than me at everything. They'd hardly got a chance to know Dad, and at his best he could cause more laughter than any trained pig. When the chill faded I remember thinking "You're the killer here, Noble." Yet all I'd actually killed to that point was one male robin with a homemade slingshot.

I didn't pause to look into rooms till I reached the kitchen at the far end. Like the bath it was way too neat. No sign of a plate nor any scrap of food. On the breakfast table there was nothing but the notepad Mother used for lists. Parallel beside it was the old ice pick, shining as new as if somebody had scrubbed it with steel wool. The top note on the pad said *Rat trap* and *Pears*. We'd never had rats and it wasn't pear season, so I was spooked to look at the next page.

But I knew I had to, and all it offered was four bars of music in my brother's hand. He was taking piano lessons that he paid for by selling peanut butter door to door in a Cub Scout uniform (he wasn't a Scout), and he was good at tunes from the start. I could tell it was already his main escape. And I knew enough about music myself to hum his short melody, nine notes long. It broke off, as high as my voice would go. So at that point I looked out the window. The car was gone.

By then I thought I knew what had happened. There was nothing to do but throw my head back and howl at the ceiling or search the house and either confirm or deny my guess. I went to Mother's shut bedroom door and knocked—no answer. I opened it and looked in. Nothing but a neat bed, clear daylight and her wedding dress laid out on the quilt. She'd always said we should bury her in that, and every few months she'd take it out and check it for mildew or mold.

My brother and sister were still young enough to sleep in the same room, between mine and Mother's. I went on there and the door was open. They were in their bunk beds, my sister on the top one. Her name was Adelle. She was nine years old and loved by all, for many good reasons. I stood in the door and called her name plainly. The least noise could wake her. She was facing my way but never moved. My brother was eleven, named Arch (for Archer)—another big favorite for his endless sweet jokes. Arch was facing the wall, away from me. A dynamite stick in his ear couldn't budge him once he was asleep. So I went over to him and knelt by his side. When I reached to shake his shoulder, he was already cold in the warm spring air. I said something like "Arch, don't tell me you're gone." He couldn't tell me anything of course.

And if she'd been there, Adelle would have spoken long since but she hadn't. I liked her too much to see her close now. I thought it might blind me. So I turned Arch to face me, pulled the cover back off him, and raised his T-shirt. In the midst of his chest, no bigger than a speck of ink, was the spot where the ice pick had pierced his heart and killed him in his sleep. When I got sufficient strength to look, Adelle had the same wound.

In those days calling the Law was a lot slower than now. First you called the Court House, they plugged you through to the local police, you told your story to whoever answered, and he decided whether you were in trouble or just drunk or fooling. For one thing he knew you weren't in mortal danger. In those safer days few people called while the Strangler was strangling. But assuming you didn't claim to be on fire, somebody would come out eventually. And if you'd had a bodily assault or a break-in, the chance was the culprit might be the officer's brother-in-law or second cousin. The Law and the crooks were that close together. The second worst thing that was ever done to me was done by a Lawman's brother-in-law, but I won't be describing that here. Still, from the instant I saw our cleaned ice pick in the kitchen, I knew who'd killed my brother and sister. It was nobody kin to any known policeman, but I couldn't make myself think the name.

I went out to the back porch and sat in a straight chair to wait for either my mother or the Law. The reason I'd called them was to get some other human opinion. Had I truly gone crazy and dreamed this up? Was I even awake? Or were two of my family dead indoors and the other one missing along with the car? I was old enough to know they'd think I caused it the minute they got here. I could prove I didn't, though. My fingerprints weren't on that ice pick or near the children, and nobody else who'd ever known me could suspect me of violence—not in those years.

It did feel strange, though, realizing that I could sit still on a bright Easter morning with most of my family dead behind me. I'd loved Arch and Adelle as much as brothers can. I understood that losing them ought to feel like a landslide. And hard as my mother's life had been, she'd never harmed me, not bodily. But seated in sunshine I felt relieved. Stunned but lighter. Feeling so free was tougher to bear than what lay behind me.

In the few minutes I was having such thoughts, I was still alone. We didn't have a dog, I was on the porch, and nobody passed on the street that ran beside us—not till somebody yelled my name out, "*Noble!*"

It was a man's voice, and it sounded like an English accent.

I wasn't ready to talk to anybody so I didn't turn.

The same voice spoke from closer by. "I say, Mr. Norfleet."

It was Jarret James, dressed for Easter in a new sharkskin suit, a red silk tie, and brown-and-white shoes so intricately worked and carefully polished they looked like a map of the Himalayan countries. Jarret and I had been real friends from the time his aunt started work as our cook, when he and I were six or seven. As we got older we'd drifted apart in the regulation way of those days, but we could still speak our childhood language when we met each other by accident somewhere. The most recent time had been at the vigil when Martin Luther King was murdered just ten days before. Now Jarret was coming across the yard toward me. He liked to imitate English actors he'd seen in movies, mostly Laurence Olivier. I tried to get ready to match his funny skill. He always went for the upper-class accents. I'd be a Cockney.

Now I wanted to tell him how sporty he looked, knowing how hard he worked for his clothes. But I also knew the Law would be here any minute, so I stood up to show I couldn't talk long. When Jarret was no more than five steps away, I said "Hold it, friend. I'm on duty here."

He stopped and looked. "Looks like you're *dead*. You wearing corpse powder?" He occasionally worked at the Negro funeral home.

I could feel I was pale, but I tried to grin to show I was fine, and my whole face collapsed. I didn't shed tears or make any noise.

Jarret came closer. "Noble, what happened?"

I tried to say "Nothing." The word broke up.

Jarret whispered "Nothing, my ass. She beat you, didn't she?" By then his English accent was slipping.

Mother had beat me once or twice years ago, but now I was way too big for that, and I shook my head No.

Jarret said "Then what the hell's happened?" He very seldom used hard language.

I waved my hand politely, meaning *Leave now*.

He didn't budge but stood on, watching me.

So I finally met his long face and deep eyes. He was truly chestnut brown and unblemished. I recalled we'd never had a cross word or argument in all the thousand games we played. Then I remembered I'd heard he had a young daughter recently and lived with the child's mother out in the country.

I said "I hear you're a father now."

He waited before he gave a low burst of laughter. "Must've heard that on the loony bin airways. I'm a virgin sacrifice like you." When I didn't respond, he said "You're still a virgin, aren't you?"

For several reasons I lacked the heart to tell him about my latest discovery (and I'd later discover he had a fine girlfriend, however chaste he had or hadn't been); so I nodded a lie. And to change the subject, I pointed behind me to the house. "Adelle and Arch are in there, dead."

"Dead? You speaking literally now?" Jarret backed three steps. "*Je - sus*. You mean it, don't you, boy?"

I nodded. "Ice pick. Straight through their hearts, I guess. Both of them, peaceful in their beds."

Jarret came very near to smiling, and his eyes were on mine. "She finally did it."

I couldn't make myself confirm him. As he started back toward me, I said "You'd better leave quick. The Law'll be here any minute." To the best of my knowledge, he'd never done anything remotely illegal. I guess I was thinking that people with dark skin ought to run from the Law.

But Jarret stood in place. In his best British accent again, he said "So you're telling the truth?"

"I wish I wasn't," I said. And oh I did.

He said "Nobe, it's Easter. Don't tell me a lie on your family today." His father had killed a white man at Easter, ten years ago and was promptly executed for it in the Raleigh gas chamber.

Jarret said "But she done it, right? Mrs. Norfleet done it? Your own birth mother?"

Despite being young as I was, I said to myself *Very few human beings have ever had to answer that, not about their mothers.* And even then I could have kept quiet, but I'd always trusted black people with my pains. They hadn't failed me yet. So finally I had to meet Jarret's big eyes and nod and say Yes. I all but expected my mother to rise up screaming that instant and finish us two with neat single thrusts that wouldn't even bleed.

Jarret actually laughed and bent over double. Then he faced me and said "I *knew* she would." He started back toward me. But when I waved him off, he ran like a healthy four-point stag. He was that strong and graceful and had always been. It took him ten seconds to vanish in the dogwood. When he did, there was nothing to see but the low trees, white as wide handfuls of snow flung up and trapped in the air.

At once the police car pulled in the driveway. Through his window I could see it was one I knew—Barber Brady. He wasn't more than ten years older than me, and he'd helped me with Mother a time or two when she got out of hand. He looked less like a young policeman than anyone you could imagine—no potbelly and sagging pants, he was nearly seven feet tall and thin as a twig. He opened his door.

Just before his foot touched the ground, something in the dogwoods made me look up. For an instant—that felt like seventeen years—I saw hundreds of hands facing palm-out toward me. In the midst of all the cross-shaped blooms, the hands were the color of normal white hands, and at first I thought they were trying to stop me from something. What was it? They looked like the *Stop* hand on school-patrol signs.

Then I noticed the central hand. It wasn't much bigger than the others, but I knew it was a male hand, and its back was turned toward me instead of the palm. Again it didn't seem to be forbidding. And though I wasn't sure, in the few seconds I had to look, I thought it was moving slightly to wave me toward it.

Until that point, except for normal childhood daydreams, I hadn't been prone to seeing things as strange as that. But the whole sight looked as real as Barber Brady and a good deal better. I was standing at the head of the steps. So with no second thought, I moved to go to it. It didn't cross my mind to think that it couldn't be real or to wonder what it meant or what it would do with me if I obeyed it.

I was down the four steps, and moving still, when Barber said "Noble, is she tensed up again?"

Of course the hands vanished. *Tense* and *tension* were the words I'd used in the past to explain what was wrong when Barber helped me with Mother. Police in general understand the word *tension*.

I said "So it seems—but worse this time."

Barber said "Is she in there?" He nodded precisely to her bedroom window.

"Gone," I said. "She took the car unless somebody drove her."

He hoisted his gunbelt and pants to his armpits and said "You saying that you and me are safe?"

Again the idea struck me as funny. I'd loved my kin but I was seventeen, with a long way to go where feelings were concerned. So I laughed a little. "Barber, you and I are safe. But Arch and Adelle are dead as hammers, not to mention the fix my mother is in wherever she's gone."

Barber was almost in reach of me, but he stopped in his tracks. "Your brother and sister—that's Arch and Adelle?"

"Yes."

"They're minors, right?"

"They were," I said.

You wouldn't have thought a tear was available anywhere in Barber's body. He stood where he was, though, and both his eyes filled. Furthermore he made no attempt to hide the moisture.

And at first I thought he looked like Bert Lahr as the Cowardly Lion. But then I realized I was dry as any hot brick, and I felt a little shamed. In fact, for the first time in my life, I felt truly horrified.

It was well before the days when Lawmen wouldn't so much as search a baby carriage without guns drawn. They more or less assumed a safe world and were mostly right. So Barber didn't touch his pistol. But when we got indoors, he did wave me forward and say "You lead."

I led him down to the bunk bedroom.

He got to within an arm's reach of Adelle—she was eye-level to us—but he said "Noble, touch her and tell me what you feel."

It was also before the days when crime-scene contamination was much of a concern. Still, except for lifting her shirt when I found her, I hadn't really touched her alive since breakfast the previous morning. I distinctly remembered telling her she had a Grape-Nut stuck to her upper lip. She couldn't seem to find it, so I reached out and flicked it off. She was warm as toast then. Now I laid a slow hand on her forehead. She was cool—not as cold as Arch but way under normal—and I told Barber so.

Then he came closer and knelt by Arch's head. Under his breath Barber said "Help me, Lord." He touched the spot under Arch's jaw where they check for pulses in good police movies. "You're right about one thing," he said back to me. "They're both *long* gone."

By now the whole weight was settling on me, but still my body was choosing to bear up. I'd been the man around here for so long, I couldn't think of being a child again. Yet I waited for Barber to tell me what next.

He stayed on his haunches down by Arch. "She strangled them then?"

"No, Barber, they were stabbed."

"Then where's all the blood?"

"No blood," I said. "An ice pick through the heart, neat as a surgeon. All you got to do is ease it in between the ribs, the whole way in. Then you swipe it slightly up and down and that's it. *Ball game.*" In my hitchhiking days one of my rides had described the technique and told me always to carry an icepick when I was on the road (had I ever told Mother?—I've never known).

Barber stood up and looked at me closely. For the first time, I knew, he was checking me. Had one more member of the family gone crazy? Was he in any danger? His right hand feinted toward his pistol, but he never touched it.

I said "The weapon's in the kitchen" and pointed him toward it.

But Barber shut his eyes and shook his head hard. "Much as I hate to ask you, son—show me their wounds."

So, despite the fact that Barber was the Law, I had to go through that again—Arch one more time and then Adelle. And what I remembered from Arch's example turned out to be true. His wound was a little darker now but was still no bigger than three grains of rice. Adelle's was smaller—her skin was so tender—and she had shed one thin trail of blood about four inches long. It hadn't even stained her pajamas. I looked straight at Barber as he saw the sights.

His whole face confirmed that I hadn't dreamed the worst.

From a selfish point of view, the actual worst would have been if I'd died too. I even thought it at the time—how much my joy from the previous night had left me glad that Mother had spared me. She had to have known I was in my bed, deep asleep in full fatigue; but she'd let me be. The question *Why?* would wait a good while, maybe forever. Till then, considering how long I'd dealt with a stove-in soul (my afflicted mother), I felt like Barber was my present nearby needy human in need of attention.

But the color slowly came back to his face, and he asked for a phone.

Once he'd called for more help from the station, the new men gathered what evidence there was—the ice pick of course, some letters of Mother's from various government agencies. She'd recently protested a lot of things and got form replies that more or less said she didn't know what she was talking about. Everybody from the local garbage service to the Oval Office had answered her politely but with no help at all. She probably hadn't had a truly personal letter since her own mother died in a state nursing home for the *feebleminded* as they were called. Then we saw the two bodies off to the coroner, and the other Lawmen left.

The chief of police was another tall man with a face like Abraham Lincoln's if Lincoln had shaved the afternoon before Booth shot him. As the chief left he touched my shoulder and said "I've heard some praise of you from several teachers and of course your track coach. You're too smart for this."

For an instant I thought he meant I was too smart to kill two sleeping children and also make my mother and her car disappear.

I must have looked as weak as he had a minute ago; so he gripped my shoulder and said "I'll do everything in my power to ease you through this, and I'm not a weak man." He didn't reach for his handcuffs but smiled and left as quietly as any young moth.

It was almost late afternoon by then. Barber was the last to go, and I followed him out. As he leaned to get down into his car, he thought to pause and look back at me. "Ace, you need a place to sleep tonight?"

Ace was a name left over from the World Wars. One of my sure recollections of Dad was how he called me *Ace*, more than once anyhow. It got to me now. That and the fact that I hadn't given the slightest thought to where I'd sleep. I shook my head No to Barber and pointed plainly behind me—the house, the place I'd lived since birth.

Barber said "You sure you want to sleep there?"

I didn't understand he meant was I scared of Mother.

I told him I was tired, and that much was true.

He said "You got anything left to eat?"

Considering his leanness I remember a moment of surprise that Barber valued the presence of groceries.

I told him I had some sardines and crackers. Mother always kept those on hand for me, a major component of the male diet then.

Barber must not have liked canned fish. He frowned but then he actually gave me an official salute, silent as any Canadian Mountie on splendid horseback thanking a moose for failing to charge. And he went on his way.

His car was fading before I recalled the first time I'd met him—seven years ago on Halloween night. Two friends and I had rigged up a way to stop passing cars by suddenly raising a rope across the street, a rope hung with streamers of rags and ugly masks. It hadn't dawned on us of course that we could cause serious harm, but somebody called the cops and young Barber came. He was new on the job and looked as scared as us. The other boys ran—both older than me—and I tried to join them. Barber yelled me back, read me a stiff warning and then—of all things—reached into his pocket, found a ballpoint pen with a peephole in it that showed a blond with massive boobs in a lime-green bikini. When he let me see her, in the glow of his flashlight, he said "If you give me your solemn word you'll live a clean life, I'll give you that pen." So I gave him my word and he surrendered the pen. I kept it till I was way gone in puberty and wore it out.

Before I turned back now and headed indoors, I took a slow look at the dogwoods again. Dark was settling on them like octopus ink flushed into clear water. No sign of what I'd seen before. No hands, just flowers. I've never been a man that cares much for flowers, but it was a help to know that something besides me and two or three Lawmen had survived this killing and might very well still be here tomorrow.

* * *

Once I was inside I didn't feel scared. If my mother had meant me to die, she'd have managed that. I sleep like a brick. You could treat me any way your heart desired, and I'd never stop you. I did lock the doors, though, and cook myself a fried egg sandwich and a can of red beans. Mother hadn't bought any sardines after all. What I wanted to do more than anything else was call the friend who'd cheered my body so lavishly yesterday. For reasons I'll make clear, that wasn't likely to work this soon. I had a few friends from the track team, but they were my age, and considering Mother's unpredictability I'd never been able to ask them to the house. I knew if I called them now I'd just have to lay out all I knew about this day and the recent past. I had no more close kin in hailing distance. The nearest was an uncle who might have come to get me if I'd phoned him and begged hard, but that would have taken a three-hour drive. And up till then I'd never begged anybody for anything, not since I was a baby anyhow.

So I took my second shower of the day, and that got me focused again on my body. With all the endless reserves of a boy, I stayed in that warm flood till I'd drained my mind of all its present hungers. In the circumstances, some people may condemn me still. Maybe I should have been on my knees, thanking God for my life and praying for the soul of my desperate mother, wherever she was. I thought very likely she was dead in a ditch with her own throat cut by her own hand. But I doubt most grown men will think I was wrong to console myself in absolute private in a way that cost nobody alive but me a single cent.

Even after I was dried off and lying naked on my bed in the dark, I found the strength to do it again and finally plunge myself into sleep. Surely that was no excess reward for a boy seventeen who'd just learned to enter another human being with no worse intent than the hope for warmth on both sides, a boy who'd just undergone a loss that was very nearly total. Anyhow, unpleasant as it may be for some to consider, I believe it's a fact worth setting down—a good many young boys have saved themselves from desperation and suicide through free resort to their own kind skin.

After that I only woke once, thinking I heard footsteps. Somehow it didn't scare me, and I got up to check. Once I was upright and had cleared my head, I knew I was alone. Then I said to myself "You think you're alone since that's what you asked for so many times." And I'd asked for solitude the way boys in general do. Here it was apparently, in pure black spades. But I went on and checked all the beds again to be sure I hadn't dreamt up the footsteps and the sadness.

So I was wide awake when I got back to my room and took a last look out the window toward the back. Even in the pitch dark, the trees and the whole yard were changed again. As real as the spread of hands I'd seen in the early evening, I saw our whole deep yard in moonlight populated by actual stars. At first I thought it was lightning bugs. But I knew it was too early for them. They'd show up in June. I took another long careful look, and Yes it was stars down low to the ground. Each was the size of the pure high blaze from a kerosene lamp, and each was moving slightly. This time none of them outshone the others, and nothing seemed to beckon me on. But I had the feeling that, if I could have stayed awake longer, I'd have figured that they were doing some kind of dance. Immensely slow but the answer to everything.

Tired as I was, my mind half guessed them to mean I would somehow survive and have a life that I could bear, most times at least. In sleep it seemed like a simpler proposition than my life has proved to be. It's not over yet and I'd be the last one to say it couldn't yet gutter out in smoke and fumes with heavy damage to me and others. But so far the blaze has seldom vanished for longer than a few months here and there. Like my poor mother, I'd never been given to church and prayer. As I lay down to wait for morning though, I spoke to whatever might be listening. Oddly I just said "Many thanks."

I was a senior in high school, a few weeks from graduating and hunting a job that would let me eventually go to night classes or somehow earn enough to go to maybe two years of real college. So Monday morning should have been a school day, but I'd forgot to set my clock. I slept on through till the sound of a key in the back door woke me.

Then a voice said "Nobie?"

There was no other voice in the natural world remotely like it—much higher pitched than bats could have heard. I knew it was Hesta, though—

Hesta James, Jarret's aunt who'd cooked for us years ago (you could get a good cook for seven dollars a week). She must have kept her key all this time. Not that anybody worried much about keys in our safe town. It had stayed almost incredibly safe, even this deep into Vietnam and the civil rights struggles.

I called out to say I was in my room. "Wait for me in the kitchen."

By the time I'd put on yesterday's clothes and washed my face, Hesta was cooking the breakfast we used to have before things changed. Eggs, plenty of bacon, grits, toast and homemade pear preserves. She'd brought the ingredients as her contribution. I came up behind her at the stove and hugged her. She was under five feet tall and weighed maybe seventy pounds in her heavy dark clothes, which were always good enough for church. She'd said more than once that she fully expected to be caught up into Heaven first thing at Jesus' Last Judgment, and she had no plans whatever to leave in less than the best dress she could afford on her famous *savings* that she sometimes alluded to, her one known mystery.

I held on to her firmly, but she wouldn't look back to meet my kiss. So I said "You still think you'll pass me on the fast road to Heaven?"

"Not a *shred* of doubt," she said. "You and nine out of ten white folks, not to mention every sorry black soul—man or woman."

She'd never been married nor lived with a man, and she'd never had children of her own to raise. Or so Jarret said. She was his oldest aunt, but she took him in when his mother got killed (long before his father was executed); and she raised him right, he always said. Yet I'd heard Hesta say many times that childlessness was one of God's blessings from her point of view. Now she was still turning bacon in the pan, but she finally reached up with her free hand and squeezed my wrist. "Sit down here and eat this good food. Food makes up for a lot."

I obeyed her and found I was hungry as a wolf. Back then of course I had to ask her to sit down beside me. She'd have never taken that action on her own.

She was silent but she picked up every crumb I dropped and held them all in the palm of her hand. I remembered then how she'd always done that. She'd throw them outside for the birds once I finished. I finally said "I guess Jarret told you."

Hesta shook her head No. "Radio," she said. "They had it on there early this morning."

I said "Oh Christ—"

And she put her hand across my mouth. "Beg His pardon, Nobie. He kept you alive."

I said "*Something* did, that's for sure."

Hesta said "You'll find out His name years from now."

I smiled. "You want to explain that?"

Hesta said "He'll call you when He wants you."

"You're speaking of Jesus?"

"I don't talk about no other man." But then she laughed to show she was sane. "Where you think she's gone?"

I knew she meant Mother. Hesta had quit working here the day Mother threw a butcher knife at her—and just because Hesta was drying a cheap jelly glass that fell and broke. I said "I guess she's either killed herself and is lying somewhere not far away, or she's gone off free the way she always claimed she wanted."

Hesta said "She's crazy. You know that, don't you?"

"I know she gets her blue spells a lot more often than most people. I know she has those yelling fits and flings things around till I call the Law. They calm her down."

Hesta said "You called the *Law* on your mama?"

I said "Wasn't that on the radio too? No, an officer came maybe two or three times—an old boy I know named Brady. We'd get her halfway calm and talk her into spending the night in a clean jail cell till her mind could steady itself. Then she'd be fine for a while." Hesta was nodding impatiently so I said "Surely you know all that."

Hesta said "Her demon. I told her she could flush him if she came to my preacher. Preacher Delphus Jenkins told me he could heal her any minute she asked him."

I wasn't old enough to argue with a woman as convinced as Hesta. My own guess was that, Yes, Mother was insane. But I was too young—and from the wrong time and place—to judge whether demons were involved or not. Still I knew even then that there was such a thing as evil. This house, this kitchen table where I sat eating a bountiful breakfast, had known real evil just yesterday. That hadn't quite dawned on me till then, and it went down badly. Not thinking what I meant, I said "I shouldn't stay in this house, should I?" I realized I was asking Hesta for earnest advice. Who else could I ask?

She said "No, baby, that's why I'm here." She'd always had the longest hands I'd ever known on a truly short person. Her right hand reached out now and ringed my whole left wrist. "You staying with me."

Right off, I thanked her.

She said "Are the bunk-bed sheets still bloody?"

I told her they were still on the beds—no blood.

She said "Let me strip em then, them and your mother's. Then I'll wash these dishes. You gather your things and we'll move to my place for as long as you need it. I won't take a penny of rent and won't charge a penny to feed you. The Lord's blessed me with money, and it's yours if you need it."

I said "Hesta, that's too good and you know it."

"It *is*," she said. "You right about that. But old as I am—and mean as I been—I'm buying my way into Heaven for sure."

The two of us knew she'd likely never done a wrong thing in her life. But even in that sad house, so close on the heels of mad death, we managed to laugh. And my whole life took one more new wide swerve that slowed and shaped me deeply, though in ways I couldn't imagine for years.

I've mentioned that my only known kin was an uncle, my father's brother, Stanley. He lived miles away and had shown the barest minimum of interest in us since long before Dad disappeared (if Stan had any knowledge of Dad's whereabouts, alive or dead, he'd never given the least hint). But Arch and Adelle still had to be buried; and despite the fact that I was living with an old black woman, I couldn't qualify as a pauper since the house was still in my mother's name. The year was 1968. Vietnam (as I said) was plunging on down its far-off coal chute, except it was using young men for coal. All the black people who weren't off at war, and a lonesome few white 4-Fs, were well past the midst of the civil-rights movement here in the streets; and Dr. King had been shot dead in Memphis ten days ago. I knew Uncle Stan would share the views of a great many white men that King had been on Satan's payroll and that any support for equal rights would prove you a Communist if not a comedian, showing off. And any protest of Vietnam—whatever your skin tone—was cause for prompt lynching in numerous states across the land. So I settled myself in firmly at Hesta's before I called Stan—I didn't want to risk being asked to live with him.

When I'd told him the truth as fast as I could, he at once said "Where are you living now?" At the news of me in a Negro house, he said "First thing—get yourself out of there before you catch something that'll kill you too. Then sell that pitiful house of your mother's and fund your life—I know your daddy paid off the mortgage before he flew the coop: I guaranteed his note. You're no spring chicken, are you? You need to get *moving*. Don't plan college do you?"

I said I'd hoped for at least two years now and maybe night school eventually.

Stan said "Better find you a good business school instead—learn how to keep books, be a public accountant. You can do that fast with the Norfleet mind."

I asked what that was.

"Mathematical genius."

Stan was a carpet salesman. Owned his own store. Dad had worked as a salesman in a men's clothing store, lived on salary and commissions so small you couldn't count them. But I didn't try to contradict my uncle. I needed six hundred dollars, that day if possible, to pay the undertaker. So I said "You're right. I hadn't thought of it. But now that you say so, I've whizzed through math ever since the first grade"—a sizable lie. Right now I was barely passing trigonometry. But I went on and made my request for tangible help.

Stan said "That's the best deal you could make on a funeral for two?"

I told him I'd argued the mortician down from eleven hundred dollars, which was not strictly true.

I'll have to give it to him—Stan took one long breath, then simply said "I'll wire it to you at noon. You can pay me back when you sell the damned house." I'd forgot the time he paid us a visit one Christmas Eve and called the house *dinky* when we offered him a pallet by the decorated tree (otherwise he'd have had to sleep with me, and I was just six). So he pushed off at midnight after too much eggnog; and before he was out of earshot on the porch, Mother said "Everybody thank Jesus he's *gone.*" Even Dad put his hands up to imitate prayer and said "Oh yes. Thank you, Jesus."

I was maybe more stunned by his meanness than by what Mother did. She at least had a history of sanity problems. Uncle Stan was a genius, as he'd just confirmed—any scrap of paper turned to money in his hands. He didn't ask when the funeral would be or what I'd be doing in the months to come. So I thanked him for promising to wire me the money.

It turned out he did have a single question. "She's not any threat to us, is she, Nobe?" *Us* was him and his poodle wife, Loretta. They had no children.

"Mother, you mean?"

"Yes."

I had to say "Her name was Edith."

Stan said "*Was?* Now you're saying she's dead?"

I hadn't planned to say the word *was.* It had just come out. So I said to Stan "I believe she is. She couldn't live long, knowing what she'd done."

He said "So she's no harm to anybody left?"

"None at all," I said. "You sleep in peace."

Stan had the grace to say he was much obliged for that. Then he had a last thought. "Loretta hasn't slept a whole hour for long years."

I suddenly felt I was old enough to say "Then you're very likely the cause of that."

I'll hand it to Stan. He waited calmly to think that through. Then he said he'd pray for me in church next Sunday.

I said "Why wait?" and was almost ready to ask if my father was alive, but Stan was gone by then.

I did, though, mention out loud at the funeral that we owed him thanks for practical help. Since there were under thirty mourners in attendance, the thanks didn't go too far toward glorifying Stan.

That was all in April. The third week in May, the Law in Maryland found Mother's car in a parking lot fifty yards from the ocean. When they forced it open, it was neat as our whole house had been on Easter morning, and on the front seat was a fresh white envelope addressed to me in her normal fine handwriting. I'd always loved its beautiful strength and upright energy, strong as a young tree. It hadn't weakened at all from the weight of what she'd done nor however many miles she'd wandered to wind up two states away from home by the green Atlantic.

Barber Brady, my policeman friend, brought me the news at school. There were only three more weeks to go till Commencement was on us. When he and the principal came to the classroom and asked for me, everybody's eyes went out on lobster stalks. That was the first time I realized they mostly thought I was guilty of what happened.

But all Barber wanted was to tell the news about the car and get me to phone the Maryland Law. All three of us went to the principal's office, and the other two men stood there and watched me while I placed the call. I thought Barber said that they hadn't found Mother, but maybe I invented that. With the two men watching me, I dreaded the chance that Mother would suddenly come to the telephone and be there, alive, for me to deal with down a long-distance wire—long-distance calls had been non-existent in my whole life except for that one time with Uncle Stan.

But this time it was an older man's voice, deep as my father's. He called me Noble right away, said he was holding a sealed envelope with my name on it and did I want him to open and read it to me now.

First I said "Sir, do you know what my mother's done?"

He said "Call me Dellum. Yes, son, I do. Or I've heard the main theory. Young Officer Brady down there, your policeman, has outlined the incident. Have you had any recent word from your mother?"

It slipped from me too fast. "Thank God, not a word."

He said "Then we better see what this letter says."

I braced myself. "Thank you, Dellum."

He said "You may not thank me when I'm done." But then he said "How old are you?" When I told him he said "Noble, hang on now." His voice was more like Dad's by the instant. I could hear him cut the envelope open. Then he paused a long time.

I knew it would say she'd drowned herself and was out of our way so far as trials and worry were concerned.

But Dellum finally said "It's nothing but the title to her car signed over to you—you're Noble Redden Norfleet, correct?"

I told him I was.

"Then now you're the owner of a '59 Buick that looked in fine condition to me. When do you plan to come up and get it? It's clean as your hand." He took a long pause. "—Assuming your hand is cleaner than mine."

I didn't pause as long as I should have over that last remark—what was the dirt on Dellum's hand? I was thinking ahead to how I could get to Maryland fast. It was a Thursday afternoon. I told him I'd hitchhike up there tomorrow evening after school. I'd thumbed my way to Washington more than once, so I figured on maybe a seven-hour trip to Ocean City.

He gave me directions and said I should ask for Dellum Stillman when I got to the station. They'd phone him if he was off duty at the time.

That part seemed important to him, so I promised I would.

When I got back to class—it was Spanish class—my teacher's eyes filled up with tears as she watched me walk all the way to my desk.

Everybody else watched too, in awful silence. A teacher in tears was a major event.

So before I sat down, I quietly told her they'd found my mother's car parked by the ocean. I said that it seemed very much like Mother had washed out to sea and that I would be heading up there late tomorrow to bring the Buick home. I knew I'd have to sell it, but I was still boy enough to feel excited at the prospect of the trip and of driving the Buick home with the title in my pocket.

At least half the other boys said "Noble, take me."

But the teacher said "Enough now. Open your books." Her name was Anita Acheson from South Carolina. She was twenty-six years old, called Nita. Her husband was a master sergeant, at present in Vietnam. And Nita was the one who had lent me her body the night my brother and sister were killed. With her cooperation I'd plowed her up and down a whole room with more than one picture of her husband on view in expensive frames. That first night anyhow it hadn't looked to me as if he grudged me the pleasure of his wife's fine body and kindly manners. He kept on smiling beneath his various military caps with the Stars and Stripes at rest behind him. But I hadn't tested his patience again in succeeding weeks. I'd been in some kind of natural mourning.

Still it was his wife's idea to drive me to Maryland the next afternoon. I drove most of the way of course, but we took Nita's car. She wouldn't hear of me hitchhiking in the dark, though those were the last days of hitching in America—safe hitching anyhow. The serial killers weren't yet staked out in every third car, trolling for lovely girls or boys or mere human skin to chew or lick and then leave cold in a rest-stop Dumpster with the Popsicle sticks and hairspray cans. Oh if you were a free young man on the road, you might get your thigh massaged or hear more dirty jokes than you could digest; but death was unlikely (whereas just the other day a friend told me he'd recently passed an official roadsign in Oklahoma that said *Warning! Hitchhikers may be escaped convicts*).

So I'd already done a lot of free wandering at the sole expense of drivers who were no worse than lonesome or on the verge of falling asleep with no one to talk to. They'd buy you big meals at the next truckstop. On my summer trips out west, several of them offered to pay for motel rooms. A guy in Missouri, a Baptist religious-education director, tried to climb in with me—the room had twin beds. Off the top of my head, I made up a claim that has stood me in good stead ever since with unwelcome guests. I said I had no hard feelings whatever, but I did have a case of penile pellagra and felt I should just declare my condition as a form of fair warning.

I wasn't that sure of what constituted pellagra; but ever since I heard of it in childhood, it had always sounded like a dread affliction, and I'll have to say it's worked as a shield around me every time I've mentioned it. Not that I mentioned it all that often from this point onward in my life. From the time my family left me, for years I just got more and more like some ferret on partial rations in a solitary cell on the back of the moon. No food that I could find on Earth filled my endless need.

I can say Nita tried though. This early in the story, I don't want to lose you with excess descriptions of my body at work, but I honestly know it's part of what I need to say about my life—a part that not everybody can say. Permit me then to note the plain fact that—between Chatham, North Carolina and Ocean City, Maryland—we exerted ourselves a number of times. I didn't have to beg. Nita was every bit as ready as I was; and despite the fact that a lot of the trip was on two-lane roads with slow-moving farmers or dazed housewives before or behind us, we stopped the car just twice in all the hours. That was for gas, peanuts and Cokes only. Nita drank more Cokes than the first patent-holder, that wily pharmacist from Atlanta who spiked the first recipe with coca leaves. She could also retain them for longer than a camel.

When we did it for the last time, we were south of D.C. before the traffic thickened. I was still at the wheel with Nita in my lap, facing me. The whole way through, it went as fine as ever. But right toward the end, as we both took off on our separate flights to the sun and the other stars, I suddenly thought I could see something coming at us from the road up ahead. At that point in my life, I'd never seen a chariot except in books and in the movie *Ben-Hur*. What was coming, though, was a wide troop of chariots all loaded with angels. They had to be angels, bright as they were. They got so near I could see they had fairly normal faces—tilted eyes and notched lips, just all ablaze—and each one was bearing an original expression that I saw (maybe wrongly) as a smile, a very original kind of smile. Still no two expressions were alike, and they all aimed past the back of Nita's head straight at me. When I said the words "Thank you," I was thanking the angels, who were still streaming past.

Nita thought I meant her and returned the thanks.

As the years have gone by, I've thought more than once that I was wrong to read those faces as smiling on me. Weren't they more likely bearing me some kind of speechless warning that I was launched on a life that would ruin me, trusting skin as much as I did? Well, whatever, after every chariot flew on past us, I noticed that Anita and I were slightly tired. God knew we had every reason to be.

While we were bypassing Washington at nearly dusk, Nita was at the wheel. I was dozing briefly. Then some clear voice woke me and said *Look now before it's too late*. I looked to Nita, who was simply driving in a shade of light that was kinder than any light I'd seen. Right off, I knew it was not natural light. I also knew it didn't come from any manmade source. It was truly unearthly. Startled as I was, Nita looked like something I'd have instantly died for. Beautiful wasn't exactly the word. She was fine but not in the final running with the movie stars of those years. Still I knew that, even on tiring days, she looked more alive than most people ever manage at a dance.

What had changed here, this minute, was her actual charge—the pure voltage in her. Till now she'd put out a sparking heat that had caught and thrilled me. Now, though, she was suddenly calmer than any mountain yet not a bit distant. Before, her face and body had pulled on me like waves. Now she was drawing me toward her steadily like the strongest tide in the history of the ocean. If that, and some of my other descriptions, sound ridiculous, please recall that I'm trying to tell you how it felt back then, to a boy young as I was—a recent virgin. I stayed where I'd been, by the passenger door. But I said "I'm never going to leave you again."

Nita watched the road, then suddenly laughed. "Oh yes you are."

"No, I mean it," I said. In principle I knew she was married and would have other duties if her husband got back from Vietnam; but drunk as I was on my own hormones and her kind welcome, I was blind to every obstacle and danger. The finest eye surgeon couldn't have helped me see, not then and there. I thought I could somehow wait through her marriage and meet her on the far side if it took ninety years.

A smile had lasted on Nita's face, and she turned it to me now. When we were alone, she almost never called my name. I think just the plain sounds reminded her of calling the roll in school. But now she said the whole name, full out—"Noble Redden Norfleet." Then she waited through a whole mile of road and tried again. "Noble, I like you way too much. You know how wrong I'm treating you, old as I am with a good-hearted husband and the solemn duty to be your teacher and lead you right—" Her voice stopped itself.

I said "Nobody's ever given me one percent of what you've given me. I'll be needing you forever."

But she said "My darling, I'm a good Catholic girl—a true cradle Catholic. I started this thing with you and me before I knew what a loss you'd suffer. If I've helped you any in all your grief, then may God forgive me for all the rest. But once we're safely back home tomorrow, I've got to repent and change my life—both our lives. I'm leading you wrong, Noble. Please help me stop that."

Repent? For what? What had we done wrong? And it wasn't just my youth that made me wonder such things. I strongly suspect that if I could sit beside her today, this many years later, I'd feel the same merciless tide and would ask the same questions. And I'm still not convinced that God has ever condemned me, one moment, or that he blamed Nita who lost her first child in a dreadful way. That was some years later, and the child was not mine, but by then we'd lost all direct contact, and I couldn't even send her a note in sympathy.

Even though I figured I could ease her mind tonight by the ocean, I was still deeply saddened by Nita's surprise. I sat in her car through all the last miles and scarcely spoke again. Looking back, I can see that I'd somehow postponed most of my grief for all that had happened—in my life and near me—in the past few weeks. I'd surely postponed any realization of how lonely I was and would likely remain for years to come. After all, who wants to spend much time, not to mention an entire loyal life, with a man whose mother killed her two other children and somehow left him alive and alone to stand as the worst scarecrow in the field?

By the time we got to Ocean City, it was early in the night. Dellum Stillman, the policeman who phoned me, had gone for the day. But when I mentioned my name and the car, the sergeant at the desk said "In that case, he'll be right back. He told me most definitely to call him if you showed up."

By then I had little left to say to Nita. Still we were both starving, so we crossed the street and ate seafood at a reasonable place. I was trying hard not to act childish and freeze her out. But that close to her, the prospect of her shutting down our joy was even more depressing than it was in the car with an arm's reach between us. Scary even. If she meant what she said, I was now abandoned by everybody except old Hesta; and I figured that Hesta couldn't last me many years longer, not the way her mind seemed to be failing.

Nita saw how low I was and touched one finger to the back of my hand that was spread on the table. "Noble, please try to see it my way. All Al's hopes are pinned on me. I'm keeping him alive."

"Who's Al?"

"My husband—Albert Lee Acheson."

I was sorry I'd forced her. Till then she'd never said his name, and that made all we'd done a little easier—entirely unreal, for me anyhow. Al was nobody but a round face in those framed photographs in Nita's bedroom. I still couldn't feel I'd stolen anything that Al rightly owned. I said "Look here, there's enough of you for more than one man and one high-school senior." I meant it of course as a compliment. She was not overweight and had never seemed vulgar in any way.

At first her face went hard; and she said "I'm not a man-sized bargain platter, Noble—'All you can eat for a dollar ninety-eight.'" But she calmed in a minute. Then she grinned and thanked me. "The trouble is I lack enough brains."

"You're a schoolteacher, girl. You're bright as a searchlight."

She said "What I mean is, I can't think of anything but you now. And that's got to quit. Simple as that."

Nothing seems simple to any boy except his own will—simple and *right.* And when I looked up at Nita again, she was lit by the same unnatural shine I'd seen on the highway. Here she was with a neon beer sign behind her left ear, and still she looked like the goal of that band of angels I'd seen on the highway. I couldn't have her, though. And I couldn't imagine living without her. So I stood up suddenly, meaning to leave.

A hand on my shoulder and a man's voice stopped me, a deep voice that I seemed to know. It said "Noble Norfleet?"

When I turned it was a grizzle-haired man, medium-size and in normal street clothes, unusually neat. He looked like Spencer Tracy portraying a rock.

By then I'd forgot all about Dellum Stillman, and the sight of him shocked me. In a truly weird way, my first thought was *I'm looking at a mirror forty years from now*—he looked that much like an older me or somebody kin to me that I'd never met. Still I just said "I'm Noble." Strangers generally laughed when I said it. Ever seen a noble boy?

But Dellum said "You mind if I sit down here with your lady friend and wait till you're back?" He must have thought I was headed for the Gents'. I introduced him to Nita and called her a family friend.

She didn't correct me and shook his hand too.

I thought her face, for an instant, showed the same feeling as mine—this man looked like he might be my father. But of course neither one of us mentioned it.

Dellum called to the waitress for coffee and a grilled cheese sandwich. That was my own favorite, and it helped me trust him.

So we both sat down.

He asked in detail about our trip north as if he cared how it might have gone. He said he hoped we'd stay the night and not rush straight home. We had to be *whipped* from the drive, he said—it was always harder to drive *up* the map than *down*. That was an idea I'd had as a child, but I'd never heard anyone else claim he thought the same thing. Then he laughed and asked if Nita and I were kin to each other.

Before I could speak Nita said "No sir, I'm his Spanish teacher."

Dellum waited awhile before he suddenly leaned over right in my face. "Are you that good a student?"

When I didn't answer Nita said "He's got a good mind. I've tried to help him. You know what he's been through lately, don't you?"

Dellum was swallowing coffee by then. He waited. Then he spoke straight to Nita. "I've heard he lost the bulk of his family. Now his mother's vanished one more time."

I was sitting on Nita's side of the booth, wondering what he meant by *one more time*.

Dellum finally looked to me. "She hasn't contacted you then since you and I talked on the phone?"

I'd more than half figured her body had washed up by now and was in a box, waiting for me to haul home. I said "Cap'n Stillman, I'm praying none of us ever sights her again. She's a desperate—" I know I meant to say "desperate soul." But after my weeks of keeping intact, I came apart there in fluorescent light at a Formica table in a mom-and-pop seafood joint by the sea. I didn't shed tears, though, or make the least sound. I just couldn't make my mind work at all. It might as well have been the dumb white heart of one of the french-fried potatoes I was bolting down.

When I wasn't better in another long minute, Dellum asked the waitress to save him the check.

She didn't seem to have a problem with that, and I guess it helped me trust him even more. In fact she said "Is this boy your nephew?"

Dellum said "No kin, I'm sad to say."

The waitress said "You've mentioned a good-looking nephew so often, and knowing how stuck on your *own* looks you are, I thought this was him—he looks enough like you."

Dellum actually thanked her. "That's a compliment, Patsy" and put another dollar on top of her tip.

Then everybody laughed and we all stood up. With only the briefest words to Nita, in five more minutes Dellum was driving us somewhere in her car.

The whole house was his. Nobody lived with him and, without the usual male mess, it was still male space. Every wall was paneled in dark knotty pine. And the resin smell was pleasantly strong, though the house was maybe fifty years old. There were no family pictures or other signs of a wife, children or even dead parents. The only decorations were a few stuffed deep-sea fish on the walls, a few certificates of heroism and commendations from children's clubs. The kitchen shelves held nothing but coffee cups and two white plates as if he had a mate or at least the hope of a visitor at times. Not even a frying pan or a toaster in sight on the stove. Not so much as an ashtray anywhere. Quiet as it seemed, it might have been the final blast-off pad for some saint leaving this world, unburdened.

Yet it soon turned out that Dellum had more reasons than one to care about my problems. He said his own wife and son had drowned twenty years ago, north of here in New Jersey. They'd gone out for a Sunday afternoon stroll on the beach, to find seashells, and hadn't come back. No trace of their bodies had ever been found, and Dellum said he'd moved on south slowly in various jobs with the small-town Law. He said he had no realistic hope they'd finally turn up.

But he also said he kept having one dream that led him onward. In the dream he'd be patrolling the beach. His eye would catch a small arm calling toward him from the surf. He'd stop and run down. It would almost certainly be his son, who had died at age eight. The boy in the surf would still be barely alive, and Dellum would save him. The boy's mother, Dellum's wife, would be nothing but rags left over from her last bathing suit all knotted around the boy's pale legs. At last Dellum had given up hope here in Maryland and found a good job. "Preventing mischief and genuine harm and aiding the helpless" was how he described it with no smile at all.

By the time he'd told us that and toured us through most of the small house, Nita was showing how tired she was. Her eyes kept going dead as glass eyes. Dellum noticed it first and asked if she wanted to nap on the sofa in his den. When she declined he turned to me. "I got you a room at a boardinghouse, but it's just for one person. See, I didn't know—"

Nita broke right in. "I didn't know I could bring him up here till the very last minute."

Dellum said "Glad you could. No, all I'm saying is, this boy's got a single room waiting for him. But you both are welcome to doss down here for as long as you want. I've got beds enough, in separate rooms, for more than one family."

Not knowing Dellum long, and new as I was at the ancient game of who-sleeps-where, I produced one of my famous slow blushes that wind up resembling prairie fires way out of control. I've never completely put them behind me.

Nita had never seen one till then; and she stood there speechless, watching me.

For all the years he'd spent with the Law, still Dellum just smiled. "I'll show you the rooms. You two sort em out."

The first room he showed us had one narrow cot. Against my hopes Nita said "This is mine. All my childhood I slept on a cot like this. I was going to be a nun, and my mother loved the idea."

Dellum said "Fine. I'm a Catholic myself. Converted last year—because it's so hard. Any mad-dog felon can be a Baptist. I like a *hard* church."

It was Nita's turn to look caught-out. She said "It's hard all right and I'm afraid the nun plan failed me. Or I failed it." But she moved toward the cot, sat down on the edge and said "If you two will please forgive me, I'll turn in now. That drive really *got* me."

I brought her suitcase in from the car and tried to sneak in at least a last kiss.

She stood and faced the wall.

You wouldn't have needed Law skills to feel how sick at heart I was at the prospect of picking my own room and lying alone till daylight dawned, if it chose to do so.

Dellum saw my dejection at once and said "Boss Man, you good for some TV?"

It was past eleven but I was awake as any cat burglar. I said "Lead the way, sir."

We watched the end of the local news. They were burying the township's dozenth dead soldier, with the meager honors that were all that small towns could muster, even in the worst days of Vietnam. It was finally dawning on average people now that we were already hip-deep in blood and could not slog back for a long time to come. I'd been so swamped in my own numb life that I'd barely noticed the war at all. But as Dellum and I were watching that funeral, I saw that his narrow gray eyes were full. I hadn't expected to see my second Lawman streaming tears in so short a time, but it made me understand something surprising, and it came out of me like the voice of a stranger alive down in me. I said "I've got to sign up as a medic soon as I graduate."

The thought hadn't crossed my mind till then. And once I said it, I knew I was lying. Or wrong somehow. The average citizen knew next to nothing about the rights and wrongs of that particular war, but most sane men and boys were already doing everything from blowing off body parts to hiding behind long feather boas and ropes of pearls to look like queers and dodge the draft. Before I could take back what I'd said, Dellum's hand reached out and covered my mouth.

He was near me on the sofa. When his hand came down, he said "That's one form of trouble you don't need to seek. Let em come for you with shotguns and leg irons. It's why we have a draft—men in general don't want to kill children unless they're compelled by somebody's government."

I said "Nita's husband's over there now."

Dellum said "Then let him represent your family. You keep *out* of that place."

"He might die," I said. "His name is Al."

"Pray to God Al lives." I've mentioned Dellum's deep voice. By then it was deeper than whales can dive. "You let Miss Nita lose him at that far distance, you'll *really* have something even you can't handle."

At first I thought I understood him, but then I was puzzled. "Please say what you mean."

Dellum said "You're talking to an old detective, son. You and her are so hot in love with each other, I felt like I was in a *sauna* being near you. But Nita said she was brought up to be a nun. One thing I know a whole lot about is a Catholic upbringing—my wife had one and it ruined her for life. Ruined our marriage and would have ruined our son if he hadn't drowned first. If you let Nita's husband get killed while you're cheating, she'll go crazy on you."

I felt caught and grim and hacked. I also strongly suspected Dellum was right. He'd never looked more like my father, though Dad had surely not stayed around to help me start my adult life. Or had he? For one cold instant I thought this was Dad. The instant passed but still I said "Do you know the whole story I've lived through?"

Dellum said "You heard me say all I know about you. Your brother and sister died in their beds, your mother disappeared, now her car's turned up with the title signed to you and she's still gone."

I told him at least that much was right. "—And a whole lot more."

Dellum got up, turned off the TV and sat in the far chair. At first he nearly smiled. Then he said "Call me Dell please. Not many people do but I'd like for you to."

I thanked him and just managed to get out "Dell—" It felt about as easy as calling General Washington *George*.

That moment he turned into somebody new—and maybe too near me. The deep voice said "You killed those children, didn't you? Your mother ran from you. She's hiding somewhere, scared to death you'll find her. But you know where she is. That much is true."

I said "Yes sir" and believed myself. Or believed Dellum Stillman, or whoever this was, for another weird instant.

He pointed toward Nita's room. "This woman's no real schoolteacher, is she? She's your partner in crime."

I said "Sir, she's innocent as any new baby, and she teaches two years of Spanish at my high school." When Dell grinned and frowned almost at the same time, I said again "Can I tell you what happened?"

Dell said "Looks like to me it's happening still. But go on, sure."

I'd never smoked more than three cigarettes in my life, never liked the taste. But I suddenly asked Dell if he had any.

He just shook his head. "I'm not that eager to die before my time," and he gave a little beckoning wave with his hand. His face had settled into nearly a smile.

By then I was ice-cold scared of something, and I had no idea what I would say or what the truth might turn out to be. I recall that I tried to tell myself I was safe this close to an honest man. But then it dawned on me that Dell might just be what he said he was, a good detective in a seaside town that no doubt had its share of murders.

What if Mother were alive and hidden somewhere in this same township? What if she'd told Dell some story of her own that he was concealing till I laid out my story? What if I'd inherited Mother's insanity and committed the havoc on Arch and Adelle and then forgot I'd done it because I was crazy? What about all these things I was seeing—waving hands in dogwood trees, close-up stars in a normal backyard; other men's wives turned to angels in my lap, humping like cats on interstate highways?

So I just started in. "I loved my dad but I barely knew him. He left us when I was still eight years old but paid occasional night visits for about another year (mainly to use my mother's poor body). Then she *claimed* he shot himself shortly after she wrote him that his daughter was born and had been named for his own dead mother, the first Adelle Norfleet. There was nobody else to contradict her claim, though I've sometimes doubted it. Not that I'm sure I've seen him again; and I don't think I have any true memories of him, just a few things I've heard and made pictures of. In all of them anyhow, he's as good as your best dog, which makes me think I miss him. Once he was gone, my mother never mentioned him till she started breaking up when I was twelve. That was five years ago. Soon after she weakened, I'd taken on after-school and summer jobs and had raised enough money to go to a two-week summer camp more than a hundred miles from home. It felt like Heaven, being there in the mountains. And it wasn't till then that I realized our life at home was turning bad."

When I paused a little, Dell said "You mean your mother's mind was slipping?"

I decided to challenge him. "Did Mother tell you that?"

Dell looked stunned for a second but was too good a Lawman to throw down his cards. "What in the world would make you think that?"

I said "Well, first, because it's true. I can almost tell you've met her and talked awhile with her. See, young as I was, it wasn't till I got away to summer camp that I finally put the facts together—our mother was finally cracking all over like some old plate. I could lie in a bunk in the cold pitch-dark of the Smoky Mountains and replay individual things she'd say at supper or when I was just watching cartoons with the other boys or playing cards on the raw wood floor."

Dell said "I wouldn't think she liked TV much."

I had to nod. "You're right but one of her favorite things was to turn the TV up, then face the highest corner of the ceiling, and yell out something like 'Premier Khrushchev, I know you're listening to all I say and every private thought I try to have. I hope you enjoy it and use it well. We're true-blue soldiers in this poor house—an abandoned woman and three young orphans. We're in love with our country and ready to fight if called upon! But peace to you and all your dirty Commies—and most of all to your pitiful wife. I watch her nightly on the television news and can see she suffers arthritis in her hands. Send her sympathy from me, and tell her I eat eight raisins a day soaked overnight in gin. They keep me *cured.*'"

Dell had tried to stay solemn and open-minded; but he broke up laughing then, though I could see he knew I wasn't lying. For another whole minute he seemed like the kindly man on the phone and at the fish house. He said "Was there any other adult in the house in possession of his wits?"

"No. Her own mother tried to stay with us—we called her Tall Agnes—but Mother slapped her more than once, so she packed and left and died soon after."

"Died of poisoning, you say?"

"No, Dell, I didn't mention poison. You know more than me—"

He ignored that and pushed me onward. "You were twelve when you finally knew she was cracked?"

"When I went to camp, Yes; and *cracked* really doesn't cover Mother's situation."

Dell nodded and all but smiled again. "So you had five years of craziness to take before it really *got* you?" In that one sentence, he hardened again. You wouldn't have thought a cast-iron bar could have got any harder but Dell's face did. He kept it right on me, and the six feet between us was far too close.

So then I knew I was over my head in trouble deeper than my poor mother, whether she was somewhere under the ocean or maybe even out of sight in this house, waiting for me.

I said "Dell, you brought me all the way up here. You owe me one thing. Is my mother truly missing; or has she turned up, alive or dead?"

Dell said "Let's come to that awhile later, son." Then he sat back deep in his chair. "Who paid for those years when you claim she was crazy? Who raised you children and on whose money?"

I said "She managed to keep her job, right up till last Easter. Like an after-work drunk, she could hide her symptoms all day long when she wanted to. She worked in a good-sized accounting firm—a silent clerk. But I've had to call the Law to quiet her more than once in the evening. By then the pressure would truly get to her. Usually by the time the Law arrives, though, she's in the kitchen making cream mints, as quiet-seeming as anybody's aunt."

Dell said "I've seen some killer aunts."

I said "I'm beginning to believe you have. Mother worked, like I said. I always had several small-change jobs. My skinflint uncle sent a slim check occasionally. Otherwise, we did without."

Dell said "And you hated her for that?"

I didn't think I had. Hate hadn't felt like a part of my mind. And 1968 was several years before America launched out on the great Hatred and Anger Jamboree we've been on ever since. Even now, in a whole new century, if you listen to TV for five minutes or to any conversation on the street, you'll hear at least one person say "I'm just so *angry* at so and so." And if nobody volunteers to say it, then a bystanding reporter or hack-psychologist will turn to some normally disappointed person and say "Have you had a chance to get your *anger* out?" Anger at *what* for God's sake? Who could pick out a single target from the thicket of candidates? But Dell's last question had left me puzzled. I said "I doubt I've hated anything. What for? Doesn't everybody pay for everything eventually?"

Dell said "We may get to find that out. You and me both."

That scared me even worse. This very experienced man almost certainly thought I was the red-handed felon in a big-sized interstate crime. My only thing that halfway resembled an alibi was Nita Acheson, asleep two rooms away. But she was somebody else's wife, a schoolteacher hired to keep her hands off me. And even Nita would have to swear she hadn't seen me for all of that fatal night. I'd got to the moment you've heard of before. I was tired and as guilty-feeling as any other nearly grown boy. So it dawned on me to do the quick clean thing. I smiled at Dellum. "You got some statement you want me to sign? I see you've got a big tape recorder on your stereo. Want to just go on and tape a confession?"

Dell said "If you're ready I'll call another cop. We'll read you your rights— "

My head had already started nodding Yes. My brain was racing from *scared* to *thrilled*. I even thought *Noble, this proves it. You're crazy as your mother; you never touched your brother and sister in the mildest anger, yet here you are aiming yourself toward Death Row*. But I didn't pull back or take back a word.

Right then, though, something moved against my right leg, down at the calf. It might well have shocked me, but at once it was soothing. Not so much soothing but healing. It worked instantaneously. I looked down and there, in the dim light, was a knotty face and curious eyes, fixed right on me. No special shine, though—no trace of music. Not till I reached down and actually touched it did I realize what had rescued me now.

It was Dell's ancient dog. He'd been asleep behind the sofa and had somehow picked this moment to wake up and check out who I was. His steady dark eyes confirmed I was who I thought I was—a sane boy, innocent of killing anyhow. I looked to Dell and said "What's his name?"

"Jeff. Jeffrey Dellum was my lost son's name."

As I gently scrubbed at Jeff's ridged skull, his eyes stayed open and fixed on me still. I said "Well, you've taught him to watch the world. He hasn't blinked yet."

Dell said "Blind in both eyes. Can't see anything."

I said "He sees me. He sees I'm not guilty, not of what you claim."

Dell actually laughed and for the first time lately he looked like a decent human being and not a flinty arm of the Law. Then he leaned far toward me and made a tall sign of the cross in the air. He'd said he was Catholic. I left it at that, though I've had later occasions to wonder if he knew what he meant by that vanishing cross in the air. Was he trying to steer me, and is it finally taking hold all these years later? In any case, he said "Son, I never claimed you were anything but what I could see. I just had to run you through the mill to prove I was right." He softened his voice and called to the dog. "Jeff, come here to Dellum."

Jeff wouldn't obey. By then he'd stretched out against my ankle and was gone again in peaceful sleep.

I had a space in time, then and there, when I honestly wondered if I'd died and was in some afterlife that was meant to be blessed. Or had I entered the outskirts of Hell where the rest of my life would go pretty much as it had till now—what felt like easiness, followed by torture, then spells of relief? For all I knew, I sat there for hours, days or weeks. Then I came to in nothing but dim hall light. Dell was gone but Jeff was still asleep down beside me. I crouched back on the sofa again and must have slept till the outskirts of dawn.

Then a hand woke me, laid on my head. It was Nita in the light summer bathrobe she'd brought.

At first I didn't know where I was, then I thought of Dell, then I saw that he and Jeff were gone.

Nita said "You haven't undressed all night?"

I said "I was proving my innocence." When she frowned I grinned and said "I'm clean. *Clean* bill of health. Dell believes the truth."

Nita said "Dellum's gone. His bedroom's open. His bed's made up."

I stood then and walked through the rooms, calling Dell and Jeff both. Nothing responded. Then I saw that his car was gone from the drive.

Nita had followed me, looking worried.

I told her "He's already gone to work. We'll meet him down there. He said Mother's car was in some basement, next to the station."

I was still fully dressed, but my clothes were so sour I was eager to shed them.

Nita, in her robe, was halfway gone toward being fully naked. And she stood there looking a good deal better than any goddess in the Latin textbook I'd stolen from school two years ago just because I loved one picture of Diana, Goddess of the Hunt.

How was I meant to respect Nita's word then and not reach out for guaranteed bliss? It would be a good while of course before I gave a serious thought to anybody's bliss but my own. If they gave the least sign of pleasure—the simplest moan—that was all I needed to flag me onward. So I got to my feet. The fact that Dell might turn up any second was meaningless to me. I was out of my clothes in under three seconds. When Nita stepped back I didn't think she was hesitating. I remember telling myself *She's watching my natural body.* It was good enough to look at if your standards weren't stringent. It didn't dawn on me that the sight of a stripped-bare recent orphan was maybe what moved her.

The next quarter hour, there on the floor, was the finest time I'd spent till then. At the end it felt as if I'd soared whole years ahead into my grown manhood—not the cruel kind but the kind I'd wanted all my life, a careful man that watches the world and tends to his own. And that's in spite of the fact that Nita poured out bitter tears every second of the way, though she never said No—not that I could hear. Be sure I don't report that with pride.

*   *   *

By the time we'd cleaned ourselves up and dressed, Dell still wasn't back. There were no notes anywhere explaining his absence; so I ate a bowl of his cereal and milk, and then we drove into town. When I asked for Dell at the police station, the young man on duty at first looked blank. I gave him Dell's full name and said he was holding an abandoned car that belonged to me. The man got up and spoke to an officer in the room behind him, a white-haired fellow. The fellow came toward me and Nita smiling. When he got to the counter, he said "Dell Stillman doesn't really work here on a regular basis."

I told him that came as a sizable surprise.

He actually laughed. "A lot of people say that. He just helps us sometime at big events—wrecks and parades. He used to be a private detective apparently up in New Jersey." The overhead light suddenly lit up the officer's white hair, and it felt like a boulder of ice coming at me, but then he laughed again. "I guess Dell talks a lot, but I doubt he means harm."

I said "He sure scared the hell out of me—had me almost confessing to outright slaughter."

That wiped the smile off the officer's face. "You under suspicion of something, sir?"

I told him "Absolutely not. You can call the police chief in my hometown in North Carolina, and he'll vouch for me. No sir, my mother killed my brother and sister some weeks ago and fled in her car. We had no word of her whereabouts till Dell Stillman phoned me two days ago, right at my school, and told me her car had been found up here, abandoned with a note saying now it was mine."

After the officer had searched every cell of my face for about a minute each, he said "I'm Captain Blair Henry. I know your story. The car's here, right; but I didn't know that Dell had called you. I was going to get around to that early next week. Well, here you are in any case. You plan to drive it south?"

I told him I did.

He told the younger man to go get the car, and then he asked me if I'd be kind enough to tell him a few things about my mother in case she turned up "in some form or other"—he truly said that (I guessed any Lawman who lived by the ocean had seen some fairly awful bodies washed up weeks too late).

Nita and I went back to his office. I gave him the truth as far as I knew it.

He seemed to believe me. When he'd made a few notes and got my number at Hesta's house, he shook my hand and said he'd notify me if he heard a thing about Mother.

I smiled but asked him to tell Dell Stillman not to scare good people the way he had me.

He said "Dell pretty much goes his own way. We're a small town, you see—very little in the way of serious trouble so we try to humor Dell—but I'll give him your message." Then he gave me one of the major surprises of my life till then. He was bigger than me in every respect; and he folded me in with arms that might well have crushed creatures stronger than me, saying "I can see in your eyes that you'll make better luck for yourself than you've had."

That's the kind of promise any stunned boy or girl might be glad to hear. When I got my breath I thanked him and said "Excuse me for asking a maybe dumb question, but do I look anything like Dell Stillman's son?"

He studied me carefully one last time, then said "You still look honest to me, but No I never saw Dellum's son, if he ever existed."

I figured I'd better leave it at that and head on my way, so I thanked him again.

Nita did also but still in Spanish.

I hadn't expected anything special, but the sight of that '59 Buick at the curb in the pounding sun of a late spring morning rolled over me like the nearby waves. Wild as she got, Mother always kept her car as spotlessly clean as her house. Wherever it had been in recent weeks, the car was shining now. I stopped in my tracks maybe ten yards away and stood, more than half expecting my parent to step out and bear down on me. There was no fear in what I felt. What had stopped me was a sudden longing to see her, not the awful last way but the way she looked in my first memories when we were both young and she fully understood me—as I did her.

Nita understood at once. Very gently she said "Noble, now it's nothing but a car. You've got to drive it home."

I thanked her and then realized I was hungry. Dell's cereal was thinning out in my stomach. That restaurant where we'd eaten supper was open beyond us, so we went over there, and I ate more than I'd eaten in weeks.

For some strange reason Nita chose to speak in really complicated Spanish through that whole meal. She often smiled, in short little bursts. But I hardly understood half of what she said, and I told her so. She claimed that should make me try harder on my homework. Then as I was finishing and thinking how much I dreaded the lone ride down in that Buick, Nita finally spoke English. She said "Let's at least take a walk on the beach before we leave."

I recalled Dell saying he still had hopes my mother's body might reappear one day from the sea, so I hardly relished the idea of walking where she'd disappeared. But we went anyhow.

We walked for way over an hour, several miles in both directions, north and south. I kept waiting for Nita to say something else about us two. I'll confess I'd spent a fair amount of time calculating what a life together would be like if her husband didn't come back from the war. She'd seemed so miserable when we left Dell's house, but all she did at first on the beach was comment on the things we passed. She hadn't gone to college for nothing. She knew a good deal about birds and shells and the spooky ghost crabs that scuttled around us. And she couldn't help giving me little lectures on the sights. At first I tried to hold her hand. Politely but strongly, she refused; so we walked separate but close as friends.

It was then that she gave me a little speech that felt as planned as any valedictory speech at Commencement. "Noble, you've been through some terrible hell. I don't low-rate one atom you've suffered. But I want you to know one thing I endured. It has a lot to do with why I let myself get too close to you and why I'm asking you to let me go now—back to where I belong and have made promises. See, when I was two years younger than you, my own mother died; and I was left in a crossroads town in South Carolina with a father and two brothers—all of them running The Honest Garage, which was truly its name; and it had earned it. I liked them all three; and I see them all still, every Christmas and Easter. Papa was in his early forties. My brothers were nineteen and twenty-one. I had to take over and try to run the house for the four of us, making beds anyhow and cooking our breakfast and supper. I'd never so much as fried a chicken, but I sure-God had to dive in fast and learn what I could from a few old books and a bunch of clippings my mother had left in closets and drawers.

"It seemed to come to me naturally. Pop and my brothers praised me from the start, which of course made me happy. One night I cooked the hardest meal I'd tried till then—my nearest brother Lon's favorite, Swiss steak. It was Lon's nineteenth birthday and the steak came out a lot better than Mother's. That was during the summer school-vacation; and I was awake till late, cleaning up the kitchen. I finally got to sleep and was deep unconscious when somebody got in my narrow bed beside me. Just by the feel of his coarse raven hair, I could tell it was Lon. And when I finally knew it, I didn't manage to turn him away. Mother's death had been harder on him than anybody else, and I always felt he was due more love than he'd ever got. In any case it was my first time, he said it was his, and he'd been a sweet brother.

"I still don't believe it was Lon who told the others. Maybe he didn't and they just responded to some high signal that I was putting out against my will. Anyhow once Lon had left my bed the first time, I figured he'd be back some night soon, but a long time passed, and then my older brother turned up. His name was Randal. Among all of us, he was the great beauty. Ordinary people who were more than half blind would stop in the street and watch him pass, even when he was a child. And though he was our only silent kinsman, he was also kind to be around. After his first visit he returned once a week, every Friday night for a long time to come."

I felt like I had to stop Nita there. I wasn't offended or horrified, but I somehow knew if she told me too much she'd always blame me for what I knew. So I took her elbow and said "Maybe you ought to quit right now. I think I get the message."

We went on, silent, for another few yards. And then she spoke so quietly I could hardly hear her above the mild surf. "My father was next—just once but next."

I reached out then, without breaking stride, and put my right hand over her mouth.

She shook herself free and gave a long laugh. But we both went onward.

Like a lot of boys of my generation, as long as Mother was alive and subscribing, I'd read a newspaper every day of my life from seven years old till she disappeared. So I'd read of more than one family story even harder to hear than Nita's, and I had to believe her. Who on God's Earth would make up such a story? Anyhow to fill the air with something but surf, I started whistling.

Nita let me do that for fifty more yards. Then she said "One way and another, every few weeks or months, that went on pretty much till I left for college. It got so I didn't know who it was, the room was so dark and I went so dazed. Then I met my husband in a botany class. He was working on an M.A. thesis on orchids and was the lab assistant in my senior year. He had eyes very much like your eyes. You'd be half-scared they were going to draw you right inside them if you got too close. I hope they're still that way. It's been a long time—"

She may have choked up. There were no tears or moans, but she stopped for a good while and wouldn't look toward me.

I finally said what I thought was decent. "He'll get back, Nita, with two safe eyes. I'll bet you good money."

That last sentence didn't go down too well, and she finally faced me with a hard frown.

I said I was sorry, but again I promised her Al would come back, eyes and all. I told her I felt it deep in my bones, which was actually true. The thought of his presence was a real fear by now. Then I tried to think how to change the subject.

Nita pushed on though. "I never told Al of course, but nobody ever dared touch me again while he was in sight."

I didn't want to think too hard right then about what she meant that to signify for me. So I watched the ground for many yards to come and somehow felt scared. I wasn't fool enough to think we'd come across

Mother's corpse beached at our feet, but I still couldn't shake the sadness I'd felt when I saw the Buick. That and Nita's cutting me off were making me know, for the first time really, how entirely alone I was on the Earth. It wasn't that I'd fallen in love with my teacher. Young as I was, I knew what drew me to her so strongly. Crude though it sounds, I knew it was not the rarest thing of all. But what young man—what *man* for that matter—is likely to be persuaded by that fact to walk away from a woman who's given him numerous times what Nita gave me?

This may sound too hard to believe, even by way of a belated confession; but when we'd walked about two miles north and turned to head back, I thought I should speak out in this grand scenery and beg her to keep on helping me make my way through the thicket of my near future. That of course partly meant I was begging her not to shut me out of her excellent body, the body she'd pledged to a man off at war and that men in her family had availed themselves of well before she could try to refuse.

Before I could speak, though, a man was walking toward us with his head down. He looked shrunk and huddled in on himself. And bright as it was, he was wearing a raincoat and a broad old hat.

I thought I'd wait till we got on past him before I spoke to Nita again.

And we'd got to within a few feet of him before Nita spoke. She said "Mr. Stillman, we thought we'd missed you."

Then I saw it was Dell.

He stopped in his tracks and gave a wide smile to Nita alone.

She said "We left your house the way we found it, but we thought we'd missed seeing you again."

Dell gave her a slight bow, smiling still. Then he faced me, grim as a grave.

The look felt like it lasted a week. It also felt like a giant had seized me and shaken me hard to make me cough out one important thing. Of course I figured he still thought I was guilty of everything I'd lost.

So I literally raised my hands in the air like a man surrendering.

Nita turned and laughed.

But Dell stayed grim. Then he said "You out here scrounging for your family?"

I told him I knew where my family was, except my poor mother.

Dell said "Well, you just truck on south to the pitiful state that you call home. I've got your phone number. When I find her, you'll know." In the last minute he seemed to grow a good deal younger in the face, though his body stayed crouched.

If this man bore any kinship to me, I felt like I ought to start running *now*. Still I was too young to want us to part like this, in meanness. So I made a last try. "Where's old Jeff?"

Dell said "Don't you give Jeff a thought. Jeff's fine. He might be up there with all your family in God's big lap." Dell pointed to the sky and, again, didn't smile.

Hot as the sun was, I literally shuddered. Not till then in my life had I come up against what felt like a demon, some spirit made out of pure dark malice. I wouldn't have been the least surprised if he'd gone on to say he'd strangled Jeff with his cold bare hands in the last ten minutes. In time it would turn out I was maybe right about Dell Stillman's spirit. For then, though, I took Nita's arm and we pushed on.

She turned one final time and thanked Dell again.

And Dell said "Little lady, take *extra* care," as if I might be as evil as he. He didn't look to me again.

In another half hour Nita and I were on the road south in separate cars.

I'd never been alone in a car for seven hours, so the trip was a very mixed time for me. At first of course I thought a lot about Nita pulling herself away and about her troubling story. It was still the late 1960s; and for all the free sex talk on television, the country hadn't yet owned up to the commonness of incest. By the time I bypassed Washington, I'd worked myself into a hot lather of self-pity and almost equal pity for Nita. The pity for her, I'm sorry to say, included a strong faith on my part that the best thing I could do for her now would be to offer her the kind of physical love I guessed she'd never known (green as I was, I'd had strong hints that Nita's acquaintance with the kinds of pleasure I longed to give was non-existent).

Then once I was into the rolling Virginia countryside, I underwent my next strange experience. As always it began with a change in the light. In those days car clocks never worked past the first six months; but Mother's clock was dead-right still—it was four-twelve P.M. I was bound due south, and the sun was naturally about halfway down the sky on my right. Slowly now it began to move toward the south till it was directly in front of me. Its color lightened to a pale white gold, and somehow I knew it was no longer setting but rising. I understood that was good news for me.

And then I saw the highway itself start rolling out like the longest carpet, straight south before me. It wasn't red or special in any unreal way. It was just gray concrete with yellow lines and oil stains. But I could see it as far as it went—to the tip end of Florida and the blue Gulf beyond. I could see my old home and Hesta's house, each small but clear. I could see my school and Nita's classroom. My brother's and sister's graves were in place with the flowers I'd left there the previous Sunday, still living somehow and colored more fiercely than when I'd last seen them. None of it looked toylike or cute. It looked like a world on the way to being perfect.

For the first time, with one of my recent visions, I doubted I understood what it meant. And with all the weird events of the weekend, I couldn't be sure if it boded well or was some sort of warning. So for the first time, I asked out loud. I said "Give me something better than this." It waited a good while, whatever it was. Then with the vision still clean and bright, it said "Come ahead."

The two words were at least as definite as speech, though I can't guarantee they'd have been on a tape you might have been making beside me that moment. At first I thought they must be an order to drive straight to Florida and sail out from there. But then as I kept looking forward, I saw my mother's face in the air above the end of the road. She was not quite smiling, but I thought she recognized me, and I understood I must find her first—her body at least and a decent grave for her.

The car gave me no trouble at all, and I got to my hometown about ten that Saturday night. I'd tried to keep up with Nita on the highway, but she slipped away in the traffic, so I drove straight to her house. At least I'd find out if she'd got back safely, or I'd sit at the curb and wait till she turned up.

She was already there. When I gave my usual four slow knocks on the back door, she appeared, already in her bathrobe again. You'll know that gave me a moment of hope. But she blocked the door with the firmest courtesy, saying she was bone-tired and would see me in class.

That meant I wouldn't even see her on Sunday—she was keeping her promise to herself anyhow. When she shut the door, I stood there a minute, wondering how I'd use all the energy in me. There was nobody else in town I could go to, not unless I planned to spend more cash than I had. Hesta was bound to be asleep; and asleep or awake, I couldn't talk to Hesta. She had settled every question on Earth in her cranky way and could barely listen to another opinion. Still when Nita's porch light went dark, I drove on to Hesta's. At least she'd have a billion lights on. She'd once said "Every dark corner in my house is hiding somebody I cheated or hurt, and all of them now are too old to forgive me." Nobody seemed to know what she meant. My family anyhow had never known her to do the least harm, but of course she'd lived for many years before we met her.

Yet the house was dark by the time I got there, nothing but a dim shine through the kitchen window. I parked in the yard by Hesta's Studebaker, which was twenty years old and so beautifully kept that classic-car fiends were always offering her gigantic sums to drive it away. She'd thank them profusely, then say she intended to take it to Heaven. "Heard Studebakers were the angels' favorite car; and they're scarce now, you know—not making no more."

I climbed the steps quietly and let myself in the side-porch door (she'd trusted me with keys to all her three doors). I called her name and thought I heard a single dull knock but no voice spoke. I turned left and felt my way through the hall toward the dim kitchen. Again I said Hesta's name and asked if she was all right.

A strange voice said "I'm all right, Noble."

At first I thought it came from a man. It was that clear and low and was plainly not black.

By then my eyes had opened a little, and I saw a body standing at the sink. Again it looked like a small trim man.

Hesta kept her knives in a rack just one step beyond me. I reached out and took the biggest handle I could feel.

The man said "Sit down, son. You're bound to be hungry."

For a cold instant I thought it was Dellum. He'd beat me down here, had somehow found Hesta's and was waiting with his next weird surprise. So I took awhile to compose myself and say the right thing. I finally chuckled. "Dell Stillman, you're a one-man bloodhound."

The man said "Oh son, no blood please."

Then I knew the voice. *Oh Lord God,* I said to myself. *This is my poor mother.* Sometimes her medication made her voice deepen. Still I couldn't imagine she was here. I thought she had to be a ghost turned out from Hell to bring me a personal message, or maybe she'd come to finish the job she'd left unfinished on her natural children. For a long hard moment, I stood in place with my knife loose beside me and waited for her to turn whatever weapon she held against my heart or the pit of my throat.

She stayed where she was, five yards away, still by the sink. And slowly she raised the wick on the oil lamp Hesta kept for power failures. It was like watching light itself carve a woman out of nothing but air. And yes it was Mother. No possible question on Earth. She said "Hesta's got a whole world of fresh eggs and some good sharp cheese. Let me fix you an omelet. It'll help you sleep."

A hundred questions swarmed up at me. *Can it truly be Mother? Other than Maryland, where has she been? How did she get here without the Buick? Who on Earth brought her? And where is Dellum in this whole mystery?* Strangest of all, though—scared as I was—I was half glad to see her. I also knew I was seriously hungry, and I said "All right. I'd be much obliged." I suddenly thought how strange it was that people were always wanting to cook me eggs whenever the outlook was dim. But this was my only parent after all, and up till now she'd never harmed me—not my body nor my skin.

She went on about her job as if these weeks hadn't cut a deep trench between us. I set my knife back in Hesta's rack, but I stayed upright where I was and waited. I still didn't quite want to have my mother moving behind me with cutlery near.

As she worked in the lamp light, she slowly looked younger till by the time she'd finished my meal, she was almost the girl I'd loved as far back as I could recall. For the first time in years, her hair was auburn and clean again. Her eyes didn't seem to be driven by wild dogs. Her mouth could smile. Maybe these weeks on the road, or wherever, had finally given her the rest she'd needed for so many years. Anyhow she set my food at the head of Hesta's table, and she took a seat to the right of my chair.

By then it seemed natural to sit beside her. I couldn't think of anything to say, though. But the food tasted fine, and it seemed to please her to watch me eat it. Her name was Edith Redden Norfleet, and for whatever reason that just keep sounding itself in my head. So when our eyes finally met and she smiled, I managed to say two words—"Edith Redden," her maiden name.

She said "I used to know a girl named that."

"Well, so did I." Nothing else came to me, and I kept on eating.

Eventually she said "Noble. Noble something—" Her voice trailed off. Then she said "I used to love a boy named Noble. You ever see him around here anymore?" She still seemed saner than most folks I knew.

I said "I run across him every week or so. He's bearing up all right—close to finishing high school. Sure would like to go to college for a year or so but can't see how."

None of that concerned her. She only said "You think he holds me responsible?"

"For the night before Easter?" I said.

"Don't confuse me with dates. You're almost certain to know what I mean."

I said "I don't think Noble Norfleet's any big judge of anything. Don't worry about what he thinks at all. He makes his own mistakes." And the way I felt that moment, I couldn't have blamed Edith Redden for anything, much less the killing of children I'd liked.

She stood up and her voice rose a note or two on the scale. "Son, I didn't give you your coffee."

For all I could see, no coffee was made. I'd never been much of a coffee drinker so I said "Don't worry. It's too late now." I meant it was too late at night for caffeine.

But she sat back down like a dropped sack of sand. She laid both hands flat out on the table and looked at them. Her wedding ring was still in place, half an inch wide. When I worried about what she might use for money—if she was still alive and drifting—I'd thought she could get a few dollars anyhow from this much gold. The right hand was not ten inches from mine.

But I couldn't touch it, not yet anyhow.

At last she said "I was hoping it wasn't too late."

So finally I thought I'd push on forward and see if we were alive or dead. These last ten minutes had seemed far stronger than any real dream. I said "Mother, it's been a lot too late since Easter morning."

In the minutes it took her to think through that, she got younger still. And when she finally spoke, her voice was almost back to its normal state. "Too late for what?" Then before I could give her the awful answer, she said "I stopped by the house. It's still fine. No reason at all you and I can't take back up right where we left off. I'll probably have to look for a new job, but I haven't lost a one of my skills. I'll be in demand—" She faced me and gave the smile that was harder to bear than any smile since.

I almost thought I should reach out and hold her, tightly somehow, to stop her rushing on backward through time. In a few more seconds, she'd have gone past the point where I was born; and then where would I be?

But then she looked up and met my eyes again, sane as any Supreme Court justice on the bench in robes. She said "You're going to turn me in."

I told her she'd never heard that from me.

"But you want to," she said.

That much wasn't true and I asked her who told her.

"That man up north," she managed to point precisely toward north.

"In Maryland?" I said. "A man named Dell?"

She seemed to shake her head, though she didn't say No. But she did say "Hesta." Then she nodded hard. "Hesta says you've laid all your traps for me." As a boy I'd built rabbit gums and trapped a good many wild rabbits to sell. I felt more than sure, though, that Hesta hadn't said I'd laid traps for Mother. I was about to say as much when a wave of reality swept me down.

Maybe I'd been too surprised to wonder, then too hypnotized by Mother's calm nearness; but suddenly all the questions I hadn't asked came falling in on me. Where was Hesta now? Again, how had Mother got to town? How had she managed to stay so clean and well-kept through these six weeks? What had she used for money, and where had she got the clothes she was wearing? They were plain but they fit. And if they weren't new, they still looked clean and pressed. Above all, how had she known to look for me here? So I said "Where is Hesta?"

"Upstairs in her bed."

"Alive?" I said.

"Oh very much so. She was just worn out."

By then I was worried, though I hated to be. I'd prized the last few minutes so highly. I strongly felt I should check on Hesta. She seldom got tired before two in the morning. But I didn't want to leave Mother here alone. She might be gone when I got back. So I said "Are you sleeping down here or upstairs?"

She actually smiled, more broadly than ever. "Oh son, you know I haven't slept for years. Not since my twenty-third birthday."

I said "How did you get down here from Maryland?"

She seemed truly puzzled. "I've never been to Maryland, except maybe that time we all went to D.C. when you were—what?—nine?"

I said "Have you seen the rest of our family?" It felt as cruel as anything I'd done since forcing Nita this morning at Dell's, but I didn't take it back or ask Mother's pardon.

She looked at me as if I were having the kind of dream I'd had so often in early childhood. My nights then were frequent terrors. She reached out to touch my hand.

But I took it back. Then I said "You and I need to take a short trip."

"Where to?"

I said "Not far. You wait for me now. I'll be right down. Make some coffee for me. I need some after all."

That did it. She stood and started work at the sink.

For some reason I turned the oil lamp down to the slimmest shine. Then I climbed Hesta's steps, by threes, entirely silent. At the top all the rooms were still dark as Egypt. But I called her name, and I heard the same dull knock I'd heard when I entered the house half an hour ago. Now it seemed to come from Hesta's room, a weak knock and dim yips like an old dog asleep.

When I switched on her light, Hesta was flat on her iron bed, staring toward me. She was dressed in her underwear and a long slip, and she looked much smaller than the average schoolchild. Her wrists and ankles were thin as sticks but were bound with plastic clothesline. Her mouth was covered with masking tape.

At once I knew that the worst part, for Hesta, was being half-dressed with a man in her room. I said "Don't worry. I can hardly see you." Then I went straight over and, with my pocketknife, quickly cut her loose.

She lay there still and carefully peeled the tape from her lips before she sat up. Then she studied me slowly and said "You alive?"

"Oh yes. Are you?"

Hesta put her long hand over her heart and waited till she knew. "Still beating, I *think*."

I said "She didn't stab you anywhere?"

"No, child, she was gentle as always—with me anyhow."

I said "How long you been tied up?"

Hesta said "First of all, you shut your eyes while I dress." When I did, she got up to find her clothes. But she went on whispering. "See, she and I were talking easy downstairs till not long before you walked back in. She'd got here a little after dark—knocked on the door, polite as a child—and was fine till I mentioned that you were coming soon."

"Did she say why she needed to tie you up?"

Hesta gave a parched laugh. "Said she wanted you all to herself. Like years ago when you were a baby. You bound to know that."

I said "Is she real?"

Hesta laughed again. "Oh yes, I threw some holy water at her when her back was turned. She didn't even smoke, much less disappear." Hesta ordered her holy water by the quart from a grinning cadaverous preacher on TV. It cost her plenty and she used it liberally to heal herself and needy others right here at her home. Now after a long wait, Hesta said "You can open your eyes."

I did and saw that, warm as it was, she'd dressed for church in the depths of winter—a wool dress, a sweater, one of the black caps she knitted by the dozen. I suddenly realized *She thinks we're both about to be killed. She's dressed for her funeral.* But I didn't mention that. I said "How on Earth did she get down here? I've got her car parked right outside, just drove it back from Maryland."

Hesta said "I asked her and all she told me was 'The Lord brought me. Brings me everywhere I go.' "

"You ask her anything about the—killing?" I'd nearly said *crime* but something had stopped me. However much I'd liked my brother and sister, I'd still never thought of their deaths as *murder*, as outright crimes.

Hesta said "I asked her if she'd seen the Law. She told me that's why she'd come back home. Said she had 'some business to talk over with him'—wouldn't tell me who she meant by *him*. Then she showed me that pearl-handled pistol and tied me up."

I said "She's never owned a pistol in her life."

Hesta said "She's got one now, real as a three-week case of the flu. She fired in the kitchen just to show me it worked. Shot straight overhead by my poor old stove. Went right through the roof. That'll cost me thirty dollars, if you or me ever goes back downstairs to cook another meal."

By then I'll admit I was feeling more fear. Hesta had told me weeks ago that she'd never kept a gun. I had nothing but a short pocketknife. And here we were with an insane woman, armed to the teeth, between us and safety. We couldn't even call for help since Hesta had never got an upstairs phone—nobody ever called her after dark—so at that point I was stymied.

But Hesta reached out, took both my hands and stood still and quiet for maybe ten seconds. I understood it was some form of prayer, and I knew her prayers mostly got results. When she turned me loose, she said very firmly "I'm going downstairs now and getting that pistol."

I had to say "Not alone you're not."

But she shook her head hard. "I'm an old woman, Noble. If she kills me, that's fine. I'll speed straight to Heaven. You need a long life."

For a whole moment that seemed to make sense. But then I knew that this was my mother we were talking about, she was my sole duty, nobody else should stand between her and me—not now. I told Hesta to stay up here and read her Bible, which was what she did most Saturday nights; and I said I was sure things would turn out calmly.

She accepted that and went straight to her Bible. "I'll read Psalm Seventy-seven," she said. "That'll help you."

"Remind me how that begins," I said.

Hesta said " 'I cried unto God with my voice.' "

"That's a good one," I told her. "You keep saying that and this'll go right."

Hesta said "Amen."

As I turned to leave, Hesta whispered "Step here." When I leaned down toward her, she said "You know it now, don't you?—you're fighting a demon."

I'd forgot. And I halfway thought she was right, so I begged her pardon.

"I told you the day you found those dead children—it's not Miss Edith. It's the demon down in her. He's spread roots all through her mind and her heart, he's clamped onto her like a great mad dog, you tell him to leave in the name of the Lord."

I said "Amen," turned my head to smile and left Hesta there on her thin mattress.

I reached the kitchen door in silence; and everything was the way I'd left it, except that Mother was back at the table, sitting down. I could almost have sworn she'd changed her clothes. Surely her dress hadn't been this dark.

Anyhow she'd turned the oil lamp high again. In the warm shine, she still looked young but tireder now—as tired as any child who's been trooped up and down the east-coast map against its own will for nearly two months by mysterious means. She was also wrapped in some kind of spell that kept her from noticing me in the doorway. It crossed my mind to think *She's maybe* all *demon now, when she doesn't know I'm watching.* So I stood still another minute, trying to think exactly when she'd first seemed too strange for normal life.

What I recalled was my twelfth birthday, five years ago, when I came home from school half-expecting a pound cake and two or three presents to mark the occasion. But what ambushed me was Mother in an electric-blue new dress, the whole house strung with crepe-paper streamers and my name in Christmas lights across the dining room. She'd even swept my brother and sister up in her wildness, and their glad faces were painted orange and black and dusted with dime-store glitter. The first to speak was Mother herself; and all she said was "Love of my life," pointing to me. She didn't say one more word for three days, though she never stopped smiling.

As I got to the pitiful end of that memory, she stayed at Hesta's table but slowly turned toward me—no surprise, no fear. No pistol anywhere in sight either.

She didn't quite smile but her voice was still pleasant. "You forgot your coffee." When she brought the full mug back from the sink, she laid the pistol quietly on the table. Now it was nearer to my place than hers.

So I went on and sat in the place where I'd eaten my supper. By then, again, I'd lost any fear. And as I sat I took up the pistol as if it were nothing more intriguing than a half-dollar coin.

Mother calmly said "I'd feel safer if you left it in sight."

I put it to the right of my place, on the off-side from her.

She said "Move it five inches closer to me." While my hand refused to move, she launched the kind of smile I hadn't seen for years. It lit her face like dawn on a pear tree, blooming like fury.

So again I obeyed her. I still wasn't scared. I smiled back at her, then drank nearly half the coffee straight off in a swallow. It was far and away the finest coffee I'd drunk since Easter, and I told her as much.

She said "I can make good coffee—and it's *hard.* Not everybody can." When I'd emptied the cup, her eyes fixed on me like a desperate baby's hand. And she said "Son, I ask you in deep sincerity—tell me what I did awhile back. Why I left here so fast, where I've been ever since, where I'm meant to go now?" No child in the hands of a firing squad ever looked more puzzled and plainly concerned.

I'd seen her play the kinds of games many crazy people play when they've got you off-stride (in those days we used the word *crazy* pretty freely; *mental illness* had barely been heard of in the world I frequented). But I thought I knew my mother well enough to see she was playing no games with me now. I said "First off, it's all a great mystery—to me and everybody else who knows you, in this town at least. All I can tell you is what I found when I woke up on Easter morning, the fourteenth of April, not two months ago."

She nodded and took a long slow breath. "Tell me that much then."

I said "Somebody killed both Arch and Adelle with the kitchen ice pick—in their own bunk beds back at our own home—and you and the Buick were gone by the time I woke up that morning near eleven o'clock."

That seemed to take a good while to reach her. And all through the wait her eyes never weakened their hold on me. She finally said "They're still truly dead—Arch and Adelle both?"

"Yes ma'm. God didn't make a personal appearance to resurrect them, so I saw them buried. I saw their bodies covered."

"My children?" she said.

I said "Yours and Henry Norfleet's."

Her eyes went sharp. "Henry Norfleet had no more part in those children than he did in you, and you well know it."

No I didn't know what she meant—maybe nothing—but I didn't want to ask. I nodded in silence.

She said "Archie Norfleet? Adelle Norfleet? Both young as they were?" She seemed to be asking genuine questions. It truly seemed I was giving her news she was only just learning.

I had to say "You've got it right, Mother."

She'd been a quick weeper before her troubles started, but now her eyes didn't fill with tears. They blinked slowly and then she laid both hands on the table, palms flat down. She looked aside quickly, then said "There's some coffee left—"

I shook my head No. And when she stared off into blank space, I said "Tell me one thing—who left me alive?"

She knew that at once. "Who else but the Lord?" When she faced me, she laughed—nothing crazy, just a girl's quick chuckle.

I said what I felt. "They were all I had, my brother and sister, except for you."

She said "The same thing's true for me of course. Now you're the whole story. Now you can tell it your way, with nobody else in the road between you and where you're headed." My left hand was on the table, and she reached for that.

Without meaning to, I drew it away. I thought I was hearing the crazy voice I'd heard before. And my inmost mind couldn't bear her touch, not right then.

That seemed to hurt her. Her mouth went straight as a rail but she didn't speak, and I thought she glanced at the gun beside me.

I finally said "You know we need to go to the Law now—you know that, don't you?"

Right off, she nodded. It was clearly not a new idea to her.

I said "The Buick's just outside and ready. Let's ride downtown and do what we have to."

She said "I can't get in the Buick again. That's your car now."

I said "Then we'll go in Hesta's Studebaker. She'd be glad to have us use it." I put my right hand over the pistol and pushed my chair back.

Mother stayed in place but made no effort to take the gun. And the beautiful youth she'd shown me awhile ago streamed back into her face, some kind of deep peace that she'd found somewhere I couldn't imagine.

I put the pistol into my right pocket and finally managed to hold out a hand and ask my mother to stand up now. I also asked if she had any luggage.

She laughed. "I left all that in the bin at the Salvation Army. Figured the warden would want to re-dress me."

I kept her hand in mine and led the way to the hall. She let me lead with no pulling back, and then I thought *I'm her father now.* Strange as the idea was, it was easy to take. Before we got to the outside door, there came a small clatter from the stairs and then Hesta's voice from overhead saying "Goddammit all to Hell. I *knew* it would happen."

I couldn't have been more shocked at such words from pious Hesta, but I called out "What did you know?"

"I knew if I tried to carry this goddamned gun, I'd break my skinny ass."

Mother said "*Hesta!*" Then she and I laughed. Neither of us had ever heard Hesta say an improper word in the years we'd known her.

Even Hesta joined us with a high old laugh I remembered from the good days.

Dark as it was, I still could make out Hesta's body crumpled at the foot of the stairs, child-size, with a long old shotgun thrown out beyond her. At her age, I figured, she'd broken a hip or a leg at the least. So I went right to her and leaned down to help her.

She said "Don't touch me. I'm all right, Nobie."

As it turned out all the extra clothes had padded her fall, and she wasn't really hurt.

But in that moment my mother's hand had slid out of mine.

Hesta noticed it first. She called out "*Edith!* Miss Edith, you come back here to me!"

But the front door closed. By the time I got to the porch and the yard, Edith Norfleet was long gone again by whatever means—both cars were still in sight. Behind me I could hear Hesta's voice at the front door.

She was saying, over and over to herself "Poor child, you're going to go kill yourself."

I knew of course Hesta didn't mean me. I walked back toward her.

By then she'd got the porch light on. And hot as it was, she was shivering hard in all those winter clothes—a deep black midget polar bear.

I shook my head. "You're wrong about suicide anyhow. She'd have done that at Easter, if ever. I'll find her."

But Hesta said "Edith told me she came back here to die."

When I looked up at Hesta, she nodded Yes strongly. "Told me she meant to die in my arms. Asked me would I hold her till she bled to death."

"What did you say to that?"

"I told her Yes. I saw she was right. That way she'd have spared herself and you a whole long extra heartbreak to bear."

That almost brought me down in terror and cold surprise. My knees truly buckled and I held my arms out to keep me upright. My vanished mother suddenly seemed more important to my life than the air I was gasping. And I don't mean I was dedicated, above all else, to trapping and sending her to prison forever. At that moment, then, I wanted her near me as far ahead as I could think—the only girl I'd loved all my life. I felt that, if I could find her quick, I'd take her anywhere on Earth to hide her from the Law and her own demon. I said "Hesta, tell me where you guess she's gone."

She didn't need to guess. "Those children's graves." Her face then was more trustworthy than any young hickory tree, and her guess sounded right.

So I told Hesta to take her gun, go back upstairs and lock herself in. I'd be back as soon as I'd done my duty. Then I went to the Buick and drove straight ahead. I did swerve by our old house briefly to see if any lights were on there, but it was still dark, so I kept on out to the old cemetery where Arch and Adelle were meant to be resting.

It couldn't have been half an hour since Mother had slipped away from me. But by the time I'd stopped the car at the tall locked gates and got myself up and over the wall—some five feet high—she had been there and left. I knew it for sure because, even dark as the night was by now, there were two white sprigs from somebody's shrubbery laid on the graves. One sprig on each grave, laid precisely where she'd guessed that child's head had to be lying. I gathered my courage to look all around me—nobody in sight, no sound of a human. And then it came to me that my poor mother might be in the hands of her demon now, being swept across the face of the Earth like light on the air.

I don't know whether something flung me down or I fell at last from the weight of the long day and all I'd seen. When I came to anyhow, I was lying on my side fairly neatly stretched between my brother's and sister's places. That was also scary but I was too stunned to leap up and run. I managed to sit upright, though, and take the two white flowers that Mother—or someone or some huge thing—had laid to either side of me. They smelled sweet enough to have come from God, but I knew they hadn't. Again I looked all round me—nothing. I called out again. "Edith - Redden - Norfleet?" Nothing answered, not that I could be sure of. But some suspicion rose up in me—*She's here. Or she hears me. Somehow she knows.*

So I spoke out, slightly louder than normal. "Mother, you know you've got to turn yourself in. Either that or they'll track you down with dogs. You dread dogs, remember? Either come here now and let me drive you, or go to the Law and ask for Barber Brady. He's a friend of mine. He'll treat you as kindly as he possibly can. You've met him before. He knows our whole story."

Once that last claim was out of my mouth, I thought *Nobody knows the whole story, do they?* But I didn't say that. I waited a good while to see if she answered. By then I'd started thinking of two other possibilities. She might fly at me out of the dark like a killing bird, or she might step forward from behind a tree with her best old smile and explain in detail all that had happened since Easter Sunday and how she was spotless of any real blame. Of course I badly wanted that second chance, and of course it never came.

Suddenly, more than anything else, I wanted to go back to Nita's house. I was surer than ever that, if I told Nita all that had happened since we last spoke, she'd take me in till dawn at least. I could taste her body as if it were something I'd loved since the cradle, not just a few weeks. I needed to climb back in her and stay till I was a lot more ready than now to face this world as the grown man the world seemed to think I was, though I was a child. Or so I felt at that hour of the night.

But I also thought that, if I didn't find my mother now—and that might mean alerting the Law—then I'd be responsible all my life for any further harm she caused. She might kill Hesta or somebody else's brother and sister, or she might kill herself. By then I was on my knees at the two graves but I didn't pray. I recalled the end of the vision I'd seen this afternoon on the road home from Maryland—Mother somehow calling me onward to settle her case, whether it took her to Heaven, Hell, the penitentiary or the nearest madhouse. Even as I knelt there, ready to say it, I thought *This means I'm as far gone as Mother, but let it come on.*

So I stood up and promised my brother and sister I'd find her, if she was alive on Earth. And I wouldn't turn her in to the Law. As I'd thought for that moment in Hesta's empty yard, I'd disappear with Mother, somehow forever. She'd be no danger to *nobody* else, but she'd live out however much more life God intended her to have, and she'd do it in a clean room with sheets on the bed and sufficient food. I'd be her only guard, and I'd be kinder to her than the world had been anyhow.

The instant I finished that thought, the moon broke out of a cloud as sudden as any big flare. Again I looked to all sides around me—nobody still, though the whole graveyard looked big as the Earth now and safer than the world had ever been. I waited in this new light to know if I meant what I said. Then I knew I did. So in moon glow bright enough to solve any problem in plane geometry, I got myself back over the wall and into the car.

As I leaned to turn the key in the engine, Mother's voice spoke out. "Son, drive me on to the Law now please." The sound was calm and it came from the backseat, three feet behind me.

But it didn't scare me. I even managed to think *Well, of course. She's making me do it after all.* Then I felt the side of my thigh for the pistol. It was plainly there. But she'd done so many uncanny things in these past weeks that I had to wonder *Has she got some other weapon here now?* So I faced around and asked her outright. "You got any means of turning on me?" (Dell was still in my mind somehow as a possible danger.) Before the words were out of my mouth though, I was sorry I'd said them.

She still looked fine in the moon that was almost foaming through the windows, and without a word she held both empty hands up toward me.

I took her to mean she was still unarmed. So at once, again, I wanted to keep the vow I'd made at the graves—I'd hide out with her, somewhere quiet and a long way from here, for the rest of her life. She wouldn't be able to harm another soul, and I'd be gone from my Spanish teacher's life with no more pressure on her and her marriage. I could change my name and get a halfway decent job.

Before I could go any further with that, though, Mother tapped the back of my neck very firmly. "Noble, let's don't wait any longer. Go now." She'd read my mind of course or planted the whole idea of us stealing off.

Still I really couldn't do it, not then and there. My heart had clamped down hard on its own plan. I thought of a reason. "Mother, you remember I mentioned Barber Brady. He'll be off-duty now. Let's take a ride in this good moonlight, then go in tomorrow morning by eight. He'll be there then and can help us through the details."

She waited a good while. "You're holding out on me, son. I know what I need to do. Help me do it *now.*"

As I sat there, watching the strain in her eyes and her good hands twisted together like spider legs, I saw she was right. But I also estimated I was right about Barber's work shift, and I very much wanted to surrender her to Barber—slim tender old baby. To be sure, what I mainly wanted to do was somehow have a few peaceful hours with my ruined mother before she left my world forever. So I said "I promise I'll take you in at nine on the dot tomorrow morning, but let's have this last night just to ride around and look at things under so much moon."

She said "I've gone my last mile, Noble. The next time we crank this car, we're going straight to the Law. You've had too long a day on the roads to drive around safely now. Come on back here and stretch yourself out and sleep a few hours. I'll wake you in time."

If you're not a boy who'd managed to love his mother through years of raving and two clean murders, you may well not believe what I did next. But this is my memory, and I strongly believe I'm right. I took her words literally. I locked both doors and climbed over the front seat into the back.

By then she'd moved down off her seat and was crouched on the floor way over to the side.

I said "Can't we both stretch out on the seat?"

She said "We could but you wouldn't want that. I love you too much."

At the time I didn't ask what she meant. I've wondered many times in all the years since, but I still don't know—thank God, I guess. I slid my shoes off and lay on my left side, facing her and the front of the car.

She faced forward also and folded her arms.

In less than a minute, I anyhow had sunk out of all contact with the present—this car and anyone else alive. The thought of death and danger never touched me, if I dreamt at all I don't recall it; and if my mother touched me again before dawn broke, I never felt it.

But as she'd promised, Mother touched my shoulder in the early daylight. She said "I figure it's seven o'clock, and I think it's Sunday."

I checked my watch. It was just past seven.

"You said that kind boy would be in by eight, that boy named Barber.

You really think he works on Sunday?" She was matter-of-fact as a courteous lawyer.

I sat up, clogged with the deep sleep I'd had but not too clogged to avoid a little meanness. I said "He worked on the Sunday my brother and sister died."

She didn't seem to understand, but she didn't ask again.

I said "You want to stop by Hesta's and wash your face—use the bathroom maybe?"

She said "They'll have a bathroom at the jail." I'd never heard her use that word before, even in the times she'd been there to calm down. But then she gave an actual laugh and faced me smiling. "What I really want is a pancake breakfast. Any way to get that?"

I knew I had six dollars in cash, and I knew of a little breakfast place where they wouldn't know either one of us. So we went straight there, got out of the car in the actual world, walked into the café and seated ourselves.

When the waitress came, Mother couldn't remember the word for pancakes. She asked me what she'd told me she wanted. I smiled at the waitress and ordered a short stack of buckwheat cakes with one fried egg and a side of bacon. That was her old favorite, and I thought she needed at least that much in the way of reinforcement for what came next.

As she heard me order the perfect things, she laughed once more and touched the back of my wrist where it lay on the table.

With that I was near again to heading us out of here and fleeing forever. Or trying to. But by then I was also dying to pee. It had been a very long seven or eight hours. The Men's room was twenty feet away. Could I leave Mother here and expect her to stay? The coffee arrived, we both took swallows, and then I suddenly knew what next. I said "Mother, you go in the Ladies' room. I'll go to the Gents'. Our eyes need washing."

She said "You sure you won't leave me?"

I told her that was her last worry on Earth. And off we went through separate doors. Was I hoping she'd disappear one more time? Maybe a little, yes. Anyhow I took my time in the Gents', more than half-hoping she'd be gone when I reappeared. But when I came out, she was already eating her pancakes and bacon with so much interest I doubted she'd had a full meal since Easter. She didn't see me at first, which gave me a minute to stand back and ask myself—a last time—what was my real duty.

Then the next vision came, the first I'd had since the previous afternoon on the highway. It resembled that one in several ways, except for this—I was not in a car, Mother's face was not in the sky luring me. We were both a good deal older than now and were actually eating another meal at a different table in an ordinary kitchen but lighter than this. It was eggs and dry toast—no major feast—but we both seemed mainly content where we were, and our eyes appeared to be meeting anyhow.

The only strange thing, aside from our looking some years older, was that when we moved our lips to speak, what came out was a lot like music. Not words at all but wordless music, stranger than any I'd heard before; and you could almost see it streaming through the air above us like flags meant for battle but never used that way, clean and not torn. I couldn't be sure, since it was so new, that I understood its meaning; but it turned out I did. And new as it was, I couldn't be sure it was something I'd want as a steady way to talk from here on out; but here and now it sounded welcome. And the way we looked as it came from our mouths, it seemed to mean we were sane and peacefully tending each other.

Before it faded, our waitress in the real café called out to me—I was still standing at the bathroom door. "Lost your appetite?"

Mother was too involved with her own food to turn and look.

Still I went on toward her and ate my choice for Sunday breakfast. It was cinnamon French toast with real maple syrup. To this present day I have never been to France, but I've always admired the French for their bravery, and maybe their toast was what got me on through the rest of the morning.

We'd finished our meal, got into the car and were more than halfway toward the court house as full sunlight broke through the early haze. I don't know when there's ever been a brighter day. To break the silence, I said as much. "Ever seen anything as bright as this?"

Mother said "No, but I guess Hell will be."

That stunned me enough to shut me back up for half a block. Then I couldn't help it—I burst out laughing.

And she joined me gladly.

Finally I could say "You think you're bound for Hell?" It didn't feel cruel then but now I wonder.

Whatever, she took it as a justified question. "Where else do you think I could possibly go after what I've done?"

For the first time I wondered who she might have hurt since Easter morning. She'd gone at least as far north as Maryland. Who knew where she might have gone southward? Could there be other corpses in other states? At the moment I couldn't bring myself to ask her, and I wasn't about to stop at a pay phone and call Dellum Stillman for his insights. Weird as Dell was, he might have done all her havoc single-handed and framed her with it. Here and now anyhow, she was facing me so intently that I had to answer. I said "Miss Edith, I'm no religious expert; and I know very little about the prison system, but don't you think the mental confusion you've suffered for so long will force them to send you to a treatment place?"

I might as well have struck her. Her eyes stayed on me, but her whole head flinched.

We were passing the church we'd gone to occasionally before Mother's illness kept us at home. A few early children were waiting at the crosswalk, all in the careful Sunday clothes children still wore then. I remembered how much I'd wanted to be like them when Mother kept us from going, so I paused and signaled for them to cross. The oldest boy seemed to know me suddenly. I could swear he said "Nobie, you be *careful*!" Then he made silly faces.

I waved anyhow and then I noticed a grown man standing by the boy.

Across the considerable space between us, his eyes seemed to know me better than any other grown man I'd met in years. His own hand came up and seemed on the verge of urging me toward him.

I still didn't recognize him. I slowed down all the same and tried to wave back.

But Mother reached out to take my arm and pull it down. She said "This is Hell—don't you know that yet?"

I moved the car forward. "The whole world, you mean, or just our place?"

"Oh Noble, the *world.* I thought I'd explained that when you were a child. I'm sorry I've left you so ill-informed."

I thought *At least she's clouding over. They'll see right off that she's not responsible for anything she does.*

Her right hand moved around to show me the excellent day in progress through all our windows, and she managed to smile. "This whole thing is Hell—the upper floors. It goes downhill very fast if you travel and see other places. The worst place is always the children's ward—any town you visit—or the orphans' farm. *That'll* open your eyes. Down there, you can't even pray for help. There, God is too busy laughing to hear anybody at all. The second worst level, oh darling, is the crazy house. I'll be there of course unless you shoot me now."

My left hand was already lying in my lap. I let it slide down very slowly to check. Her pistol was still in place in my pocket.

Her eyes had seen me. She nodded, dead-earnest.

I had to say "Mother, even if I obeyed you, think where I'd land. They'd dig out some cave under the orphanage just for me."

She smiled very beautifully. "Never think that, son. They'll thank you with trumpets and laurel crowns." She almost believed it.

Or so it looked and she'd seldom looked better.

But I kept us moving; and she didn't say another word till we were sitting in the little lobby, reading old magazines like average human beings waiting for the dentist. I'd given my name and asked for Barber Brady. The Sunday receptionist, younger than me, said he'd "probably be here in maybe five minutes." I figured she was substitute help, and I thought of looking for Barber myself. But then I knew I should stay by Mother.

Mother went a step closer to the dazed receptionist and said "Better tell young Barber to trim that time. What I've got for him will get him a raise if not a promotion."

The girl at the desk gave a sick little grin.

Mother pointed to me and said "Look at that fine man. He's my elder son, the smartest man in central Carolina. You're bound to know and respect him, surely."

And the girl did nod and say to me plainly "Noble, I remember you when I was in grade school. You were two whole years ahead of me, but I always remember that dark green sweater you wore on cold days." Then she went back to clipping discount coupons from the morning paper.

I was suddenly flat as an empty can that's spent all day in the road. I'd never owned a green sweater in my life; and all I could think was *She's ruining that paper for everybody else, and it's not even nine o'clock. Damn her soul.* I didn't feel horrified by what was underway between me and Mother, or by all that had fallen on my shrunk family in the past six weeks, or by who Nita Acheson was in my future, or how these moments in this public room would bend the shape of my whole coming life the way God Himself might take a lead horseshoe in His hands—lead's a soft easy metal, deadly to taste—and straighten it perfectly or tie a knot that only He could ever solve.

So I didn't see Barber walking toward us. The thing that shook me out of my sadness was Mother standing up, extending her hand and saying "Noble, here's your friend. Tell him who I am."

I actually obeyed her and shook Barber's hand. Lean as he was, the palm of his hand was soft as a pillow, despite the pistol there on his hip. Before I could say a word about Mother, I saw a strange thing that almost amused me—my mother looked more like Barber's mother than mine. Their faces were more alike at least.

Before I could speak, Barber said "Mrs. Norfleet, I'd know you anywhere." Then he turned to me. "You're saying this visit is official, am I right?"

I could only beg his pardon and ask him to explain.

His little black eyes would not look at Mother, but he looked at her shoes—clean canvas sneakers—and said "Are you saying your mother needs a place to sleep tonight?"

For a Lawman, the reasoning seemed kinder than I'd expected, even from gentle Barber Brady. I looked to Mother, thinking she might simply vanish from sight where she stood, vaguely smiling.

But she spoke straight out to Barber's face. "I'm in serious need of starting to pay my debt to society." Her words themselves were a comical speech from a high-school skit about crime and justice; but she'd said them, smiling at her own high tone. She knew as well as Barber and I that, however she phrased it, she told the truth.

So Barber looked all around the big room as if somebody stronger than he was waiting to take over now and handle this thing that I had tried so hard to decorate with maybe fake visions and ridiculous dreams of somehow sparing a pitiful lunatic who'd executed two innocent children and God knew what else.

No one volunteered to help Barber out, so it fell to him—good soul that he was—to tell my mother the news she expected. There was a warrant for her arrest, outstanding for weeks. They could lead her off, there and then, with no objection. Neither my mother nor I said nay, neither one of us even asked for a cheap attorney, so the Law took over as it had every right to do. Before that Sunday noon they led Edith Redden Norfleet to her cell, the holding pen for whatever came next.

As she raised her face to kiss me goodbye, I had to refuse her silently. I took both her hands, though, and said I'd stand right by her—whatever came, forever more. I didn't know what a lie I'd told. But when I saw her led through the last door, with Barber beside her and one other young man (likewise tall as a tree), I heard what sounded like a high metal clang. Nobody in the room but me gave any sign of hearing it, yet at once I understood it was real, and I knew what it was.

It was nothing but the old machine of calamity, grinding my mother into its first wheels, commencing at last the awful business she'd tried to trigger—for her own reasons—on Easter morning and then had been allowed to postpone, like a child on a string, till her leave ran out and she got reeled in. I'd asked some questions while she was still missing, so I understood that now she'd be examined by doctors who'd certify whether she was competent for trial. I'd been all but guaranteed that the experts were bound to find her way less than ready for a full death-penalty procedure or even a real trial of any sort. She'd likely be warehoused with others of her kind in what would amount to a permanent confinement where she couldn't harm anyone but herself or some unlucky fellow inmate or a state employee paid to guard her. Any way I studied it in my tired mind, the sound I'd heard was the end of whatever life I'd had from birth to that instant.

* * *

So by midday Sunday I was on my own again, no one alive with any big claim on me. I thought I should go on back to Hesta's, be sure she was safe, and tell her the morning's news anyhow. But once I'd walked through blinding sun, cranked the Buick, and seized that steering wheel in both dry hands, another surge of my mother's pain poured up my arms toward my chest and throat. I damn nearly drowned in the next two minutes, just sitting in a shut car, safe as any house dog. But I didn't shed a tear. I forced them down and when the pain had passed on through me, I knew I'd never be the same again. I also knew the one thing I needed above all else. And I'd get it at whatever cost to life and limb. Then I backed out carefully—my last truly careful act for years to come—and headed for Nita Acheson's house.

Her car was there but she didn't answer my knock at the back door. By the time I'd stood on the stoop, waiting hard, I was sinking in some kind of desperation I'd never known. If I couldn't see her—and beg to touch her right away—I knew I'd die. I'd prayed very seldom in recent years; but now I actually said out loud "Lord, lead me to Nita." And nothing whatever seemed wrong in my plea. When I turned to look round me, I more than half-expected she'd be there—an instant answer to my demand. But the only obvious sight was Mother's car. The sun had struck the edge of the bumper, and it looked like something about to break into scary life. I was stunned enough to think it was some kind of burning bush that would bloom any instant with guidance for me. Needless to say, the bumper didn't speak.

Still when nothing else happened, it silently drew me toward it. This Buick, and an empty five-room house I couldn't bear to visit, were all I owned. I cranked up and drove to the nearest intersection. And there at the stop sign, I heard an answer in my head—*She's gone to church.* Whatever had happened between us lately, Nita had never stopped going to mass. On such a bright morning, she'd have walked the short distance. I might even find her walking home.

I did. I could see the back of her upright body from a whole block away, and again tears nearly came. No live human being had ever looked half this fine before. This was real rescue (and maybe a guarantee God existed). I pulled up slowly to the curb beside her, leaned over and said "Your chauffeur, Madame."

At first she wouldn't turn or stop, and I thought she hadn't caught my voice. She looked so steady and self-possessed in her dark blue dress with the big white buttons and the blue pillbox hat riding her hair. You'd have known, at a glimpse, that she had to teach school. You could see she had that calm ready power at her fingertips and all up her spine. So I kept the car rolling and tried again. "Mrs. Acheson, ma'm, these subjunctive verbs are giving me *fits*." And I reeled off a badly botched conjugation of the Spanish verb for *love* in the subjunctive.

Nita stopped in her tracks and studied my face. Then without a word she opened the passenger door and stepped in.

Only when she was near me, and I drove ahead, did I suddenly feel the weight of what had happened to me since I saw her last night. Just having her in the car again, though, seemed a promise I'd survive; but for the moment I couldn't speak to tell her.

So looking straight ahead, she spoke first. "Noble, please just leave me off at the back door. You know why I can't ask you in."

Young as I was, I kept the story waiting till we'd stopped in her driveway. As she said a quick "Thanks" and turned to leave, I said "I just turned Mother in."

Of course that stopped her, and she searched my face again for the truth. Was I still joking?

I raised my right hand slightly, an oath. "When I got to Hesta's last night, Mother met me. God knows where she's been—she's well past telling—and the night's a long story, but anyhow I just left her downtown with the Law."

The first thing she said was "Did Dell Stillman bring her?"

"I'll try to find out all the secrets later, but right now the whole thing's a total mystery. She's been well cared for anyway—though God knows how—but her mind's confused. Off and on, she seemed glad to see me."

Nita's left hand started out to touch me. Then it pulled back, but she said "So she was calm?"

I said "She was fairly far-gone at first. She'd tied Hesta up and she somehow had a pistol—fired a shot through Hesta's roof." I had to laugh.

"But you're not hurt?"

I knew she meant my body. I said a fast "No" and shook my head hard. Then tears came again and I didn't try to stop them. They were real at least. They weren't just a crowbar to pry me back into Nita's grand body that I longed to crawl up in now and *hide*.

So Nita stayed in place for a good while and said kind things. She was sorry, I'd get over this somehow, all my friends would help me.

To that I had to say the plain truth. "Except for you and Hesta, name one friend I've got." There was no honest answer except *I can't*.

Nita didn't quite say it, but she did shake her head. Then she said "You look famished."

I told her I hadn't had a real meal since Maryland yesterday. I'd forgot the French toast.

That made the difference. Nita said "That's one problem I can fix," and she left the car.

When I stayed at the wheel, Nita got all the way to her door and opened it before she looked back and said "Noble, come in."

I've probably already written as much about my intimate relations with Nita as a reader can use for the purposes of harmless understanding. That's not to say that I'm opposed to pornography. As long as it doesn't involve children or actual cruelty to a living creature, I suspect it's more useful to society than not. With the aid of assorted magazines and films, don't most potential sex offenders manage to discharge their harm in their own rooms without going public?

For instance if there'd been any movies of Nita and me on that one Sunday, they'd have shown two washed and well-made young people in full employment of one another's skin among attractive domestic surroundings for what would have looked like a harmless hour (to anybody but a true friend of Nita's or a sex-crazed Christian, which so many are and which seems very weird, considering Jesus hardly mentions sex). And if I could have managed to forget the eventual pain I caused, then I might well have replayed the pictures for years to come and avoided a lot more waste with other humans, though none were underage or forced by me at gunpoint. But we were together a few decades before some ninety percent of all acts, however dull or grim, were caught forever on videotape.

So all that's left is my detailed memories from long ago, more than thirty years. And when I occasionally run them, even now, I'm compelled to wonder if they can be true. They still look so perfect—every heart's desire my skin ever knew being perfectly gratified, to the outside eye at least and in my mind. All the same I think my memories are truthful. Things really happened the way I recall, I'm virtually sure. The fact that they often gratified me alone—by letting me truly hide for whole minutes in a fine woman's body, facedown and moaning as my mouth worked to honor her—could also be said about a lot of my life through the long years that followed. Yet I think I'm saner now than I've ever been, and I finally see how I caused more than a normal share of havoc around me. I'm no ex-killer, no master of mental cruelty, though most of my harm was to people's minds. But I think I've outdone the average American male of my time—hound dogs though a very large percent of them are—in the kinds of misunderstandings and wrongs you can't repair. That part of the story is yet to come.

What's left to know about my afternoon with Nita is that, once I gave her a full account of the recent last hours with Mother and begged for her help, she gave it again. I tried hard to tell her the exact truth of what had happened so far and what was still pending. I didn't press on her for pity at all. But the news itself was hard enough to leave her feeling she owed me the single thing that might help me, then and there. And for reasons of her own, that I never questioned, she continued to let me use her that way—right on through the end of school and up till Commencement—until somebody took the first step between us.

That was Hesta. When I'd finished at Nita's that same Sunday, I went straight to Hesta's. By then it was late in the afternoon. Hesta was sitting on the porch with her Bible, facing the road. And she gave no return when I waved and smiled at her, turning in. I thought she was hurt or peeved anyhow that I'd waited so long to get back and tell her the news of Mother, and of course I felt guilty. So when I climbed the steps, I said I was sorry before I even reached her.

She kept on looking at the road and said "You're *sorry,* all right." She'd changed out of church clothes but still had her hat on, a wide black straw hat with artificial green grapes that women had worn about 1900 but seldom since. Now it looked like an alien craft that had paused here briefly and might lift up without the least warning and bear Hesta off. Still it didn't diminish the bitterness in her eyes and on her lips.

I tried to ignore it. I said "But Hesta, I'm alive—don't you see? I might *not* have been. Aren't you glad of that?" I sat on the top step, close to her feet, faced her directly and began again to tell the story of the past full hours.

I hadn't got more than a sentence out when Hesta said "I know all that—all of it that matters. I called the Law. They told me she was locked up for good and you were safe."

I said "But there's a lot they don't know about the rest of last night and the whole of this morning."

Hesta shut the Bible and laid her long right hand flat on the cover. "What I know is, you been with that evil high-school teacher."

I was nearly as stunned as when I'd first seen Mother last night. Hesta had never once mentioned Nita's name, and I had no idea she'd ever heard of it. I asked "Who please are you talking about?"

Hesta turned in a semi-circle around her, scanning the yard and the road for listeners. When she saw no one, she looked straight at me. "That woman with the pitiful husband overseas. The woman that's trying to damn you to Hell, young as you are—and her on the state payroll, eating taxes that bone-poor people like me have to pay."

A whole secret patch of my childish brain agreed with her and wanted to nod, go indoors and bathe and never see Nita Acheson again except in the classroom behind a Spanish book. That thought trailed off, though; and I tried to fight for Nita. "I'm a grown man, Hesta. Two weeks from tonight I'll graduate from high school. I'll be in Vietnam in under a year." It rolled out as if some spirit inside me had known it beforehand and told me this instant.

Hesta made her customary sound of disgust. It involved doing something with her many false teeth. "No white boy owning a house and a

Buick is going to *that* war. Niggers are the main boys fighting that war and dying like blind rats deep in a barrel."

I let the voice down in me speak again. "I'm planning on going down after Commencement and seeing if the Infantry or Navy wants me more." The longer the voice spoke, the easier it was to believe what it claimed.

Hesta said "If you sign up for this miserable war, you're taking your poor mother's track years too soon. She didn't turn crazy till your daddy left her."

Hesta was the last person alive who'd known Mother almost all her life, and I should have asked her whatever she knew, but of course I was far too drowned in myself to ask the crucial questions. There were two hot mysteries pressing me then. How had Mother survived through her weeks on the road, or wherever she'd been, and how did Hesta know about me and Nita?

I said "Who told you about Mrs. Acheson?"

She opened her mouth to tell me, then halted. Her eyes closed briefly, and she paused to spit her snuff in the clean can she kept beside her chair. "No need to strain your feeble mind to guess who told me what. More than one person knows it, and they all go to my church."

In those days, before white people stopped having maids and yard men, black people knew every secret in town. All they had to do was look and listen. I should have guessed that somebody knew what I'd been doing, knocking on Nita's door so often. No lie I could tell would alter that now. So I asked Hesta to help me with my second big question. "Can you even begin to guess how Mother lived through the last six weeks, between here and Maryland and wherever else she went, and how she got back as clean as she was and strong as a bear?"

Hesta said "If you ever darkened a church door, or got to your knees and asked God for help, you'd have known long since."

I said I was ready to believe she was right; would she tell me what she knew?

Hesta said "The Holy Ghost brought her home when it meant her to come."

It was so plain that Hesta believed herself, I all but asked her to bless me now and lead me aright. But I also told her something else I'd noticed about religion. "I can't help telling you I haven't seen one white church that's stood behind Negroes for this civil-rights business."

Hesta said "I'm glad you noticed that much. Stay on in a white church if you dare, and the fire and brimstone will rain on you *soon*. You could come to my church any Sunday of the year and get yourself right. You could also go upstairs this minute and fall to your knees and tell God the truth. He'll lead you, I promise—*He*'s promised, right here in this book on my lap." She stroked the worn Bible as if it were her own skin, a skin that God had kept in near-slavery for all Hesta's years (or so I thought then). And she quoted the words I'd heard before " 'The eternal God is my refuge, and underneath are the everlasting arms.' "

For whatever untold reason, the food I'd eaten at Nita's thrust up into my mouth. It was different from the grief that had swelled in me earlier. It was literal sour slop from my stomach. But to hide it from Hesta, I swallowed it fast.

Still Hesta had seen it. "Old demon can't stand to hear scripture read, can he?" She actually laughed, which she seldom did.

At first I didn't understand, but then I said "You're not claiming I've got the Devil in me?" I couldn't help grinning.

Then slowly, for the first time in all these weeks since she'd come to rescue me from the house where my family ended, she leaned down and pulled my warm head toward her bony knee. I let myself go and her thin old fingers combed through my hair.

It had to mean some kind of good feeling for me; and I said softly "See, I'm still good."

She waited a long while; and then as though it were the hardest chore she'd had, she leaned even nearer and whispered "Oh - child, I - wish - that - were - *so*."

I said "What have I done wrong but love a married woman?"

She said "God forgives you for that already if you're sorry you did it, and you quit it today. No, the deep trouble is, you're Edith's main child. She put the evil in you, last night if not sooner. It may have come in your blood, in her belly, before you were born."

I stayed up against her knee. "You honestly believe that can happen to a person?"

She stayed calm now, no more of her church voice. Her fingers were still prowling gently through my hair. "Of course I believe it. How else you think evil creeps on downward through the years?"

I was like most modern American boys in knowing less about philosophy, not to mention theology, than the average Airedale dog. Even in the weeks since my family nightmare, I'd gone no further in thinking about it than wondering, a time or two, if Mother's mental illness would somehow come to me through natural heredity. Good as it was to pause, then, near Hesta and be mildly stroked by a hand that wanted nothing from me but patient attention, I told myself she was deeply cracked though fairly harmless and that I'd need to find me another place to stay in the days between now and whenever I'd leave for Vietnam or the cactus plains of the Planet Mozingo.

At last Hesta said "What was that man's name at Edith's old church who tried to help yall a few years ago?"

At first I was puzzled. Then I remembered a new young minister from our former church who'd tried to call on Mother one evening two years ago when she was especially confused. I'd been in my room, reading a mystery, when I heard her start out talking calmly, then end up yelling loud demands that he leave then and there. I'd gone in just as he was almost out the front door, and I walked with him down the yard to his car. I half-lied to him to ease his nerves—saying how Mother had these spells now and then when her hormones were high, how she really didn't mean any harsh thing she said, and how I'd bring us all to his church one Sunday soon when life was more peaceful.

He'd accepted my story with no sign of suspicion and added that I might need the support of a group of good people who could help me out in my times of need. He also volunteered to meet with me privately, day or night, if I wanted to talk. Then he gave me a slow careful look and said, straight at me, "You're strong as a bow, I can readily see." He pronounced the word as in *bow and arrow*, an expression I'd not heard till then. "But the strongest bows can split if you steadily draw them too far back."

The strange words fascinated me, and I thought he might have made an offer worth pursuing, but then I plunged back into my same life and never thought of him again. I knew his name, though, and said to Hesta

"He's still in town at the same brick church. His name is Landingham." Hadn't I glimpsed him just this morning as I rode past the church with Mother?

At that, Hesta leaned entirely forward. I was shocked to think she might plan to kiss me on the crown of my head. But no, being Hesta, she did something odd. She dug her sharp chin into my hair and ground it back and forth a few times.

I took it to be her kindest move yet.

With her chin still against me, she whispered "You find him tonight. He's honor bound to lead you ahead."

Without full knowledge I was plainly in the deepest of shaky states. And from there Hesta's words sounded like an order I had to obey. No black person had ever lied to me or done me the least unkindness I could think of. The same thing holds true all these years later, though Hesta's order had outcomes she couldn't foresee.

Nita had said she would cook a waffle supper if I waited till dark and walked to her house. I still can't believe what I did instead; but I stood straight up from Hesta's step, went indoors and telephoned Nita to say I had to go see a man about my troubles.

Needless to say, she wondered who.

And I told her frankly. "His name is Tom Landingham, the man I think I mentioned before—the one who tried to help Mother out but she ran off."

"The minister?" Nita said and mentioned the church Tom served.

I won't specify the church here in writing. It was one of the mainline Protestant branches with the usual lily-white well-heeled lawyers, doctors, bank presidents and members of the Junior League still wearing hats and pale gloves in those days. You'd never hear a member head off into chattering fits of ecstasy or use the kinds of voices that change completely when they say the words *Jesus* or *God*. (You may have noticed on TV or elsewhere how certain brands of Christians say *Jeeesus* and *Gawwwd*—hang on to your wallets.) I probably ought to go on and say which brand I contacted. The Catholics get such regular public shame for child-molesting priests; yet I'd bet a sizable sum that Protestant preachers, youth leaders, choir directors and organists match them, wrong for wrong. I'll stick with my choice, though, to withhold the brand. Still I've never heard anybody wonder out loud why religious professionals—Christians anyhow—are so attracted to young children's bodies. Are rabbis and Buddhist monks similarly afflicted? Anyhow I was, as I'd just claimed to Hesta, a grown man in many ways—the dangerous ways.

And when I got to the door of the church office-building, it was past six P.M.—maybe the wrong time of the wrong day for my first real meeting with this particular person. In those days most churches still had regular Sunday-night services, so I didn't know who or what I'd find, but the door was unlocked. I let myself in and walked on down the deep wine carpet, looking for the man Hesta said I should see. The first lighted room had a middle-aged woman with tight red curls at a desk counting money.

When she looked up and saw me, she blushed and said "I'm *sorry*. I'm not supposed to do this in public. It's the morning offering. My little boy got sick as a dog and upchucked his oatmeal, and I haven't had a chance to count it till now." She seemed as guilty as if I'd caught her stealing bread from starved orphans.

I smiled. "Don't mind me at all. I'm looking for Reverend Landingham. Does he still work here?"

By then she'd got her wits collected and had no doubt noticed my wrinkled clothes, so her voice got official. "The Reverend Tom Landingham? He's here indeed. He's the minister of this church; and if I'm not mistaken, he's three doors down the hall, preparing for the service. Do you have an appointment?"

I told her I didn't.

She said "Then I'd better let him know you're here. May I have your name please?"

By the instant she was turning into a policeman, and it rubbed me wrong. I said "I heard he was a Christian and I need help. I believe that's his business, so I'll find him myself."

Her already ample bosoms grew about three sizes as I said that.

I thought she might explode on the spot, but I said "He's a Christian—am I wrong?"

She nodded. "As fine a one as I've known."

I thanked her.

And that seemed to let her deflate a little.

It also freed me to walk on alone in the carpet that was now more than ever like quicksand. Likely it was trying to tell me something, the way everything from my weird visions to the whole Atlantic Ocean in Maryland to derelict Buicks and bizarre nuts posing as full-fledged Lawmen—not to mention a mother so swamped in tragedy she couldn't be saved by her last living child—had tried to guide me in recent days and had so far failed.

The door was spotless mahogany, and the nameplate was probably brass but looked gold. It was his—and it said *Tom* not *Thomas*—so I worried right off that I might have come to one of those *Jesus Can Be Your Best Friend Too* fellows—and when I knocked once lightly, a voice said "Come."

I might well have laughed. But again the events of the past two days bore down on me. I just stood there. And when the door at last opened from inside, I must have looked in serious trouble.

The man said "Lord, son, step inside." His smooth hand took my bare left wrist and drew me in. With the door shut behind us, he led me straight to a kind of prayer desk that stood in a corner. It was wide enough for two people to kneel on a velvet cushion, and he silently gestured for me to kneel beside him. It had a shelf you could lean your elbows on, and on the shelf was a book that as I discovered later contained many dozen pictures of people Tom prayed for daily. What I noticed most, though, was the single thing on the wall above us—a picture I'd later recognize as the negative image of the Shroud of Turin.

Whatever the truth about that peculiar long piece of linen, I recognized the face as Jesus. He was plainly in far more dreadful trouble than I'd ever been in. His nose was broken, his cheek was badly swollen, blood streaked down his forehead and all through his hair from the crown of thorns. But the main thing I thought as I looked up at him was *Thank God his eyes are shut.* I couldn't have stood to meet those eyes, not then anyhow.

Tom Landingham was maybe four inches to my left, not quite touching my side at any point. Finally he said, in a clear low voice, "Sir, give us calm strength. Fix our eyes so we can see that hope exists for this young man and for me." He waited a good while, then said "Amen."

Till that last word I hadn't been sure he was actually praying, and I took to the businesslike tone and words.

Again not touching me, he stood upright, indicated an armchair beside his desk and sat in his own tall chair, surrounded by more books and papers than I'd seen near anybody since the Wizard Merlin in King Arthur movies. He looked me carefully in the face for a long five seconds. His own face was well-made but, to my eyes, it seemed to have a fine-gauged veil that moved around it as he stared or talked. It would half-hide his eyes for seconds, then his moving lips, then sometimes the whole face would seem to retreat and hide out from you. Once he'd studied me, though, he smiled a little. "You're Noble, am I right?"

"Yes sir, Noble Norfleet. I guess I glimpsed you this morning as I drove by, but I haven't really seen you since my poor mother mistreated you two years ago."

He nodded. "I'm in the *mistreated* business. No need to apologize."

I hadn't, and hadn't intended to; but that didn't seem worth lingering over. I said "You may have heard the sad news about my family through the past six weeks."

He nodded again. "I have. I was waiting for you to contact me. I see I was wrong."

Wrong about what? He hadn't smiled again, but he seemed in no hurry, so I took the chance to study him a little more. He was somewhere in his middle thirties with a full head of sandy hair that might have been shorter in another decade. He hadn't quite gone the whole hippie way to shoulder-length curls—I hadn't either—but his head gave signs of considerable sympathy for the new youthful ways. A lot of preachers did back then. Some even indulged in the beads and elaborate belt buckles that were signs of mild rebellion, though almost none of them stepped out and said what Jesus would have said about rights for black people or about the filthy war. His eyes, when you could really see them, were an almost shockingly pale blue and had the kind of hungriness I'd seen in truly lonely men during my earlier hitchhiking days. Still he had a spread of family pictures framed behind him, an airbrushed wife and two almost incredibly pretty young daughters.

After a while I saw he was waiting for me to reply to what he'd said last. So I said "Oh you weren't wrong, I guess. Maybe I just wasn't ready for you."

Tom said "And you think you are now?" With all that came afterward, I'll say this much—he started out with the right intentions. His face was as solemn as it should have been, and the flickering hunger had gone from his eyes.

But still I didn't know what he meant—*Was I ready for him now?* I was after all a grown man in a lot of the ways that counted. I was a few weeks away from being old enough to "die for my country" in Southeast Asia, girls seemed to smell some odor around me that I couldn't smell, and I could have already fathered dozens of children (if I'd started fathering as soon as my cock worked). Still I told Tom Landingham I guessed I believed in God but that I and my family hadn't been good about going to church.

"God doesn't care if you go to church, Noble."

I thought about that for a moment, then laughed. "Where'd you be, though, if everybody knew that?"

Tom finally smiled again. "I don't tell everybody that. I'd soon be selling used cars in the broiling sun. But you're in deep trouble."

I was starting to wonder if I'd turned into clear glass. Twice in the last hour both he and Hesta had looked directly into my mind and read me right. I said "You know everything that happened in my life today?"

He said "I know this much. Your mother is finally in custody—you took her in."

I asked how he knew.

"A member of the church works down at the jail. He phoned me with the news. I was going to try to find you after the service tonight."

I asked him if he thought they'd harm Mother—truly I hadn't thought of that till now. Had some part of me wanted them to pay her back with pain for all the havoc she'd made?

Tom said "From all I've seen and heard, she'll go fairly straight to a mental institution and likely spend the rest of her life there."

Somehow—in Tom Landingham's level voice, in this clean room with the blind and battered face of Jesus—I finally knew what I'd only guessed in bearable snatches. I was now entirely alone on Earth, except for the friendship Hesta provided and the parts of Nita Acheson's body that I'd been rubbing against me like drugs. At that hard moment I thought I suddenly saw the whole line of my life to come, and that's what it was—a narrow single straight line onward past the end of the sky. It was not even the string of loops and tangles that most people get, and it certainly wasn't the scary cat's-cradle network that any boy with half a brain hopes he'll survive with no worse loss than the odd arm or leg before it kills him. By then I'd gone, or something had hauled me, well past tears. I doubt I've shed a tablespoon of tears in sorrow since that Sunday evening.

Tom finally took a quick look at his watch. "Lord, I've got to preach in fifteen minutes."

I knew I was too disheveled to enter that cool sanctuary with the beige wall-to-wall and the blond oak pews. I honestly wanted to lie down now on the floor of his office and wait till he was back and could lead me on to whatever seemed the next best path for me. But that seemed childish.

By then he was standing up and holding the black gown he wore in church. He said "Tell me where I can find you tonight. My wife and daughters will expect me for bedtime prayers at ten o'clock in the house, but till then I'll be free."

I couldn't make myself want to see Hesta again before I'd got some strength in my weak knees. I couldn't yet bear the prospect of trying to see my mother behind iron bars. And I thought if I just drove around town idly, I'd likely wind up at Nita's back door, a cunt-struck dog. So I put my hands out and shrugged in blank confusion.

Tom did me the finest service yet. He took one more long look at my eyes. Then he said "Look, Noble—you need a real pause now; and there's not a safer place in this town than the room you're in. These shelves are full of good books. That leather couch is ideal for naps. Wait here till I'm back. It may be nine o'clock." He didn't touch me as he left the room, and he never said one word to warn me against theft or the kind of frenzy my family was known for—one of us at least, the one I'd surrendered half a day ago to an enforced lifetime in a Hell even she could hardly have foreseen.

Tom had told me to lock the door when he left. I gladly did that and spent twenty minutes dutifully thumbing through various books before the sight of that long couch overcame me. I stretched out there and was gone in dreamless oblivion fast. I doubt I flinched for the whole two hours. I didn't even hear Tom let himself in. The first thing I knew was the sound of his voice softly calling my name and the touch of his hand on my shoulder. I've always been an easy waker, but that one time I woke up scared.

Later Tom claimed I actually struck him on the side of the head and said a name he wouldn't reveal in all the time I knew him, though I asked him many times. But once I knew where I was, he sat at the far end from me and asked where I was living at the moment.

I told him about my recent weeks at Hesta's.

He said "That might not be a good place to talk, right?"

When I agreed he asked if I knew of a private place. Before I thought carefully I said "My home—the house where I lived till Easter anyhow. You've been there briefly." When Tom looked puzzled I told him I owned it still but had just not decided on whether to sell it. I also told him it was in good shape—I checked on it every few days—and that I didn't have any real objections to us going there and talking awhile if he wanted that. I know I didn't have any conscious thoughts of doing more than talking, but I won't claim the back of my mind may not have had thoughts of its own. At that point I was nearer to an outcast timber wolf prowling on his own than the boy I'd been till yesterday.

But like good Americans swilling down gasoline and fouling the Universe, both Tom and I went alone in separate cars. I led the way and waited, as he'd asked me to, while he stopped off at a service station and bought cold beer. I'd never thought a minister would do that publicly but I was wrong.

* * *

And Tom surprised me even more, right off when we got to the house, by asking if I had a picture of Mother before she "took the first steps toward confusion." He used those words and I've never forgot them.

So I brought out the albums she'd kept right up till my father left. I started trying to show him the pictures. They started when she was an infant, held in a black woman's arms—was it possibly Hesta? And they focused on her almost completely through the two whole volumes she managed to fill till she was abandoned. The first thing Tom said as I turned the pages was "See how neat she is. All the pictures are laid down exactly parallel. There's no mess or clutter, no silly captions, no pressed corsages from the senior prom."

I hadn't ever quite noticed the fact, though of course I'd known how orderly she was right up through Easter morning. By then, though, the albums were turning sad for me. I shifted them onto Tom's lap and moved to the nearest facing chair.

Tom plainly understood but went on turning till he reached the last page. I knew that page had the picture of me standing by Mother outside on the porch the day Dad left. Dad snapped it with her old box Kodak that afternoon, then left in the night. And it was only as I thought about it, sitting eight feet away, that I realized what day it was in the picture—another Easter. She and I were dressed in new light-colored clothes. My sport coat had the buttons I've liked best in my whole life. The salesman had said they were genuine stag horn, and I still believe him. Mother's suit was canary yellow, she wore the purple orchid my father had given her that same morning, and her whole face was tilted up from me to drink in the bright day—till almost the end she loved sunshine and said more than once that she more than half thought the sun was a god and required her worship.

Tom didn't look up and didn't say a word, but I could suddenly feel exactly who I'd been on that very day nearly ten years ago. It had been a cold Sunday, and we had just got home from church. I was eight years old, and Mother's hand was frozen when I reached up for it as Dad said "Smile!" I'd heard that dead people got cold fast, and I thought "My mother will die before I do." It was the worst thing I'd known till then; and it still seemed hard as I sat there—a seventeen-year-old man with the smell of a hot woman still on my hands, though I'd washed them three times since I left Nita's.

Tom shut the last album, laid both of them on the table that stretched between us and said "She was actually lovely, wasn't she?" as if that were some kind of big surprise.

It almost offended me but I couldn't explain her first beauty to him. I couldn't say another word about her that day. So I said "Let's please don't talk about her now. Let that come later."

Tom nodded and leaned a little toward me. "There's something you need to tell me though—"

I said "Well, is there?" For a long instant I wasn't sure what.

"You came to my study in some distress more than two hours ago."

It all came back to me slowly. I finally said "I'm fucking my high-school Spanish teacher, and it's bound to be wrong." I'd pretty much prided myself up till now in not using rough words, even with my school friends, but now they seemed right.

Tom showed no sign of alarm or pity or even disapproval. He just said "Whose idea was it to start with?"

That struck me as an interesting tack, and I may have half-laughed. But then I tried to think it out truly. He was likely assuming the teacher had outright seduced the pupil. At the time I felt like hiding behind some such misconception. Still I finally told him "I guess it came on us both at the same time. We wound up alone at her house one afternoon when I had offered to trim the ivy that was eating the gutters."

Tom said "It's a woman then—your teacher?"

That surprised me. "Very much so. A woman nine years older than me with a healthy husband in Vietnam."

"Why did it cave in on you today? Something to do with your poor mother's fate?"

"The black lady I live with said I was mired up in evil and that I should see you."

The strangest moment of a crowded day may have been the next. Tom leaned back on Mother's sofa, wiped his lean face in his two dry hands and spread his long arms out beside him. For only the second time today, his eyes and mouth were entirely clear. I could see him plainly, and he spoke straight at me. "If you haven't killed or beat your teacher or mailed her soldier a hateful letter, you've done no wrong."

I don't know where I got the wits to wonder, but I said "In whose eyes, please, have I done no wrong—God's or just yours?"

Tom said "Either one."

"What about the husband if he found out?"

Tom still didn't smile. "He might be surprised. He might shoot you dead. But who knows how many Vietnamese women he's bought or raped? Who knows what he expects from his wife? There are more than a few very average-seeming men who like to watch other men screw their wives."

To say the least this was not what I'd expected. Tom was moving much faster than I could follow. I said "Back up a minute here. You believe in God, right?"

He said "Completely. God's with us this minute in this sad room. He always is, though sometimes he'll go silent on you, silent as a road-rock for months on end. I've known him to stand and stare at good people for numerous years—and them in ghastly heart-killing pain."

I had to laugh. "If he was in this house when Mother lived here, he must have been deaf-and-dumb for sure—also a big fan of horror stories."

Tom said "I don't doubt anything you say."

"But God says a lot against sex in the Bible, right?"

Tom said "In the Old Testament God seems to lay down a few thousand rules about who can touch who and who gets stoned if their wife starts her period while they're making sweet love. But after Jesus rose from the tomb and vanished, St. Paul said all the Old Testament laws were finished, done, *canceled.* And if you read every word Jesus says in all four gospels—and it's *all* we know about what he thought—he seems not to think sex matters much. Not nearly as much as total kindness to every living creature and sharing your blessings with those who have less."

I said "So I can leave you sitting here right now, speed back around to Nita Acheson's and fuck till the school bell rings in the morning?"

Tom said "You *can.* You can cut off her head and shoot hoops with it—till they catch you at least."

I said "Hold on. That's a low blow, coming at the end of today."

He waited a good while. "It is. I'm sorry. What I mean to say is, you're free to do anything Nita lets you do or your mind doesn't veto. Jesus appears to advise against it. He told the woman taken in adultery—and he'd just saved her life from the mob that would stone her—he told her to go 'and sin no more.' But he didn't call out his own sex police or chain her thighs together as she left him."

I said "But she knew Hell would wait for her, right?"

"Not for cheating on her husband, no. Jesus didn't tell her that. He forgave her first and *then*—only then—he advised her to quit."

We both stayed quiet a considerable time. Gradually Tom looked around in a sweep at everything in the room, though he didn't stand up. He seemed to be saving mental pictures of each chair and lamp, each magazine, my sister's last doll, my brother's green cap, the framed school pictures of us all grinning proudly as if we had a trace of hope to be proud of.

He was plainly so interested, I almost thought if I kept still long enough, he'd make me an offer to buy the place.

But he finally said "Excuse me for asking this private question; but you haven't washed since you left your teacher, have you?"

I must have turned a ferocious red. Even I could smell mine and Nita's leavings after all these hours. I begged his pardon.

Tom said "Not at all." He gave the whole room another broad sweep of his wide eyes. They stopped on me. By now they'd veiled over again; but still they looked like a big cat's eyes—a lion's or panther's, not in a scary way, just not quite a human's eyes. Then very slowly he said "Noble, if I may, I would like to do something that could be new to you. I'm going to risk doing what I feel I need to do, here and now. It's partly for me, I freely admit; but it's mainly for you. It'll show what I'm trying to tell you better than any words I've got."

Again out of nowhere I heard myself say "It won't involve touching me, will it?"

Tom laughed a little. "It very well might. Would that throw you badly?"

"Sir," I said, "it's been a full day. I may just need to find my way back to Hesta's and wash these tired bones and sleep about a week."

But before I finished that, Tom had stood and moved to within a yard of where my feet met the floor. He stood there, looking up toward the ceiling with his arms out beside him, riding the air.

For a moment I thought of the times when Mother would gaze up at the same blank ceiling and shout out messages to Khrushchev, Lyndon Johnson or God Himself. And I wondered who Tom might be addressing.

But without a word he closed his eyes and knelt where he stood. If he'd reached out toward me, he'd have touched my knees. With what I'd learned in my hitchhiking days, and from hearing other boys talk about preachers, I more than half knew that something to do with my body was pending. Or trying to pend. To this very day I can honestly claim that I've never actively desired a man's body—in my private thoughts and dreams, I mean. I can see from pictures and from visits to gyms that the full male package can be impressive, but for me it's never given off the thrilling high sound that women's bodies can—a sound like some kind of homing beacon for lost airplanes that calls me in (and God knows I've been lost for a good part of every day of my life). Not to mention that the beacon is also the world's most powerful magnet.

Still it had truly been an awful day, a dreadful weekend that might well have killed a normal person much older than me; and by the time Tom Landingham knelt before me, I was feeling at least as marooned and useless as a young man can feel. Here apparently was an educated man who was widely admired for good sense and kindness, and he seemed to be needing something I might have, so I had no major difficulty in meeting his eyes.

He finally said "May I approach?"

In my head I could only hear phrases I'd heard in school, maybe quotes from Shakespeare—*approach the altar* or *approach the throne*—and I had to keep from laughing. Who was I but a teenage orphan with all but no money, no exceptional mind, no striking talents and slumped in an old chair not ten yards from where two murders had recently occurred and me in clothes that were two-days old and ripe as bear meat? So I must have felt ready for any form of tribute, short of physical mayhem. And I must have shown no sign of refusal.

On his knees Tom moved the final way onward, laid his hands on the sides of my knees and slowly lowered his head into my lap. Then he stayed there, motionless, completely quiet.

However often in recent weeks I'd tried to tell people I was thoroughly grown, I still had the blind sexual readiness of a fourteen-year-old. So, under my clothes, I promptly produced an iron-bar erection in the general whereabouts of the minister's nose. My mind was thinking numerous things simultaneously—*Oh Noble, you've flat betrayed yourself now* plus *Noble, you're about to get your first authentic blow job* (Nita had been reserved about that) plus *This is the most ridiculous fix you've ever been in—an ordained preacher, with a wife and daughters, snorting your crotch for God knows what reason.*

I was on the verge of realizing a bedrock truth which is inexplicably far from well known—physical desire which is powered by any purpose but the making of actual children is God's biggest joke on the Planet Earth and the big majority of all its creatures, but I wasn't quite old enough to think that far ahead and shape my life accordingly—and I wouldn't be for decades, if ever. None of which is to say that I don't still value the physical joy my body can make—or has made—almost as highly as any feeling but unselfish love.

Anyhow at that point I didn't move or ask Tom to quit, and my hands stayed beside me on the arms of the chair. Part of my mind was nothing but an *eye*, watching this weird event in a room that had seen far more than its share of the weird; so I stayed in place and truly watched. Young as I was and unaccustomed to having my skin tended to so lavishly by another human being, of whatever sex or persuasion, I reached my own peak fairly fast.

After maybe three more minutes, though, when Tom still hadn't moved or spoken, I thought I'd better get some information. I didn't want to touch him for fear of launching some next step that I was too tired for. But I said "Sir, do you think your God enjoys watching this?" At first it didn't break whatever spell he was under, and I started thinking he'd fallen asleep.

But at last he raised back up very slowly. His eyes didn't meet me.

I figured they couldn't, not from that nearby. I said "Why don't you sit on the sofa? My legs have gone to sleep."

Tom obeyed me but even from there he looked ashamed.

I suddenly knew how completely exhausted my mind and bones were. Still I had to know a last thing before leaving here. I said "Now was that supposed to help me somehow with the problem I brought you?"

He managed to face me but didn't speak.

I said "I'm the last one to judge anybody alive, but help me know how to use my body in the actual world—I've already made big mistakes in private. That's all I ask, tonight anyhow" (I may not have talked that well back then, but I'm still convinced it's what I meant).

And eventually Tom seemed to know what he meant by the whole last act. He said "Well, first, I wanted to kiss your flesh but something stopped me. And then I was showing you what I deeply *know* is true—short of harming children, sex is seldom ever wrong. And even children aren't always hurt. I don't think I was hurt at all when my Aunt Florence feasted on me. She was only six years older than I, her true love had died in the war, she said she was way more lonesome than the last dodo on the plains of Mauritius." He took a plainly thoughtful wait, then said what he'd apparently just now discovered. "It's a way to praise God."

I said "Have you told your congregation that?"

"No I haven't. Most of them wouldn't understand."

I said "Does your wife know you're here with me?"

"She knows that I'm here right now, yes—trying to help you through a tragic time. But she has a frail mind herself, and I don't try to crowd it with thoughts that she can't—and shouldn't—handle."

After that I halfway thought Tom Landingham was sicker than Mother, but I also partly welcomed what he said. Wouldn't many young men, even now, when free sex is easy to find? I was more than half serious, then, when I said "So I can go back and spend the night inside a married woman who's also my teacher?"

Tom said "It might well get her fired if the wrong people see you. Her nerves might break. *Yours* might break, in time. Her husband might kill you, or you and her both, if he comes back and finds out. You'll need to run that part of your business with considerable care. If you like, I can do my best to guide you forward. I'm in my study each afternoon late. If anybody stops you, say I asked you to visit."

By then I was ready to thank him but also never to see him again. I stood up and pointed him toward the back door.

But he said "Could I take a last minute and go to the rooms where your siblings died?"

I barely knew what *siblings* were, and I halted a minute. Did he have some other strange rite in mind? Still I took the lead, walked the few yards and turned on the light. In the weeks since Easter, it had got so I could look in there without strong pain. Hesta came by here at least once a week now to sweep and dust, so the room was clean and the bunk beds were neatly spread. It was no harder to bear than the average motel room unless you paused to think. I planned to leave quickly, and I stayed by the light switch to hurry Tom up.

He stood in the doorway, taking it in. "They both slept here?" When I said "They did," he made a slow way over to the corner, laid a hand on the top bunk and then on the bottom. It was not one of his major meticulous radar sweeps, but he was plainly more than impressed. Then he looked back to me. "They're in good shape," he said. "They have no memory at all of what happened."

I said "Are you telling me you know that for sure?"

"Absolutely. I am."

I'd seen enough phony psychics on TV to halfway wish I could hurl him through the window, but I'd had my own credible visions lately, so I said "Can you actually hear their voices?"

Tom saved the day. He said "Oh no, Noble. I'm not that wild but I'm speaking from the depths of a lifetime's faith. Arch and Adelle Norfleet are alive wherever God means them to be this minute. They'll be there forever."

However confused I'd been by all he'd said in the previous hours, I was suddenly truly grateful to him. His face and eyes were clear as pure water when he made me that promise of their good whereabouts. For whatever reason, then and there, I chose to believe him and have never since doubted it for more than a day or two at a time. I would have gone a long way to repay him.

* * *

And of course I did, over weeks to come; but that same night I stopped by the jail, went in and tried to at least see Mother even if we couldn't talk.

The jailer said that wouldn't be possible and turned his back to finish a whole chess pie he was eating.

Then a pleasant-faced woman, maybe thirty years old, in uniform appeared and took a little time to ease my mind, as far as she could. She said that Mrs. Norfleet was long since asleep in a private cell and had seemed very peaceful ever since she got there. When I asked the woman what she thought would happen, she took me into a dim low cubicle with mustard-color walls, shut the door behind us and whispered the rest. "I shouldn't be saying a word of this; but if what we've heard about her is true, they'll take her pretty straight to a state hospital for the feebleminded with anti-social histories and keep her there."

I must have looked a little stunned by that, though it was the most I hoped for. *Feebleminded* did seem a little mild for Mother's condition, but I didn't say that.

So the woman took the back of my neck in a hand as strong as any weightlifter's and literally massaged it for maybe a minute as I stood there with my eyes shut, thanking God or whatever power was responsible and wondering if we wouldn't be arrested for inappropriate behavior if anybody barged in. Nobody did, though, and finally the woman said "You go on now and get some rest. You can see her tomorrow, if she's still at peace." As I went through the door, she asked another question. "You got a home, right?"

Before I could think, I told her I did. If I'd said *No* would she have invited me to her place, and if so would it have been just a trailer with nobody else but her or a full-fledged house with a husband and children and a color TV? In any case I had just enough strength left to thank her as I left alone. My mind was so whipped I couldn't even linger on a normal boy's pleasure in the fact that his body had drawn two fairly sane human beings, and maybe a third, in the course of a day. Then I drove back to Hesta's, told her I'd been to church as she suggested and now was *safe*.

She saw how exhausted I was and didn't ask for further proof.

So I climbed to my room and slept like a hypnotized rock under ether in the depths of a mineshaft long since abandoned by all forms of life.

Then I had two more weeks of school to finish before graduation. I put every private concern in cold storage while I got through the numerous duties of the present. I had to find a lawyer for Mother and help lead her through the various tests and hearings before the State could agree she was incurably insane and dangerous. Then I went to the jail and watched them lead her out to a car so Barber Brady and another officer could drive her to the state hospital prison where she'd be confined till she got sane enough to indict or died of natural causes first.

She was not handcuffed and they'd let her wear the clothes she'd worn when I turned her in. But her face and eyes were all unstrung since I'd seen her last, only four days ago; and I was not entirely sure she knew who I was when I bent to kiss her. Anyhow she pulled back and pressed me gently away with both hands.

I told her I'd come to see her very soon and that she'd like her new home.

But she said "I'm not sure I'll want to have company. I think I may have got worn out by all these weddings and baby showers and other such nonsense they've forced on me lately. They compelled me to get baptized this morning!" But then she laughed in her old way that had you wondering if it wasn't all put-on to make a fool of you.

So that left me with nothing to do but press her hands lightly and say goodbye. As the car pulled away, I thought she might kill herself at the hospital. I'll have to admit that it felt like a hope.

Next I had to go through the complications of having myself declared the administrator of her estate and the sole recipient of the quite surprising savings account she'd managed to keep (nearly $10,000), the lump sum payment from her pension plan (another $8,000) and of course the owner of the car and the house with its staggering freight—decades of stuff that ranged in importance from a million old checks and recipes, through Adelle's doll collection and Arch's thousand toy soldiers, to the hidden volumes of handwritten diaries and poems I found in Mother's trunk but couldn't bear to read.

I'd got to the point of starting in on the cleanup job when Commencement night arrived. I'd told Hesta I'd need to be moving back in at home and getting it ready for whatever came next—I still hadn't quite decided what I'd do. There was not enough money to send me to college for long, if a college would have had such as me with my B minus grades and my scary background. I didn't have a job yet. The draft might very well swoop down on me if I didn't haul ass to enlist myself first and have some say in whether I'd go to the U.S. Infantry and stand a strong chance of dying in a boggy rice field or into the Navy and let the Vietcong select my river boat for mortar practice or be a Marine and go screaming wild, trimming scalps and ears off teenage Asians who wanted nothing worse than to flush crazy white men out of their country and get on with buying their own motorbikes, boom boxes and rickshaws.

Well before the Sunday night in question, I'd asked Hesta to go with me to school and sit up front as the nearest thing I had to a parent and watch me start life as a certified man. She'd accepted with the solemn dignity of a person who's merely receiving her due. And when time came to go, she was waiting on the porch in a new dress that I had no idea she'd bought—the first piece of white clothes I'd ever seen on her and a wide white hat with the best imitation white rose ever made. It looked fresh enough to speak out loud and declare its name. I knew that Hesta had been to the jail to see Mother more than once, but it came as a shock when we were more than halfway to school and she said "You're not going to stop by the graves?"

I said "No, why?"

She said "I just thought they'd enjoy a short visit."

Neither one of us said the two children's names, but of course I knew her meaning. And I glanced at my watch. We were short on time, so I said "I planned to climb over the fence late tonight and leave them some flowers from the stage decorations."

Hesta said "You promise?"

I promised her Yes.

And she only had one other question. "Am I going to have to meet that Spaniard?"

I forced a grin down and said I doubted the chance would arise.

"I hope to God not," Hesta said, "—now you've seen the light."

I hadn't quite viewed it in those terms, but then I hadn't seen Nita outside of class since the day I turned Mother in and met Tom Landingham. The separation from Nita hadn't been all that painful for me, and I assumed it had been a welcome change for her. I'd heard that Tom would say the benediction at tonight's ceremony—this was back before prayer disappeared from schools, near us anyhow—and Nita would surely have to be there, but I didn't feel any sense of dread at what might happen with either one of them. Maybe Hesta was partly right anyhow. If I hadn't seen the light, it did seem I'd got a gram of horse sense from somewhere.

And Commencement went off smoothly enough, though of course it went on for the standard ninety hours and had sufficient quantities of both sobriety and silliness to last me for life. I surprised myself by enjoying the time as part of a herd of healthy young people, all glad of something. But I didn't get any medals or special commendations, though they gave out what felt like several hundred. In fact my name was not called aloud at any point, though it was spelled right in the printed program (a lot of people spell it *Nobel* as if I'm the inventor of dynamite and the famous Swedish prize). I couldn't complain—I'd never stretched myself in my studies, and I'd seldom tried to fix any memory of me and my brain or my dazzling personality in teachers' minds.

I did glimpse Nita way back in the audience with a few other teachers and Tom on stage, but I didn't meet either one face to face. At the lime-punch reception I shepherded Hesta past a good many pale old maids and mothers and well-brought-up American racist males who tried, by raised eyebrows and frowns, to show my valiant lady-companion she was out of her element. But if she saw them, she ignored them grandly and continued to carry herself like a woman accepting the small gold watch she'd earned for years of honest labor. The people who treated her the way she deserved were my friends from the track team. Every single one of them shook her hand, and more than one hugged her.

So on the way home in the car, Hesta said "Do those boys know about your life up till now?"

"What part of my life?"

Hesta said "I guess I mean the terrible parts."

I said "Well, they're bound to know about Easter Sunday and Mother in jail. If they know anything about me and the Spaniard, they heard it from some of your spies, not from me." I smiled as I said it; and then as we pulled up by her back door, I reminded her I'd be moving out tomorrow.

She said "You don't think I know that?"

I told her it was just a little reminder.

Dark as the night was, she looked out her window at her little garden that was totally hid—she wouldn't face me—and she said "Noble, I'm not feebleminded *yet*. You think I'm about to forget I'm losing the only person I ever loved that shared my house?"

If she'd suddenly stripped, revealing a dancer's jeweled G-string, I couldn't have been any more amazed. I'd never heard the word *love* from her mouth in all the years I'd known her, and I'd seen no signs of her loving another soul on Earth, much less Noble Norfleet. I guess I'd just assumed she was offering food and shelter to a half-drowned orphan these past few weeks. So once I'd stopped the car, I reached down to take her left hand and thank her.

But she drew it back as if I'd scorched her, opened her door and stepped to the ground. Before I could get out, she leaned back in. "Now you go on to the children's graves, you hear? It's your last promise to me." And with that she left as quickly as one of the spirits she saw everywhere in our lives.

I had no doubt she was not a demon.

When I'd climbed the wall and reached the graves, though, I half-expected to find Mother waiting. There was nothing, except the two low mounds of local dirt that the crabgrass still hadn't captured and hid. At first I knelt and said my goodbye—I said the one word. Then I wondered if I would truly ever leave, so I stood back up and tried to think of better words to say. Finally I managed to think it out. It was just the word *Thanks*, and I still wonder why. I mean, they'd given me a few years of laughter and almost equal amounts of typical older-brother frustration.

Was I saying I was glad they were gone from my life? Had they somehow cleared a path for me? God knew, their likable compact bodies had been the occasion for clearing Edith Norfleet off my screen forever. Or so I believed. As I said, I still wonder where I'd have wound up if they'd lived on.

But that was all I could do at the graves. I'd kept my promise to Hesta and myself. I could go home to bed. My track friends had asked me to drink beer with them at an old place of ours deep back in the woods on black granite bluffs by a serious stream, but I faced a whole long day of cleaning out the house. I should get a night's sleep; so I cleared the cemetery wall again, opened the car door and got the next shock.

Tom Landingham said "Don't be afraid." He was waiting in the front passenger seat.

Though Mother had played the same trick on me, it still scared me more than anything yet, and I don't know why. I wasn't mad. I had nothing against him. Still I'd put him so far out of mind as a personal guide that I think I expected Tom less than any living soul or ghost I knew. When I got my heart back into my body, I said "How the hell did you know I was here?"

He'd changed into khakis, a burgundy polo shirt and bare feet, another real surprise (it's illegal to drive without shoes in Carolina, a sane regulation). He'd gone by Hesta's, she'd sent him on here, he had a gift for me, and I'd got away from Commencement before he could hand it over. That was the first thing that passed between us then. The gift was enclosed in a small velvet box with no special wrapping. Tom reached up to turn on the ceiling light as I lifted the lid, and there was a silver medal with a man I took to be Jesus displaying his world-famed profile. When I turned it over, yes I could see it was Jesus again—standing up full length at the head of a table with numerous diners. There were women as well as men, which meant it couldn't be the Last Supper (an all-boy event so far as I knew and still suspect, though if you read the gospels you can easily surmise a few women were present, to wash the dishes if nothing else—in any case of course they never said a word).

Tom said "It was what my mother gave me when I finished college and was on my way to divinity school. I thought you should have it."

I thanked him sincerely but said "I'm far from bound for preacher school—you know that, don't you?"

He said he did. Then he pointed to the medal and said "Do you know who all the guests are at the dinner table here?"

I told him I didn't.

Tom said "I've never been sure myself; but I've always thought it was one of those meals where he ate with the whores and tax collectors, the real guttersnipes that everybody else despised and shunned but that he sought out on numerous occasions."

It hadn't really dawned on me till then, but this was the only Commencement gift I'd got or was ever likely to get. I thanked him again and asked if I couldn't take him to the Waffle House for coffee at least.

He declined the offer. What he wanted, for now, was just to talk; so we turned out the light and sat in the dark by the cemetery wall and talked for the better part of an hour. Tom showed some understandable concern about my future—where was a man as young as I headed next? By that point in American history, very few boys with high-school diplomas from the white middle class weren't bound for college after some fairly lightweight summer job to defray the cost of the small incidentals like rock 'n' roll LPs, hippie beads, bell-bottoms and condoms of course for the Age of Free Love.

Anyhow I brought Tom up to date on financial realities and my vague plan to join the service before the draft suddenly vacuumed me up.

He was the first adult I'd told who didn't look at me as if I were crazier than my poor mother. He went on about how they might not send me to Vietnam but then raised an idea I hadn't yet considered in earnest. "Noble, have you thought about serving as a medic?"

He couldn't have known that I'd surprised myself by mentioning the same idea to evil old Dellum in Maryland, so I told Tom I hadn't. That was mainly just to see where it would lead him.

He said "Then you'd better give it some thought."

I remember laughing. "Don't medics have the shortest life expectancy of all?"

He thought that over. "It's dangerous business, sure; but maybe you need it next."

He hadn't done anything weird or unwelcome yet, aside from being here at all; so I asked him to expand a little on the medic idea.

Then was the first time tonight he really turned those strange eyes on me, those detection devices. He searched me thoroughly like a lost soul in dire need of instant care; then he said "There's no way you can help your mother now. She's gone on past your reach forever. You can make up for it, though, by helping others."

Today it may sound more than farfetched. In the crowded air of the late 1960s, it didn't seem strange—not with the Asian war, the civil-rights murders, Martin King's assassination only two months ago and now Bobby Kennedy's a few days past plus the red-hot discovery by my generation of drugs and fucking as harmless pastimes—it didn't seem strange. In fact Tom's suggestion all but chimed in my mind. *Yes.* Yet I didn't think of offering substitute help to make up for my mother's havoc. What I thought of was Adelle and Arch in their bunks and how I'd been nowhere in reach when harm walked through their open door. I could pay, a little anyhow, on my debt to them. And if I died in a bamboo thicket, giving blood to a boy maybe younger than me, then so much the better. So I said to Tom "Well, thank you for that. It sounds dead right."

He waited awhile. Then he said "Say *right* if it feels right, Noble. Omit the word *dead*."

We both laughed hard.

After that I was tired. But like most people my age, then and now, I couldn't be the first to say so and leave for something as meaningless as sleep. It's only fair to put on record that what came next came honest and aboveboard between two adults. No alcohol or drugs were involved, not in my body anyhow. No sleazy hand was placed on my thigh.

Tom simply said "I'd like to give you one more thing, or maybe it's more for me than you. But if you can accept it, I think it'll teach you one last thing that you can use from the weeks you knew me."

Of course I knew he was looping back to sex and the way he'd acted that night at my old home. I've mentioned that I was still as subject to instant ignition in the genital department as a boy in the first throes of puberty. There was also the fact that, since the day I turned Mother in and received consolations from Nita and Tom, the only reward my cock had received was from my own hand. So I said to myself *I may just sit here and let this happen, if no pain is involved.*

In the wide front seat of a mystery Buick that had been God-knew-where since Mother took flight, I leaned back and let this mystery man—who claimed to minister from God to humanity—loosen my good pants and bend to feed on my hot skin and drink my spirit as if that much of me anyhow bore some direct kinship with the bread and wine he served on Sundays to ladies and gents in linen dresses and starched shirts and ties.

Tom was good at his work as before. Again it didn't take long, and that simple transaction was all he asked of me. I wasn't expected to reciprocate with so much as a hand on the top of his head or a word of thanks. (I say none of that with a trace of pride. In long retrospect I say it with regret and no little shame—not for what I accepted but for the unrelieved stinginess I showed, the sealed blindness of an average boy, despite my being grown.)

When Tom had sat back up and paused, he owned up to feeling something similar to what I've described. He said "You ever been worshiped before?"

We were deep in the country three miles from town, and there were no street lamps or car lights passing. Still I couldn't make myself face this man for fear of actually meeting those eyes, full force in the dark. But nothing in the sound of his voice suggested he was joking.

I said "No sir," just to see where this led.

And he said "That's what I gave you then. The bare human body is the altar of God on this Earth at least. That's all I meant to teach you. Take it with you when you go on into the world. Almost nobody knows it or believes it anyhow. It ought to be taught from every pulpit every Sunday forever, every synagogue and temple on the whole planet Earth; but of course anybody who taught it would be burned."

The previous time we'd ended an evening, I'd come away more than half sure Tom Landingham was crazy—maybe criminally so. But here and now it suddenly seemed like the vital truth he claimed it was; and even with what came too soon afterward, it shaped my life for the whole stretch ahead. So much so that when Tom sat quietly another long minute, then touched one finger to the back of my right hand, opened the door and stepped outside, I said "I thank you" just loud enough to hear.

But he didn't answer.

By then I was wider awake than I'd been in a good many weeks. And with my new knowledge, it felt as though I ought to go to Nita and try to help her understand what she'd meant to me, even if we never touched or met after this. I'd be lying if I didn't also admit I hoped she'd change her mind and wave me in. When I parked in her backyard, it was nearly midnight; but the usual dim bulb was on in the kitchen. Though I hadn't been here since the day Mother went to jail, I still had my key. Nita had never asked for it back. I tapped on the glass, though, so I didn't scare her. Then I let myself in.

I stood in the kitchen and called her name lightly, then a little louder. No answer, no sound of anybody moving. She had insomnia and seldom managed to sleep before two or three in the morning. Maybe she was in her bed, reading with the radio on. I softly whistled my favorite song, which was "Help!" by the Beatles, and moved toward the bedroom. The door was open but the light was out. I stood there silent while my eyes slowly opened.

But Nita's bed was empty. I stepped to a lamp. The whole room was neater than the White House parlor. On the bed where I'd known the first ecstasy ever, and I'm not jeering now, was a small package wrapped in silver paper with a dark blue bow. Propped beside it was a white envelope with the one word *Noble* in Nita's handwriting but large, almost as if she were writing for the blackboard in school.

It almost scared me. I suddenly wondered if it might not warn me she was dead in the bathtub or hid on the floor beyond the bed with both her wrists cut. Still I had to read it. It hurt so much I burned it that night, but I can recall it far too well.

It said she had left for her old family home. One of her brothers had come to drive her to South Carolina, which explained why her car was still in the yard. She didn't try to lay a word of blame on me. In fact she said she'd learned a lot from knowing me. She didn't say what that was nor when she'd come back here, if ever. She wished me "the best on Earth" and hoped that I would accept the gift in the spirit in which it was intended. I stood there, wondering how she'd known I would show up tonight; and I tested my mind to see how I felt about this strange turn. At first I almost felt relief. It would simplify my immediate future; and by then I'd partly learned how to ignore everything that lay more than two minutes ahead.

So I sat on the edge of the bed and opened the silver package. Of course it was a book, the poems of Federico García Lorca. Nita had mentioned him several times before, stressing the various pains of his life and his final murder. I turned the pages far enough to see that Lorca's Spanish was still a good deal more advanced than I could read without a dictionary. Then as I rose up to start back out, something fell from the book to the floor at my feet—another envelope, another letter.

This one had passed through the mail, I could see—airmail stationery, addressed to Nita in a small tight hand in coal-black ink. When I turned it over, I got the next surprise. It bore her husband's name and return address—an APO address but from Vietnam, I knew of course. Nita was bound to have put it there for me. She meant me to read it, so a whole lobe of my brain said *No*, but I sat back down and took out the pages of paper so thin you could see your fingers through it. After all these years, I have it still. With all I've lost I still have Albert Acheson's letter, and I read it every year or so.

My dearest Anita,

Your letter has reached me with the hardest news I ever hope to hear. I had a short leave not two weeks ago, went to Saigon with two other guys and spent the whole time <u>not</u> fucking the teenage whores that they kept buying. You say you think it is best I should know what you've been doing with that poor kid. But sitting here in the deep pig shit that is all this war is, I can't help wishing you'd kept your mean secret.

As it is I'm still at the point where I want to hurt you just as bad in return. I'm hoping that will change before I get home if I ever do. Right now there doesn't seem to be a lot of point in trying. But if you can hang on to the promise you made in your awful letter, maybe I can. You will need to keep on writing me every day and telling me honestly every time that you are true to me again and will always be.

Just pray I don't die out here, Anita. I would haunt you every breath you draw from that minute on.

Keep strong and keep talking, by mail I mean,

To your faithful husband—Albert

If I'd ever had a serious doubt about volunteering for Vietnam, it vanished on the spot. Not that I wanted to meet Albert Acheson face to face—oh far from it—but that night at least, if you'd pushed me hard I'd have almost surely told you that I wanted to go and die in pain to pay for my wrong in cheating on him. I'd consoled myself for my mother's crime by rubbing my cock again and again on my numb brain with the partial assistance of another man's wife, so I told myself before I ever left Nita's house that this was a crime I wouldn't repeat. But while I'd taken a small piece of pride in refusing the drugs of my generation, I'd addicted myself without full knowledge to the world's cheapest drug.

All the downstairs lights were on at Hesta's at one in the morning. That was strange, considering the fact that she tired early. But when I walked in, she was in the kitchen, still in her new dress but wearing her shocking-pink bedroom shoes with the rabbit eyes and ears. They looked about as appropriate on a woman of her strong dignity as they would have on the pope. I asked her what had kept her up so late.

She said "First, tell me you got to the graves."

I told her I'd just spent a long time there, no reason to trouble her with what else happened.

That freed her up for the rest of her plan. She said "All right then. Sit down here." She pointed to my usual place at the table. Then she went to her old refrigerator, brought out a full bottle of scuppernong wine and two chilled jelly glasses and poured us each a heavy slug. Then she sat across from me and raised a toast. "Here's to you, son." With that she threw her head back and downed every drop of the potent syrup.

She'd never called me *son* before. I'd never seen her take a drink stronger than coffee, and I had to guess that she'd learned how to make a toast from watching TV, but I followed her lead.

When she'd wiped her mouth with the back of her hand, she reached deep into her bosom and brought out a small envelope.

I almost flinched at the thought of another hard letter so soon.

But Hesta said "This is just something to help you on past the place where I can reach you still."

I expected one of her usual offerings—a thin Bible tract of the sort old men pass out in bus stations or one of the laminated plastic healing cards she got from sending five dollars a week to some howling radio preacher—but I opened it anyhow as if it might surprise me.

Imagine the feeling when it turned out to be a yellow bank check in her strong upright hand for five thousand dollars. When I could speak I said "You can't do this, Hesta."

"I've *done* it," she said. "Can't cancel it now." By then she was back on her feet and rinsing our glasses at the sink.

So I said "Any idea what I ought to do with it?"

"No," she said. "It's a present from me to you—that's all. You can cash it tomorrow and burn all the money if that'll help you any."

I laughed. "Not likely."

"Then get you a savings account," she said. "Put it in there and use it to send yourself to college—*fast.* But since you say you're going to this war, let it make you some interest till you get back and learn how to train your mind and lead a good life."

I told Hesta I'd do exactly that and would put her name on the bank account with mine so she could have it back if I died in service.

She stood at the sink with her back turned to me and was silent a long time. Then, not facing me, she said "Noble, Hesta's going to be long dead when you get back."

Again I laughed. "You'll be here forever."

Her head shook hard. "I guarantee *not.* My work is finished now, this very night."

By the flare of strength that burned from her firm arms and shoulders, I knew she meant it. And I knew she'd accomplished her meaning in the time she'd just foretold. Then, as now, Hesta James was the only person

I'd known who'd done her own will every day of her life—all the days I'd known her anyhow.

I'd have stood up and ringed my arms around her for the kind of thanks you normally give a big benefactor you've known all your life, but I knew she'd hate that. I only said "Nobody's ever been good as you are."

"Not to *you* they haven't," Hesta said. "That little bit is true. I'm a rattlesnake sinner otherwise. Now you get your rest."

It served as a benediction I obeyed. I didn't wake till noon the next day.

As it turned out I had another few weeks left at home, and I managed to stay fairly busy through the time. It took me the best part of six weeks to clean out the home place. I've mentioned that ordeal. But if you've never had to go through the piled-up leavings of a family—in our case, the decades since my parents got married just before Dad went to the war in Korea—you may not know what a hard job is. The first trick is you can't just go in with an iron rake, pull stuff out and burn it in the yard. Young as I was, I knew that there might be papers I'd need in future years. And considering Mother's mental state, I suspected there could well be uncashed checks or fifty-dollar bills she'd hid in books or drawers or stuffed down inside the ten million brown-paper bags she'd carefully folded and saved.

And then you're likely to turn up occasional secrets that can be fairly rough on your nerves. For instance I found the letters my father sent home from the war. I doubt many boys under fire can have written about love and loyalty better than he and then have turned out, not many years later, to be the coward who walked off and left three helpless children to manage a raving woman. I even found, tightly bound up in an old silk stocking, the Polaroid pictures he'd taken of Mother (buck-naked and flagrant, stretched back on their bed) and the ones she'd taken of him (ditto with a gigantic smile and a huge hard-on wearing one of her bras and his little Army cap). Thank God there were none of them actually joined up together.

I've spoken of the pain of sorting my brother's and sister's belongings. Arch had barely made it to eleven, and I halfway feared he might have started keeping the kind of diary I kept as puberty seized me, day by day, but No he hadn't. As for Adelle, I'm told that girls today in the twenty-first century aren't nearly as stuck on dolls as they once were; oh but my sister had a world of dolls, every size and color and every age. You might have thought with Mother being odd, Adelle would have wanted nothing to do with adults; but she had a whole department of grown-woman dolls, mostly dressed in earnest Joan-Crawford-type suits with stacked shoulder pads. One by one as I touched each doll and boxed it away for the orphanage, they felt like raw and outraged nerves.

The orphanage, the Salvation Army store, yard sales every weekend, a steady fire in the backyard oil drums—by the time I was done, I'd left myself nothing but my bed, a kitchen table and two straight chairs, enough tools to make a sandwich or fry an egg, a pair of bathroom towels and some soap, my usual bed, and two easy chairs in the living room plus the radio and TV. I even stripped my personal possessions to the barest bone. I kept sufficient clothes to be decent, Dad's shaving brush which he'd somehow forgot and a dozen books that had been real props in the hardest times of Mother's troubles.

There was *Ivanhoe, Tarzan and the Leopard Men, Treasure Island, The Illustrated Man, The Martian Chronicles* and—as I got older—a well-thumbed stack of pornographic paperbacks I'd bought downtown at the old poolhall. There was nothing too randy and nothing at all sadistic; and by today's standards of what seems thrilling, the whole sad stack was sweetly tame, but it fired my brain through dozens of single-handed raids on my skin. Just seeing them again, hid back in my closet, reminded me that my dead brother never got to the age where that sort of scot-free absolute ecstasy is every boy's instant right.

Otherwise I spent a lot of time alone and a lot of it asleep. It seemed as if I hadn't slept since Easter. So I'd clean house at night when it was cooler, then sleep all day—twelve or fourteen hours. The phone never rang and nobody knocked. I was that nearly dead as far as the rest of the world was concerned. I'd occasionally go to a movie with one of my track-team friends, but I'd always be the one to make that arrangement. Also by then I'd got a weekend job in the local hospital's emergency room. With the recent improvements in my financial picture, I didn't need the money. But Tom Landingham pushed it on me in line with his early suggestion that I somehow owed it to Arch and Adelle. He arranged it through a doctor he knew on the ER staff, and I thought I'd go along with it a time or two to see how I liked it.

At first I was very much the low-man on the ladder—*sub-basement* low—and the chores I got were the ones involving blood and shit and chunks of hair. Then I graduated to washing the males who arrived without open wounds but who needed deodorization or body-shaving before the doctors felt ready to see them. You wouldn't want to know what that was like. I hadn't imagined there were men on Earth, not to mention my neat-looking town, who'd clung onto dirt in their folds and creases that was absolutely petrified with age. But I guarantee there were, and not all of them were poor and surely not crazy. Looking back I can see one blessing at least—I didn't have to guard against patients' blood or body fluids. AIDS hadn't landed yet.

Still I can't really say that, that summer anyhow, I had time to feel I was helping anybody—alive or dead. Aside from the minimum wage I got, the only other result of the job was that Tom Landingham met me most Sunday mornings at one o'clock as I staggered out of the hospital door. He'd have to preside at Sunday school and church just a few hours later, but he'd take me out to an all-night diner and drink coffee with me. Then he'd take me home—my all-but-empty house.

I freely admit I never tried to stop him. And every time he took my elbow and steered me toward my room, I'd lie back on the bed I'd used since I left the crib and accept the service he seemed so endlessly ready to give. By then, though I'd never said a word about it to him, I'd reached the point where it meant even more to my dark mind than it had at the start. I've mentioned that, with no special guidance, Tom knew how to trigger my pleasure—he never once failed, though it wasn't exactly rocket science—and that I was still at a point in my life when a little proof that I mattered even this much to some other human beyond old Hesta was no small matter. What got more interesting steadily was trying to guess what it all meant to Tom.

To the best of my knowledge, he never climaxed in the times he was with me. At least he never took his clothes off or bared his equipment; but I never failed to see, from the heat in his eyes, how urgent it was for him to swallow me down, time after time. And to me it felt literally terrific in the world I entered every time we were together—together in our peculiar way, though I'd be as alone as a blind mute astronaut adrift outside his distant craft (like most boys I'd been alone with my competent body for three or four years before I met another human who'd cooperate).

That night by the graveyard, Tom had said my body was the *altar of God*; and by the time we were deep into summer, I no longer thought the idea was funny. I'd learned that much from remembering Nita and what she'd taught me, wrong as we were to cheat on her husband. I didn't even have serious qualms about giving a member of my own gender the use of my intimate facilities to please, and somehow console, the two of us. And with all that together, during such a full summer, I was on my way to seizing between my powerful teeth the bit I would run with for so long to come—the notion that sex is the fast way to God. Before I left home I'd even receive, in one more vision, a proof that seemed to come from God that Nita and Tom and I were *right*, but that's still a few weeks ahead in the story.

Except for the numerous times with Tom, and alone with myself, I touched no other human body that summer. There were girls in town that I'd dated in school, and I'd see them as I went about my chores. The sight of some of them, and the chats we'd have, would set me tingling for a half hour or so; but I never felt compelled to book a real date with any one of them, and I even suspected I might get refused. Their parents would likely have warned them off any private time with a boy whose family had, only last Easter, undergone insane murder (insanity was widely considered to run in families, maybe rightly so). The important thing, looking back, was that what Tom Landingham provided was seeing me through till I took the next leap.

I made the main preparations for that on the afternoon I watched Mother leave. I'd thought a good deal about which service to join. Hesta's nephew Jarret James with the funny English accent, had said "Join the Navy. If you're in the Navy, they shoot at the boat. In the Army they shoot at *you.*" It didn't seem a negligible point, but the longer I thought—and talked with Tom and worked in the emergency room—the more my mind began to aim at the Army. Above all I wanted the plain old Infantry with me as a medic, so I went to the Army recruiting place and set the plan in motion. I wouldn't be eighteen till early August, but they were more than glad to see me. They'd do all the paperwork now and wait till my birthday came.

In the next few days, I passed the various written tests and the physical with no real hitch. They asked about a thousand questions on my medical history. Did I still wet the bed? Had I ever had sex with a man? (I said Yes and they didn't miss a beat). Had I ever wanted to have sex with my mother? (not since I was three, I told them). Had I ever wanted to kill anybody? (of course). Did I have screaming nightmares and walk in my sleep? (not more than once a month). All my answers were true; and I managed to satisfy them completely, though they never asked if my mother had killed anybody; and I didn't tell them. In a quick ten days they'd accepted me for a three-year enlistment. They couldn't guarantee I'd be a medic, but they said good medics were always in demand. I knew that meant medics died like flies, but of course they didn't say it.

When I told Tom the deal was set, he seemed proud of me. It was then he suggested we needed to make a trip together as a kind of farewell. He used the word *farewell,* but he didn't say he suspected he'd never see me again once I left for training camp. Because of church he couldn't leave town on a weekend, but could I get away from my job for two nights at the first of a week? That wasn't hard to arrange; and on the Monday after my enlistment, I stopped by in the Buick to get him—he and his wife only had one car.

It was the first time I met his wife. Her name was Alma and she was a good deal lovelier than the picture Tom kept in his office, a tall woman with long raven hair and rich brown eyes that seemed to know a lot more about the real world than Tom ever had and to see no need to hide any of it the way he did.

She came as far as the side porch to see us off; and when I shook her hand, I could tell she was straining hard to read my face for danger, so I told her I was a careful driver.

She nodded and said "Please be careful with everything else too." When I looked a little puzzled, she said "We have two beautiful daughters who love him deeply. I do as well."

I said I could understand what she meant.

That was somehow the worst thing I could have said. Her eyes brimmed full and she turned and rushed indoors.

Tom surprised me by not going back to reassure her. He just said "I always call her Ruby Falls—she weeps so much." Ruby Falls was a tourist site in Tennessee. Tom had grown up a few miles away, a mountain boy from a half-starved family with eight other children.

I could only be glad the Landingham daughters were off at a summer camp somewhere deep in the mountains. I doubt I could have met them without feeling way too guilty to make the trip I'd planned with their strange father.

We were bound due east all the way to the ocean. Through our childhoods, with Mother in her fragile state, Arch and Adelle and I had never gone anywhere, and all but a few of my hitchhike journeys had led me south and west of home; so the whole right-hand half of North Carolina was news to me. And by the time we got an hour down the road, we'd left the last foothill behind and were in the pinewoods and dish-flat fields of the coastal plain. In those days tobacco was still the state's chief money crop and its pride. Though I'd never smoked I could still look out at the thousands of acres of pale green plants and not feel what I can't help feeling today—that humankind begs it to poison millions of them.

And the people that you saw working the fields were ninety-nine percent Afro-Americans—not a single Mexican in sight (three decades later it would be at least a hundred percent Mexicans, short men with the stark straight raven hair and the hard-carved curving profiles of their Mayan and Aztec forebears). For a man who hadn't gone five miles from home for more than a year, except that miserable errand to Maryland, a sight as simple as tall green plants with leaves as broad and leathery as bomber jackets was a steady relief.

Then in early afternoon, we got to the place, unmarked on the map, where the soil starts looking more like sand than dirt and the whiff of salt in the air starts to strengthen with every roll of the tires. The Maryland ocean hadn't smelled this potent—it was too assaulted by the smells of fried fish and mom-and-pop factories making saltwater taffy and other dental disasters, so my feelings began to rise by the mile. I was almost pleasantly excited, which was quite a switch for me in recent years. I was no longer even worried about where we'd land or sleep.

Tom hadn't told me our exact destination. He clearly had some surprise up his sleeve, and I hadn't tried to force it out of him. If somebody wanted to plan something truly entertaining on my behalf at this point, I was hardly the boy to stop them. It turned out our goal was the Outer Banks, that frail chain of islands the mainland has thrust out to bear the brunt of the hardest weather the Atlantic Ocean can stage at its worst. By two in the afternoon, Tom had guided me right up against a big old house, tall as a silo and covered with pale green wood shingles.

When I killed the motor, he said "Here's a place you'll be truly safe in—nobody for miles but you and me."

Even that didn't faze me. The presence of others in my life, or my presence among them, had caused very little except real pain and yelling or tears since I was scarcely ten years old. Being all but alone felt like a true blessing.

The house belonged to a rich insurance man in Tom's congregation. It had been right here, through storm and strife, for fifty years and had never even lost its roof. Or so Tom claimed. Isolated as it was, we were no more than a couple of miles from Kill Devil Hills, the giant sand dunes. As I stepped from the car, my whole body instantly felt regenerated—*rewired* to be exact. I felt as if I might yet survive to have a good life and maybe be a good man, and that was a brand-new feeling for me.

It wasn't till we were indoors and started climbing upstairs with our slim luggage that I smelled a possible hitch, and I thought *I trust there's more than one bed involved here.* If Tom had led us toward some master bedroom with one big bed, I knew I'd have to plead some problem. I'd claim I had "nervous leg syndrome," which had plagued my father. (It's a little-known but maddening ailment. One of your legs will jump, in the night, as if lightning struck it. You can easily kick yourself out of bed, not to mention your partner.) It would be a small lie, but I was primed to tell it. Tom led me to a private room, though, on the front of the house with six floor-to-ceiling windows on the ocean, its own bathroom and a narrow single bed.

So it was a mostly good two days. Tom went out right away, bought a world of groceries and did some fine cooking (he did all the cooking for his own family, saying he'd learned to cook both well and cheaply as a mountaineer child). Oddly enough Mother had been a good cook till right up to the end, but since Easter I'd barely had a decent meal—neither Hesta nor Nita was a power in the kitchen. And again, to my surprise, Tom left me free to spend a lot of time walking alone on the beach and swimming in the vicious but thrilling surf. That whole stretch of water isn't called "The Graveyard of the Atlantic" for nothing.

There was one twenty-minute stretch when I got caught in a riptide—or what felt like my own private vortex—and I thought I might truly have bought the farm, for good and all. After the first few panicky seconds, it did seem for *good.* I couldn't make any headway at all in returning to the shore, and I was known as a strong young man to others my age. When I looked to the beach, there was not a single human in sight. So I lay on my back in water that felt like a million ropes all pulling in opposite ways. I thought *It's weaving something beneath me.* Was it a net to support and save me or some kind of cage to trap and drown me?

I looked straight up at a sky so blue it seemed like a vision in itself—not an actual creature but something purer and older than that. Maybe God or whatever lay back of the short word *God.* I thought *Well, pray to that for your life. That'll save you if it wants to.* But I couldn't do it. I wasn't out of breath and I wasn't scared, but I couldn't make myself want to live. Grand as the day was, and with all the years I had to expect, I couldn't even think of changing the serious fix I was in. *Let it happen on its own with no push from me in any direction.*

And then very slowly I knew I was happy. *Happy* was a word that had hardly crossed my mind for long months, maybe for years. And there on my back, in the hands of an ocean that cared as much for me as it did for the nearest rag of dead seaweed, I somehow found the calm leisure to wonder why. I found it had nothing to do with my recent freedom from Mother, nothing to do with the prospects of serving in an evil war, nothing whatever to do with the thought that an ordained minister was in a big house a few hundred yards off preparing a bountiful dinner for me. It was simple love. *But love for what?*

I didn't strain to know. I lay on, supported by the strong ropes beneath me. And then I knew I loved Noble Norfleet, a boy who didn't even seem to be me. It didn't feel remotely like self-love in any dangerous sense. I didn't think *I* weighed one gram more on the great scale of things than the meanest beggar. But there at the genuine point of death, when I could have breathed out and laid my head beneath the green salt, I knew that Noble Norfleet somehow needed to last till the endless spread of blue overhead had signaled it was done with this one boy. With that I rolled over onto my side and had no trouble whatever in stroking my way straight in to solid ground.

By the time I got back to the house, Tom had the big meal almost ready. If I looked a little exhausted, he didn't mention it; and I didn't mention my recent experience in the famous local undertow. I took a quick shower, managed a ten-minute nap and then heard the dinner bell. When I got back downstairs, the dining table was handsomely set and a huge copper candelabra was lighted. The food was all spread—deviled crabs in their shells, broiled red snapper, corn on the cob, green beans cooked the old way with ham, handmade biscuits and a bottle of cold white wine.

Tom asked me if I'd like to "give thanks." I hadn't heard anybody request a dinner blessing that way since my grandmother died, and it silenced me for an awkward stretch. But we sat there calmly till I finally said "Let's thank the blue sky—" That was as far as I could honestly get.

Tom kept his head down for a few more seconds, then laughed and said "Do you want to say what we thank it *for*?"

I honestly tried to think but no words came. I knew the sky had strengthened me to face the prospect of death not an hour before, but I still didn't want to discuss that moment.

So Tom served our plates and waited till I'd bit deep into the first ear of corn. Then he said "How about we thank it for the Earth that grew this corn and for saving your life?"

My near-drowning had occurred way down the beach from the house, well out of sight. I couldn't imagine how he'd even glimpsed that so I laughed too. "That was you then in the little submarine that refused to help me?"

Tom said "No." He looked genuinely puzzled. "Did you see a sub?"

I finally said "No" but couldn't let the subject drop—why had so many mysteries surrounded me in the past few months, from Easter morning to small-town Maryland to my mother turning back home unscathed from weeks on the road to this recent rescue that happened with nobody watching but me and the sky itself and any mind or eye that might lie beyond it? I knew that even Tom would have no answer to that, so I asked something simpler. "Why do you think my life got saved?"

He faced me steadily and said a word nobody had ever said to me. "Because you look beautiful now."

Not only had nobody ever said the word to me, but I'd never heard a man called *beautiful* before. *Handsome* was what good-looking men were called in the world I came from, if anybody happened to see them at all (which they seldom did—women were the main things people seemed to dwell on). Then I must have burst out in one of my prairie brushfire blushes.

Tom reached in his water glass and flicked a few cold drops at my redness. Then he said "No, you do look amazing, Noble. Don't contradict me. Something happened to you since you went swimming, and it changed your looks. You looked fine before but now you've turned golden."

If he'd reached out then and touched me anywhere, even on the back of the hand, I think I'd either have struck him or run—I felt that momentarily sick. But I managed to get through a few more mouthfuls of his first-rate food before I spoke again. I said "You swear you weren't spying on me out there in the surf?"

Tom raised his right hand in a silent oath.

So I went on and told him. "I very nearly drowned and I gave up fighting to stay alive, but something outside me turned the tide." Then with Tom's eyes on me, I flinched a little. "It was likely just a natural change in the water."

At first Tom gave an agreeing nod. After a minute, though, he said "No way."

I said "Tell me why."

"Noble, if I could tell you why, I wouldn't be here on a Carolina beach in a borrowed house, cooking supper for two men. I'd be the unquestioned King of the World. So no, I don't understand your path at all"—he raised his swearing hand again—"but I know you've got one. You can twist it right or wrong. It's plainly on the ground before you, as of today."

I've mentioned that Mother had subjected me to very little in the way of church, but I'd listened to enough preachers on the radio to suspect that the standard holy-Joe song could break out from Tom any instant now. To balk it I raised both arms out beside me like balancing wings. Then I gazed toward the ceiling, blared my eyes wide and gave a brief preview of navigating my destined path.

Tom laughed for a moment. Then he said "Shame, *shame*." And though I hadn't quite eaten my fill, he stood up and began to clear the table—not another word.

I didn't try to help him but went out and sat on the long front porch and watched the evening flood in around me.

Indoors behind me Tom played the piano for more than an hour. I wasn't an expert on any kind of music. Except for Arch's sweet melodies, Mother mostly hadn't allowed music at home. It could make her too happy, and happiness was one of the hardest things for her to handle. But even I could tell Tom Landingham was good at whatever he was playing. I still think he was making it up. In all the years since, I've never again heard any tune he played. But the testosterone that's likely to pound through the veins of any two men who've had so much as a mild confrontation went on barring each of us from joining the other for any kind of peaceful words before dark fell.

So when exhaustion suddenly seized me, I walked through the living room and said a calm "Good night" toward his chair in the farthest corner. He was reading *The Glass Bead Game* by Hermann Hesse, a major hit with hippies back then; and he looked up and nodded with the thinnest smile. But he still didn't speak.

I'm sorry to say my last conscious thought before I slept was *He'll wake me up about three* A.M. *and wolf me down like warm lemon sherbet.*

But he didn't. He may have glided on bat wings over the ocean till dawn or fed all the homeless camped out under bridges between here and home, but he didn't visit me.

I slept straight through the night as deep as if the ocean had taken me after all and swept me toward the sands of the Sahara, which was after all only four thousand miles due east of my slim bed.

The second day would be our last. When I woke I could hear Tom puttering quietly in the kitchen; so I pulled on my shorts and joined him, half sheepish.

He gave no sign of bearing a grudge. He was cooking corn fritters, a half pound of bacon, scrambled eggs, baked tomatoes and biscuits again. I've mentioned how little good food I'd had in recent years, but I think it's worth stressing how nearly miraculous it seemed to return to a pleasure that was easy enough for a human being with modest skills to bring about. And since I'm a generally grateful soul, it's honest to say that—these years later—a main component of my good memories of Tom Landingham is of just such gifts from an old cookstove.

Then the long day passed in normal beach fashion. We took a long walk to the north and south. We horsed around in the ocean, which was calmer than yesterday. We lay on the sand and read our books—I had my copy of *Treasure Island,* which I was repeating for the ninety-ninth time. I understood it was a boy's book; but I had no trouble thinking of myself as still a kind of boy, with all I'd been through and done to others. We had a late lunch of cheese and crackers back at the house, and then we parted for separate naps.

So it was well into dusk before Tom came to my door and spoke to wake me. I'd assumed we were going to eat at the house again. But Tom said "Better get shaved, put your best clothes on and let's be out of here in under half an hour." He'd told me to bring one pair of long trousers and a decent shirt with a jacket and tie. I hadn't imagined what the need would be, but it soon appeared we were headed for the finest restaurant anywhere near. Needless to say, when Mother was at home we never ate out. And on my various hitchhike ventures, I'd never got into anything grander than a Howard Johnson's when a traveling salesman decided to treat me to fried clams or baked beans.

It was my introduction, then, to starched white napkins the size of big diapers; crisp cold shrimp cocktails with horseradish sauce, tossed salads in bowls the size of wash basins with Roquefort dressing as rich as an oilman, prime ribs wider than full cross-sections of Texas steers, baked potatoes with chives and bacon and sour cream, strawberry shortcake on fresh short biscuits with real whipped cream and black espresso so strong you could stand your spoon upright in the cup and it wouldn't fall. Not to mention waiters as awed as altar boys and a full-time maitre d' who took himself as seriously as any grand duke on the last czar's staff. I was almost as awed myself and certainly fuller than I'd ever been when we finished after two slow hours.

We hadn't talked about anything nearly as strange as usual in the past two days, and we didn't talk at dinner or in the car as Tom drove us out into the night. He didn't take the normal turn for our place but kept on northward. I didn't ask where we were headed but assumed we were getting a final dose of salt air before we had to leave in the morning. By the time Tom finally slowed and turned, we were well past the reach of any human lights, and the stars were burning almost savagely. I leaned out to see if the sight was normal or whether I was undergoing some brand-new revelation. It seemed to be normal. And after maybe another mile we stopped in what seemed a small parking lot, but still I could see no human lights.

Tom opened his door and finally spoke. "Welcome to your farewell event." The good cheer he'd managed throughout our dinner sounded even higher, and he led the way to a narrow paved walk uphill. We got to what felt like a stone platform. Then Tom led me on by the elbow till we actually came up against a great vertical something also made of stone—very smooth with no detectable joints.

After I'd stroked my way a few yards to right and left, I finally said "OK, I give up. Are we in Egypt? Whose tomb is it?"

I'd long since learned how Tom loved mysteries, and now he actually began to moan like ghosts in old-time radio stories of the kind that scared me irresistibly before I had even scarier things in my own house. At first I laughed and then he kept it up so long that the hair began to rise on my neck; so I said "Tom, I'll be scared enough in Vietnam. Give me a break here." Then I realized I couldn't make out his presence anywhere, just the moaning voice; and it was growing more distant by the second. I called out again—"Tell me where we are." There were maybe three minutes of silence, and I didn't enjoy a single second.

Then a far-off voice that might or might not be Tom spoke out. "You're at the famous Wright Brothers' Monument where man first flew."

I'd known of course that two very peculiar bachelor brothers had left their bicycle shop in Dayton, Ohio to try to fly their matchstick-and-canvas plane off the windy dunes down here, and I'd seen many pictures of the monument. It was a tall bird's wing in gray granite so I tried to relax. I said "They ought to light it up at night."

The voice said "I've caused the lights *not* to shine."

By then I could believe it. But chilled as I was, I chose to walk straight toward the voice. It led me off the stone platform and the narrow walk into sand and scrub, and finally I came up against a body, upright and tall. I could smell it was Tom by the lime cologne, and the upper half of his body was bare. I said "Whoa, man. What's going on?"

He said "I want to honor you a last time."

I told him he'd done far more for me than I'd ever deserved.

He persisted though. He said he felt it was his duty to God to thank me for all I'd meant to him in these recent weeks. He sounded sane again.

But how sane was I? Just the sound of those words made me believe him. At the time I felt—and I don't expect applause—that I and my slender competent body had done this smart man a genuine favor by yielding to him a few dozen hot times. I thanked him and said "Let's go to the house then."

It turned out that, while he was moaning and groaning like a spook, he'd also managed to get a cotton blanket out of my car. Mother had won it in a bingo game and had always kept it in the trunk in case we had some emergency that called for a blanket. He also produced a small flashlight, led us farther out from the monument, spread the blanket, sat down on it and asked me to join him.

I did, with no reservation whatever. I lay flat and stared dead-up at the stars again. And then it started. I hadn't had an authentic vision since I stepped out of the restroom at the breakfast café the morning I turned Mother in to the Law. But now when the whole dark sky was suddenly sewn, not only with stars but with silently roaring open shafts onto what lay beyond them, I knew I'd been selected again to see what must be useful news for my ongoing life.

So I kept watching as Tom got down to performing what he claimed was his duty to God. I could just make out that he'd kept his trousers on. I hadn't so much as loosened a button, but of course Tom had to uncover as much of me as proved necessary. I helped him a little, and of course my cock cooperated with its usual reliability, but I mainly kept gazing overhead at the actual news. Behind the shafts that opened out behind the stars, I could gradually make out scattered glimpses of a huge body moving in long loose clothes that rose and fell in the slowest slow motion. I'd see the sweep of a great arm and hand, then a leg would lift and stride out toward me or turn and recede.

I kept waiting for sight of the head and face that surely managed the body, and I'm almost certain I saw the outer boundaries of a long fall of hair. After that, very silently in my mind, I tried to speak to it. I said *Am I set to have a long life?* It went on moving. I said *Why am I allowed to see this tonight?* At that it stopped and held in place, though the clothes still moved a little on the limbs. But when I heard no words of answer, I said *Please show me the side of your face.* I recalled, from Sunday school years before, that even Moses on Mount Sinai was not allowed to see God's face, only his back.

At that the various shafts were slowly shaded over as if the thinnest grade of pale cloth had been pulled across them. Then I could see, through numerous openings, the dim outline of a profile that seemed to be a strong man's or a woman's at least as self-possessed as the woman who posed for the Statue of Liberty. And then I heard a voice in my head that was not my own voice and surely not Tom's. It said *Keep on.* Did I have any choice but to think it meant *Keep on the way you're headed tonight?*

By the time I'd asked myself that question and mulled it an instant or two, Tom had finished. He'd returned what he claimed were his thanks to God, and I'd given him the tangible proof he seemed to require. By then I'd thought of my cum as the receipt he'd keep inside him to prove he'd done his duty. I'll have to say that, with all the pleasure I'd taken in Nita's own good arms, this last stretch of minutes was the finest actual gift my skin had yet received. But I didn't say that or anything else.

So Tom stood up and said he thanked me *profoundly*. I'm sure of that last word. I didn't put any special weight on it at the time, but he also said something very much like "I've done the last thing I know to do for God." Then he headed for the Buick.

By then my eyes had opened to the dark so fully I could see Tom fairly plain. At first I thought that final sentence was nearly as crazy as anything Mother had said at her worst—I'm still not sure I was all that wrong—but then I recalled how this whole quarter hour had triggered my vision of what ruled the sky: the arms and legs and face that had urged me forward but offered no trace of a map. So I looked again at Tom's vanishing body, and his back and shoulders and his high-held head looked young as a runner's breaking the tape.

Two mornings later I was waked by a knock on the front door at home. Nobody but strangers ever came to the front door, so I struggled into some pants and ran to answer. My watch seemed to say it was 6 A.M., but I thought it was wrong.

Tom Landingham's wife was there on the stoop. Whatever time it was, she was wearing an immaculate coal-black dress with a big white collar; and her long hair was pulled back tightly from her face. She said "I'm Tom's wife, Alma Landingham, and I'm very sorry to wake you so early—" Then her voice failed.

Though I was bare from the waist up and still addled from sleep, I somehow had the wits to ask her in.

But she shook her head hard, then managed to say "I've got three billion things to do. I just have to ask you one question first." Again she shut down.

I reached out and took her cool white hand and drew her inside. She sat on one of my last two chairs, and I even volunteered to make coffee for her. When she declined that I sat at her feet and said "What's the question please?" Of course I figured it was somehow connected with the beach trip and Tom's feelings for me. I could suddenly feel my soul crouching down the way it had in the old days when Mother would start raving at me. I thought of just turning and bolting out the back door. Maybe it was some kind of pure curiosity that kept me in place.

Then she said "Can you imagine a single reason why Tom just killed himself in the night?"

Somehow I couldn't hear her. I couldn't process her meaning at all. I said "What night are you talking about?" I could only think of the pitch-dark time at the Wright Brothers' Monument and my glad vision.

She said my name then, for the first time in my hearing. "Noble, wake up please. This is as serious as possible."

I begged her pardon.

"He must have died by three A.M. When I woke at five, he was cool beside me." When I looked puzzled she said "I'm a trained nurse. I know such things."

To this very day I seldom say *Jesus* (Mother asked me not to, as a sign of respect); but I said it then in pure amazement and—I guess—the need for help. Then I called Alma's name. "What did he take?" I was just assuming he hadn't bled, or she'd have been even more shocked than she was.

Alma said "The pill bottle was there by the bed. It was empty and it didn't have a label." After we both sat silent awhile, she said "Do you understand *anything* about it?" No child in a picture from the world's worst orphanage had ever looked more cruelly baffled.

With what felt like absolute honesty, I told her plain No.

But by noon—once I'd gone to the parsonage with Alma, seen Tom cold in his bed, helped her call the authorities and then the church staff—I knew I'd played a sizable part in Tom's calamity. And I buckled under that latest crime. In another half hour I was back in the Buick and bound down the map toward South Carolina. Nita Acheson was literally the only adult I knew left alive, above ground, who'd have the good sense to help me in this particular bind; and I had no reason to think she'd see me, assuming I could find her. All I knew was the name of the town and the fact that her father and both of her brothers had run a place called The Honest Garage back when she was a girl.

I'd made no plans and hadn't brought so much as a toothbrush or a change of clothes. I hadn't even estimated that the drive itself would take a long four hours, but I found the little town, and The Honest Garage was still in business in the midst of Main Street. When I pulled in and stopped, I realized I didn't even know Nita's maiden name.

The man who came out to fill my gas tank was snow-white haired and as distinguished looking as any senior diplomat. The nametag on his uniform said *Belford.* He had a kind of life in his eyes and hands that seemed familiar; so when I paid him, I said "I'm looking for a wonderful lady who was my Spanish teacher in high school, named Anita Acheson. Does she live around here by any chance?"

Belford smiled as he handed me my change, but he said "You wanting to give her a prize she's won in some contest?"

I thought for a second and then had to laugh. "In a manner of speaking, yes sir, I do."

With that he turned back toward the station and started to point.

But when we both looked, Nita stood there in the doorway. She was wearing a dress I'd never seen on her, a vivid green; and while I could tell she recognized me, she didn't smile or wave.

Belford said "I'm her daddy. Be kind. She's having a hard time."

I suddenly thought *Albert's been killed.* It almost made me climb back in the car right then and speed off.

But Nita walked toward me—or toward the two of us. Her father was still there with me, and as she came I had little choice but to stand and think of the story she'd told me about the years when her mother died and the men in her family climbed aboard her. By the time she reached us, I was studying her father's face and hardly seeing her.

So she stopped there and waited.

Then Belford said "This young fellow says you taught him all he knows."

Nita smiled at last and said "I may have."

So I held out my hand and said "*Buenos días, señora.*"

She accepted the touch and kept on smiling, but I knew it was the only touch we'd share that day or ever after. I could see that clearly in her eyes, and I felt it in my own mind.

I said "*¿Cómo está?*" and prayed she wouldn't say Albert was dead.

But she changed into English as if she didn't want to leave her father out. "I'm fine, thank you, Noble. I've just got a miserable summer cold."

Pure gratitude almost bowled me over.

At first it seemed as if we were going to have to talk, standing there in the open public. It seemed she was staying at her father's house. He had never remarried. She was cleaning up for him and cooking his meals, but I could soon see that we weren't going there. She didn't even suggest it. Her father stood with us through the first few minutes, so I figured I'd have to state my purpose in his presence.

When I told Nita I was in serious trouble and needed her help, she took a three-second pause. Then she looked to old Belford who was cleaning my windshield for at least the third time. "Dad, I'll take this boy to the café and be back here by the time you shut down."

Belford looked at me closely, then shook my hand. "She helped me out of a deep ditch, bud, a long time ago. I'm sure she'll help you."

She tried anyhow. First she saw I was starving, which I hadn't noticed. And when we got to the nearest café, she made me eat an entire meal—a hot turkey sandwich soused with good gravy, french fries as light as clouds in the spring sky and homemade slaw with no sugar in it (sugar ruins all the slaw it's ever been in). Then she said "I guess you got my graduation present."

I thanked her and told her I'd read Albert's letter and would try to keep it as long as I lived. I told her I'd signed up for the Army and would be going shortly after my birthday. I told her all about leaving Hesta's and stripping Mother's house, and then I ran out of any way to tell her about

Tom Landingham and me. I just sat and faced her like the schoolboy she'd first met two years ago in elementary Spanish.

She said "Well, it's clear you've had your hands full; but none of it sounds like serious trouble. What's gone wrong, Noble?"

I said "Nita, it's not you; and don't think I'm down here begging for what I know you can't give."

She thanked me for that and smiled outright for the first full time.

That nearly derailed me—she looked so grand—but then it gave me the strength I needed to tell her the truth I'd so far omitted. I knew she'd met Tom Landingham at school events long before my Commencement; and that also freed me to think I could lay out the whole story, start to finish—if it truly was finished. Just then and there I suddenly wondered if Tom had left any kind of letter or diary that Alma hadn't found yet. And if so, would the Law be waiting to question me when I got home? Still I started to talk to Nita. And the first help was seeing how her well-trained face showed no trace of shock as I told the whole truth so far as I knew it. The last thing before I thought I'd finished was something I hadn't admitted till I said it. "Nita, am I some kind of demon on the loose?"

She calmly said "Why would you think that?"

I said "Count it up. Since Easter Sunday I've been responsible for one dead brother, one dead sister, a wonderful teacher I pressed too hard, a mother in prison for criminal insanity, a badly cheated husband off in Vietnam and now a dead preacher. That's not average for a boy my age, is it?"

At first Nita seemed to shake her head No, but then she said "Don't take *all* the credit."

I had to laugh. "All right if you say so. But answer me this please—and I'm truly serious—am I some kind of born troublemaker, or is this all just a stretch of bad luck?"

At that point Nita changed her mind. She called the waitress and ordered a cup of black coffee, hot as the day was. While she waited she moved things around on the table. She was making temporary patterns with her paper napkin, the sugar bowl, the salt and pepper shakers. Once she'd drunk two swallows of coffee, though, she knew her answer. "I've thought about this ever since I left and came down here. In your case, Noble, it's both things surely. You've certainly had the bad luck of Job, but there's something down in you that turns people dangerous—makes them think they can do everything they've wanted, from the cradle upward, with you and your wild eyes." She was clearly finished but she still hadn't smiled.

I ate a few mouthfuls and then had to say "So I drove all this way for that? What good is that to me? I guess I should just plow off the first bridge when I head back north." I was truly in earnest.

Nita finally let the hint of a smile lift her eyes, but when she spoke she said "Maybe you should."

We went on talking about small matters till I finished the meal. Then she said she had to meet her father and cook his supper. Since she'd been so honest with me, weeks ago and now, I thought I'd ask her one last question. "Your dad and brothers are good to you, I hope."

But she lowered an iron fire-curtain on that. "I wouldn't be down here, Noble, if they weren't."

That also told me nothing I could use, so I gave up wondering and drove her back to the filling station. I didn't go in.

But Belford came out and invited me to supper.

I thanked him and said I had a job to get to. I'll have to say he was nicer than Nita. Still I'd given her cause enough to act any way she wanted to me. She and I shook hands and exchanged good wishes.

And as she and her father turned and went toward the station, a younger man was standing in the door. He looked so much like Nita I knew he had to be a brother—very dark-haired and, like her, hot as a pistol. She'd mentioned that one of her brothers had left for a job in Detroit, but the man standing in the doorway now had heard about me, or he glared like a dragon for unspecified reasons.

So I hit the road. And when I got to the first long bridge, I honestly thought for maybe three seconds I'd swerve sharp right and put myself and a good many people yet to come in my life well out of harm's way. But of course I didn't. Wasn't I licensed just two nights ago to give the world whatever I had by God Himself or whatever had shown itself to me, in moving fragments, through the stars near Kill Devil Hills, N.C.? How crazy was that and who was I to say, or how was I to tell?

* * *

The main thing, though, that got me home intact was a highway sign I saw right after crossing back over into North Carolina. It was so small it just managed to clear the pine trees around it, and all it said in green neon was "All Girl Staff." It hadn't been many years since such places were legal in the state—massage parlors that could actually give what the Law called "hand relief" and places with "movie mates," which were women who'd sit beside you in a cubicle while you watched a pornographic movie and give you whatever assistance you might need, within limits that I never tested.

Anyhow I was still sufficiently wiped out to get off the highway at that point and park at All Girl Staff before it dawned on me that I didn't have so much as twenty dollars in my pocket. The building itself was plainly an old gas station where the gas pumps had been removed and the windows had been boarded up. Besides my Buick there were only two other cars and a gigantic classic Indian motorcycle. I had no idea what the Staff would be selling or how soon I'd get kicked out the door for inadequate funds, but I was too discouraged by everything else today not to try my luck.

The entrance around back had a lighted doorbell with a tiny sign that said "Ring for Possible Admission." The sign was handwritten on a three-by-five card, and the script was so neat and legible that it had to have been made by a really gifted student of penmanship or a public schoolteacher. Had I been missing out on a goldmine, not getting to know my teachers sooner? Anyhow something about the word *possible* cheered me a little and I rang.

It took a long time but finally the door opened fast and wide, and there stood the biggest man I'd seen till that point in my life. He was nearly seven feet tall and must have weighed close to three hundred pounds. He also had a beard that would have done full credit to anybody in the Book of Genesis, from God Himself to Abraham or Methuselah. He spent about ten seconds studying me up and down and then said "Show me some authentic ID with proof of age."

I showed him my authentic driver's license.

He shook his head, handed it back and said "You won't be eighteen for several days."

I said "That's a fact but I sure need help."

He said "Tell me why?"

"Well, my brother and sister have recently died, I've just had to put my mother in prison, a good friend committed suicide last night, and the woman I love in South Carolina has just shut me out."

Even that list didn't make him slam the door. The man took another long survey of my looks. Finally he said "My name's Hog Arnie. I'm sergeant-at-arms of the local Devastator Angels, honest to God. We run this business on very strict lines. Answer me this—have you killed anybody, are you packing a gun or illegal drugs, and what have you got against the female sex?"

I told him I was innocent of all the above and was nothing worse than a man in a terrible run of luck.

At that Arnie said "Come in and shut the door."

I stepped in, shut the door and was briefly in what seemed to be pitch darkness with no sounds but a mild gurgle of water. When my eyes opened a little I could see we were in a small room with a huge dimly lighted aquarium, one of the best-kept I'd ever seen. If you hadn't seen as many aquariums as me, you'd have thought it was the most peaceful world ever made and not just the hangout for killers and cannibals. There were three or four straight chairs and a low table with a stack of brand-new magazines, mostly *Mechanix Illustrated* and *Knitting Times*.

Arnie said "Take a load off your feet" and pointed to a chair.

I told him I'd been driving all day.

But he said "Sit down" emphatically.

Somehow I wasn't scared so I took the farthest chair.

Arnie sat just opposite and said "It sounds like you may qualify for a merciful waiver of regulations under Clause 6D."

He hadn't smiled so I took him seriously. I said "I'd be glad for any kind of waiver at this point but I'm almost broke."

Arnie shook his head again. This might prove a higher hurdle than my age. "What's the most you can spend?"

He looked so honest I took out my wallet and counted the bills. "I'm going to need gas in another few miles—I'd say I could spend ten dollars max."

Arnie shook his head harder than ever, then grinned. "One of the girls might clip your toenails for ten dollars—*might.*"

I started to rise. I said "Thanks for the rest. It was nice to see your fish—"

Arnie said "Hold on. Let me speak to Dipper." He stood up, vanished through a door I hadn't noticed; and a long wait followed.

I think I dozed off for maybe ten minutes.

Then Arnie was back with a woman that looked like the old-maid principal from my grade school. At least I now knew who'd written that sign.

This one, though, was wearing short shorts and a tank-top shirt that said "Call Me Dipper If You're A Big Tipper." She regarded me very sternly, then looked to Arnie. "You *sure* he's a few days shy of eighteen?"

Arnie said "Dead sure."

Dipper said "All right. Take his ten dollars then." She watched intently as the money passed from me to Arnie and into Arnie's pocket. Then she faced me and actually smiled. "In light of your being so young and broke, I think you'd better go to Antoinette" (I later saw the name spelled that way on the girl's own T-shirt, like the queen of France that went to the guillotine; but Dipper pronounced it *Anton-et*).

So I stood up, not knowing what was coming next and surely expecting some pitiful country girl with at least one wall-eye and buck teeth parallel to the ground.

Then Dipper led me down a short hall, knocked lightly on a door, opened it a little and nudged me inward.

I don't expect anybody to believe this—I didn't at the time—but Antoinette was the finest-looking woman I'd ever been in the same room with. If she was older than me, I'd be surprised to know it, though she claimed she was twenty-three. In any case she was almost as tall as me and I wasn't short. Her face was in perfect order, her ash-blond hair was long and straight in the fashion of the time, and her eyes were green. You hear a lot about people with green eyes, but she was the only human I've ever seen whose eyes were not some weird color of blue or gray but were actually a genuine emerald green. Honest to God, my first thought was *I want to adopt her.* I still don't know why I thought that, maybe because she looked a little like what my sister might have looked like if she'd had the chance. Anyhow I was speechless, standing there.

She gave me a smile that could crush huge boulders if the need arose. "Take your clothes off, son."

All I could say was "Please don't call me *son*. My real name is Noble."

Her smile hadn't faded. "All right—Noble, peel off as many layers as you want to. It's plenty warm in here."

So I stripped down to my Jockey shorts.

And she pointed for me to lie on a tall bench near the wall.

I lay on my belly, wondering briefly if Arnie and the principal might not burst in any minute now and fillet me quicker than a freshwater fish. But just the act of stretching out had me all but overwhelmed with tiredness in a very few seconds.

Antoinette turned on some slow restful music, lowered the light, put warm sweet oil in both her hands and began to stroke my shoulders and neck.

I had just enough consciousness left to think *These soft hands have rubbed down how many truckers, Devastator Angels, Baptist ministers in disguise and husbands who claimed to have "gone out to buy a carton of cigarettes"?* And I thought for three seconds some helpful new vision might shine for me here the way they had in past rough times, but No I was deep asleep before anything else could reach me.

—Anything except what Antoinette did at some later date when she'd worked her way down the breadth of my back and the length of my spine. She leaned and whispered into my ear "Hunch your pelvis up."

I managed to do so, too far gone to understand entirely what she meant.

She shinnied my underwear down my legs, off my bare feet and then stroked southward through my meat and gristle with hands that were waking me up by the instant. She worked all the way to the soles of my feet, then worked on back up toward my butt. Then not lifting her hands at all, she stopped and waited so long I thought she had to be finished.

I figured this was what I got for ten dollars. It was not everything my friend Phil Gilmer had got at the All Girl Staff at home—Phil holds the state pole-vault title to this day—but he admitted he'd paid every penny of the fifty dollars he got for Christmas. So I half-rose and turned to thank Antoinette.

Her face was as strangely veiled as Tom's had ever been at such silent moments. I could truly not see her plainly enough to be sure she was even the same girl I'd seen when I entered the room and before I dozed, but the voice was the same when she gently said "Roll over please whenever that suits you."

Please and *whenever it suited me*? I'd have given her pure gold bars to turn over if I'd had any handy. Of course I was harder than a railroad spike, but I felt no embarrassment or shame. Nothing in this woman's voice or touch allowed me to think I might surprise her or let her down with the facts of my body and I was right.

She worked around my upper thighs awhile, and then without stopping she said "You seem like an educated man. You know who I'm named for?"

I shut my eyes and said "If you're truly Antoinette, I'm guessing you're named for the queen of France that lost her head."

She didn't say whether I was right or not, but she gave a laugh as fine as her face had been at the start, and what she went on and did to me was more than any normal human woman could have done without some claim to royal powers.

When I'd reached the goal she worked me toward, I lay still as she carefully dried me. All but one cell in my body was blissful, and that was a single cell in my brain that dreaded to open my eyes and see some different woman standing above me. But when the same voice said "All right," I knew I had to leave. I sat upright and slid my legs around.

Then she laughed again. "Boy, open your eyes. You'll fall and break your noggin."

So I looked at last, and there she was—the original girl, fine and real as before. That one reluctant cell in my brain said silently *To thank this girl, you'll worship women from this day onward.* And in sometimes awful but always well-meaning ways, I've done it, though when I left Antoinette then and there, I didn't even reach out and shake her hand. Still I did turn back when I opened the door, and I said "I hope you'll have the best life anybody can have."

She was already changing the sheet on the bench, and she didn't look up. But she said "I'm working at it day and night," and her face was calm.

Later on here I'll try to explain my line of reasoning for occasional visits through the years to women who may have been doing such work under various forms of mental or even physical duress, but I hope your patience will hold you in place while I say that—there in my early manhood—I left Antoinette with pure gratitude; and I feel it today, three decades later.

Once I was back home, I had under a month before the Army took me. In the time remaining I went to Tom Landingham's funeral. Nobody there but Alma knew me, so I didn't have to say anything but *Sorry* to her and the daughters who'd been rushed back from summer camp and looked rightly stunned. They were roughly the ages of Arch and Adelle, so I didn't offer my hand to shake. I strongly suspected the feel of skin that young and smooth might hurt me too much. Nobody I knew from the Law was there, and nobody said a word to me in those last weeks about the mystery of what Tom had done and how and why.

Two days after the funeral, I went alone to his grave and tried to talk to him. I don't mean literally. But I did stand there and ask him silent questions, most of which you can imagine. I more than half-hoped I could get some reliable help with the ones that felt especially urgent (some still do). *Was this tragedy of his also about me?* and *Did he know now, wherever he was, whether he'd been right about whatever it was he was doing with me—my skin and the gist of who I was and what I had to give? And what on Earth was so fine down inside me to make him bow before me as he had? Had he seen his own version of what I saw that night in the sky? If so, did the same voice that told me to live also tell him to die?* But no help came.

On the last weekend I'd have at home, I went to see Mother. I hadn't seen her since they took her away. She hadn't tried to phone me, and I didn't phone her. In the early weeks I did get a small handful of notes from her. She knew my address and her handwriting still was as strong as ever, entirely controlled and as soaked with power as any battlefield general's at dawn. At first she plainly knew where she was; and while she never mentioned why she was there, she gave clear descriptions of the living conditions. She had a clean cubicle of her own, she almost praised the food (I recalled how little she'd eaten since Easter), she said the "nurses" were "respectful Negro men and a few big but kindly women." And she said the doctors seemed "very well up" on everything they needed to know.

Fairly soon, though, she was sending me detailed plans for her upcoming Christmas vacation in Mexico. I *seemed* to be included. That wasn't always clear and after a while she was sending reports, with very nice drawings in the margins, from her solo rambles through the mountains of Peru and camping out with the "butt-naked natives" of Tierra del Fuego. She also added what sounded true—that Charles Darwin on the voyage of the *Beagle* had seen the same natives sleeping in the snow, still naked as jaybirds with no trace of blankets. She didn't make the connection for me, but I assumed she was trying to cheer the two of us up—her powers of adjustment were at least as elastic as the nudist natives.

After that she continued to write in detail about life with the natives and how much she loved the wild ocean down there in the Straits of Magellan. They'd built her a fair-sized boat, and she sailed alone a good part of each day. By then I'd given up the idea of even mentioning my enlistment and what had become the actual hope that I'd go to Vietnam. Still a great many reasons gathered force in me; so early that last week I phoned the prison and, after being shunted through six or eight attendants and guards, I finally talked to a warden who claimed to be a doctor. He sounded more than a little confused himself and said "She's here for depression, right?"

I said "You could call it that, but it caused her to murder two children in their beds. Otherwise she's a likable soul."

He said Mrs. Norfleet had been very calm so far, was doing great work in her painting class and that I could see her for half an hour on Wednesday morning if she approved my visit.

I told him "At the moment she's sailing her boat off the Straits of Magellan; but if you get her back, I'll be there Wednesday."

That didn't even faze him. He gave me matter-of-fact directions on how to get to the right entrance at the regulation time, and he said "She'll be here. That much is sure at least. Or so you imply."

After the uncanny powers she'd shown in recent months, I'd never have claimed I was sure of anything where Mother was concerned, and I'd never once thought any *implication* I might have given had a thing to do with my mother's fate.

But on the appointed Wednesday, they led me to a low narrow room where the walls were painted the shade of milky green that always has me wishing I were dead in under two minutes. There were no magazines, I hadn't brought a book, and the room was soundproof. So by the time my mother appeared, I was on the far edge of sanity myself—so much so that I didn't stand up when she entered but stayed in my chair and gazed up at her like a crippled child.

The black male orderly's nametag said *Darwin*, and for a quick moment I wondered if we were in Tierra del Fuego after all.

Wherever I was in real time and space, Mother came straight to me. She seemed to need a few seconds to know me. Then she laid a flat hand on the crown of my head and said "You might want to think about standing when your mother walks in. She's been through a lot just to get you here alive."

With her there above me, I was suddenly scared. But scared of what, especially in view of the weight she'd lost since I'd last seen her and the fact that the life in her eyes was all but dead? Anyhow I wasn't entirely sure what she meant—that she'd *got me alive*—but I stood to my feet. And since I was at a loss to think what next, I gave a semi-military salute in her direction.

Mother said "When is it they come to get you?"

Was she thinking I'd be here to join her soon? I asked her who *they* were.

"The Forces," she said. And just when I thought she was off on another wild tack, she said "This war you'll fight."

For the first time in years, I wanted to know how she knew what she knew. "Who told you I'd enlisted in the Army?"

"Noble," she said, "I read the newspaper. I know there's a war on. I know your mother is a lunatic killer in prison for life—and the life to come. I know that uncle of yours wouldn't give you cold spit in the midst of a desert, so I know you're entirely alone in the world. Where else would you go?"

I hadn't heard a saner chain of sentences since Commencement night, and they made me laugh. But in case she had any worry for me, I said "It's not guaranteed I'll have to fight. I could stay fifty miles away in Fort Bragg and pick up cigarette stubs for three years. I could go to the war and be a medic and never fire a shot—"

She put a cold finger to my lips. "Don't say the word *medic* please or *shot.* Ask God to forget you mentioned either one."

I said "God's keeping close watch on me."

She stepped back then and studied me closely. She hadn't looked clearer-headed for years.

And for an instant I even wondered if her new short haircut had somehow helped her.

Then at last she said "God's watching *you*, Yes; but he turned His back on me the very day you were born, so you try to keep a watch on *me* from here on out. You're the last soul not in Heaven or Hell who cares if I breathe. Remember me somehow."

I told her there'd be no possible way I could put her out of my mind for two seconds, and I thought it was true.

Mother said "You don't know it but you're lying through your teeth." She frowned slightly and tried to explain. "I've forgot every hard thing that happened to me in my whole life." Then very slowly she produced a broad smile.

And I caught sight for the final time in many years of the girl who'd "got me here alive," whatever on Earth that meant.

I rushed through the last few days by doing just two things. I slept as many hours as I could manage, and I kept on doing the necessary chores. I knew I could keep the Buick right up till the final minute. Any second-hand lot in town would give me a decent price for it. When it came to selling my family home, though, I finally balked. Technically the deed was still in my father's name. Who knew whether he was alive, though; and either way, how would an eighteen-year-old son go about getting the necessary permissions from a lost man or an insane felon? So I found a real-estate woman to act as my rental agent and see to repairs while I was gone.

She agreed to do it all for a slim five percent of the income, and she said "It's a sturdy place. I can see you love it."

I had to say "You may be seriously wrong about that much." Still I had the savings to pay for occasional roof repairs or a new water heater when the need arose, so she and I shook hands on our little deal. I might need a bolt hole, for a few weeks anyhow, if I came back alive.

Then the last day dawned. I planned to spend it in Mother's house, and I'd kept exactly enough clothes to wear till the Army could hand me my free uniform. Jarret James, Hesta's nephew, had helped me through the final week; and I'd told him to borrow Hesta's key and take the few sticks of furniture and kitchen tools once I was gone. It was not till four o'clock that last afternoon, though—when Jarret and I had finished all the chores I had on my list—that he calmly said "Aunt Hesta's cooking us a big feed tonight."

I was somehow annoyed that he'd just assumed I might not have something else planned, so I said I was planning to stay in alone and get a long rest.

But Jarret said "It's your birthday, fool. You can't stay alone."

I'd forgot it entirely, despite the fact that my whole enlistment depended on it; but I found I was more than half glad to say Yes. It seemed right to eat my last free meal with two black people, not because—for all my recent bad luck—I felt like any kind of honorary Negro but because no black man, woman or child had truly disappointed me in my whole life; and at that point my young life felt longer than the Amazon River.

At six o'clock then I showed up at Hesta's in the best clothes I had, and of course she had to count the missing buttons and remark on how wrinkled I was. I told her the Army would take care of that.

She said "Oh yes, they'll take care of *you*; but before you eat here under my table, strip off that shirt and let me press it. I can't stand to watch it through a whole good meal."

I knew it was pointless to argue against her; so I stripped off the shirt and sat at the table, drinking iced tea, while she put the shirt into band-box shape. By the time she was finished, I was relishing this final taste of Hesta's rough care.

Then Jarret arrived, dressed like our ambassador to Britain, in a new-looking black suit, a starched white shirt and a gray silk tie. When we both had the glasses of cranberry juice that Hesta served first, Jarret reached in a pocket and gave me a present wrapped in numerous layers of stiff aluminum foil.

It had to be the world's finest knife. It was at least seven inches long, the blade was plainly hand-forged, the sides were covered with old deer-horn, and it had all the dignity of age and long use.

Jarret said "It belonged to Aunt Hesta's father, my own grandfather Augustus James. She gave it to me when I turned sixteen, but you'll need it now."

Hesta turned from the stove for her usual correction. "No, it belonged to my great-great-grandfather Roger Nevers who came here from Africa in a boatload of slaves. They were bootleg men brought over here to work long after white folks stopped bringing in the legal slaves. And you be careful with it. It killed a man."

I said "You want to tell me how?"

She thought about it. "I don't, no sir. But I'll tell you the one he killed was white."

"Did they lynch Roger for it?"

Hesta shook her head firmly. "He died in bed, peaceful as me, not two miles from here." She pointed due west. "Nobody ever caught him. Nobody ever knew."

Jarret said "How come you never told *me* this?"

Hesta said "I still haven't told you more than two facts from the past, and I'm not going to say one word more about it between this minute and my own grave. Roger Nevers saved his own precious life. Let him rest where he is."

Jarret said "You know where he's at?"

Hesta said "He's behind the preposition *at*," and that was it. She'd finished with the subject.

When she had all the plates and bowls on the table, she took her own seat. "Noble, that's a handsome knife you got now. But this is *my* present—every dish I ever heard you say you liked."

And it very nearly was, plus Hesta had somehow improved her kitchen skills for the occasion. We had baked chicken with a sauce that vanished from the Earth when Hesta died, fried okra, fresh corn pudding and fresh butter beans, tomato aspic, cornbread sticks and biscuits with scraps of country ham, then peach pie with actual hand-whipped cream.

It was well past dark before we finished, and I had to meet the Army bus at sunup. So once it seemed polite to leave, I said my thanks and stood to go. Then it just came to me, and I turned to Jarret. "You think you could drive Aunt Hesta to visit my mother now and then, maybe once a month? I'll be glad to send you the money for gas."

While Jarret was nodding agreement, Hesta said—in almost a whisper—"Nobie, I been seeing Edith once a week ever since they took her."

Jarret looked almost as amazed as I.

But Hesta just said "I go on the bus every Friday morning. She thinks I'm her mother now, and that seems to ease her some."

Even as I stood there at eighteen years old, I understood that—of all the things this strange old woman had done for me (and for Mother and God and God-knew-who-else)—none would cut deeper and last me longer than that plain news. I wanted to take her into my arms, but I knew she'd stop me, so I put a quick kiss onto my fingers and laid it on her right wrist.

As Jarret walked me out to the door, I could see Hesta standing stock-still where I'd left her, secretly trying to scrub the dry kiss off her skin.

And when I got home it was hardly ten o'clock, but I was suddenly so tired that I fell half-dressed across my bed and plunged into sleep that must have been as deep as the average coma. I woke at two in the morning, though, and lay there in the same place I'd lain in the night my brother and sister died. I doubt I shed any actual tears, but I lived through a fairly exact equivalent of earnest weeping from then till the time I had to get up.

To this very day I still don't believe I wept for myself, stunned as I was by my own hungers and by something wrong in the ground or the sky. Lord knows, there were plenty of other humans to whom I hadn't paid my earthly dues—all of them already dead but my mother and Nita's husband

Albert. Still by the time the alarm clock rang, all those debts seemed canceled but one. Or so I believed. I'd paid them by accepting the blame outright for the misery I'd caused those people or the pain they'd suffered at another's hand which I could have stopped if I'd been where I should have been the moment they suffered. But despite my burning every picture of Mother, young or older, that I could lay my busy hands on, I clung to the vivid indelible memories of every atom of her face and voice that were stored forever in the core of my mind as I rose and left that terrible house—forever, I thought. For good and all.

TWO

Even in the Army, from the first day of being yelled at and low-rated, I reminded my brain of how I managed to live with Mother through the wilder days—to hunker down low, obey all orders that weren't truly harmful, then to scrounge out at least two minutes per hour when I could tell myself who I was and where I hoped to go when the present rough weather ended. Not that I had a big career plan, just that I hoped somehow to repay Arch and Adelle for their early losses and to try to keep my own life calm for as long as it lasted. For whatever reason, I hoped it would last a very long time. One thing I was born with, that some people lack, is a will to live as strong as the average wolverine's.

It's also true that if you've been alive in America at any point in the past hundred years, you're hardly likely to need the story of my military training. It had all the laughs of the *Gomer Pyle* show and long moments of the dull toothaching meanness of *From Here to Eternity* or *Full Metal Jacket.* The boys I trained with almost all seemed younger than me, though none of them were. I decided the summer had put at least ten extra years on my head, but that didn't stop me from mostly enjoying the various youngsters. They were black and white, brown, red, yellow and numerous shades in between. And while I certainly was no Ph.D. in any subject, I was steadily amazed by how many of them had only the slimmest grip on the way the world worked, especially the human body and mind.

We had everything from college graduates with plans to teach nuclear physics for life, to agreeable grade-school-playground drug pushers, to decent-looking tall boys from Kentucky and cheerful stocky runts from Manhattan who all nonetheless held views on race and God that made Hitler look like your sweet Uncle Jake. They'd spew out a line of unmitigated hate, and then an hour later you'd notice that they were helping a coal-black boy from Georgia bandage a dangerous blister on his heel or loudly encouraging a fledgling Orthodox Jew through the minefields of non-kosher food. And even though it was still the "swinging sixties," I was steadily surprised by how many of them confessed to being snow-pure virgins.

For whatever reason I wound up as the unofficial barracks father-confessor. Boys would wait till I was more or less alone and then start asking me amazing questions about an infinite range of subjects, all dealing with sex. Young as we were, there were frequent questions about masturbation. The remains of Victorian guilt and Catholic education were still thick in the air, and a lot of the thinking was truly bizarre. But generally it tended to run along the lines of concluding that—however sinful and damaging to a boy's mental, spiritual and physical health—"self-abuse" was more or less steadily permissible to prevent the buildup of even more dangerous "pressure." So anytime you woke up in the nighttime barracks, you were assured of hearing one or more of the invisible cots squeaking rhythmically.

And most of their theories about women were even more exotic, if not outright alarming. All these years later, well after the women's revolution and a constant media diet of long-overdue consciousness-raising about the harm men can so easily do to women, I'll have to say I'm still not surprised at the daily crop of news accounts of almost unimaginable havoc by men against the bodies of women, not to mention their minds. In the barracks and later in Vietnam, there at the end of the 1960s, I heard hundreds of questions, jokes and fantasies and alleged true stories about hetero fucking that left me trained forever in the devastating powers of testosterone and the terror of women which even I, with a murderous mother behind me, still find all but utterly mysterious.

I'll record just two stories by way of illustration. In the midst of basic training, one of our sergeants got a few days of "compassionate leave"—his mother had died and her funeral was pending. A couple of us were standing at the door when he walked out with his bag, and a tiny boy from Utah said "Sarge, we'll be praying for you, minute by minute." The sergeant barely broke stride but grinned and gave us a wave. "Son," he said, "don't waste your prayers. I hated my mother's guts and couldn't be gladder we're shoveling her under. What I'm looking forward to is my wife Ardis. She's put on weight but she does my will. I plan to spend this entire leave sucking her pussy till her face caves in." Of course we laughed. I honestly think he was trying to prove to us he loved her, and most of us believed he was truly sincere.

Then in Vietnam eighteen months later, I was taking the IV blood plasma needle from the arm of a dying boy. The whole lower half of his body was mostly gone. He'd stepped on a mine. I could see he was a Catholic—he was wearing a rosary—so I asked if he wanted to say a prayer with me. I sometimes joined the ones who were desperate in the Lord's Prayer or the Twenty-third Psalm. Far more often than you might think, they'd want to say "Now I lay me down to sleep." And I'd whisper right with them; but this one boy said "Noble, I just want to say 'Thank God.'" I nodded to that and wondered what reason on Earth he had to thank God now. Then he said "See, I'll never have any more nightmares of crawling back up deep inside my sister's body and lying there, stifling." He said "Thanks" again and that ended it for him.

Wild as both stories sound, they are honestly typical of so much I heard. I won't claim I tried to correct many boys. I didn't know enough myself; and though I've learned a few things since, I'm still far from fully-informed. Then, though, I had my own fears like other young men; and I had my share of the same blind hunger that would drive me through the whole midst of my life, but every so often I would say the word *love* to some otherwise benign soul who seemed especially confused about sex. They'd sometimes pause as if I'd struck them, occasionally as if I'd shone a light on them; but mostly I'd say it when I was alone—aloud to the hot air or silently deep inside my head. I'd say it as a promise that I'd live and get to learn what *love* might mean when I could freely touch a fine woman and how a prize like *love* might feel in a life like mine. My luck would prove very slow in coming, but that's years ahead of what I'm describing.

* * *

When basic training ended I was sent to San Antonio, Texas for the next important round. The everyday facts of Army life hardly changed at all—the endless waste of time, the bone-cracking boredom, the always surprising daily array of humans from flat-out monsters to genuine saints (and I don't just mean village-idiot saints)—but two things were new. First, when we finally got a chance to fill out the notoriously unlikely form, requesting what we'd like to do by way of special duty, I specified "medical corpsman" (which of course was commonly called "corpse man"). If the standard perverse military luck had held, I'd have been assigned to something like funeral-florist duties; but since I slightly exaggerated my summer job in the emergency room at home, I actually got assigned to medic training. And the second new thing was that women came back into my life. That was well after my training started.

Strangely my special training consisted mainly of working in an Army hospital as, of all things, the assistant to a gynecologist, Captain Waterman. I spent a good many hours on wards with normal patients, but a lot of the time I was filing papers for Captain Waterman. There weren't nearly as many women in the service as now, so most of his patients were officers' wives. And even in those days, before women had made it clear how very peculiar it was that gynecology was such a male profession, I had no duties that were even mildly offensive. In the whole time I was there, I never saw a woman naked, not in the doctor's office anyhow. All that preparation and stand-by assistance was done by female nurses, so my scope for harm or mischief was narrow. All the same, I hope people are relaxed enough now to excuse me and two or three other boys—none of us out of our teens yet, and we called ourselves *boys*—for the jokes we sometimes played on the job.

For instance, our doctor had a model of the female organs on a shelf behind his desk. It consisted of a life-sized transparent statue of a woman from just below the breasts to mid-thigh level. Every part was there in minute detail, in various realistic tints; and the whole thing could be disassembled to demonstrate scientific points. Needless to say it was manufactured in Germany, had cost Captain Waterman two thousand dollars and he was most attentive to its needs. He'd never let any of us on the staff even dust it for example.

So of course one Sunday night a friend of mine from Rockford, Illinois took one of the doctor's fine cigars from the humidor on his desk and inserted it you-know-where. Nobody noticed it for a whole busy day. Then on Tuesday afternoon a major's wife was sitting in the chair opposite the doctor, answering his questions about a gynecological problem, when all of a sudden she cried out "What is the meaning of *that*?" And before Captain Waterman could discover what she'd seen and invent an explanation, she stalked out of the building, never to return.

We also used the loudspeaker system for occasional high jinks. Captain Waterman had a younger partner named Dr. John Mehoff; so we'd brighten up slow days by getting the really dim corporal who read announcements on the PA system to say things like "Paging Dr. Mehoff, Dr. Jack Mehoff." I saw quite a few patients break up laughing at such moments; but I literally never saw a single doctor or nurse appear to catch on, though one very senior nurse did say "It would be a good deal more respectful to call him *John*, don't you think?"

Otherwise we spent our work time in classes on the treatment of combat injuries of all kinds from gunshot wounds to total-body burns. Since we were stationed in relatively peaceful Texas, we got almost no experience with actual young male bodies in trouble. As far as young men were concerned, in fact, the worst illness you're likely to meet in a stateside hospital is strep throat or appendicitis. So what I'd learned in my few weeks in a round-the-clock emergency room at home turned out to be a lot more useful under fire than anything they taught me in Texas. But then it turned out, as every medic knows, that nothing planned by the Mind of Man can prepare you for war wounds and the reactions of the people that get them (and no fully-fledged MD that I ever ran across seemed to have been prepared either, however all-knowing they're trained to pose as).

Then I've mentioned that women re-entered my life. Not that I had extensive experience with them before, considering that the only live grown woman I'd ever seen with all her clothes off was Nita Acheson. And the only woman near my own age that I'd had intimate relations with was Antoinette at the All Girl Staff. So the first brief times I got to go to town with another few boys, I passed up the main thing they were looking for—

a beer joint with maximal ear-killing music—and hunted down the cheapest cleanest places I could find that would let me strip, lie down and be rubbed back to something like *life* by whatever girl or woman I could bother with my slender resources.

And some did seem bothered. Not one was mean or greedy. They were mostly big country girls who were worn out from a long day's work that surely gave them few real rewards, not to mention entertainment. Since I couldn't think of my body or my stellar personality as a consolation—and since I couldn't afford to tip big—I generally left them with the glum feeling that I'd made their lives that much harder to live. Still from Nita and Antoinette and my weird visions—and of course from the pints of testosterone cooking in me and the round-the-clock Army talk of pussy, tits and tail—I couldn't quite make myself stop prowling in the hope of one more round of what I'd got in the past from two women who had somehow been in the path I was taking on a given day.

Young as I was, and short on brain power, I'd already spent a good many hours wondering what I *had* got from Nita and Antoinette and why it had me so awe-struck. And once I'd ticked off the explanations I've listed above, I'd find myself wondering if Tom Landingham hadn't mainly been right. Maybe the sexual parts of any grown body are an actual altar of God, and aren't we meant to worship there? I don't claim that I thought of the matter in such distant terms, but I guarantee I felt it fairly steadily; and it drove me through those years of my life, and long years ahead, as one of the principal engines in my mind. In my Texas months, with a war coming down the road straight at me, of course I was simply praying for a woman who'd let me use her the way I needed. Even Nita hadn't granted me that, not entire free range of her hair and skin and the quick of her lovely head.

Understand, I'm sure I was the only boy I knew who never got one single personal letter during our slow months of training—not *one*, though I turned up at every mail call like a starved-out hound. Mother stopped writing to me after my last visit; so I didn't try to edge into her mind, wherever it was in those hard days. I did write several times to Hesta and even Jarret, but I got no answers. For some reason I couldn't bring myself to phone Hesta. Maybe I thought the sound of her voice would plunge me deeper than I could stand to go. Maybe also I was scared of what she'd tell me about her visits to Mother. So when I say I *prayed* for the right kind of woman, I mean I truly prayed. It didn't seem remotely sinful to me to ask God Himself for what I thought He'd licensed me to do, and for whatever reason—whether it was answered prayer or not—I met Kealy Curtis.

She was a nurse in the same hospital where I did my training, and like Anita she was older than me, exactly twice as old—age thirty-six. But since she'd never been married and had no boyfriend to speak of, we had no problem with lying or cheating on anybody else. In fact the only problem we had, at the start anyhow, was that Kealy shared a house with her mother. But that comes later. Since we met on the job, we knew each other for several weeks before she began to dawn on me as the excellent person she truly was and how much she might promise if I got to know her in after hours.

It was longer than that before I got the least sign from Kealy that she had any similar feelings for me. Like all the truly great nurses I've met, she was a very salty dog on the surface and a deep well of goodness beneath. She kept us trainees on a three-inch leash—making sure we got patients' medications right, keeping our public jokes to a minimum and maintaining dignity when that was called for but above all demanding that we treat every patient like a human being, whether he might be a bone-dumb private with his first case of clap or a toothless black vet from World War I who couldn't write his name.

She'd also take just so much in the way of teasing from us, and then she'd rear up like a diamondback and shake her rattles till we blushed and backed off. Though we all wore nametags, she gave no sign of ever knowing our names but called every one of us *Young Sir*. So the first time I wound up alone with her, she surprised me several ways. We were working a late shift, substituting for friends; and we'd gone in the medications closet at the same time on separate errands. It was called a closet but was really a medium-sized room, and she was over at the narcotics safe (being one of the rare staff who knew the combination).

I'd been sorting through the milder pills in search of some ancient remedy a Spanish-American War vet was requesting for his bloated ankles.

When I didn't find it, I was in no special hurry to clear out; and I walked up behind Kealy and stood there looking into the safe. It was nothing but more vials and bottles—stuff that a few million Americans would have killed both of us to get at—but it was at least worth seeing, if only to say I had.

I must have been standing too close to Kealy because she rocked back on her haunches and waited silently. When I didn't move she said "Young Sir, you're way out of line here."

Still without moving I said "I'm sorry. Believe me, ma'm, I'm no rapist—not even a molester." I attempted a chuckle but it dropped down, helpless as any shot bird.

Kealy waited again, then said "I'm *waiting,* Young Sir" (it turned out later that she meant I was too near the drugs, not her).

So I stomped loudly as I backed off a few steps. Still I didn't turn and leave the room. I knew the door behind us was closed.

Kealy stayed in place till she'd finished her errand. Then she stood up, faced me and met my eyes.

Mine stayed right on her and didn't skitter. Hers were such a pale gray that it almost seemed she didn't have pupils, and for a bad moment I thought she'd somehow gone blind since the last time I saw her.

But No, she looked me up and down slowly; and I suddenly thought what most boys think at such a time *My fly's unzipped.* My right hand tried to make a stealthy zipper check.

Kealy said "Don't worry. It's under wraps."

Army-issue underwear in those days was olive-drab boxers, and that meant your private equipment often showed fairly plainly down whichever side of your crotch you arranged it. I've heard that expensive tailors used to ask a real gentleman which side he "dressed" on. For whatever reason, in boxer shorts I "dressed" to the left; and I reached down quickly and flicked the spot to confirm I was fully at-ease. Till that moment, there in front of Kealy, I'd never felt ashamed of my body; and I said "Ma'm, *I'm* sorry."

"*Ma'm?*" she said. "Do I look that ancient?" And before I could answer, she said "And *sorry?*—sorry for what? How's the rest of your family?" (*sorry* in the South back then could also mean *no-count*).

I wasn't asking for pity but merely answering her question when I said "They're all dead."

It didn't embarrass her. She waited and then said "How did that happen?"

I thought *Well, she's a nurse. She's heard worse than this.* So I gave her the quick two-minute version.

When I'd finished she said "And that's it? That was truly all your family?"

I said "Every last soul but one black lady that used to cook for Mother. She won't answer my mail, and I'm thinking she may have died since I left home."

Kealy said "Your mother's not up to writing letters?"

I could finally smile and shake my head. "That's something I haven't attempted to start. I doubt I could stand it, especially under fire."

Kealy said "You're hoping you're bound for Vietnam?"

I told her I was.

And that gave her a chance to shake her head in disbelief. "How old are you?"

"Eighteen last August."

She looked down at the drugs on her small tray. "Maybe I ought to just shoot you up now with all this morphine—" She still didn't smile but she did look at me again with those pale eyes. "You want a home-cooked meal this Sunday afternoon about five o'clock?"

I nodded fiercely. "—A whole lot more than any shot of morphine."

"Who's your sergeant?" she said.

When I told her she said "It's a done deal then. He owes me ten favors." She gestured for me to leave the room first.

I felt a lot better than I'd felt at dawn. Still I didn't expect the goodness that followed.

First, though, her mother was crazy too. Kealy didn't mention it before I came to dinner, and I didn't notice anything for several hours. Mrs. Curtis was not an old woman, maybe sixty; and as soon as we met, she told me just to call her Eileen. Then she worked with Kealy back in the kitchen while I watched a King Arthur movie on TV and drank red wine (a first for me and ever since, I've strongly endorsed the French proverb that says "All wine is red"). But both women were in and out of the living room, and Eileen seemed like a normal mother—eager for me to feel at ease. Oncc we sat down to eat, she watched my plate like a kindly hawk and replenished my helpings every few minutes.

It was only when we finished dessert, which was Eileen's homemade pineapple upside-down cake, that I got the first clue. Kealy had stood up to clear the plates and told Eileen to just sit still while Kealy got the coffee. But Eileen's face clouded up, she glanced to me, and then in an almost normal voice she said to Kealy "When does the screwing start?"

Kealy froze in place, no glance at me. Then at last she laid a hand on her mother's shoulder and broke out laughing. "Mother, what did you say?"

Eileen whispered the question again.

Kealy said "Darling, don't you trouble your mind about that at all. This is not a whorehouse, this boy is a *child*, and speaking of which it's way past your bedtime."

It was seven P.M. Whose bedtime was that? But Eileen folded her napkin neatly and smiled across the table at me. When she stood to leave—and I halfway stood to be polite—she only said "Child, sit right where you are. Your coffee's on the way." And she left for bed.

She was hardly out of sight when Kealy looked to me and said "Noble, her name is not *Eileen*—it's Rona Dee. She's a little demented as you must have seen."

I had to admit I hadn't seen that. So we spent pretty much the rest of the evening discussing our mothers. Rona/Eileen was entering premature senility and promised to be harmless till she reached the point of wandering out of the house on her own and would have to be put in some kind of total care. Kealy seemed very calm at the prospect; and when we got down to nine o'clock and were still in the living room on separate chairs, she quietly told me she'd drive me back to base.

I realized I hadn't expected much more, so I wasn't seriously disappointed.

When she put me out, though, Kealy touched my left arm and said "I hope we can do this again."

A fine kind of warmth ran through me for the first time since I left Nita months ago, and of course I told Kealy to name the day.

She said "We can talk about that a little later." And when I opened the car door to leave, she said "You know I don't run a screwing parlor or anything remotely resembling one?"

I looked back and said "I was kind of hoping you did." Then I laughed and trotted toward the gate. Behind me I could hear Kealy join in. She had the most genuine laugh I'd ever heard in the world; and even as I walked away from her, I knew how glad I'd be to see her again in the morning.

From then till my last week in Texas, it was mostly good talk between us while we were holding down late-night shifts, plus two or three more dinners at her house. Since few of our patients required much attention once they'd gone to sleep, Kealy and I could sit at the ward desk, update the charts and tell each other anything we dared. It was only then in my life that I learned how much better it is to tell your dark truths in the deep of the night than at any other time.

So for the first time, I told another human the whole long tale of my life since Easter morning. Kealy's eyes took in every word I said; and they never once frowned or crouched in disgust or even disapproval—not even when I told her about what I'd done to Anita's husband and the times I'd accepted, and eventually welcomed, the strange worship Tom Landingham felt compelled to give me, though it somehow killed him. Not only did she never flinch but Kealy almost never breathed a word, except to say "How sad" at the news of Arch and Adelle; and I'd got through my entire bill of goods before I realized she hadn't described one step of the way down the road she'd traveled. In politeness then I asked her.

It turned out she'd been in the Army for years. She even served as a very young nurse in Korea, in that old war that's nearly forgot but that killed almost more men than Vietnam. Since she'd grown up poor in the farming country of east Texas, she'd seen a lot of pain before Korea—she'd seen children starving at the end of the Depression—so the pain she saw in combat conditions was no big surprise. The thing that had really stove her in was the job she had not long before I met her. She'd worked for three years in a pediatric polio ward; and tough as she'd always thought she was, those tormented children nearly shut her down. She'd left the Army some years before. Now she got out of nursing completely, lived on her savings for nearly a year and let her mother run the place.

She said "I know it was what broke Mother. I stayed in my room most of the time, staring up at the ceiling, or out on the porch just watching strangers pass in the street. She'd come and sit by me and occasionally say 'Kealy, go take a walk.' Or 'Let me toast you a slice of the pound cake I just now made and add a scoop of homemade ice cream with warm chocolate syrup.' Then she started saying, two or three times a day, 'Kealy, you need to buy you a *dog*. The TV says they've got cheap dogs at the city shelter—big grateful fellows that will do what you tell em.' And I started thinking she was losing her own mind under the strain of nursing me; so I had to stand up and tell myself life must *start* again, like it or not. The only other choice was to cut my throat, but then who would take care of my poor mother?"

Late as it was, I was maybe feeling zoomy. Anyhow I said "Well, couldn't you train one of those shelter dogs to tend your mama and you go on and do yourself in?"

Kealy's eyes held on me a good ten seconds. Then she picked up a pen and worked on the chart of the Spanish-American-War vet who had died that afternoon.

I tried to follow suit with another chart, but then Kealy's pen shot past my head and hit the glass wall behind me. Recalling my mother, I said to myself *Keep working. This will likely calm itself.* When more silence passed and I could half-see that Kealy was staring at me again, I kept on writing but said "I'm sorry. All that ever helped me when my mother failed was a chance to laugh." Another long silence.

Then Kealy broke down into her fine laugh. It lasted long enough for tears to fill her eyes and stream down, and then a serious change began.

I sat and watched it progress the whole way.

She underwent some alteration that had her whole body pulsing with light—not the kind of light that streams from saints in the best church windows nor light that a meter or a camera could have captured but a genuine shine that changed Kealy Curtis then and before my eyes and forever in my mind. I can feel it right now. It was not the kind of streaming power that Nita had poured out on me in the car as we bypassed Washington the time that seemed so many years ago. But then Anita was younger than Kealy, and Nita and I had known each other to the hot bonequick many times already.

This was no kind of magnetic voltage that meant to draw me in or jolt me backward. Kealy didn't manage what happened at all. She had no notion it was happening, I'm sure. No, she stayed what she was—a pleasant woman on the verge of middle age with an excellent body still—but there at her desk under fluorescent light in a hospital ward, she endured the change that made her a new kind of vision entirely, a long minute's turn through all grades of beauty that told me this was the grandest woman I'd known till that moment and how I must find my way to tell her that much at least and to thank her fully before I went to Southeast Asia and maybe died with the truth locked in me.

Inexperienced as I was in how to thank other creatures alive and anywhere near me, I waited till Kealy's laugh had settled. Then I stood, walked behind her and handed her some Kleenex to dry her eyes. Then still behind her I said "Can I take you to the movies this Friday?"

She said "Oh son, you save your few pennies."

I said "Listen, Kealy, I am not your son. I'm nobody's son in the whole world now—thank God Almighty. I'm a man bound for trouble, and I need your help."

She didn't look back but she whispered "You got it."

And it turned out I had.

Strange as it may seem, I've hardly mentioned any events of that full time beyond the ones in my own life. It was a fairly terrible stretch, outdoors as well as in; but I was so drowned in my own concerns that I paid little notice to world-sized disasters or the ones closer by but outside my head. I've mentioned the murders of Robert Kennedy and Dr. King (with the riots that followed in so many cities). In addition, back in January the North Vietnamese had launched what was called the Tet Offensive, a time when they struck—all at once—most of the major cities in South Vietnam, wreaked vast destruction and killed many thousands, both

Asian and American. In late March President Lyndon Johnson had announced that he wouldn't run for re-election—too many Democrats were hot on his heels because of the war—and the Democratic nominating convention in Chicago later that summer was a violent circus.

By then the TV news from Vietnam had taken the turn that made it worse by the day—but still with a whole seven years to go. Among the wildest campaigns of 1968 was the old-fashioned siege of U.S. Marines in a small mountain valley post called Khe Sanh. There forty thousand North Vietnamese soldiers bombarded five thousand Marines who were dug in, with maybe more rats than humans, and who came out eleven weeks later with only a ten percent mortality rate (through it all the North Vietnamese were hammered so hard by American bombers that they took up to ninety percent deaths).

With that kind of news, the anti-war protests at home were heating up fast—though as far as I could see, they also were happening mainly on TV. The Southern states were more inclined to support the military than most other regions, but still I did once or twice see elderly women outside a post office with fairly polite signs against the killing. If I was in uniform, though, they always smiled at me and said "Good luck." Since I'd seldom known what good luck was, I enjoyed the greeting.

And I somehow managed not to get alarmed by the news reports. In fact they made me all the more curious to see the action close up and in service. I'd sometimes wonder if my mind was following Tom Landingham's urging that I do something sizable to help other people and repay my mother's errors, but the truth was it never really felt like that. On the rare times I watched any war news on TV, I'd occasionally glimpse a pair of medics hunched down under fire holding plasma bags or racing to haul a wounded boy toward a helicopter under mortar shells; and I'd always think *That's got to be me before this thing ends.* It seemed as simple and mysterious as that and it still does.

But I had five weeks left in Texas, and in that time I got to know better the truth I'd seen come over Kealy Curtis that night in the ward. In the early weeks of knowing her, I'd still kept up my visits to the girls in town—lying down for an oily rub that generally ended in "hand relief," not anything closer—but I never felt called on to try to see any one of the girls when they got off work or even to ask what extra services might be available then and there and at what price. I mostly never even knew the girls' names. When you asked they'd give some name like Brandy or Crystal that you knew was fake, so I quit asking. That alone made it difficult to use them in my head in the private times I got alone with myself.

Even so, I wasn't completely focused on ways to get Kealy to bed. Nothing about her turned me off—her age or the few extra pounds she carried—and sometimes when I'd walk up close behind her at her desk or wind up alone with her in the medications closet, I'd hear that low ring in my head and the heat seeping all down through my body that meant I was ready, if she'd ever have me, to pay her the respect I knew she deserved (through my later years with women, I tended to hope I was showing them *respect* instead of the *worship* that Tom had mentioned so often with me; but that didn't mean I thought my intimacies with them were sacrilegious or even sinful, not more than a half dozen times anyhow). But even the last time I went to her house, I didn't go expecting to "grease my piston" as a boy from Idaho yelled out to me when I left the barracks.

It was a Saturday night, and neither Kealy nor I was on duty, so I'd asked to take her out for some barbecue in town and then to a movie. But she'd begun to get concerned about her mother. Eileen had recently wandered off from the house a time or two, and Kealy had panicked when she got home and couldn't find her, so Kealy said we'd have to stay in and keep an eye on her mother. When I said I was sorry not to be able to buy her so much as a barbecue plate before we parted company, she told me I could bring the groceries if I wanted to. When I asked what I should get, she'd only say "You choose. Just bring your favorites and I'll invent a way to cook em, even if I've never seem em before."

I didn't have any exotic tastes at the time, not in food; so I got the kinds of boy's foods that I still loved and missed in the Army—a big chicken for frying, genuine Kraft macaroni and cheese in the cardboard box, really ripe tomatoes, bottled blue cheese dressing, and buttered pecan ice cream with oatmeal-and-raisin cookies. I even got the kind of paper napkins Mother had always kept at home—huge pale green ones with embossed swirling patterns—and a pound of Eight O'Clock fresh-ground coffee. Mother had always said it had the most caffeine of any brand, and caffeine was still the only drug I used on a regular basis. I was, and have remained, cautious most of the time with anything that could derail my mind.

Anyhow Kealy cooked everything I brought just as carefully as if they'd been the finest items available east of the Rockies. Eileen helped out with what seemed a full deck of wits, and it wasn't till nine o'clock when we'd finished eating that she gave any sign of being unusual for a woman her age. As Kealy was back in the kitchen, serving up the ice cream, Eileen gave me a long unblinking look that was far and away the kindest expression I could ever remember getting from an older woman. Then she said "It's my greatest comfort that you live here now and can watch over Kealy once I'm gone. Kealy's never had nothing, though she's earned precious diamonds and crowns of gold just for living with me—I'm an actual serpent." With that her kind face suddenly went all dark, and she gave an actual imitation of a snake hissing. It was more convincing than I could have guessed. Then before I could get out any response, Eileen laid her head right down on the table in my direction, shut her eyes and was deep asleep in under thirty seconds, breathing like a baby.

Without thinking why, I got to my feet, went round behind her and laid my own head down on her narrow back for maybe five seconds. She was plainly alive, very warm to my cheek. I wished I'd known her in her clearer days. When I raised back up, there was Kealy in the kitchen door, quietly watching. I faced her and said the first thing I thought. "I wish I lived here."

She didn't frown or smile. She only said "Well, why don't you live here tonight anyhow?"

My next thought was *If I do I'll get in serious trouble.*

Kealy saw that on my face. She said "I can fix things up with your captain, if you want to."

I told her I'd appreciate that.

She said "You can sleep on the sofa in the living room. It folds out into a fairly decent bed."

That wasn't entirely what I'd expected, but then I hadn't expected much from anybody for a long time now. I thanked her, helped her clear the table; and while she got Eileen to her room, I washed the last dishes. Then Kealy and I watched the late news on her tiny TV; and well before midnight she put clean sheets on the pull-out bed, told me "Good night" calmly—without looking back at where I stood—and left me there with the new toothbrush and the clean wash rag she'd also found in some distant drawer.

To my surprise I went to sleep almost as fast as Eileen, and it was ten past two in the morning when I woke up—I could see my watch by a dim light from the hallway. I didn't really have to, but I thought I'd get up and pee and see if the rest of the house was unconscious. I wasn't all swollen up with blind lust—I'd even put on my trousers before I headed for the john—but the possibility of immediate sex is never more than two seconds away from the thoughts of the average young man (I mean that literally, which is a fact that very few women I've known can credit).

Anyhow I peed and while the commode was flushing, I took the opportunity to open Kealy's medicine cabinet and survey the contents, a practice I've never been able to outgrow. There were no big surprises in the way of drugs, sex toys or the kinds of rubber goods that could fire my hopes in those early days. Strangely there was a small display of snapshots of Kealy through the years. Somebody—likely Eileen—had taped them up there long ago, and they were so curled and yellow that I could see they no longer mattered to anybody.

So I carefully peeled loose a picture of Kealy and two other young women in spanking clean white civilian nurse uniforms with the old-fashioned starched caps that have disappeared now in the same way as the spooky but wondrous old outfits nuns wore in my childhood, like white and black bats. I suspected it was taken at the time of my friend's graduation from nurse's training; and though it wasn't a real antique, it had that winning quality of making you want to race back yourself through the intervening years and actually touch your friend at that age before time got to her first and wore on her. I even brought it up to my dry lips and kissed it lightly, then put it in my wallet and walked back out into the hall.

By then a light was coming from Kealy's room, though her door was four-fifths shut. No sound, surely no words; but I went there anyhow and waited what seemed like a year of my life. At last when nobody spoke or moved, I tapped on the doorframe.

Kealy's voice said "Mother?"

I didn't want to wake Eileen, wherever she was; so I whispered "No, it's Young Sir Norfleet."

Kealy's voice stayed normal. "Step on in." They were the same exact words my mother would have used at the sound of a welcome knock.

That somehow didn't faze me. I pressed the door open and stepped inside the room I'd never seen before. It was bigger than I'd expected, considering the rest of the house; and at first I couldn't locate Kealy's whereabouts. She was in her wide bed, but somehow my eyes couldn't see her. I was still way more than half asleep. When I finally realized she was propped up reading but was covered to the neck with the white sheets and spread, I was so embarrassed that I said the first thing that came to my drowsy mind. "Kealy, why in the world did I spend the night here?"

She had her horn-rimmed glasses on and slowly lowered those to study me clearly. It took her so long I was about to turn and dress fully and make my way back to base when she finally said, again at normal volume, "Because I was hoping you understood you're a humdinger of a young man and I'll miss you when you're gone."

Humdinger was an ancient word, even in 1968. I was just old enough, though, to be half sure it was a compliment. Anyhow it woke me up enough for me to bend from the waist and give her the kind of old-time bow that seemed appropriate.

Kealy nodded deeply from where she was but made no other move or gesture, not even a smile. She put on her glasses and returned to her book.

But suddenly I couldn't make myself turn and go. By then I was conscious enough to rerun clearly in my mind the moment, or hour, I sat in the hospital ward and watched this normal woman become a light-bearing splendid creature at a government-issue metal desk. That almost thrilled me as much as before; but then I had a terrible thought that—honest to God—I hadn't had till then, however realistic it was. *Noble, you'll be dead before you can even hope to see this lady again.* I know I thought of Kealy as a *lady*, which was plainly a response to the decades between us. But the whole thought wouldn't cancel itself, and it washed back on me again—*Son, you're dead.* The fact that, by then in just the last minute, my cock had gone hard was the only evidence on Earth I was wrong. *You're not dead yet anyhow. Move, son.* Why was I calling myself *son* here and now? I still don't know but I know I took the last steps to enter the bedroom, I quietly closed the door behind me and turned the key. That simple turn chilled me worse than being in Hesta James's kitchen—a room full of knives—with my poor mother and the pistol she'd got somewhere on the road.

The chill might have been enough to change my mind and send me running backward, but my body stayed strong. Still when I found words all I could say was "Kealy, I'm cold. Could I climb in your covers?"

She said "You recall I'm a trained nurse, don't you? Would a registered nurse let a man freeze to death?" With that she began to smooth the spare pillows; and before I even shucked my pants, she'd switched off the light.

Through the open blinds there was bright moonlight. Since I've always had a cat's eye for darkness, I could see my way through the room very clearly. And in no more than two steps, my chill had faded; so when I could hear Kealy's covers spread open, I felt no further temptation to leave.

Till now I haven't described any sex act in close detail, and I don't plan to start at this late date or at least not till further details are important. Nobody's words, least of all mine, can take you inside anybody's brain—not down to the kernel where sex acts happen—so I've figured that anybody reading this and feeling disappointed by my lukewarm sex pages can find him or herself a magazine or X-rated movie that will turn their trick without my help (I don't condemn that, don't get me wrong). I'm just not eager to try it here—not at this point—in my life history.

Actually this one night with Kealy didn't come that late in my own *mental* history. I've mentioned the occasional fact about my times with Nita, Tom and Antoinette; but the one thing I haven't tried to convey yet is important to my whole story. That thing was my realization that—up till this time with Kealy Curtis—I'd never got my whole *mind* satisfied with any other human, but I did that time with her. If I'd turned on a light and set up a camera to follow my body and hers through the hour, you'd see a young man being given free rein to go where he needed to—with arms, hands, fingers, lips, tongue, teeth, cock and legs—on the body of a smart and kind and attractive woman who knew what she had to give and gave it without stint and with gentle laughter at all the right points.

In brief then I wound up worshiping a woman for the first time ever in my life. At least it felt like worship to me, it felt right as sleep on your tiredest night, it still does in my memory all these years later, and Kealy politely said she liked it when I finally got up and said I'd better go to base before they sent out the MPs to find me. But I'll have to admit our meeting was the main thing that set me off on a long career of trying to rerun that perfect hour again and again with a whole line of others—all of them volunteers, not one was drugged or hypnotized or tied or chained in any sense of those words. And I take full blame for whatever harm was involved in that. Kealy Curtis only did me good, and I thank her every time I try to say a prayer.

I wrote her from overseas through the early months. Then there came a time when she didn't answer. I figured she'd found a man her age or her mother was taking all her spare time or she'd come to her senses and wondered what on Earth she'd seen in a raw lonesome puppy for the few weeks we had, and I didn't write another letter after that. It was almost surely a real mistake, as it's often been when I've let good people vanish. I likely never knew a finer person than Kealy Curtis, but then I've lined the road behind me with excellent women who either sent me on my richly-deserved crooked way or that I left with no forwarding address. At least when I left, every one of them was standing; and as I recall every one was dry-eyed. Thank Christ for that much.

Hard as it is to believe, a lot of adult men and women have no idea of what our years in Vietnam meant to several million Afro, Anglo, Hispanic, Asian, Jewish and Native Americans who went to a country as beautiful as any on Earth, though not as big as California. The famous Wall in Washington is at least a public record that some sixty thousand men died in those thirteen years (the most frequent names, in order, are Smith,

Johnson, Williams, Brown and Jones—there are two Norfleets); and if you read a good history of the war or see the good movies, like *Apocalypse Now*, you'll maybe have some feeling for the unique grind of guerilla war in a tropical climate. Your enemies there, for instance, could range from ten-year-old boys weighing sixty pounds in black pajamas who could plant a land mine in under three minutes (that would blow both legs plus your testicles off) to eighty-year-old grandmothers wearing ditto with grenades in their pockets (that could strip the face off your skull in an instant and leave you upright holding your rifle that was useless now as a broke toothpick). Not to mention the beautiful young housewives who ran devastating anti-aircraft batteries or their five-year-old sons who could toss hand grenades or the dead-earnest grown men whose every intent was to kill all the Yanks they could see, hear or *sense* at whatever cost to their own life and limb.

But my war was not like most people's war. I had pretty much the standard array of nightmare times in my thirteen months. I tended to men with everything from a bad case of dandruff or a syphilitic chancre, to tropical-foot-rot with symptoms straight out of a crazed science-fiction tale, to abdominal direct strikes from a mortar shell that left yards of gut outside their bodies in stinking gray senior-prom-type festoons. I tended to boys in fields where the gunfire came so thick it sounded like sleet blowing past your ears. More than once I single-handedly ran for yards toward a waiting helicopter with a badly damaged man in my arms under gunfire, I even hunched down and trotted more than a hundred yards with a bloody boy back into the cover of a bamboo thicket and laid him down before I noticed he didn't have a head—not a trace of a head, torn off at the neck by a shell before I touched him. Haste was a medic's first enemy of course. It was also your main hope of keeping your own self alive in a pinch, but you weren't supposed to think of that till you'd saved all your wounded.

I turned out to love it. In spite of the nightmares, I loved almost every waking minute for more than a year; and I'd be lying like a lot of other people—men and women both—if I didn't say so. I don't mean I loved watching agony and blood, but what Tom Landingham had said came true in a strong way out there. I honestly think I wolfed down every chance I got in that little country so far from home to repay somehow my mother's crime to a lost and trapped part of the human race that looked like her and my dead young kin (well, the black boys didn't; but you've already heard my praise for their people).

I can't say I had much feeling that God or angels or anything outside me was guiding my duties, not for most of the time. In the first ten months, I had no single experience that resembled the visions that had come so thick in the months back home after Mother did her worst plus the one where Kealy was glorified. I didn't even go to the rare worship services provided by various baldheaded chaplains—they seemed to spend much more time with the fly boys (bombers and fighters) than with grunts like me and my boys on the ground.

I can recall that three or four boys, mostly teenaged Catholics, were so near to dying that—once I'd popped them with a shot of morphine—they'd look up at me, think I was a priest, and begin to confess sins that didn't amount to a hill of dry beans. Rubbing some girl's nipples, stealing rubbers from their father's sock drawer in hopes of getting laid, thinking "impure" thoughts during Mass on Sundays. I didn't know that the Catholic Church had stopped using Latin in its formal rites, so I'd make up solemn words that sounded like my idea of Latin, and none of the boys ever seemed to know the difference. I even knew how to make a convincing sign of the cross, and I think I'm right in saying each of them died smiling or at least in more peace than they might have felt without my presence.

It was a good thing, for me and—I honestly think—the many men I tried to help, that there was something alive at that time on the Earth for me to care for. There surely was no woman or girl I could spend my powerful feelings on. The war was famous in that decade for having more available whores than any conflict since the Greeks beat the Trojans. And three separate times in my Asian phase, I got into towns—Da Nang and Saigon—with a few other boys and had my chance at a great lot of women from the age of my sister to way past Kealy in looks and years. My friends found partners that seemed to ease their faculties and send them back into action stronger, almost every time. Starved as my own mind and body were, I never found a woman—not to mention a girl—that looked like somebody I ought to know.

Maybe that was the trouble, the plain word *know*. Then, and always afterward, I never just wanted to *know* a woman in the old-time Biblical sense of the word—a quick hit off her breasts and crotch. No, in those months I was rapidly turning into the kind of absolute lonesome ranger who'd throw his head back and wail at the moon for months on end in bone-rattling solitude before I'd spend a quick half hour—or even a whole night that cost fifty dollars—with a woman that couldn't pronounce my name and sure-God wouldn't recall my face or the width of my shoulders once I'd shut the door and gone my way.

Oh I'd sit, nursing five or six beers, and talk to a bar girl all night long (and pay for her presence) while my friends got their ashes hauled spectacularly or so they claimed. Some of the women were lovely as a small pond at daybreak or week-old fawns; and I always liked to stroke their skin, just the underside of an arm or their neck right back of their chin—that magic Asian hairless skin that's like some seamless uninterrupted fabric for Martian glider wings or angel suits. But I'd always still be waiting in the bar when my friends finished their own private errands and came out with grins on their faces to find me.

They'd tease me of course and call me queer. I'd never mentioned my time with Tom Landingham, though a few others—mainly from New Jersey—insisted on telling how many queers had sucked their dicks in bus-station men's rooms or up against walls in ratty alleys where they had to vomit afterward, which I much doubted. Just to shut them up, I finally told one of them I was neutered accidentally by the doctor that delivered me—a drunk old fool that was my mother's brother who was working by lamp light in a hard northeaster on the Outer Banks. I never got a word of teasing after that. Of course it was a substantial lie, as you already know—the *neutered* part, I mean, though I might have been a happier man (and a better one likely) if it had truly happened.

The remainder of that year is hardly worth describing, from the point of view of world history or my own life, with one exception I'll mention shortly. Apart from that, it was just the job of trying to help men in many kinds of trouble without giving in to any one fear. If I learned a thing in Vietnam that I hadn't known before—at the hands of my sorry father, my mother, Nita, Hesta, Tom and Kealy—it was likely the fact that I wasn't really scared of anything but fire. And by *fire* I just mean actual flames. When it came to gunshots or mortar rounds, it turned out I could stand straight up and walk right through them as if they were rice at my own wedding.

It didn't feel like any brand of heroism. I could also wade into bottomless swamps where poisonous snakes were close enough to strike, I could walk three inches from booby traps and never flinch, I could blow live breath into boys' mouths when their teeth were nothing but splinters of bone and I'd inhale their blood and mucus—none of that felt brave for even a moment; and it still doesn't now. What I couldn't face, in daylight or dream, was the danger of fire, actual flames.

We Americans had all the fiery weapons on our side of the war. Napalm sprayed on human beings produces flames that can't be extinguished by any sure means short of underground burial. You can jump in a lake, but the napalm goes on flaming under water. I couldn't really have been afraid of enemy flames then—they didn't have any more flames than it took to cook their rice—so I don't know where my fear came from; but lately I've wondered if it wasn't the punishment I gave myself, or God Himself gave me, for lending the little strength I had to a war at least as evil as any.

The one amazing thing that happened waited for the final weeks of my war. Any veteran or student of the war in Vietnam knows that, because of the overwhelming number of bombers we flew against guerilla fighters who traveled mainly by foot and bicycle, the guerillas were forced underground. Before the war ended the Vietcong had dug more than a thousand miles of man-sized tunnels that honeycombed a big part of the country. The record says that as many as ten thousand people were in those tunnels at any given time in the final years and that all those intersecting networks contained an array of facilities that included numerous full hospitals and kitchens, schools for the soldiers' children and clothing factories, not to mention such obvious needs as munitions dumps and communications centers.

As rumors about the tunnels spread among our boys, and then as we began to encounter the real thing in daily action, they became a nightmare obsession among a lot of us. Certain boys, especially short and narrow-hipped boys, were designated to be "tunnel rats." When the concealed entrances were discovered, almost always accidentally, those slim boys would be sent down to explore for any signs of habitation and to capture or kill anybody they came across who was still alive after we'd lobbed in the usual preliminary hand grenades and incendiary devices.

More than one of the "rats" approached me, secretly, after such hair-raising missions and asked if I had any kind of drugs that could bolster their nerves or calm them down afterward. One of them even developed foot sores that looked suspiciously self-inflicted (all you have to do is make a small cut and dab it once a day with your feces); but I never turned in one single soul with a self-inflicted wound—not even the meanest bastard of all, a Bible-spewing macho Methodist from Ann Arbor, Michigan who finally managed to cut off his thumb after trying for weeks and crying about it.

Anyhow—very late in my year, as I mentioned—the real thing happened. My outfit was operating over in a heavily undermined region. It was right up near the Cambodian border, a more than normally dangerous place to be. The second day after we got there, a decent boy from Rock Wall, Texas tumbled straight out of sight on daytime patrol. We all saw him walking, more or less at ease; then one instant later he just wasn't there, as sudden as if the air erased him. Such falls often turned out to be terrible. The Vietcong would build "tiger pits" in pathways and cover them with vines. At the bottom of the pit there would be sharpened bamboo sticks, smeared with shit—imagine your landing—and of course your wounds might well be incurable short of amputation.

On this day, though, the boy from Rock Wall hit no sharp sticks; and he scrambled back out in under three minutes, wide-eyed and pale. He'd landed in what seemed like a huge tunnel, but he hadn't explored more of it than the part he landed in. As best we could make out from his high chatter, the ceiling was higher than his own tall head, the walls were wider apart than his arm-stretch; and it seemed to reach backward into darkness for quite a distance. Most such tunnels were decidedly smaller, so of course the lieutenant's curiosity was up—and his thoughts of getting spectacular credit for such a find. But of course he didn't volunteer to lead a scouting patrol to test the discovery.

He arranged for two men to roll in a few grenades to announce our presence if nothing else. Then he called on the last "rat" who'd asked me for nerve-drugs and sent him down (our only other experienced "rat" was on a brief leave). The boy's name was Ruiz; his family was Cuban from Ibor City, Florida; and he had the kind of bright black eyes that could see a lit pocket-match five miles away through the thickest tar. He'd also never stopped smiling in all the months I'd known him. I'd even walked past him during daytime naps, and his good face would be smiling away as if there were no such thing as hard dreams. So now he made three signs of the cross down the length of his body, gave us a wave and entered the hole.

The rest of us sat around and waited a long time. I even seem to recall I took a long nap to the sound of soothing dirty jokes all around me and one black guy humming "Lovely to Look At" and "Rock of Ages." Then the same guy shook me awake, and at once I heard some distant moaning. Everybody else had stood up, raised their rifles and was circling the tunnel hole. I haven't yet mentioned the fact that medics had a choice about guns—we could carry them or not, according to our wishes. Several of the medics I'd worked with up till then had been members of the Seventh Day Adventist Church, and they were all conscientious objectors who wouldn't even so much as carry a pistol (all a medic could manage and still do his job).

So, early in the year, I followed suit. I'd turned my pistol back in and served with just my hands. In those days before AIDS threatened every drop of blood, we didn't wear gloves, not to mention face masks; and many times I'd lie down at night with blood caked deep as mud on my arms, right up to the elbows, and nowhere to wash them (our platoon once went for three blistering days in the field with not one drop of *drinking* water). Anyhow while the others were waiting round the hole with enough rifle power to take out a town, I and my partner were quietly checking out our supplies. Every second that passed with no sign of Ruiz was likely to mean he couldn't come up of his own accord. We'd need to go get him.

With all I'd done up till now, I'd never had to enter a tunnel. I thought about fire. Would the Vietcong start a gasoline fire to drive us back, or maybe lure us far in and then throw gas? Before I could work up a big head of fear, the lieutenant turned toward me and my partner and pointed us silently downward. Right then I said the first prayer I'd said in Vietnam, and even more surprising than the fact that I chose to pray then was what I prayed for. I didn't ask to be spared getting burned or killed or captured.

In silence I said *Let me see my locked-up mother again. I'm the last thing she's got.* I hadn't heard a syllable from her or from any of her keepers, much less a doctor. I've mentioned not hearing a word from Hesta, and Mother hadn't occupied my conscious thoughts or even my dreams for a long time now, but that was my prayer. Then I had a flash of recalling my late-night vision with Tom under the stars by the Wright Brothers' Monument to flight—the vision that said *Keep on* and that seemed to give me permission to move straight onward with my natural path. I was inside the tunnel where Ruiz had vanished before I managed to say *Amen.*

My partner Dan Snyder had gone down fifteen seconds before me; but when I got down and paused a moment to let my eyes begin to widen, Dan was nowhere near me. I called his name and got no answer. The moaning we'd heard hadn't stopped, though. It just sounded farther off than it had. So I told myself it truly was Ruiz and that Dan had already gone on toward him. Of course I followed. They hadn't issued flashlights to us, which meant I was in the deepest dark I'd ever known within a few steps. I kept on calling Dan's and Ruiz's names for another ten steps. Then I thought two things.

By making any sound I was risking the chance of flaming gasoline thrown in my face. But I also suddenly realized I was calmer than I'd ever been in my life. For whatever reason I thought I was in a whole new world where none of the past hard months had happened—Mother had never done her worst, I'd never cheated on Nita's husband nor done my part in Tom's suicide nor *nothing* else bad. I could walk straight onward, darker and darker, and be entirely free of the past. Nobody would know my history, and I could lead a long charmed life from here on out.

Part of my mind knew how crazy that was, but even the realization didn't rile my calm. Then I could hear that the moaning had stopped. Maybe Ruiz was dead or maybe Dan had finally got to him and managed to ease him. It must have been then that I felt swept over by a great wave of tiredness. In Vietnam everybody was tired twenty-four hours a day—Americans at least—and I'd already gone so far beyond any normal duty stretch that I know I squatted in the midst of the tunnel and waited for my head to clear. I also know I put my arms out, one straight on each side, to see if I could touch the tunnel walls; but my arms waved in empty space—there were no walls in reach. At that point I'm almost sure I thought I'd stretch out for a quick five-minute nap, and then I'd be ready to head back to duty.

That may be the last thing I know for certain, if that much is certain. I can't guarantee what I more than halfway believe happened next, but here it is anyhow. I came to, God knows how many minutes later—or hours or days. A warm hand shook me; and when I looked up, there was Dan crouched above me with the stump of a candle. He looked rested too. He'd had a good bath, his hair was combed neatly; and I'm almost sure he was in a light blue civilian shirt and plaid Bermuda shorts, no medic's equipment whatsoever.

Before I could ask him about the change, Dan said he was headed back to the *world*.

For us in Nam the *world* meant the States, but at the time I understood him to mean he was just climbing back to join our company, so I began to gather myself and my pack to join him.

Dan didn't speak but he shook his head No, helped me get to my feet, then pointed me onward into the tunnel. At last he craned right up to my ear—Dan was fairly short—and he whispered "Ruiz wants to tell you his wishes."

In the circumstances, that didn't seem stranger than a whole lot else I'd lived through lately, so I did something else entirely new for me in Nam. I hugged young Dan and said "Good luck," which was generally considered a terrible thing to say over there. That could make Fate notice you and send you the worst luck you'd ever known, just to keep Itself from dying of boredom as It watched the whole spectacle we made in the world.

But Dan didn't comment on my mistake. He just said "Thanks, Noble, for everything" and went toward the mouth of the tunnel beyond us.

I couldn't imagine what *everything* he was thanking me for—we'd hardly exchanged fifteen private words outside our work—but once Dan was out of my hearing range, I obeyed his instructions and went on inward to hear the wishes Ruiz meant to tell me. Were they some last wishes I should send his mother (I knew he wasn't married)? I'd heard all the awful tunnel rumors, and I knew the saner intelligence reports that claimed the Vietcong already had literally hundreds of miles of these networks all under our feet everywhere we went. But my calm lasted as I walked ahead, and my hope for a fresh new future world—somehow in this absence of sound and light—was stronger still.

Again I may have walked for days. I never got hungry, though. I never got tired and once Dan was gone, I never once thought of the Army again or my duties there. I never thought I might be deserting since I was on my way to Ruiz. Ruiz was hardly my main aim of course. I was hungry for life, and nothing whatever suggested to me that I was dreaming or lost in the midst of some new kind of vision or swamped at last by Mother's kind of madness. I just went onward in no light at all—or whatever light was coming from my own eyes and body. I could see that the packed dirt floor was dry, and the walls were braced every few yards with stout wood uprights and ceiling beams.

And eventually I thought I saw Ruiz. There was one small lantern on a dugout shelf in the wall some fifty yards ahead, and the feeble glow showed a man on the floor. He was flat on his back with his feet toward me, and he seemed as well-composed as a corpse laid out by a loving family member. But when I got closer, the body stirred a little; and when I stopped to watch, the man rose slowly up on his elbows and looked my way. Yes, it was Ruiz and he seemed fairly strong. He said my whole name and then he said a few words in Spanish that I understood as a prayer of thanks—I thought I could make out the words *Dios* and *gracias* anyhow.

Before I could let him try to stand, I checked him out and patted him down—no sign of blood, though there did seem to be a big bruise on his temple; and his pulse was thready, but that was hardly alarming, considering where we were. He was understandably eager to rise, so I helped him up.

Ruiz was decidedly woozy so he took hold of my arm and slowly drew me deep on inward, steadily pointing as we left the lantern light.

Another stretch of days or years passed—again I know this sounds deranged—till we saw the next glow of light far head. I said to Ruiz "This is bound to be them—our pals, the VC." The main thing American soldiers called the enemy was *gooks*, sometimes *slopes*; but that was old-fashioned, from the tilt of their eyes. I'd use the word *gook* more times than I should when talking to the boys in my company, but in my own mind I called them *pals* for some reason having nothing whatever to do with saintly tendencies on my part or theirs. I likely just thought if I met one and called him *pal*, he might stand a better chance of leaving me alive—not that I thought they'd know the word *pal*. Who knew what the sound meant in Vietnamese?

Ruiz understood the thing I'd said about the VC being our pals, though. He said "Yeah it's them, straight ahead, not far at all. You think you could carry me the rest of the way?"

I'd figured his bruise might mean a concussion; so sure, I had no problem with that. Turned out he was light as an armload of sheets and pillows bound for the laundry; and he smelled like cedar or pine back home, that fresh and evergreen. When we got within ten yards of the light, I could see it came from a door in the tunnel wall—a wide tall door on my right. And then I could hear the sound of soft footsteps and clicks from some kind of metal tool. When I got there I paused in the doorway to let my eyes adjust; and when I looked down at Ruiz again, he was either asleep or dead or passed out. It didn't disturb me. I knew I could fix whatever was wrong.

Then a woman's voice said, in clear but strange English, "Bring him in here."

I was calm enough, maybe childish enough, to think *Say "please."* But I walked on into the room that was still filled with near-blinding light. When I finally could see, there was one clean cot, a narrow table with bandages and so forth and two small basins of what seemed clean water. Thirsty as I was, I was tempted to drink; but first I laid Ruiz down on his back and arranged his arms and legs very neatly. His eyes were shut. Still his eyelids jittered as if he were dreaming, and his skin was soft and warm to the touch. Then I looked all around for the woman whose voice had called us in.

She was in a far corner, standing upright and as still as if she'd frozen in place. She was short and black-haired, wearing the typical black smock and trousers; and straight off, I could see that her face was pretty and her eyes were dark. But however hard I've tried through the years to recall her likeness, I still can't see any trace of Asian skin or features—very much to the contrary, as I'll explain. And in my memory, her voice is light and remarkably pleasant; and I no longer hear any Asian accent if she ever had one.

I was standing by Ruiz, so I touched his chest. "I think he may have suffered a concussion. Let's sponge him down with that cool water and let him rest."

That seemed like the right combination of words to set the woman free. She gave a gentle shake like a young dog waking up. Then she did everything I asked her to do but with an economical grace that I couldn't have matched in a hundred years. When I thought we were finished cleaning Ruiz up, and the color had begun coming back to his face, the woman said "Now you check his feet."

His boots looked fine to me, muddy but whole. I said "His feet are fine."

But the woman shook her head and took her own lead. As easy as skinning an over-ripe peach—but entirely gentle—she slid the shoes off Ruiz's feet.

They were worse off than any feet I'd seen in Nam or anywhere else. It looked like the cruelest man alive had raked them back and forth through barbed wire for awful hours. For the first time in my medical experience, I felt like running in the opposite direction and never returning—they were that destroyed, past all treatment. But then the woman ringed a hand around my elbow, which made me stay. I couldn't move, though. I still saw no way to help at all.

The woman silently went to work. She washed the feet clean of the blood and maggots that were pulsing in every scrape and wound. Then with tools as simple as something you'd find in an elementary classroom—old-time scissors, a needle-and-thread that any grandmother might use to darn socks, flannel bandages that were clean but cut from ancient thin cloth—she did the best any human could have done in the circumstances.

I'm glad to say I thanked her; and when I looked past her shoulders toward Ruiz, his eyes were open and his breathing was strong again. His dream was over. He didn't speak, though, and I only smiled at him. I thought *You're going to live to go home, son.* By that I meant Eduardo M. Ruiz, not me—*Fast Eddie* as we called him. That far at least, I turned out right. He's alive to this day in rural California. I get a big Christmas card from him every year, though I've never seen him since the time I must have shut my eyes in that bright room in a dark dirt tunnel where I'd gone to save him.

He was gone when I came to, at whatever point in time. The next thing I remember anyhow is being quietly shuffled along the last few yards of tunnel toward what seemed daylight. The ones who were guiding me forward were boys in black pants and no shirts and with the strong smell of the fermented fish paste beloved in Vietnam by all sides of the war, except our own. They were so much shorter than me, so much gentler, that I felt like the human beings at the end of *Close Encounters* being gently but firmly handed aboard the great spaceship by child-sized aliens (the movie came later but that's how it felt).

Just as we got almost in reach of the natural daylight filtered through vines at the tunnel door, two of the boys pulled down on me hard till I got to my knees. Then one of the boys took a most impressive knife and raked it, not so lightly, across the whole width of my throat. I also thought somebody said "Never," and I thought *Good night* and assumed I was dead.

But no, one voice from somewhere behind me said "Goodbye, Noble."

I knew right off it was that young woman's voice; but when I turned and tried to see her, there was nothing behind me but dark and the outlines of those short boys headed back toward God-knew-where I'd been for how long.

So when I climbed on back up and out, at first I thought I was alone in the world. Then my eyes settled down, and my ears heard a welcome familiar sound. It was my black friend that had shook me awake when Dan disappeared however long ago. Then, remember, he'd been singing "Lovely to Look At" and "Rock of Ages," two mainly white songs. This time he was singing a truly black song, a big-time hit of Aretha Franklin's called "Think!" that Aretha sang like mortar fire synchronized by God Himself if God is black—which, even to this day, I'm ready to believe.

My friend, though, was singing it like some lullaby. His full name was Randolph Junior Randleman (a lot of both white and black men in those days had Junior as a middle name); and when Randy saw me coming, he sang straight on but managed a grin.

I went right up till my toes touched his boot soles, and I thanked him for waiting.

He said "You been gone somewhere, sporty?"

I tried to think of what to tell him but knew it was too soon—I didn't know myself. I pointed to a low stand of strange red flowers and just said "I went over yonder to take me a good long leak."

Randy said "Then we better hump our slow asses and catch up with all our fine white brothers."

My recent history had been so bizarre, I actually glanced down at my hands and arms to see if I'd turned Afro-American since I last looked. But no, I was white—or strictly speaking, reddish beige. So I said "Hump on, bro. You know the way."

To this day I don't know where I'd been, if I'd been anywhere outside my mind. I don't know how Ruiz got out of the tunnel and safely back home eventually. I never once asked a soul about him, not even my partner Dan who'd been with me (I still half-believe) for some of the time at least underground. Of course the reason I didn't ask was because I didn't want to know the cold hard facts of what had really happened. I believed that strongly in what I believed, and at times I still do.

The strongest thing of all I believe is this, after all the mostly sane years since—that helpful young woman who healed Fast Eddie Ruiz's feet with such quiet care in my helpless presence was somehow my young mother, long years before I'd known her and time had done its will on her mind. And I also know that the memory of that small girl in the tunnel became another big part of who I've been in every year since. It made me place an even higher worth on women, almost all women; and it played its part in the few scarce honorable things I've done in the past thirty years, not to mention the bad.

From the time I rejoined my company till the day I left it to start the process of flying out of Nam, I never had to treat one other gravely wounded man, though two more boys in our company died instantly—shot through the head. We met very little more hot opposition; and the few times we did, it seemed that Dan always put himself forward to handle the hard stuff and left me with minor supporting chores. It was also Dan who seemed to know the subsequent times when I'd get shaky, and then he'd manage to sit the two of us down somewhere, quietly bring out a marijuana joint and puff along with me till the shakes passed off. That was my only drug use in Nam, and once I left I've seldom availed myself of things stronger than heavy-duty aspirin, occasional wines and beers and cough syrup with a little codeine for my rare chest colds. Considering the line of mistakes I made once I returned home, though, I likely should have put myself to sleep with slugs of morphine for weeks on end.

Maybe I foresaw my forthcoming long desert trek from the damps and thickets of Vietnam. I know anyhow I was sorry to leave, so sorry I had to conceal my feelings; or I'd have been thought to be even crazier than I was. The only others who wanted to stay were widely thought to be psycho killers or secret felons with crimes they might be fried for back home—a murdered wife or a string of armed robberies. What I hated to leave was the family life, the presence around me of a few dozen men I knew I could trust in the surest way, awake or asleep. You understand I'd never had anything remotely like that in my prior life, and I never have since.

Even so, like American men in general, I've made no serious effort to keep up with any one of the guys who'd have flat-out died to save me. I've mentioned hearing from Ruiz at Christmas. Through the seventies and eighties a few other men's wives would send me Christmas letters, describing their bone-crushing daily lives and including photos of the in-laws and children and a big stout man set down in their midst whom I'd barely recognize as Dan, say, or Randy. I doubt I ever reciprocated a single time. I could never think of one word to send from the life I was living.

And of course I've never been back to the country. I still get frequent junk-mail offers of trips for vets to the "Land of Smiles" or some such fiction. One or two men I've worked with lately have gone on organized tourist visits and come back saying I couldn't believe how things have changed—how much they've improved things over there (made life more American) and how amazingly unvindictive the locals are for all the mammoth havoc we caused. If I thought I could talk Dan Snyder into leaving his wife behind for a week or so and going back with me, we could maybe find the mouth of that tunnel; and then I could finally face Dan squarely and ask for his version of what he thought happened. Maybe what's stopped me, and will stop me forever, is the fear I'll be compelled to surrender the main good dream—was it my last vision?—that's kept me going when all else has dimmed.

I've not been a truly unhappy man, however grim I've made my life sound up till this point. That's a shock to hear, I feel fairly sure, if you've listened this long. Most of my Army time after I got back from Nam was the first real stretch of outright youthful pleasure I'd known. I still had nearly a year to serve; and I spent most of it in the District of Columbia, working at another military hospital for various doctors and in various wards—it was gigantic. But first I took a long weekend out of the two weeks' leave I had. I swallowed hard and went home to check on the situation there.

I've mentioned that Hesta, and even Jarret, hadn't replied when I tried to write to them. It turned out that Hesta was understandably furious that I hadn't come home on the leave I got after basic training. What I'd done instead was rent a cheap room at a motel near base, sleep practically round the clock and then just watch TV with occasional visits to likable girls at the local massage and movie-mate places. Also after I'd wondered if I had the right to do it (I'd seldom written to her, though she mostly replied), I tried to phone Kealy at her old home number in San Antonio. A deep hoarse voice picked up the phone; and when I rudely asked who was speaking, the voice said "Who the hell do you think it is?"

By then I was fairly sure it had to be a man, so I told him I seemed to have the wrong number—I was looking for a lady named Kealy Curtis.

He said "This is her."

At first I had the awful feeling that Kealy had undergone some hard illness—like uterine cancer that can cause you to take strong male hormones and turn gruff and mannish—and that this was she. Anyhow I said "Kealy, this is Noble Norfleet."

The person on the other phone broke up laughing, then finally calmed enough to say "Pal, I'm sorry for your pitiful ass; but I've just sucked down a case of cheap beer, and your friend Kealy passed away last month. Cold dead in the ground, or so I think the realtor told me. The one sure thing is I've just bought her house, her trash is still on the floor all around me, and I'm drunk as a lord."

I didn't have the stomach to push a step further for more information. Of course I might have tried to make a few more calls and get the true story; and if Kealy was gone, I might have found out about Eileen, her mother. What could I have done for Eileen, though, if she was alive so many miles away? I still hadn't seen my own mother, locked up and—so far as I knew—all alone. In just the days I'd been in the States, I'd let myself build a high inner wall of dread about seeing Mother or hearing news about her, and what my dread amounted to was that I'd disappeared so far as she was concerned.

Yet once I finally got back home, I made myself do what I knew was my duty. I walked up on Hesta's porch without warning, knocked; and she appeared eventually at the little side window, pulling back her curtain and staring out at me for at least a whole minute.

Finally she opened the door, gave me a long slow look and said "I know who you are, but I'm not your mother."

I told her I understood that all too well, but could I come in anyhow?

Before I'd said it I noticed her old hand creep down and hook the screen-door lock against me.

With all I'd seen in the recent past, still that little old-woman deed actually hurt me. I shook like a wet child, and then I said it clearer. "I need to come in please and be near you. You're all I've got." It was true but I guessed it would sound like a whine and so it did.

Hesta said "Let a cold snake into my house? You tell me why."

I was mad enough by then to tell her. "Because you let me go all the way to this war and live through the whole worst part of two years without one word of help from you—you or Jarret either. Shame on you both."

That gave her a real chance to pause and think. She studied me up and down again. "It did you good, I see. You put on some flesh."

I'd gained ten pounds on the steady free meals—that far, she was right. But my sudden anger surprised me again. "No thanks to you," I said. "Let me in now."

And then she did, but she didn't thaw by more than two degrees till three days later when I bought a used Buick and drove us to see Edith Redden Norfleet, my mother in the prison asylum where I'd left her.

It had been nearly two years since I'd seen Mother, but she'd changed almost none at all. When I heard the guard bringing her toward us down the hall, I recalled she'd asked me to stand up last time. So I was on my feet when she walked in, and she gave a slight smile as she motioned for me to take a seat again. She even went over to Hesta, who was standing still, and gave her a hug that lasted so long the orderly tapped her shoulder and said "Mrs. Norfleet, sit." He said it very quietly, but it sounded like orders to a dog all the same.

Mother turned her face on him with a look that might have baked bricks in an instant. She let him lead her to the opposite wall, though; and he sat her down there on a gray metal stool. For a while she didn't look up at all. She was deeply involved in smoothing the tan-colored dress she wore (I thought it was likely prison-issue, but I later discovered Hesta had made it). When she had the lay of the dress just right by her own secret standards, she finally looked to Hesta and grinned—a clear, sane-looking sign of recognition.

Hesta gave her a wave as if they were greeting across miles of water.

Then Mother's eyes drifted over and paused on me. The grin slowly faded but she didn't wince or frown.

I surprised myself by being glad to see her—the way I'd felt as a small boy, long before her troubles, when she'd come home from the store with some little thing for me—a single lead-soldier in the uniform of World War I or a bag of potato chips the size of my hand. To sober my feelings I suddenly tried to recall how Arch and Adelle's skin had felt when I first touched them that Easter morning—cool and dry as a china plate set out near a desert at the break of day. I could feel that exactly, but it still didn't swamp my curious gladness to see this dazed woman. As I was just about to say my name, Mother raised a hand to stall me. She said the word "Son."

You can likely imagine it took me a good while to find my voice. Then all I could think to say was "Nobe" and to nod my agreement. She'd seldom called me *Nobe*; it was Dad's name for me.

She said "When is it you head for the Army?"

I was wearing civilian clothes of course—khaki pants and a dark blue shirt. At first I thought that was what had confused her. I said "I'm safely back from Vietnam, Mother. I'm all but a free man, just got a few more months to serve."

She said "They keep us real up to date on the war—in here, I mean. We watch TV round the clock day and night, I read every paper and magazine, Dean Rusk phones us every few days" (Rusk had been Secretary of State till recently). Then she gave me the kind of look that generally has some kind of love in it; it made her clamp her eyes shut tightly. When she looked again she said "Do whatever it takes not to go to Vietnam."

I'd spent a big part of my childhood going along with Mother's cracked ideas, so I went along now. I said "I've certainly heard it's a war worth missing."

She nodded fiercely. "The worst part of it is *underground.* A lot of the boys have to fight entirely underground."

I wanted to see where this might lead, so I said "Why is that?"

That finally made her smile in my direction. "I'm not really sure I'm permitted to tell you."

I somehow knew I should push on ahead. "Oh you are," I told her. "I'm the main one you're supposed to tell."

She looked to Hesta as if for assurance.

Hesta looked to me and nodded.

So Mother said to me "If you go over there—I can see you mean to go—recall everything they tell you in the dark." Then she covered her face with her hands. I'd forgot how broad they were; she was hid completely. Then she laughed very softly for a long time. Her voice was exactly like Adelle's.

It shook me considerably and I actually said "Stop."

So the orderly winked at me from a face that was otherwise dead and told us it was time to leave.

Both Hesta and I stood and waited for Mother to look up and tell us goodbye.

But her hands stayed over her face till the orderly finally said "Mrs. Norfleet, your family is leaving."

It surprised me that a white man of his time and place would call Hesta, dark as she was, our kinsman; but it also pleased me.

And it made Mother look out at least and quit laughing. When Hesta and I had waved again and told her we'd see her as soon as we could, she said to Hesta "You need to compel him to *help* me." She wouldn't look to me.

And I didn't try to force her. I was that ashamed of my neglect.

Hesta said "He's back now, Edith. He'll help you."

Mother said "All the same, you keep up *your* visits." She was speaking to Hesta, her one loyal friend. Even as we left, she never looked to me again.

As I led Hesta out, I told myself *You may well need to live near here as soon as you can and for some years to come. My mother knows things I can use.* As soon as I thought it, it seemed dumb to me; but as it turned out, I couldn't quite shake it—not then nor later.

After two more sleepy days with Hesta—Hesta told me Jarret was "out of town on business"—and then a beery meeting with two school friends from my track-team days, I thought I should check on the old family house. It was rented to two extremely pale graduate students in nuclear medicine, a man and a woman so remarkably thin I wondered if the nuclei they were studying weren't somehow wasting them away by the week; but they had painted the whole inside a pale shade of yellow, so it seemed almost a different place and didn't spook me as much as I expected. In fact the main thing it made me remember was not Mother's crime but Tom Landingham and the mystery of his last weeks and my part in it.

Then I drove myself back up the map to the District of Columbia for my final stint among sick soldiers and veterans. The hospital itself was as big as a small city, with a big enough staff so I could just be a small bolt on the wheel. That suited me fine after all the responsibility I had in treating my boys in Vietnam. But it also proved to be an interesting place for numerous reasons—not the least of which, for a change, was my bosses. The doctors covered the usual range from raging egomaniacs (some brilliant, some morons) to apparently competent men so silent you wondered if they weren't serial killers in their rare off-hours. I managed to learn things from even the maniacs.

But me? By then I was a competent medic in emergency situations and even, when the pressure was off, a fair-enough giver of pills and shots. I was also growing the patch in my brain that Tom Landingham had encouraged me to grow, back when I was maybe more to him than a lap to root in—the part of my mind that helped me want to ease pain and worry in other human beings. By now, then, I hope you can trust that I proved well-suited, not just for treating sudden physical wounds but also for tending the many men we had in all our psychiatric wards. Some of them were also recent returnees and were struggling with what we later learned to call post-traumatic stress disorder. (People who remembered World Wars I and II called it shell shock, and I often still do. If you've worked with troubled vets from Vietnam for instance, they're never *post* traumatic. The problem is that the trauma's never finished. Whatever the awful original scene, it truly never quits. It's an endless movie that you can sometimes ignore or forget; but when you least need it, it'll tap on the deep inside of your skull and start rerunning its actual scene, in matchless 3-D and perfect sound.)

Anyhow my first awareness that such a thing existed had come in memories of my long-gone father. His own dad had fought in the First World War, had got considerably more than a whiff of mustard gas that left his lungs in awful shape, but what had taken the worst hit of all was of course his mind. Dad said his father could get through six or eight months in fair shape. Granddad was not a true tailor; but in his little town, you could go in the cubicle he kept as a shop, get very elaborate measurements taken, pick out your fine cloth, and he'd send the order off to Philadelphia and have you a dandy suit back in three weeks.

Generally, that job kept Granddad calm; but whenever a client (he wouldn't call them *customers*) spoke the mildest complaint, he wouldn't show a trace of concern. That night at home, though, he might sit down with the wife and children to hear some show on the radio and quietly start tearing strips off that day's local newspaper, chewing them thoroughly and choking them down. Or once when somebody's overcoat got wildly mismade and the client came back to show that the pockets were somehow stuffed with old-fashioned fuck-comic-books from that time—the ones where Superman is screwing Lois Lane or Fay Wray is valiantly trying to service King Kong on the peak of the Empire State Building—Granddad calmly took the coat back, with the promise to fix it. Then he gnashed out and swallowed all the pornographic stuffing and nearly died of some chemical poison in the ink.

After that, he gave up selling clothes and patiently learned how to do people's income taxes in his own home. He prided himself on saving them enviable sums of money yet never getting a client in trouble with the Feds or the State. That tended to keep him on a steady keel, especially since he only had to work hard from late December through early spring. But it also meant his wife and children had to work; and whenever they came home and gave him their paychecks, which my dad said they gladly did in light of his goodness, he'd likely break down completely and sob—sometimes through a whole weekend before he could bear to deposit the money (so Yes I have madness on both sides of my family).

The men I dealt with in D.C. were worse off. I don't know whether jungle combat with Star Wars weapons in Southeast Asia was harder than trench warfare in Belgium and France or in South Pacific foxholes, but even the oldest nurses on our staff said they'd never seen boys in deeper trouble than the ones we treated. Their symptoms went all the way from endlessly upset bowels and revolting skin eruptions that would suddenly appear and rage for days, then disappear in hours, to restagings of actual firefights with full-tilt screaming and sudden arrivals of uncanny strength that could throw any number of nurses and orderlies flat on the floor (one man broke my wrist) and would surely have killed whole rafts of bystanders if any guns or knives had been near.

Two of them managed to kill themselves while I was on duty. One strangled himself with his bathrobe belt. Since there were no locks on the toilet doors and nowhere else he could really get private, he crawled under his bed, rigged the belt to his throat and his bedsprings, then lay down and *pulled* till he was gone. There were people walking by not six feet away—but not a sound from him, not the softest moan—and we didn't find him for a whole afternoon. The other boy came from near my hometown. He could play every Protestant hymn ever written, by ear, on a beat-up saloon piano in the lobby.

Right when we thought he was almost stable, he apparently played from sundown through supper, then walked through the front doors and lay down under the wheels of a bus so neatly that the bus had passed across him and was gone before a nun, walking by at random, heard him speaking his name. It was *Whitley Ragsdale*. I'd promised him that he and I could run together when we both got home in the months to come. We'd competed a few times in our high-school days. He'd won several medals in our regional meets and had dreams of going to the next Olympics, which hadn't seemed completely unlikely at the time he quit.

I don't mean to say, by those quick descriptions, that the trouble these men brought back with them from our little jaunt to Southeast Asia didn't get my thorough belief and respect. I've gone in the Men's room, locked a stall and undergone genuine bouts of the shakes at knowing how generally helpless I was to give them anything close to relief. But personally somehow I was spared the kind of prolonged horror that had come home with so many men, like the black-haired dolls they brought their girlfriends and infant daughters.

To this late day I've still never had a dream about the hard part of Nam—the sights I saw, the things my arms and hands did for human beings on the near edge of death or worse. It's easy to think I'd gone through my own siege in Hell before I got there. But however sad the sight of my brother and sister was that Easter morning, or of Tom Landingham's wife on my doorstep not all that many weeks later, those weren't gory sights; and they've never haunted me either, thank God. Whyever, I've gone on having the luck of untroubled sleep every night I've tried with few exceptions. And most of the rare sleepless spells were caused by the presence of excellent women too fine to shut my eyes on and ignore.

I've mentioned the pleasure I had once I got home. It didn't come on duty of course or not very often. It came from two things. First was the brand-new (for me) experience of living with four other men my age in a big old private house we rented in Arlington. I'd spent two years with nothing but boys my age. Still most of that time was spent outdoors, and that's an entirely different business from life inside. With my friends in Virginia, we didn't do anything half as crazy as the average college fraternity does most weekends; but we kept up a steady assortment of jokes on one another that sometimes reached all but epic proportions, and we had one truly hair-raising Sunday that I'll describe later. What we mostly did—and the others didn't know it, though it was a real accomplishment—was to slowly convince me I could live on the Planet Earth with fairly normal humans and not freak out more than once or twice a month nor spook my housemates on a regular basis.

The second fresh pleasure came from knowing the first young woman I spent much quality time with, a girl only two years older than me and better educated than anybody else I'd ever known well. Her name was Farren Langston—called Fare—and I never could have met her if she hadn't recently got her degree in psychology from Mary Washington College in Fredericksburg, Virginia and come to D.C. for her first job as a social worker. Very soon she was doing contract work in the wards with me.

As a well-brought-up Virginia white girl from the horse-farm country near Lexington, she'd had very little direct experience with anybody in trouble more serious than saddle burn and country-club hangovers. But she had a core of strength built in her, like an extra coat of some fine fabric on her spine, that I should have recognized the first time I saw her and mistakenly thought "Oh Christ, here's a girl that'll be in the Ladies' room losing her breakfast twenty minutes from now." At the time she was interviewing a man whose fingers had started disappearing—literally. We'd notice every now and then that one of his fingers was missing a joint, and his skin would show little sign of a cut or other form of wound. Even the doctors couldn't understand it, though of course they wouldn't say so.

But once Fare Langston had talked to him twice, she calmly suggested the man had a case of Shadrach-Wilmerding syndrome—a condition in which people slowly eat themselves up, a bite or two at a time (it's rare but maybe not as rare as it ought to be). We treated the condition with insulin and massive assaults of vitamin E; and within two weeks, we had the man practically normal again, though considerably docked in the digits. Before he got better I'd had a chance to talk with Fare in the cafeteria several times; and she'd got my attention seriously.

Four years of college of course had left her knowing a lot more than me about a number of things. I certainly didn't begrudge her that knowledge, and she never flaunted it to me or anybody else I knew, but it wasn't her mind that caught me nor even her looks. Her looks, by the way, were well above average—very smooth, very white skin with a tiny dent right beneath her left eye that kept her from looking scarily perfect, promising full lips and the long straight hair that was then in fashion. It was ash-blond hair, and her eyes were an excellent walnut brown. What was out of fashion at the time were her truly impressive breasts—she apologized for them when she got to know me better—but I had very little problem in adjusting to their presence in our lives. I'll praise her other fine points later.

What surprised me more than those real blessings was the sizable fact that she'd notice me at all. The family I came from was hardly white trash or even "common" (Mother wouldn't let us call people *common*; the Bible forbade it). With all our failings we were what is now called the middle middle-class. But the main line of Fare's people, as I soon learned, were from old Virginia stock. They owned a large spread of country land that included one entire handsome mountain, and I've mentioned the horses. The college she'd attended was also famous back then for training the cream of Southern womanhood. Hippie values, drugs and Vietnam protest were unheard of at Mary Washington College—not in the 1960s and early seventies.

Fare was no prim stuck-up aristocrat, though. One of the first things she told me was that her mother's mother was a Jew from Massachusetts, and technically anyhow that made Fare a Jew. Sometimes she actually called herself a *Jewess* (we hadn't got around to dropping the *esses* off words like *Jewess, poetess* and *actress* by then). Given her credentials I must have looked a little shocked at the news; so she quickly followed with further revelations. She'd gone to a fraternity party at a gentleman's college when she was a freshman, had drunk "about a gallon" of grain alcohol (lightly disguised with grapefruit juice); and before the bus returned to Mary Washington, she wound up in a dark room where upwards of six or eight of the gentlemen availed themselves of her virgin favors.

At the news I automatically reached out to cover her hand that was lying on the table in the cafeteria; and she tolerated my touch for ten seconds, then pulled back free and met my eyes steadily.

"Do you believe that?" she said.

I told her I did, barring further notice.

She held her eyes on me till I could hardly stand it, but then she broke loose and genuinely laughed—a good strong laugh, no Southern-belle giggle.

After that I thought she was going to say she'd made the whole thing up, but she finally calmed down and said "I'll keep you posted on that as the need arises." Then she laughed again.

And we went calmly on back to the ward like two dead-earnest professionals; but before the day was over, I asked her to go to the movies with me soon. It felt like a long wait before she answered, and I told myself *If she says Yes it'll be the first time since my junior prom that a woman my age has agreed to spend any time with me except for cash payment, so it surely can't happen.* I was truly that cowed.

But Fare said "Oh I was hoping you'd ask me. I haven't seen an actual movie since I got scared and screamed during Disney's *Snow White* when I was four."

Turned out that was the unvarnished truth. She'd cried for the better part of a night at the thought of those trees that come to life and reach down for Snow White when she's on the run from the first man sent to kill her, so Fare's father had laid down the law that she couldn't go to the movies again till she was convinced she could hold her own, and she'd never felt entirely convinced.

Plainly I chose our movie with care and some trepidation. I polled all my roommates, most of whom of course suggested what I discovered were monster movies when I did a little research. All the female nurses suggested *Love Story,* but I knew that was a weeper, and in any case I didn't want to push the word *love* too early in Fare's and my friendship. I couldn't remember saying the word *love,* outright and sincerely, to another human being since the last valentine I sent to Adelle just before she died; and I couldn't start up saying it again, not yet anyhow. So I kept hunting for the right movie.

Aside from what I might *say* in any case, what I felt for Farren at that point was surely not love. The sight of her face and body, especially the draw of her several odors (from light perfume and powder to honest sweat to the briny ocean she seemed to hide far up inside her)—any or all those could have me up and ready in an instant, the most excitement I'd felt around a girl since the seventh and eighth grades when I'd have boners four or five times an hour just from seeing a girl reach down by her desk and pick up a pencil. But I knew I was—and ought to be—many months or years away from trusting myself to make the slightest promise to a good human being, much less a woman of the marrying age. Still my hope wasn't only grounded in outright hound-dog lust. From the time Fare told me that story about her frat-boy experience, she began to shine out for me with the kind of light I hadn't seen from any woman since I last saw Anita, my Spanish teacher (the light from Kealy had been very different; but Kealy was older and, after all, a finer creature). That was the thing that drew me onward. I knew it came straight from her body, though.

The movie I finally picked was *Butch Cassidy and the Sundance Kid*. It turned out nearly perfect. We went on a Saturday night, ate high-class burgers at a really good place up near the National Zoo, talked till the café shut down at midnight, then walked up and down Connecticut Avenue for another good hour till I took Fare home and said good night with a hug but no more. It was our clear, and mutual, choice to go extra easy on that first night. We didn't say as much of course. In fact once we finished eating, and with no prior planning, I suddenly knew I had to tell Fare as much as she'd told me.

As we were passing the entrance to the Zoo for the second time, and in deep darkness, we heard an enormous roaring match between two lions. They were hid from our eyes, and neither one of us jumped or flinched, but I knew they were my signal. So I just let it all come out, the whole story—my first sex with Nita, what I found when I woke up on Easter morning, and the rest of that summer till Mother turned back up and went off to crazy prison. Fare listened in a way that, from most people, would have thrown me badly—she never broke step but she also never took her eyes off the side of my face while I was talking. I got through it anyhow; and when I finished, I could finally meet her eyes. Then I actually reached in my pocket and took out a handful of change. I said "There's a phone booth in that next block ahead. You can take money now, run on up there and call a taxi home if you feel like you need to." I meant if she was scared of me now.

Fare said "I've got plenty change of my own."

I said "Well, I just meant you might not ever have met a man with my story."

Her eyes had stayed utterly calm, they'd never looked finer; and what she said was "I knew the story, Noble."

I'll have to say that threw me. If I'd been hurled through the darkness straight into hungry lion jaws, I couldn't have been any more surprised. Of course I said "How?" and my mind raced hard to recall if I'd told anybody in the state of Virginia or the District of Columbia. No I hadn't and it wasn't on any of my Army records so far as I knew. I had to ask her how she knew.

Fare said "I didn't know the details exactly, but I knew somebody had cut you to the bone long before I met you."

"You want to say how you knew?"

"Your hands," she said.

Dark as it was, I couldn't help holding my hands out before me and turning them over. I almost expected to see nail holes, but they mainly looked normal, and I knew she hadn't tried to read my palm in the short time I'd known her.

Before I could say anything else, though, Fare reached out, took my left hand and started walking us ahead. So to this day I've never known what she meant, but that didn't really slow us down.

No, it started me thinking about her full time. In Nam I'd let my old rule down and allowed myself to masturbate to magazine pictures, mental scenes from my time with Nita and the various women I'd known before I left for Asia. Once I got back home I'd tried to return to my old policy—not to make mental raids on women's bodies when they hadn't given me full permission to use them that way. Once Fare had taken my hand so bravely, though, that policy underwent heavy bombardment. For the whole next week, I managed—strictly speaking—to spare her in my mind; but it was truly all I could do to get my lonesome body through the days and nights till the Saturday afternoon when I'd invited her to join me at the house I lived in with my five friends.

Up till then we'd all lived together in good fun and mutual agreement to stay out of each other's way if anybody seemed to be down or otherwise ornery at any given point. The only boy who seemed to be more complicated than the rest was named Franco Derba, so of course he was the one I liked most. He talked a lot less than everybody else; and on weekends when we'd drink a few beers, he wouldn't touch a drop—just poured down endless amounts of soft grape juice in a big wine glass he said had belonged to his mother who died when he was a child. I'd asked him once why he only drank the juice (the Italians I've known seldom have drinking problems), and he just said he liked the unfermented taste.

Anyhow I brought Fare into the house about two in the afternoon to watch a basketball game on TV—Maryland vs. somebody pitiful. Three of the other boys also had dates; and we were all calmly enjoying ourselves, not noticing what Franco was doing till the game wound up. At that point somebody turned off the TV and switched on the overhead lights in the den. Some of us stood up and looked around, and there was Franco seated behind us in full fatigue uniform with a combat rifle across his knees. We'd known he kept the rifle in the basement—he'd bought it under the counter at a shady Army surplus store as a souvenir of his days in Nam (or so he'd told us; I had reasons to wonder if he'd ever left the States, but I never challenged him)—and he'd been outside, working on his car while the game was on; but he'd never brought the weapon upstairs before.

Nobody except me seemed to think it was strange, even Fare. She even made a jokey remark about how lucky we were in a crime-ridden city to have an armed guard, and everybody else was moving around as if the air in the room was normal.

Then Franco quietly said "Every one of you sit down please"—quiet but firm.

The youngest boy and his date were by the door; they slipped out neatly. That left three of us roommates, plus girls and Franco, in the room.

Franco raised his rifle and sighted toward the door. Somehow none of us could speak a word or make a lunge to stop his next move; but after at least ten frozen seconds, the gun came down. And again Franco spoke just above a whisper. "I asked politely for the rest of you to sit."

By then Farren had taken my hand and pulled me back down on the sofa. The others likewise obeyed on other chairs. All of us had our backs more or less toward Franco. We'd rented the house, completely furnished including sheets and pillows, from an alcoholic widower; so the few books and pictures I could see from where I sat had nothing to do with any of us. I tried to fasten on a faded scene involving a country lane and tall poplars; but since it was Europe two hundred years ago, it helped very little. And for the next however many long minutes, the room was as silent as my home had been that Easter morning when I first woke up, suspecting nothing. I'd begun to be scared, I couldn't look to Fare (having got her into this), still I finally managed to say a few words. I didn't turn to face him; but I said "Franc, pal, is there something I can get you?" I had no idea what I might mean.

Still calmly he said "I'm nobody's pal on this whole Earth—"

—Which shut me up. When Fare turned my hand loose at that point, I felt more alone than at any other time since I joined the Army. I reached to find and hold it again.

But she was turning slowly in place till she faced Franco; and when she spoke, I could tell from her voice that she was smiling very slightly. She said "Franc, remember our eighth-grade teacher?" When Franco didn't answer, she said "Her name was Mrs. Susan Sandilos, and remember she liked you much better than me?" Still nothing from Franco but Fare kept on. "Remember how you and I would come to school early, and you'd help me through the math homework I could never understand?"

By then I couldn't decide whether Fare was braver than anybody I'd known in combat or whether she'd joined Franco in the kind of insane partnership you sometimes see under really hard pressure—I once saw two men, on a risky patrol, walking onward through a thicket with their little fingers linked together, identical tattoos on the backs of their hands and their faces turned in opposite directions with looks in their eyes that were very likely killing the *greenery* with purified hate if we'd come back and checked hours later. I was very near to reaching out, pressing Fare down low; then taking the risk of standing up, walking to Franco and requesting the gun. I'm not quite sure what my thinking was, but it was truly not heroic. I've never been scareder in my life since, and I've been in some subsequent corners.

Then Franco's voice said "You weren't really dumb, Fare. You were just scared of numbers."

Fare said "I'm scared again, right now. Right here in this room."

Franco said "Well, join the club. *I'm* scared to death twenty-four hours a day."

Fare said "No, you're not. You were the bravest boy I knew. Your face is still brave." When I made a move then to stand and go toward him, Fare stopped me with a strong hand and stood up herself.

Franco said "Girl, I used to like you. Don't count on that, though. That was long past. You sit back down."

One of the other boys' dates started sobbing.

And then the loudest sound I'd heard in many a week exploded behind me. Franco had fired a single shot. It went not more than a foot above me and passed through the oak-paneled wall like wet tissue paper. Roommates and dates were sobbing all around me.

Fare never sat down. She stood in place beside our sofa, facing Franco another ten seconds. Then she slowly walked toward him.

With all the sights I'd seen in the past two years of my life, I couldn't turn to watch. I didn't even ask her to sit back down, and I surely didn't tackle her. I put my face deep into my hands, then onto my knees and said the word *coward* silently, again and again, till I heard Fare's voice.

She said "Franc, remember I took care of you. I owed it to you for the times you helped me. I've got you safe now."

Franco didn't speak but neither did his rifle.

And when I looked finally, Fare was holding his shoulder with her left hand and his gun in her right. It was well over half as big as she. Tears were running down both of their faces, though the whole room was silent again.

By dark we had Franco peacefully checked in at the hospital for "rest and observation." He wouldn't let anybody but me and Fare drive him in; and he didn't say more than five words on the trip, not till we were ready to leave him in the hands of an orderly that we knew and two others that we'd never seen before.

Franc gave us both soft handshakes. Then he looked at me, dead-serious, and said "I never met this woman before in my life; but if you didn't already have your mark on her, son, I'd kidnap her right here on the spot and treat her better than even God could." Then he smiled and left, and none of us ever saw him again. In a few days he was transferred to a heavier-duty psychiatric clinic, a few weeks later we heard he'd been discharged and sent home, and then we got a short letter from his father, asking us to pack Franc's foot locker and send it to him and also to sell his car and donate the proceeds to a Catholic charity. Franco was dead. I never had the heart to write and ask if he'd died by his own hand or some other way; but right to this day, I can see him at his best, laughing in that crowded Arlington kitchen while he boiled a thousand pounds of shrimp we'd bought for a backyard party. You'd have thought he'd live to be ninety-five and leave a townful of gorgeous grandchildren as happy as he.

By the time Fare and I headed back to the house on the Saturday night after she'd calmed him briefly and saved all our lives, it was past ten o'clock; and I was suddenly so exhausted I couldn't imagine doing much else but taking her home and hoping for better luck a few days ahead. I hadn't yet learned what a healing nearness she had to give. No woman had offered anything like that since I was four or five years old when Mother was riding on top of her life with what seemed endless attention to give. For now anyhow Fare was sitting beside me in my car but not really close. When I glanced at the side of her face a few times, I thought I could see she was also tired. So before I took the last turn for Arlington, I turned to say "Shall I take you home?"

But she turned too and held a hushing finger to her lips.

At that very moment I understood how Franco Derba's last words to us as he left were a message that well might make my life a better place than it had ever been.

Fare and I went back to my place then and found my housemates either as tired as us or asleep, so she and I sat alone at the kitchen table and drank a little wine. Strangely it helped to wake me a little as it eased my nerves, and it helped Fare too. Somehow we agreed, without saying so, not to talk about Franc yet. At first we talked about *Butch Cassidy*, the movie we'd seen a week before. I'd seen a TV program which claimed that Butch didn't really finish as the movie implied but had lived on, unbeknownst to the Law for many decades till he died an old man. He even had an ancient living sister who came on the program and swore she'd seen him quite a few times in his secret years.

I could see the story fascinated Farren, and she proceeded to ask me numerous questions as to whether I believed what I'd seen. Could old Butch truly have fooled the Law for that many years? Since those were the days before you could test people's DNA, I had to say I didn't think the program *proved* its claim; but I did believe the pictures it showed of the old man looked very much like Butch. And at that point I started to change the subject—it didn't seem that promising.

But Fare said "Wait please." She paused awhile, then laid both hands palm up on the table.

They were only an easy reach from me and were very fine hands, but somehow I didn't reach out and take them. Maybe I was scared of a big mistake.

She left them in place though; and looking down at them, at last she said "I guess I'm a kind of Cassidy too."

I had to laugh. "You about to tell me you've robbed a string of banks?"

Fare also laughed. "No, but I've been hiding from you, behind a lie, for several weeks now."

I'd told enough lies of my own for two decades, covering up for a family with a vamoosed father and a crazy mother at its heart. So I wasn't fazed, not then at least. "You ready to confess?" I sounded nonchalant.

Fare said "I think I may have told you a lie about me being gang raped."

I said "I hope it wasn't worse than that." I was not at all sure what *worse* would be; but by then I'd managed to wake up sufficiently to feel a hard-on creeping up on me in the best slow way like a coiled old reptile warming his blood in a rare beam of sunlight, extending his reach and declaring his solemn power again (laughable as that may sound to some women, and even some men, it describes my own feeling and the feelings of a lot of men I've talked to).

Fare said "It may not have happened at all, not the way I told you anyhow."

I had to say "Did you *mean* it as a lie?"

She could finally face me. "No, honest to God." Then she balked for a while. Finally she could say "Did you ever imagine some bad thing happened, and then you woke up and thought it never did—that for some reason you might have made it all up?"

At once I thought of the tunnel in Nam, my time underground or wherever I'd gone in that strange time; but I didn't bring it up. It was still too private a subject for me. Instead I told her about a suspicion that I'd seen my dad beating my mother when I was an infant—a beating that Mother, even at her worst, had always denied when I asked her about it.

Fare seemed oddly relieved to hear it, and it freed her up to tell me more. "I truly suspect I dreamed that story to punish myself for something or other. I still can't swear it didn't really happen—see, I dream it still and I always wake up with trails of hot tears down my face."

I figured I'd better touch her then, so I laid both my hands over hers, and she closed her fingers around me. I said "Fare, if all I dreamed had truly happened, I'd have killed myself a long time ago or else I'd be in a maximum-security prison in chains."

That calmed her further and she asked if we shouldn't drink a little more wine.

"No," I said. "I think we need sleep." By then of course I was thinking of a good deal else between now and any future sleep I might get.

And everything I had in mind happened very nearly as I hoped it would. Since returning to the States, I'd availed myself some three or four times of women at well-run clean massage parlors. To be precise the word *availed* means that they gave me, for reasonable sums of money, what the Law says is entirely legal—"hand relief." The women weren't always in the first blush of youth, but they were certainly skillful at their line of work; and they seemed glad to see me, though none of them put on the gruesome fake enthusiasm of the bar girls in Nam (most of those girls gave sad indications of having been forced to watch Shirley Temple movies every morning of their lives and then go out and try to be a Shirley who'd sell her little twat for narrow pieces of green-and-gray paper called U.S. dollars). So I paid each one of the Stateside masseuses a small extra sum to remove their shirts and show me their breasts, but touching was supposed to be against the rules, or that's what the signs in the cubicles said, and I'm a mainly law-abiding type—or I was that early in my career as a minister intending to worship women's bodies. Still I enjoyed looking (looking as steady as a spy satellite with the keenest lens) and smelling the welcome human smells (smells as varied as faces in a crowd, some cleaner than others, but each one welcome) as they crossed the legal space between me and the skin beyond me.

I was clean as a well-washed whistle then as I lay down with Farren at the end of that Saturday. And for the first time since I'd been with Kealy in San Antonio, I got to thank a woman in the absolute way I wanted to. Again, for now, I'll spare you the full details; but I need to mention a thing which happened that first time with Fare and—maybe because she welcomed it—soon became a pattern in my life that held on for years. I'll just say I found myself serving Fare more directly than I served myself, or that's how I understood it at the time. I mainly used my lips, my tongue and the gentle but busy fingers I'd learned as a medic. That left me with one hand entirely for myself.

At first I told myself I'd start that way with Fare in case she really had been misused by a train of college boys; but as I worked, in total dark for the same reason, I gradually saw how perfect a way I thought I'd found to give the most valuable gift I had. As I'd got to know Fare through recent weeks and seen how quickly she could calm sick patients who'd seemed nearly hopeless—as I'd watched with all my scared housemates while she calmed poor Franco—and since her face and body were so fine, I knew she was worthy of real adoration. So that's what I gave her, a long visit from my head and face and competent mouth that (as I still remember) brought her off three separate times. It may have been selfish and blind or worse; but it seemed to please Farren, then at least. She thanked me three times anyhow.

* * *

And we were together, thick and thin, for most of the rest of my Army time. Though a lot of people our age had kicked over all conventional traces and were living together in houses, barns, Volkswagen vans and fishnet hammocks if nothing more, Farren and I never quite moved into the same space together—not for longer than a two-night weekend. Part of the reason was shared between us, some built-in shyness each one of us felt at the prospect of flinging ourselves on each other at steady close range till we'd thought our way out as clearly as we could. Another powerful part was her parents.

I've said that they were horse people from the Shenandoah Valley, and they paid close attention not only to Fare's well-being on a day-to-day basis but also to the state of health of the Langston Family Name in all circumstances (I never heard anybody but Fare mention the Jewish connection). When Fare and I had been together for three months, she outright asked me if I'd like to go home with her for an overnight visit—it was not far ahead—but I begged off, claiming my duties on the ward. Not long after that, though, her mother came down to D.C. to attend a convention of some woman's club.

On the second night Fare invited me to dinner with her and her mother at the Mayflower Hotel. Her mother was named Camilla Gunter Langston, and she introduced herself with all three names. I liked her right off for owning up to *Gunter* as her maiden name. The Gunters, in Carolina and Virginia, are nowhere near as genetically ambitious as the bourbon-soaked Langstons—and *Camilla* seemed like a gesture in the direction of upgrading *Gunter* and concealing the Jewish blood. In any case Camilla had the kind of leanness in her face and neck that confesses—however well-fed you are now—to a family history of hardscrabble eating and hookworm infections two generations back. Still she was good to see in her red dress. There was no doubt whatever she was Fare's natural mother.

She was good to me too—not a single fishy look at my face, hands or clothes and not a trace of disapproval at the dishes I ordered or the various forks and spoons I chose to eat the most elaborate dinner I'd encountered up till then. I even suspect she knew Fare and I were sleeping together. Within ten minutes of our sitting down, Camilla had set up around us an invisible net of three-souled conspiracy to have a good time—right here and now, and the future be damned. It seemed to me, and Fare agreed later, to indicate that Camilla understood much more than was said about what had brought her daughter and me together and was holding us close, for now at least.

Anyhow she showed sincere interest in my Vietnam experience, and I found myself—to my own surprise—saying a little about my entrance into that dark tunnel in search of my wounded friend, though I didn't dwell on it. And Camilla asked what I had in mind for myself once I'd left the Army. It's hard to believe, I know; but till that moment, I hadn't given more than very brief thoughts to that grave question. I didn't want to admit it of course, so I said "I'm planning a medical career." The instant I said it, it sounded right—a kind of destiny I'd discovered on the spot.

Camilla plainly thought I planned to be a doctor, and I didn't tell her No, but I silently knew I'd find some other way to stay with the sick and not have to wear a starched white coat and pretend I was a medical god, however kindly. The rest of the evening went better still; and it was only when I finished my coffee and stood up to leave that I heard the first weird chord. Camilla took my hand and pressed it warmly as she met my eyes, smiling. To my considerable shock, she suddenly moved forward into my arms and hugged me close. Then she stepped back just far enough to see me; and she said in a low voice "Noble, we're sorry you've got such sadness in your background."

From the word *background* onward, I thought I was finished—with Fare anyhow, whatever long-term hopes I might have had about her. In a way I was wrong. She and I lasted a good while longer; and what brought us down was my fault, not anything Camilla Gunter Langston thought or said.

Shortly after Camilla's visit, Fare finished her stint of work alongside me and moved on into the black ghetto schools of east D.C. to work with "troubled" kids. *Troubled,* then and now, is a code word of course for children who've grown up in situations that make your worst nightmares look tame as a bedtime story from the world's kindest aunt. But then I'd worked steadily, in Nam and Stateside, with young white men from the finest neighborhoods in Upper East Side New York City or the Stockbroker Belt in Connecticut; and they very often had stories to tell that rivaled any nightmares Fare heard in D.C. But anyhow the job separation only helped our relations. We were that much gladder to see each other at suppertime.

And from my point of view, our intimate time was almost better than I could believe. I was gradually able to move on out from the mainly sexual parts of Fare's body and love the rest, though the sexual parts were always the core of what I was after. (It's generally difficult for me to write down the words for *vagina,* medical or casual; so try to bear with me. I have no trouble with *saying* the words to other men or to a good many of the women I've known, but setting them out in black and white is trickier business since all the words have been so mauled by so many hands.) I also learned to take full pleasure from actual fucking—that's a word I've never had trouble saying somehow, maybe because my brother Arch loved to whisper it to me when he was in the third grade and learned it on the playground at school. The new pleasure, though, didn't keep me from paying scrupulous attention to birth control whenever I was with Fare in any close way.

It likewise seemed that she was growing also, right along with me. She never again referred to what might or might not have happened with the drunk college boys. Any early shyness about her body or mine seemed to drift away as we spent more close-up nights together; and whenever I drifted back toward my old need to focus on her body alone and appear to forget that her fine skin and hair contained a creature named Farren Langston, she'd mostly be patient and let me work through the minutes I needed to graze around her like a stag at a salt lick. And mostly I could please her.

But sometimes she'd need to make her kind of joke, like "Hey, boy, you're *not* alone in this room. Please notice I'm the local girl, and I'm partly enjoying the concentration on my private parts but would likely be gladder if you'd join me up here for a bedtime chat" (she actually talked very much like that, the smartest friend I'd had to that point).

So I'd grin and rush to finish my worship; and then I'd go up and lie beside her, face to face, and wonder what I'd done to have this tremendous good fortune and how to hold it without pressing too tight and harming Fare or scaring her away.

It seemed I was succeeding. The main proof for me was when, once again, Fare invited me to drive home with her and spend a weekend with her mother and father—I'd never met him. This time I didn't invent an excuse; I told her outright that I'd liked her mother but really felt I wasn't ready to visit her home. I said I was too close to Vietnam and needed to get my mind fully settled before I tried to enter "domestic life" again—I used that phrase.

Fare said "You've never really had much domestic life, have you?"

At first that felt a little mean, but then I saw she was more than half right. I'd had a home life—a life in a house with other people kin to me by blood—and honest to God, it hadn't felt all that bad till the end. I still didn't claim it had stove me in to any great extent; but though I'd been to a war and back, I still hadn't had my twenty-first birthday. So I couldn't let Fare show the least pity. I told her "I had a fairly good life till the very last minute," and I didn't think I'd told a lie.

She took a real pause before she said "Will you take me down please to meet your mother?"

When I turned to see her face, she'd never looked finer. And I knew I had to grant her wish, though right away I dreaded the trip—it could go any one of a thousand bad ways, but no other woman in my whole life had done more for me except my mother, not even old Hesta. So I told Fare Yes.

Two weeks later I drove us south on a Friday evening. We couldn't have stayed with Hesta of course—Hesta would have all but asked to see our marriage license—so I'd made a motel reservation. It would be the first time Fare and I had stayed in an actual public facility; and despite the trouble I'd seen in the world, native and foreign, I was still a little skittish as we traveled southward. With all the famous freedoms of the time, my part of the old world was still fairly strict on human relations that were not in accord with the letter of the Law. Would the desk clerk ask us to display the wedding rings we clearly weren't wearing? Would some old acquaintance recognize us in the motel lobby and force me to lie and say Fare was my wife; and if so, what reaction would Fare have to that?

I know it seems silly, but it drilled in on me like an abscessed tooth the whole way down, and it may have been the reason I focused in closely on a few of the truly strange things I saw as we sped through the long stretch of unbroken pinewoods south of Petersburg—in "Southside Virginia," as we always called it, a region as drowned in the distant past as any vine-wrapped temple in Yucatán swarming with snakes. There were almost no other cars in sight by the time we got an hour down from Petersburg—big trucks hadn't yet swamped American roads—so my headlights were the only thing shining in a darkness deeper than any I'd seen since Vietnam. Back then there were still a few hitchhikers working most every highway. You'd pass young hippies in clothes so wild you couldn't imagine who would risk stopping for them, but everybody stopped except Ku Klux Klansmen. There were also plenty of the same old men you occasionally zoom past even now, homeless and heading north or south (depending on the season) with very little in the way of luggage and insufficient clothes.

What was stranger this night—and it got even stranger—was that I kept passing men walking northward on my side of the road, and it was still way too cold up north for the short-sleeved shirts they were wearing that night. I must have passed three men, spaced miles apart, before I started to notice their faces. And the first one I noticed was looking right toward me. He seemed to be a white man maybe sixty years old with stiff red hair the color of my dad's the day he left home. I didn't think that was worth mentioning to Fare.

Nor the next fellow, taller and thin as a knife blade. He was walking fast, almost a slow run; and he didn't really look much like anyone I knew. But both his arms were up like a soul surrendering at last after some long hunt that had him out here—desperate in the midst of Nowhere, Virginia. Dell Stillman's name and face shot through my mind for the first time in years. Was this weird Dell, fallen on hard times or—worse—somehow Dell out hunting me down again? I shook myself slightly and knew I was way too tired at the wheel.

Then just as we crossed the Carolina line, my lights hit the famous Welcome sign with the big male cardinal on a spray of white dogwood, the official state bird and flower. And standing beside the tall sign was the final man with his thumb stuck out, hitching a ride—except that he was on my southbound side of the road but was thumbing toward the north in serious confusion. I had no intention of picking him up or pausing even to set him straight, but for some reason I was compelled to slow down and get a good look at his big old body and his long broad face. For a cold instant it seemed half likely to be my long-gone father, Henry Norfleet.

I hadn't laid eyes on him since the day he walked out on the family and me; but when I'd cleaned out the house before I left, I'd found hundreds of pictures of him in Mother's belongings. She'd known him since they were in grade school together; and she had him in everything from his baptism suit (all-white at age ten) to the tux he'd worn at their senior prom and the knit cap he'd worn as a Merchant Marine, not to mention the homemade Polaroid porn. So I was well aware of how he'd looked, in his best days anyhow. He didn't look all that much older now, though he seemed deeply baffled about his whereabouts and of course his destination. My foot was already off the gas pedal and was hovering now above the brake. Dad had after all never done me any real harm except the act of leaving us children to manage our mother with nothing between our minds and bodies and her bad sickness but our own soft hands. In general I'd liked him; and he seemed to like me, when he paused at home long enough to focus his deep brown eyes on anybody kin to him.

Fare noticed the change in our speed and faced toward me. When I couldn't face her, she said "Was that somebody we ought to know?"

I knew the answer very likely was Yes, but she'd said it so strangely—someone we *ought* to know—that it freed me to tell her my first real lie. I said "No ma'm, just an addled old gypsy."

Fare said "I didn't think gypsies got addled. I thought you couldn't lose a gypsy if you tried."

I knew she'd recognized my lie but I could explain. I just said "There's people with nothing to live for," and I knew I was right so far as I went. But that moment then, I had no doubt—and every time since when I see that man's broad face in my dreams, I have no single trace of doubt—that the man I'd seen was my only father; and I'd passed him by.

On the following morning anyhow, with very little sleep for either one of us because of the hungers I put us through once we lay down, Fare and I went to the Farmer's Market in a field beyond town and filled the car trunk with azalea plants in rusty tin cans. I guessed there was nothing else money could buy that would please Hesta more, old as she was.

When we got to her house, she was out on the porch, though the air was chilly. She was wearing the bottle-green coat my mother had bought for the final Easter of her freedom. It was several sizes too big for Hesta and had been in the numerous boxes of clothes I'd taken to the Salvation Army three years ago. Still I didn't ask when Hesta had found it and what it had cost. I just said it looked good but was she really cold?

She said "I've been cold every minute of my life. You ought to know why."

With Farren standing awkward beside me, I didn't follow up on the *why*. I said "Hesta, this is my friend Farren Langston. She's been helping me at my job in D.C., and we've come down here to see you and Mother."

Hesta made a hard effort to get to her feet. I'd never seen her so feeble before, so I laid a hand on her shoulder to stop her.

She pushed it away with her best old power but stayed in her chair. Then she looked to Farren with the first trace of a smile I'd seen her attempt in years. "Welcome here, Miss Langston. My last name is James. I'm Miss Wilhelmina Hesta James."

I'd never heard the *Wilhelmina* before and suspected she'd made that up, then and there. But the tone of her voice had let me know jokes would not be proper. I said "When have you seen Mother?"

Hesta looked to Fare again and said "Excuse me, Miss Langston, for the truth I've got to tell this boy right *now*."

Then she turned fierce eyes on me. "Since you don't pay me to visit *nobody*, I don't owe you a report, now do I?"

I was rightly stung and said "No ma'm."

Hesta said "All *right.*" Then she told me to bring the folding chair that was propped nearby, and she asked Fare to sit. No word about any chair for me.

Fare sat and the two of them started to talk while I went to the car and hauled the azaleas to the stone front steps. I arranged them neatly with plenty of room for people to pass. Then I sat on the top step, facing the road and not really hearing the women's words. Hesta anyhow was more than half-whispering. At a pause in their talk, I leaned back and offered to plant the bushes.

Hesta had taken no notice of them, and even now she didn't say thanks. She said "What color will they turn out to be?"

I'd known to ask about that at the Market. "I know every flower you've got blooms red. I made sure every one of these is red."

Hesta said "I'll plant them later today."

I said "You sure you can manage this many?"

She said "I've managed my whole life till now and a big part of yours and your sad mother's. You get yourself on down the road and see her, you hear? I know she's got something you need to know—she told me last week."

I said "You want to give me a clue?"

Hesta said "No sir."

I sat in the quiet air and studied her closely for the first time today. Not only was Mother's coat way too big, but Hesta had shrunk severely since I'd seen her. Her hair was thin as a month-old baby's, her skin itself was pale as milk, and her eyes had seemed to triple in size in her palm-sized face. I ought to have known what was coming but selfishness stopped me. Since this old woman had been rude to me for the millionth time, and since I was not her child anymore, all I wanted to do was take my girlfriend and leave.

Where we went of course was to Mother. It had been four months since my last visit, and I was shocked when the guard led her in—she'd gained at least twenty pounds in that short time. My face must have showed how surprised I was. Mother gave me one glance, then went straight to Farren, shook her hand and said "I used to be his mother, Edith Norfleet. But I've buried her now." She dropped Fare's hand but was still focused on her. "Buried her almost completely, I think. That's my intention at least." Finally she turned to me and said "What do you think, sir?"

I put out my hand and offered to shake hers.

She didn't quite refuse me but she didn't accept, and she gave no sign of knowing me at all.

I said "Mother, it's Noble."

She gave my face a long close search. "I have a son named Archer," she said. "He's long since dead."

I nodded. "You did. It wasn't so long ago either."

The guard was standing very close by, as always. I guess he had to be sure we didn't pass anything dangerous or illegal to the prisoner. At that point, for whatever silent reason, he shook his head at me. Wasn't I allowed to remind my mother that she'd murdered her younger son not long ago? Anyhow the next thing he said was "Mrs. Norfleet, you know where you've got to sit at."

I thought I knew what her answer would be—*behind the preposition at* (she'd learned it from Hesta).

But when the guard took her by the elbow and guided her over to the usual table, she didn't fight him; and she finally faced us as if she had no other choice. But then she spread her hands before her and studied her palms. Her friend Loraine, whose death a few years back had made Mother worse, was a weirdly skilled palmist and had taught Mother secrets about the meaning of lines and folds in the average hand. At last now Mother looked up, dead at me, and said "Your father is hunting for you."

No bullet in Nam had got to within fifteen inches of me. This one hit just below my left eye and angled upward into my brain—I felt it that precisely. Of course, after what I'd seen on the highway, I'd meant to ask her what she knew about him.

Fare seemed to know how hard I was hit. Her hand came out and covered mine. We were seated on separate chairs, facing Mother.

Mother told Fare "You can keep your hand to yourself, girl. Noble's all right. He's as tough as he looks."

I apparently was. So I said "Dad's been here to see you then?"

Mother nodded. "Every Friday of the year—five-thirty, like the worst clockwork—expecting me to feed him. We can't have *guests* here. What does he *think*?" Wild as she sounded, I had to believe her.

I glanced to the guard. He turned out to look so much like Dad that I must have flinched.

Mother understood. She looked back toward the guard, then smiled at me. "It's not him," she said.

But I spoke to the man. "Has she had visits from Mr. Norfleet?"

The guard took enough time to search every memory he'd ever stored. Then he said "Sir, I'm not allowed to answer questions about anything but the rules in this room."

Three-fourths of my mind knew this had to be some kind of sad, or cruel, dementia. Still I had no choice but to ask Mother more. "Is he truly a homeless tramp on the roads?"

Mother nodded—"You've seen him then"—and shut her eyes awhile.

Oh Christ, I truly passed him by, no more than twenty-some hours ago, after all these years. At first it hurt at least half as much as finding my brother and sister, Easter morning. When I faced her again, Mother's eyes were still shut; and I somehow couldn't make a sound to win her notice.

Fare spoke up then. "Mrs. Norfleet, please—have you got some message for Noble from his dad?"

Mother calmly looked out and searched the whole room as if Fare were plainly a hard thing to find. Then she settled on her, all but glaring. "Nothing I'd be prepared to share with you, young woman."

Woman in those days was still an insulting way of addressing a clean white female in this part of the States—*lady* was the word. I said "Edith, this young lady here is the finest I know. You owe her much thanks."

Mother tried to look puzzled. "Thanks? For what on Earth please? I've never laid an eye on her, not till this moment."

I said "She's saving your son Noble's life by the hour and the minute." It even felt true—and maybe it was, considering Fare's recent bravery with Franco.

Mother looked as if she'd never seen me either.

I tapped my own forehead more than once. "This son right here, the one you didn't kill—God knows why."

Edith Redden Norfleet took that in with little lip motions that looked like bird swallows of rain. Finally she turned to Farren and said "*I* know why but can never tell him."

Honest to Christ, I'd never spent ten seconds wondering why she'd spared my life, if in fact I'd even been at home when she killed the others. I knew she was wild, that Easter and now; and I never thought she'd had a real reason. But weak as I was from what she'd just now said about Dad, I wanted to push her onward. I said "You'd better tell, if you want to save me." I had no idea what I meant.

But the guard seemed sure. He was already on his feet before my sentence ended. "Mrs. Norfleet needs her rest, right now."

I said "We haven't been here five minutes, sir."

But Mother was also standing up and had turned toward the door. As she left she said—not to anybody really, just aloud to the air—my father's whole name, Henry Manning Norfleet.

So I said to her vanishing back "Is he truly alive now please?"

She stopped and stood in place a long moment. Then when the guard touched her shoulder lightly, she turned instead of moving forward. And she faced me intently. "Noble," she said, "your father's on the roads. I hear from him still, like I said, on schedule. He's out there right by himself alone, hitching up and down the world, mainly looking for you. I've told him and told him you are in deep hiding from him, told him you'd gone halfway round the globe, just to hide from him and all he means; but he still wants you." She waited to see if she'd said all she knew—or could make up on the spot—and then she turned back and took the next step away.

To her back again I said "Is there some way you could help me reach him?"

For many years afterward I thought she said "No."

But by then the guard was closing the door, and a woman was ushering me and Fare out the opposite side of the room I wouldn't revisit till both my mother and I were different souls.

When we got to the car, Farren said "Let me drive." The sun was brighter than I'd remembered. It seemed more like radiation than simple light, so maybe I was looking a little stunned. Anyhow I paused by the driver's door and gave it some thought. *Sure, let her take over for the next few minutes.* I opened the door, slid under the wheel and waited for Fare.

She made no comment on my rudeness but reached to my right hand and took the keys from me.

We were halfway back down a crowded highway that I barely recognized toward our motel before I swam a little out of my trance. I couldn't face Farren but I managed to say "Am I truly bad off?"

She said "I think we'd better say Yes."

I laughed. By then I could look at her profile.

She looked at least as pale as I felt.

I said "Who is *We*?"

She smiled but didn't face me. "Oh, you and me. You had a hard meeting, I watched it all, I'd have been shocked too—I *am* shocked. Or maybe I still can't quite believe what I saw that woman do to you. Maybe I'm mainly *sad*."

I said "Well, it's not like you didn't know she was capable of plunging ice picks into two kids' hearts—her two youngest children."

Fare was already well-trained enough not to answer my heat with any excitement of her own. Very coolly but kindly she said "That's correct." She was watching the road as closely as if some armed Marine might lurch up onto the median, firing dead at us. Or maybe as if my dad might suddenly show up, hunkered down by another road sign, merely waiting. But then she said "I could call the Highway Patrol from the motel and get them to try to find your father."

"Yes you could," I said. Please recall here one more time—at that strange moment Farren Langston was twenty-two years old, a recent college graduate with very little experience of life outside a rich home and a rich girls' school (though, come to think of it, she had disarmed my scary roommate awhile back, hadn't she?).

Back in the motel I flung myself down and slept like some half-drowned old dog for three blank hours. Fare sat up in a chair the whole time and read the stack of books she'd brought. She never once tried to wake me, though she later said she'd leaned right down to my lips several times just to feel the damp of my breath on her hand and be half sure I was still alive—I was that far-gone. When I finally surfaced it was night outside, and I was hungrier than any blast furnace. We found a new Italian place open, they were glad for late customers, and we both ate bountiful platters of pasta and several loaves of bread. We'd literally got to the homemade gelato before either one of us mentioned my mother.

That was when Fare touched the back of my hand with a single finger and said "Your mother was either lying or badly hallucinating—you know that, don't you?"

I didn't know that. I said "They have her stoked on these new anti-hallucinogens, night and day. You know they work but they also crank your appetite high and slow your metabolism down to zero. That's why she's gained weight."

"Then it's vicious lying," Fare said as if that was absolute truth delivered from God.

I knew she was two years older than me but was acting like a pompous child, so I suddenly amazed myself and got hot mad. "How the hell are you so sure, girl? You barely even met her." It was how I'd answer when kids at school would tell me they'd seen Mother do something weird at the grocery store.

But Fare stayed calm. "I don't think there's any serious chance your father is coming in off the roads—a ragged wino—and getting admitted, as a family guest, to a state mental prison near suppertime every Friday that comes. That can't even be a possibility, can it? They'd put him in a holding cell fast."

I wanted to believe her—she was so fine to look at, she had to be right—but I still wasn't ready to give up the mixture of hope and dread I'd felt since passing that man on the highway last night. What swept across me stronger than anything else that instant was the need to take this woman back to our room and thank her fully for all she'd meant and could mean years from now, if I only could manage to honor her rightly.

To me, of course, that meant giving her body all the pleasure I knew how to give. And through a long part of that night, it seemed to work for Farren—God knows it did for me. I'd left a small light on in the bathroom and nearly shut the door, so each one of us could see at least the outline of the other. And it truly seemed like we never stopped moving—not in some moaning furious way, not climbing across and over and under each other, not struggling to ride topmost in the various times we claimed to reach a pitch in the goal I thought we were aiming toward. It steadily seemed we were almost finding the perfect way to boost each other to the highest peak our bodies could reach. At the very least, Fare never said No at any point in the time we moved, not that I heard or felt in my hands as I roved across her. And as far as I could see, she took my gifts and turned them into immediate rewards.

I know it was three in the morning when we finished that part of the job—when *I* finished anyhow. I'd reached the place where, if I'd had a gram of energy left, I'd have asked her to take me then and there—in marriage for good—but young as I was and with a young man's faith that daylight might dawn, after all, and that Fare and I would be the same people we were right now and could make real plans for a long life together, I slid off into sleep again.

Then the bedside phone rang two separate times, right near my head. Groggy as I was, I answered.

The first time nobody spoke a word, though a man seemed to be breathing deeply and listening hard.

A good while later a man's voice spoke and said—I can almost swear to God—"Is Delle really gone?" *Delle* was what we called my sister, but it's also the name of several million other women and men, so the question didn't strike me hard. I just said "No" and hung the phone up.

I remember Fare's voice asking "Who was that?"

I said "Some old drunk asking for Delle" (I still don't know where I got the *drunk* idea).

Fare said "Wasn't Adelle your sister?"

I told her Yes and she said nothing more.

No more phone calls either and I slept on.

When I finally woke, my watch said ten o'clock. The room was still dim and completely quiet, so I thought Fare was asleep behind me (I was on my right side). In that much peace then, I took my time and thought out the words I'd say when I turned. Finally I was ready. I reached to the nightstand and took a mint I'd brought from the restaurant after dinner. I thumbed my eyes as clean as I could manage, and I silently practiced the sentence I'd made—"I hope you can take this boy for good." Then I rolled over slowly.

I should have known that waking up late on Sunday mornings was dangerous for me.

Fare was not in her place. She was not in the room. The bathroom door was open; the light was off. When I sat up to call her name, she didn't answer. In recent years, as you know by now, I'd prayed very seldom. Something made me pray now, a very few words—*Don't do this to me, Sir.* One more time, though, He'd done it in spades. Or let it be done. And before I even laid eyes on Fare's letter, I truly knew why. No mystery this time.

The letter was sealed in a motel envelope bearing my name in her clear hand and propped against one of my new track shoes which she'd set on the narrow desk so I wouldn't miss it.

Dear Noble,

It's just past daylight now, and I'm leaving to get myself back to D.C. so I can breathe deep again and think. I know you had a hard day yesterday, but it turned out pretty hard for me too. I never saw a man be abused the way you were by Hesta and then your awful mother.

Then the night was rough for me. See, I think I can understand how much you need somebody to give to, *but I'm not anything resembling God, I'm not a licensed charity, and I can't take the smallest part of all you need to give. Not in the way you choose to give it. I'm not a church, Noble. That may well be a weakness in me, but at least I know what I can't take.*

I'm taking my bag and walking to the bus station now. Please don't follow me. I'll be all right. I want a quiet day with strangers around me and nothing but a strange man driving me north. You can call me if you ever want to again. I'll be at my place, but I'll be a different person.

Thanks for the kindness you've shown me right along. If I'm one more person that's let you down for no good reason, I apologize. But frankly I don't know anything else to do.

Good luck
from Farren

That's almost certainly the way she expressed it. I very nearly memorized the letter that day, then I lost it long since. Or maybe I burned it. Honest to Christ I don't recall. But it was the last fact that brought me down—those truthful words from a person as good as Farren Langston all pressed on top of my life up till then and sent it tumbling in on itself.

I didn't break up, not then and there. I had a calm meal in the motel dining room. The parents of one of my track-team friends had come in after Sunday school for the big breakfast buffet; and when they saw me, they came over nicely and asked edgy questions about my life and my mother's present health.

I gave them pleasant lies.

So the woman asked if Mother was "subject" to visits from friends.

I told her No, she was way past such contacts.

And then the man said "Nobe, we haven't felt like good *Christians*, letting you just drift off alone in the world and us not so much as sending your mother a card or a box of candy or *nothing*."

I hadn't heard the word *Christian* used for some years now without feeling some need to gag. Way too many of the "Christians" I'd run across were powerful haters, and I don't know what it was in this tall man's thin high voice or in the squinched face of his squatty wife, but I felt a rush of tears to my eyes, and I let them stream till the woman took up my napkin from the table and wiped them as shamelessly as if I'd been her own helpless son (he was still in college, a civil engineer).

The father said "Boy, do you need a job?"

By then I'd got a fair grip on myself—I was wearing civilian clothes of course—so I thanked them both, explained I still owed Uncle Sam some time, but said I'd be back down here soon and very well might need their help with my life. Their names were Phyllis and Arthur Fann; and though I never saw them again or called for their help, I've always thought they did me a Christian deed that morning—a good deed anyhow (would Jesus have done it?). Otherwise, I can't imagine why I said what I did—about returning to work in a town I thought I'd fled forever.

Once I checked out I took a ride past my old house, then paid my respects to Arch and Adelle's slim outlines in the graveyard. I thought I might report to Hesta on Mother's behavior, but on second thought I decided to let Hesta rest for a while. I even spent a minute wondering whether I ought to see if Tom Landingham's wife was still in town, but then I knew I wouldn't have three clear words to tell her, so I hit the road for D.C. in midafternoon. And for the first fifty miles, I almost felt better—a stripped-down man again anyhow, no human being who needed me personally, nobody I could say I loved who loved me back. I knew I'd phone Farren one more time to be sure the bus got her safely back north, but I wouldn't trouble her again after that.

Then when I crossed on into Virginia in broad daylight—I saw a man coming down the shoulder toward me, my side of the road. When I first glimpsed him, he was quite a ways distant; and my mind clenched on itself like a fist. As I got nearer to him, though, I could breathe free—he was plainly a homeless soul headed south, but he looked very nearly my age and bore no resemblance whatever to Dad. In another twenty miles, here came another man—my age again. This time I slowed down to get a good look, and he looked enough like me to be close kin. He even waved at me, but he kept on moving.

By the time I was well into northern Virginia, I'd passed another three or four men very similar to me in size and age and other features. Each one of them looked completely real—no special light around them, no transparent chests, no identical sets of clothes and shoes. Maybe half of them waved when they saw me looking, but that never seemed unnatural or wrong. It was dusk and I was a half hour from Arlington before I realized what I'd seen. These lonely men, all headed south with nothing but their bodies and clothes and slim luggage, had to be the first real vision I'd had since maybe what happened in that strange tunnel in Vietnam. And wasn't my glimpse of Dad on Friday and my belief that Mother had claimed he was hunting me down—weren't they also part of some news that was being pressed on me from the same old unpredictable source?

I knew the answer had to be Yes, no doubt whatever. I still don't doubt it. And what I thought the news truly meant for me and my life was nothing but this—I'd be a man walking down the road, with the main world passing, and I'd be strictly on my own. I don't know why that news swamped me then, so badly. It wasn't as if I'd lived in the bosom of a large loving family in recent years—never in my whole life, to be merely accurate. It wasn't as if I'd asked any one human being for special pity or extra credit just because of my background. And surely I hadn't lain out in the jungles of Nam, gazing up at stars as bright as arc lamps and seeing myself in a well-loved future plus Thanksgiving banquets with a wife and children smiling back at me in spasms of gratitude they couldn't resist. Hadn't I been the kid who laughed and told the others in kindergarten that Santa Claus was an outright lie (because I'd never got more than the odd set of pencils for Christmas, even when I had a resident father)?

But as I said, it swamped me now. I managed to get myself to the backyard in Arlington and lock the car behind me. I think I managed to get myself unseen to my own room and stay in the shower for the hour it took to get my face halfway back to normal before I saw my roommates. I'd broken down the middle, though, like any dry stick; and I stayed broke for a long stretch of days that made the memory of Vietnam feel like the memory of a pleasant childhood trip I had before things wrecked. I don't think any normal person noticed I was split into several pieces.

But one of my patients at the hospital did, and he wasn't even a Vietnam vet. He'd been in Korea for nearly two years, and it bothered him that the country had completely forgot Korea and the men who went over there. He was talking about that with me shortly after I broke. We were at the far end of a small ward where nobody could hear us; so after he'd gone on a little too long about his neglect, I said something mildly impatient—his name was Kelvin.

And he said "Noble, sit down here just a second please; and I'll change the subject."

I was in no hurry and, though it was against the rules, I sat on the edge of a chair.

Kelvin cranked his big West Virginia voice down to a whisper. "Do you think garlic is as scary as I do?"

His general problem had been depression. I'd never heard previous signs of dementia, so I humored him now. I said "No, I'm very fond of garlic. Tell me why it's scary."

He whispered even lower. "Well, the Chinese Communists downright loved it. They'd eat a raw head of garlic the way I'd eat a hard green apple, and then I could smell em across the lines in the dead of night. Scared me shitless for nearly two years." He thought a long moment and then laughed, silent and toothless.

I waited and nothing else came, so I stood back up.

But Kelvin said "Please" and motioned me down again.

I said "Better tell me the point. It's a busy morning, Kel."

He spoke even quieter. "Son, I can see you're scared to death of something. Just wanted to say you're far from alone. I lie here every night and call out the names of fifty-two thousand men as bad off as me—I know every name and can spell em right. We're all still living. We swap Christmas cards. You'll make it, if you want to. *Wanting to* is the hard trick, though."

Those were still the days when people sent you telegrams with urgent news, an expensive means of communication where you paid by the word. For months to come when things were bad—and they got a lot badder than they were that day—I'd try to imagine getting a telegram from Kelvin. And of course it would just say his main seven words. *Wanting to is the hard trick, Nobe.*

In the few months left till I finished the Army, I did three things with the most attention I'd paid to anything since I tried not to flunk trigonometry in my senior year—I performed my hospital duties to the letter, I wolfed down all the sleep I could manage when I was off-duty, and I found a good many women to know (as far as they'd let me). Don't misunderstand me—I truly think I never hurt one, in body or mind. I did every kind thing I could imagine to earn their presence and insure their trust. That's not to say I wanted nothing but their skin and hair.

I met some of them in massage studios (*studios* was the D.C. word at the time, maybe classier than *parlors*). Two of those women were actually working on college degrees. They proved it to me by showing me textbooks and lecture notes. I met some others in my line of work. They ranged anywhere from medical residents (already MDs) and registered nurses on through women I met in the waiting rooms or the cafeteria or out on the steps. I never told anybody one small lie about who I was or what I was after, though I always tried to avoid describing my family history so as not to ask for excess pity. I never laid a bruising finger on anybody nor said a harsh word.

To the best of my memory, I got well acquainted with nine women in that stretch of time. A few of them may not have been any grander specimens of humankind than I myself was. But there was certainly more than one of them I'd have liked to try to spend my whole life with. Yet because of my failings, nothing very substantial worked out except some literally fabulous sexual time for me and—I honestly think—a few of them. More than once it felt like healing, and by then I knew I was one grown man in earnest need of serious healing. Whatever happened I managed to last till the U.S. Government formally thanked me for doing a duty I'd sworn to do. Then it turned me out onto the world.

THREE

That's not to say I crawled out of the service as a foaming humanoid who should have been penned up for strict observation before being trusted with normal rations and visiting rights with full-fledged humans in the open air. At least I didn't think I was that bad off, and neither did anyone I knew at the time. If so they didn't tell me. Of course I didn't have any close friends for a good while after my discharge. I stayed around D.C. for maybe ten days, mainly to see the sights I hadn't managed to see in the previous year. The Vietnam Wall hadn't been built yet, and even today I can hardly stand to go there for longer than it takes to press my fingers against the names of the men who actually died in my arms. So my favorite place turned out to be a bench on the north edge of Jackson Square, across from the White House.

Even with Richard Nixon in it and all the hairy war protestors and the homeless demented, the sight of the President's house always helped me—the thought that every chief executive since John Adams has lived in those walls and done his share of good and evil is about as much as America offers in the way of deep history, unless you're into geology and delving for mastodon molars. And what's more help, when you're down and depressed, than realizing how time keeps moving, with or without *your* moaning lips? In those years of course, with Russia and China still clenched against us, I could also look at the small trim mansion—it's really not big compared to a palace—and imagine it vaporizing any instant in a nuclear strike. I don't know why I thought my eyes would last long enough to see the house vanish before I melted.

Then I packed everything I wanted to keep into two small bags; and for lack of any firmer target, I headed back to my ex-hometown. I had no plan to stay there—I had no *plan* whatever—but I thought I could at least stow my bags somewhere, then sit down long enough to look at the state of my slender finances and decide whether I could, say, take the slow drive to New Mexico that I'd always hoped for or whether I needed to tuck my chin right away and find some temporary job till I knew whether I should apply for the GI money I could get to go to college or some technical school. And if so, what would I try to learn and when and where? After all, with the thanks of a grateful nation behind me, I could theoretically be anything from a neurosurgeon to a TV repairman, not to mention career possibilities in crime (selling drugs, selling guns).

I knew well before I crossed the state line again that I wouldn't ask Wilhelmina Hesta James to lend me an inch of her precious space. After her recent meanness I didn't plan to see her anytime soon. I had no intention of seeing Mother either, not till a prison doctor could assure me she wouldn't try killing me soon again with crazy mean talk. Her old house of course was still rented to the couple who'd painted the inside yellow, and that monthly rent was welcome—I couldn't turn them out. And I certainly wouldn't check to see if Anita Acheson was still teaching Spanish and might have a bed. All through Nam I'd halfway expected to run into her husband and have some tall explaining to do, if not some blood to shed—mine, that is—but we never crossed each other's paths; and I'd never heard another syllable about him or Anita. So I thought I'd just rent a motel room, sort through my business and try to think of how to use the new freedom. I'd never really had to learn to use freedom.

I went to a place on the south side of town, checked into my room and guess who knocked on the door—with a bottle of cold California pink champagne and a giant bag of chips—ten minutes later? It was Jarret James, my boyhood friend, Hesta's nephew. He greeted me with his best English accent as if we'd laughed with each other last night, not three full years ago. He'd been driving past the motel, seen me checking in alone, gone to the nearest grocery store, bought the wine and taken a chance on ambushing me. I was glad enough to see him, but right off I asked him why he'd never answered the several letters I wrote him once I left.

All he could say was that writing to distant friends made him "miss them too much."

The look in his eyes convinced me right off. Though he was nattily dressed as always, Jarret had aged ten years in three but not as if he'd been drunk or drugged. It looked more like a big toll of sadness, and I remembered for the first time in years how his father had died in the electric chair when we were boys. We both got a prison postcard from him, mailed three days before he died. So Jarret had his version of Vietnam long before mine, and I didn't press the point about letters. I sat him down, popped the cork on his bottle, and we drank every drop while we told each other the stories we'd lived through. You already know what I told him.

In light of Nita's story about her brothers and her father, what Jarret told me was maybe no surprise, but it held me in place as long as he talked, and it had slow results that I only now realize (why did it strike me harder than Nita's—because we were both men or because Jarret was black and I wasn't?). That day was still a decade before child abuse became the open American wound that it's been since the late 1980s. People hadn't yet stood up on TV and elsewhere in public to say their childhoods had been long nightmares of having the literal shit beat out of them, time after time, by some adult—most generally a parent or other close kin. And of course the word *incest* had still not been so much as whispered in daylight. On the rare occasions any such behavior got into the paper, it was simply called "carnal knowledge of a minor." With all I'd seen and lived through as a child, I'd never quite managed to think of myself as a battered boy. And to the best of my knowledge, I'd never been touched below the waist by any adult before I took Spanish. By my own standards, up till Jarret spoke, I'd just been the slightly premature manager of a full household that needed a pilot.

His memories were way too long to set down here. The result of what he'd been through is what counts (it would lean considerable weight on me eventually). Suffice it to say that the boy I'd known as always ready for cheerful play had been through a steady siege of Hell from almost the cradle till after I left town and he got a good enough job to let him rent his own room and start his own life. We were almost down to the last of the champagne before Jarret brought out the single memory that I think bears summarizing here.

Throughout our childhoods I'd always heard that his mother had died when he was born, which was the reason he spent so much time with his Aunt Hesta and came along to our house so often when she was working there. What I hadn't known was that, when he was a baby, his mother had gone off to work as a maid with a white family moving north to Pittsburgh. She left him with the man who she said was his father. The man worked in pulpwood logging and was also gone a lot. At those times Jarret was kept by Hesta and various other women, mainly his father's mother. One way and another—but never from Hesta, Jarret claimed—he took a lot of steady walloping. Walloping so hard that it included blood and broken teeth.

By the time he got almost to his teens, his father had died; and his mother had never come back from Pittsburgh, though every birthday and Christmas the mother sent him money—"never more than three dollars." She was always on time with a card and the cash, and that was the main thing Jarret could safely look forward to. Then the night before his thirteenth birthday, he was staying alone at his grandmother's when a man who was maybe his cousin came by the house with some takeout fish he shared with Jarret—the grandmother was off in Winston with yet another daughter.

Along with the fish, the cousin had brought a half gallon of wine; and that was Jarret's introduction to spirits. At some point he passed out on the floor. When he finally came to, he was still on the floor and it was daylight. He looked round for the cousin, no signs of anybody. Then when he tried to get up, he found he was chained at the ankles in a complicated knot to two legs of his grandmother's big iron bed. At first he laughed and thought it was a joke. Turned out it wasn't and for three more days he stayed right where he was—no food or water, lying there in his own piss and shit, dreaming off and on but mainly sure he'd die any minute.

Every afternoon, once the postman came, he'd hear his cousin's footsteps on the porch, checking for the birthday card. Jarret would yell out then and beg for help. He said, and I can still believe him, that he counted on me to be his rescue. I'd been to his house the week before to borrow a bicycle pump he had, and he kept thinking I'd bring it back and untie his knots. He said he yelled my name a thousand times, but I didn't hear him. I was well over half a mile away and giving no thought whatever to him. Nobody came, not till his grandmother got home from Winston and set him loose with a big bolt-cutter.

The instant he finished telling me that, I knew two things. First, I'd heard a story at least as bad as any I'd witnessed; and second, somehow Jarret had thrown me a lifeline that I could choose to grab on to and maybe survive. At the time I had no idea why I knew it that clearly, and I'm still not sure. But the sight and presence of a man my age who'd stayed in our hometown and lasted through the life he'd described was the rescue *I* needed (diabetes had kept Jarret out of the Army, but it didn't seem to stop him drinking pink wine). On the spot, with the two of us pleasantly looped and with Jarret needing to head on back to his wife Irene who'd just had a baby daughter, still I managed to thank him.

When he left I fell across the bed, fully dressed, and slept twelve hours—the longest time I'd been unconscious in my life till then. Some people who'd know me through the coming years might say I was unconscious all that time. God knows, my life has felt like sleep way too many times.

I woke up in that motel room and saw Jarret's empty champagne bottle and our two glasses which proved what had happened and where I was. I showered and went to the café where I'd taken Mother the day I turned her in. I ordered the same thing I'd got for her then—buckwheat cakes with a fried egg and bacon—though I ate a lot more than she managed that morning. I even had the same quick waitress.

She recognized my face anyhow and asked if I wasn't in there with my mother last week.

I told her Yes and No. I'd been here with my mother, but it had been more than three years ago.

She said "Oh, sugar, it's all one to me—two days or ten years. All I know for sure is, I've been on these two flat feet at least a century; and I never forget a face." Then she paused and looked me dead in the eye. "Is your mother alive?"

I told her Yes and then couldn't help asking why she wondered.

She lowered her voice and her face went kind. "I couldn't help thinking I recognized her as that poor lady who lost her mind and had to kill her children."

I told her she was right. "But why do you say she *had* to do it?"

There were only two other customers in the place, so she gave it some thought. And when she reached her conclusion, she was forced to smile slightly. "I guess just because I'm a mother too," she said. When I nodded but was silent, she said "Does that hurt you?"

"Oh no, I gave up hurting way back."

The waitress also nodded and said "She left *you* alive, I seem to notice." Then as if she'd passed me the secret of the ages, she went about her business.

In all the years since, I've heard people say that numerous times as if it's some kind of key I can use to the secrets of Time and the Universe. I've heard whole TV programs about how guilty people feel when *they* survive but their twin brother dies or their wife or child, and how they've triumphed over the guilt and learned to serve mankind and love God and all the pets on Earth. Honest to God, till that moment there with my pancakes, the fact of my survival had never really dawned on me as something strange. When the waitress turned and went about her business, I wondered if she'd thrown the second lifeline and—if so—what I was meant to do now I was no longer drowning maybe?

Right after breakfast, for no particular reason, I drove back into the middle of town. I parked in a big lot off Main Street and began walking around. Of course this was the place I'd spent my whole life up till the time I left for the Army. I'd never especially loved it, but I hadn't hated it either. In spite of my numerous hitchhiking trips, I'd never thought of fleeing the place. If I hadn't been a sure bet to be drafted, I probably wouldn't have left, even after what Mother and Tom Landingham did. I've mentioned that I had no family nearby, no lasting friend from my school days and no man or woman but Jarret and Hesta that I'd known well. Also I'd grown a good deal, both upward in height and outward in muscles; so I didn't expect many people to know me. And nobody did or, if so, they didn't speak.

That didn't bother me a bit. With all the lonely time I'd had, I learned to crave loneliness the way dumb creatures crave salt. So after a stretch of aimless walking—looking in at the old drugstore where I used to get hot pimento cheese sandwiches and the bookstore where I used to stand for half an hour at a time and, day after day, read chapters of a book that I couldn't buy—I realized I was a block away from my high school. I went on toward it and circled the empty field where I'd put in my track and field time, a few thousand hours. A distant black man was raking gravel at the far end, and he waved at me. It was nobody I recognized from my day, but I waved back and banked off to the north so I wouldn't have to stop and tell him who I was. As I went I slowly realized that none of this had any feeling for me. I might as well have been walking through strange parts of Bismarck, North Dakota or downtown Syracuse—New York or Sicily or anywhere else they have a Syracuse.

Going north, though, meant I was in my own old neighborhood in two short blocks. Up there I knew every crack in the sidewalk, every limb in each tree, even the knots in ropes by which children's swings were hanging from the limbs. But I stopped on the corner nearest our old house and gave myself a fair chance to refuse. If anything was going to jumpstart any feelings in me, it would surely be the house. I hadn't talked to the rental agent for quite a while; and as far as I knew the pale couple in nuclear medicine were still there, in the all-yellow rooms, so on the spot I decided to walk by and see if they were in.

Not only *in*, the woman was out on the porch in a rocking chair my Grandmother Redden had bought for my own mother, when she first got disturbed, in the hope that rocking would help calm her down. I walked up slowly and paused a safe ten yards from the steps. Then I saw that the woman was holding a very small child up against her. At first she didn't see me, and then I realized she had to be nursing. Even as a medic in an Army hospital, I'd never had to deal with a bare-breasted woman; and I figured this one would be embarrassed.

But when she looked up, she said "Well, *hey*" and made only slight adjustments in her clothes.

I thought that meant she recognized me from my one brief visit, so I stepped on forward and paused again.

Her face stayed pleasant but she said "May I help you?"

Then I knew I was a stranger. At first I thought I'd just pretend I needed directions and would scoot on away, but something made me hold my ground. I said "My name is Norfleet. I met you a few months back. I grew up here." I pointed to the house behind and around her. She was so much at ease, I could tell she felt like the place was hers and this child's she was holding. To my hot amazement it made me mad. *This goddamned hell-hole is mine—get out!* Of course I didn't say it. I held my ground, though.

At that point she stood and said "*Noble!* Forgive me. I haven't got my glasses on. Come up and sit down and meet the young master."

The word *master* threw me for another loss but a smaller one. Anyhow I went up, talked a little baby talk to the remarkably homely boy (even paler than both his parents) and sat down long enough for the woman to get me a Seven Up and some saltines. Her name turned out to be Alma Steed. *Alma* had been the name of Tom Landingham's wife. And when I asked if she by any chance knew if a Mrs. Alma Landingham still lived in town, she surprised me again.

"Very much so," she said. "We go to her church." Alma Steed went on to make it clear that Tom's wife hadn't become a minister herself but was what she'd been from the start—the Sunday-school pianist and junior-choir director. Apparently she was doing all right. Then Alma Steed said "You knew poor Tom, I've heard Alma say."

That was her biggest surprise yet. What on Earth had she heard?

I told her I'd only known Tom in his last few weeks.

And she nodded. "That's what Alma told me. She said you did all you could to save him."

"I tried," I said. Then my throat closed.

Alma Steed said "Oh, she says she couldn't have made it through that awful time without your help. My husband and I are proud to live here, knowing you own it."

By then I was sitting in a plastic-strap chair I'd never seen before. She was standing up, a few feet beyond me (she'd left the baby asleep indoors). I still felt the need not to speak awhile longer, but I also didn't want to leave yet. I looked at this pale creature's blue eyes, trying to see if she'd told me the truth about Tom's wife. Had Tom's Alma lost her mind about me, or had she made up a string of stories to help her through the mystery?

Alma Steed said "Have you seen her yet?"

I said I hadn't seen her since Tom's funeral.

"Well, I'm sure she'll want to see you soon as possible." Then the way people almost always did when speaking of Mother, she lowered her voice. "I know she visits your mother when she can."

This Alma before me still looked sane. But that last detail had to be wrong. I'd given the warden a list of the people Mother could see, and Mrs. Tom Landingham wasn't on the list. I stood up to go, but to be polite I asked if the house was holding up.

She said "Oh Noble, we love this house. I know it wasn't a happy place in your last days here, but I hope the day will come when you can love it again the way we do now."

I couldn't help saying I doubted I'd loved it at any point in my whole life but was glad she and her husband did.

Then her eyes filled up. When she'd wiped them with her hand, she said "We're going to miss it when we have to leave."

"Will that be soon?" I said.

She went on to give me a fuller account than I needed of how Nuggett would finish his Ph.D. this summer—his name was Nuggett (honest to God, I'd forgot that detail)—and they'd move on to West Virginia where he had a job.

She seemed to think they were somehow letting me down by leaving. I assured her the agent could rent the house promptly, and I wished her and her new family well.

At that point she asked me to stay for lunch. Nugg would be here any minute. We could finally get to know each other, and I could see what they'd done to the place by way of improvements.

I had no doubt of her good intentions, but I had to get out fast. Hot as I was to leave, I could already see that Alma Steed had given me the next two things to do. First I needed to see Tom Landingham's wife; and depending on what she said or claimed, I might well have to see my mother. That was still something I dreaded worse than another year of war.

* * *

Alma Landingham had moved from the parsonage into a smaller house a few blocks away; and it took a big load of curiosity, or some other fuel, to send me forward to knock on her door. Surely she was off at some job or other. Her little job with the church couldn't fund her and both the girls. But I knocked anyhow and the older girl came—named Priscilla and twelve years old. She'd never known me and there was no reason to give her any real information now. I just said I was an old family friend and was her mother at home?

Being a minister's child, Priscilla had the formal good manners to trust me and lead me into the living room—small and dim, even in the early afternoon. She said her mother was resting but would surely want to see me.

I wasn't entirely sure about the *surely*; but in three minutes, Alma Landingham walked in, even finer-looking than I recalled. After all this time she was still dressed in black; and her raven hair had two symmetrical streaks of gray, one on each side like wings that might unfurl with no warning and do their will. Her deep-set eyes were as hungry as ever. By that I don't mean sexual hunger. I'd always thought she had the eyes of a very smart child that's already figured out how life is a riddle, instant by instant, but that somewhere an answer is waiting to be found. Despite all that, she had to be thirty-five; so what on Earth did she know about me, or me and Tom, not to mention my mother?

When I'd politely declined a beverage, she sat in the absolute center of the sofa—I was in a leather armchair—and met me, head on, with all her voltage. "Noble, please forgive me. I tried many times to get a working address for you while you were overseas. But nobody knew, nobody I could find."

I smiled and thanked her and said I'd pretty much tried to cut my wires to the town when I headed out. Then I risked saying "Was there something you needed to ask me about?"

She waited a good while, looking past me out the side window. Then she said to the daylight that suddenly appeared "Oh no, I wanted to *thank* you in writing for all you did."

I told her she owed me nothing at all, and then I told her what at first

I figured was a pleasant lie. Before I finished, though, I knew it was the truth. "I tried my best to save him but I failed."

Alma said "Every *one* of us failed. Even God Above failed. Imagine a man of Tom's gifts and youth with a vicious growth the size of a lemon deep down in his brain."

That was fresh news to me, and it came as a shock. "When did you learn that?"

Alma said "After you left town. See, the girls suffered worse than anybody else from it being suicide. And as weeks went by, and they just worried more about their own guilt in whatever drove him to it, our family doctor came by to see me and said maybe we really should disinter Tom and perform an autopsy after all. If we could just find a single thing wrong with his mind or body that could help explain it, then the girls might forgive him—" She broke off there.

I nodded, startled by the cool relief that was pouring through me too.

Alma said "Had you known it? Had he hinted it to you?"

I was flying blind here, but I said "In a way—not in so many words but he managed to show me he was in deep trouble."

Alma said "You mattered a great deal to him. When he left for those days you spent at the beach, he told me you were 'helping immensely in a very bad time.' Those were truly his words."

I thanked her for telling me. "But you say his doctor didn't even know—then how did Tom?"

Alma said "That seemed his biggest secret of all. Then once the autopsy report came in—the rapidest kind of malignant brain tumor—I absolutely sifted Tom's papers again and found a letter from a doctor at Duke. Tom had gone over there to keep us from knowing he suspected trouble, and they had told him he had maybe three months."

If I'd learned one useful thing in Nam, it was simply to let the shocks strike me full-force, then roll on past me and pause in the background—or stack up somewhere inside my skull—and wait till I had a half-quiet moment and then sort through them. Sitting there with Alma Landingham and this real news, all I could think was *You've got the rest of your life to* think, *Noble. Ask your next question and then leave politely.* So I told her I was glad I could help him a little, I asked a few questions about the girls, and then I said "Alma Steed says you may have seen my mother lately."

"Noble, I *have,*" she said. Her whole face crouched as if I might lunge. "Is that all right?"

I said "Your name's not even on the list to see her. How did you manage to break in on her?" It came out sounding harder than I meant to, but I let it stand. At the moment it seemed true enough. Still I almost smiled at the idea of Alma Landingham breaking *into* a prison for the criminally insane—this beautiful white Christian lady here before me, every last hair tamed into place and no doubt lovingly *named.*

In the silent wait, I could see she was having trouble finding her voice.

In that brief spell I could feel my cock stir in my pants. Not since Kealy, in San Antonio, had any woman this much older than me caused such a response; and it shamed me—partly because it was Tom's widowed wife but, right then, because it seemed to break my decision to be my body's own proprietor for the visible future. If any part of me meant to love her—or hurt her for any wrong Tom had done—I managed at least to refuse to obey it.

And finally Alma said "The visits started by accident, Noble. A group of women from the church and I have been going to the facility up there every two weeks. We've generally had a group of men that the warden lets us meet with—a Bible-study group—and there are always several guards in the room in case somebody gets nervous or loud. It almost never happens. Anyhow we talk about mostly their spiritual questions, and we're allowed to give them good gentle books to read—once the guards have searched them for knives and files!" She stopped with her little joke, and that seemed to be her answer. But she paused to remember and then she laughed. "You'd laugh, I know, at some of the questions the poor men ask us—*Is God baldheaded?*" She laughed again.

I couldn't let her off that easy. I said "Alma, my mother is not a man; and she never had the slightest interest in the Bible or God."

Alma calmly said "Please—I wasn't finished. As the months went by and our visits seemed soothing, the warden asked us—*he* approached *us*—to provide the same kinds of visits to the women." That really was as far as Alma meant to go.

We both sat silent for almost a minute; but hard as my cock still was, I didn't want to stand up yet.

So Alma stood. "Let me get you some apple juice."

I said "No, but if you can just give me two more minutes, I'll get out of your way."

She sat back down, looking wary by now.

"Are you claiming you've had any private words with my mother?"

"Noble, I'm not *claiming*. I'm telling the plain truth—I've said a few words with your mother, yes, but with guards all around us."

That helped me a little. "Did you mention me? Did my name come up?"

"I told her I knew you. That seemed to please her."

I said "Alma, how did you know her? Surely you never met her here in town."

Alma said "Oh no, I did—I thought you remembered. She came to a few women's lunches at the church just before your family tragedy."

That was stark news to me. My face must have showed it.

"I even checked the minutes of the women's circle recently. She came to all three Wednesday luncheons for the last three weeks before she—"

I raised a hand to stop her. I don't think I'd ever stopped a human being from using words before. I couldn't bear to hear this woman find a way to name the crime. Then I had two questions. "Did she say anything that sounded wild? Did she mention me at all—at the lunches, I mean?"

"I think she said she was glad to have finally joined our group. I know she said she hoped I'd get to meet you three children."

"But nothing special about me?" I said. I guess I was following up on the question of why I survived.

Alma paused and honestly tried to remember. "No, she and I shared no secrets whatever, not back in those luncheons nor at any time since. And now I doubt she has the faintest idea who I am or what I'm doing there at the facility."

"It's a prison," I said.

She said "I understand that. Forgive me if I've pained you."

I said "You specialize in paining people, don't you?" She'd hurt me and that was meant to hurt her.

If it did, again Alma hid the damage. I'd of course meant Tom—any ways she'd hurt him, though he'd never mentioned any—but I think she'd built up such a legend about Tom and their marriage that I couldn't have hurt her if I'd brought out Polaroid pictures of him nuzzling my crotch (there weren't any, thank God, unless some Martian was hovering unseen overhead with the latest equipment). She didn't ask me to specify the damage I referred to. After all Tom might have cataloged marital grievances to me every time I saw him. What she said was "I've hurt a great many people, yes. I try, every hour, to repair my wrongs."

The way her whole face and body looked then, suddenly stronger and better than ever, I couldn't doubt her meaning. I told her so and left with only a few words more but they were polite.

I felt compelled to see my mother as soon as I could, though I'd vowed to wait a good safe while before the risk of another visit. At the least I had to wait through forty-eight hours till visiting day at the so-called facility, and I spent a lot of that time asleep. Before in my life I hadn't been a major sloth, not as young men go; but now I more than half-understood I was likely doing two things. Something in me was still trying to cure itself, and something else was trying to die—or stay as nearly unconscious as possible till I could find the guts to truly kill it off or stand and use it.

Maybe the main thing I'd learned in Nam was that I was sane. I hadn't buckled and boredom was likely my worst emotion in that whole year. All I'd read about schizophrenia—a good deal by now—suggested that I had pretty well got past the age where a man goes incurably schizoid if it's on the cards for him. So I didn't need to study my mother for any signs of damaged genes that might be ticking in me. I didn't believe she'd had any contact with my sorry father, and I didn't really suspect she'd had any sensible reason for sparing me when she killed my brother and sister. Why put myself through another visit then, this soon anyhow?

Mainly, she was the only close kin I had left. It's hard to give up on the idea that even the sickest mind may improve, and all my memories of our years together were far from bad. Up till maybe two years before the bad Easter, Edith Norfleet was still a generally kind funny person. She took her maternal duties seriously. God knows, she worked night and day to support us, cook good meals for us, wash our clothes, keep our home in reasonable shape. It was not till I was sixteen years old and she began to bring out the finger paintings I'd done in the first grade and tape them up again in the kitchen—I had no idea she'd saved them for years—that I finally admitted, though just to myself, that she was drifting off the road.

And even in the times she was rattled and talking to cobwebs up on the ceiling, she almost never lost her temper or said a harsh word to any of us children. The weekend before Easter she'd taken Arch and Adelle downtown and bought them new clothes for the big day; and she'd given me twenty dollars to buy my own new duds, even though I had a little job of my own. A twenty-dollar bill was a handsome piece of money at the time, and I bought one of the pin-striped pale blue seersucker suits that older Southern men wore. Old-timey as they were, I'd always liked what they did for you—making you look tall and cool (temperature-wise) and in full control of whatever might happen.

It turned out I just got to wear it twice, to the family funeral and my high-school Commencement, before I sent it to the Salvation Army. Anyhow the more I thought in my conscious hours during those two days after Alma Landingham compelled me to see Mother again, the more I thought she'd been a better parent than any of my friends had ever had, right up to Easter that ended us all. In the aftermath I talked to her doctor; and Yes he'd renewed her tranquilizers, at her request, just a week before; but he had no clue as to where her mind was driving her, and he wasn't a fool.

I got to the facility then with fewer qualms than I usually had; and I'd even dressed in the best clothes I had, hoping somehow to please her or rouse some memory in her of her old best ways.

Though I'd phoned ahead and got permission, the guard kept me waiting for half an hour in the bone-bare room with nothing to read and no snack machine—I'd failed to eat lunch.

In the midst of my wait, another guard came out and said "She says she's never heard of you and is scared to see you." It was Darwin, the one who'd been here forever and had seen me several times.

I said "You well know I'm her last of kin. What's the usual procedure at times like this?"

Darwin said "You understand I can't force her."

I said "Of course." But then I had an idea. I said "Just tell her that Noble is out here with a knot in his chain." Darwin was puzzled but I told him "I bet you five dollars she'll understand."

He said "We can't take cash from you people," but he went out again.

What I meant was, I used to wear a silver chain with a cross she'd given me when I finished grade school. I'd always take it off before I showered, and it would get tangled, and only she could untie the knots.

In another ten minutes she came out with Darwin. She was still encased in the extra pounds she'd gained on her medicine (I thought the weight was a form of *hiding*, her latest disguise); but her face was under better control. Her eyes were calm and steady. She seemed to know the room we were in and went straight to the table where inmates had to sit. When she'd carefully adjusted the chair to her liking, she looked out and faced me.

I smiled and said "Good morning, Miss Edith. You're looking much better." I meant it as a genuine compliment.

And she smiled back, an excellent smile from her long-ago days. But then she asked me the kind of question I hadn't heard since elementary math class. "Please say better than *what*?"

I said "Last time you seemed worried about me. Today you look glad—"

She had put up both hands, palm-out, to stop me. "Sir, I've never laid eyes on you in my life."

I actually laughed.

And Mother joined in with the nearest approach to real pleasure I'd seen on her face, and in her whole body, in a number of years.

Even Darwin smiled.

So I asked if she minded if I came closer. There was another chair at the table where she sat, and visitors were allowed to perch there if the inmate and the guard agreed. When she and Darwin both nodded and pointed to the chair, I sat as near to her as I'd been in what felt like a century, maybe since supper that last Saturday night—a quiet meal, as I recalled.

Her smile slowly faded but her eyes were steady on me.

In the next quiet seconds, I realized that my visit to Alma Landingham had got me worried for no real reason. I couldn't think of any question that truly mattered to me, so I said something harmless. "Do you need anything?"

She looked to Darwin as if for suggestions.

He was shining his fingernails against his pants leg.

She looked back to me and lowered her voice again to nearly a whisper. "Sir, why did you feel it was necessary?"

I let the *sir* slide without comment. "Why was what necessary?"

"Your young lady friend that was with you last time—"

"Yes ma'm—Farren Langston. What about her?"

"She's missing," Mother said.

I said "She's in Washington. That's where she works."

"Why isn't she with you?" By now Mother's face looked mildly concerned.

I said "She's a social worker. She's busy." I tried my best smile.

Mother said "I heard you finished her." Except for her faded gray blouse and shirt, she looked entirely sane.

I had to laugh. "No ma'm, she finished *me*. I had fairly serious hopes we would last, but Farren thought otherwise. She left the night after our last visit, yours and mine."

Mother said "You smothered her—I know that much."

Darwin looked as completely uninterested as if this lady and I were planning our next croquet game instead of discussing an apparent murder.

At first of course I thought she had some demented notion that I'd killed Farren. Then I thought she was probably halfway right. I said "You've got a point, yes ma'm. I loved her too much."

Mother said "I could see that. You get that from me."

For the first time since her killings, I wanted to actually *talk* to this woman and ask her full meaning. But I just nodded and told her "Yes ma'm."

She almost smiled again and then, of all things, she asked me how the house was doing.

"Our old homeplace?"

She smiled for an instant. "Our only place, right?"

I had to say Yes, though that was far from easy. "I haven't lived there for three years now."

She nodded and said "—While you were underground." She'd remembered some version of her memory that I'd be forced to go to Vietnam, fighting.

"We've got nice tenants," I said. I hadn't said *We* to my mother in a long time.

Mother said "Get em out." I'd never heard her say *em* before. She'd always hated slang.

"Ma'm?"

"Clear em out as soon as their lease expires and claim it again." She still looked unusually calm, almost like her best old self; but her tone was new to me.

I said "I'm not sure where I'll be living."

She waited, glanced to Darwin as if for permission and then launched a grin that took me back to the afternoon I won the first race for my eighth-grade track team and she was proud of me as I crossed the line.

It nearly poleaxed me now—the smile itself and what the woman behind it had meant in bringing me to life and keeping me alive, even when the wildness clawed her down.

Before I could think how to use such a feeling, though—with her in this place for long years to come—her eyes went blank as poker chips; and she said "Well, if you still plan to roam the Earth like some stray cur, just leave here now and don't come back again."

Coming on the heels of the grin she'd awarded me moments ago, that mowed me down. But before I could think, my legs obeyed her promptly. I stood up and said "I'll spare you then."

Mother said "I'm thankful for that at least." By then she looked farther gone from me than the planet Pluto, which is so far out that scientists—even in the year 2000—can't decide whether it's a planet or not.

All I knew as I left Edith Norfleet that crucial day was this—whoever she was in her own small skull, whoever she might have been in the strict account books of any watching God, she was still the only close kin I had. And she'd forced me away.

Where I went was straight to the motel room. Again I managed to sleep a whole night and day with no hard dreams. When I woke up and gave myself another good meal at the same old diner on the edge of town, I drove back to my room and placed the first phone call to Farren since the single time when I'd checked on her safety after her lone bus ride back to D.C. By then it was eight o'clock at night, but she was at home. I asked polite questions about her work and how she was doing. I didn't allude to our past times together, even the good ones. I didn't ask about any private life she might be having, and she volunteered nothing in that department. I told her where I was and that I'd just seen Mother. I mentioned that Mother had asked about her kindly, but I didn't really say how weird the visit was.

Fare's voice was friendly—a little cautious naturally but willing to talk along, fairly aimlessly, a good calm while.

So within ten minutes I was deep into my old longing to see her. My whole body, there in a room as safe as a hammock on a cool night in Heaven, was ringing in every socket and cell with the wish to be naked against her again, giving her all I had to repay her beauty and her natural goodness. I was on the absolute verge of asking if I could drive up there and see her tomorrow, for however little or long a time she'd grant me and at however close or distant range. But I waited ten seconds.

And then Fare said "Noble, what are you planning to do from now on?"

The word *plan* somehow struck me as new. I'd understood that I had no certain future for myself, but the idea of a plan stuck into my mind like a painless dart. And right away I gave her an answer that seemed as ready as tomorrow's sunrise. "I'm going for a nursing degree down here."

No doubt her well-heeled background was talking when she said "Can you get a big enough scholarship?"

I didn't bother to mention the fact that her own tax dollars (and her rich daddy's) would partly fund me—Uncle Sam's generous GI Bill. I just said "I'll work my way through. Don't worry." And by the time I'd got that far,

I had my plan for life. It felt right at least; and I knew I could do it, barring Acts of God. The realization had also calmed my highly keyed body and mind; and the need to beg a chance to see Farren Langston, then speed myself up the interstate, praying she'd let me worship her skin—that need was *gone,* fast as my plan had come. We talked awhile longer and finally hung up, well-wishing one another still.

Then I did what I told her. I postponed my thoughts of a drive to New Mexico. The whole Southwest had waited for me a few billion years. I doubted it would get up and go anywhere in a fit of impatience. I spent the whole next day gathering myself to *jump* into the new life I was glimpsing. I got full details on the savings account I'd started with Hesta's gift—I had purposely not checked on it for three years, and it had grown nicely—and I spent two hours on the phone finding out just what the Veterans Administration would pay me to better my mind and soul with further education (even more than I thought).

Then I went to the personnel office in the main University Hospital. It was where I'd worked, just before I left home, on Emergency duty. I got the job application forms and found out exactly what I expected—that I could start work as a nursing assistant any minute. It's one piece of work you can do anywhere and anytime—there's a universal shortage. Of course I wouldn't make a lot more than I'd made in the Army, but I could work more or less on my own schedule—the graveyard shift or whenever. Once I left there I nearly walked over to the Nursing School to get information on admissions, but something told me to start that tomorrow. I'd done enough for one day, and I suddenly felt the need not to eat another supper alone.

Unless I meant to call one of the new escort services that had turned up in the hometown yellow pages since I went to Nam, I had a very small range of partners to call—partners that I could still imagine talking to. The old track-team friends had either scattered or were unimaginable now. There were no school teachers (beyond Nita Acheson) that I still cared about, no real neighbors. Mother had scared them off long years ago.

So it came down to this—I could try to phone Jarret or Alma and Nuggett or Alma Landingham or Hesta James. Alma and Nuggett and their bleached-white baby had seemed kind enough but a little too bland for the present occasion. Alma Landingham was very likely too *warm* for me to see again now. By *warm* I mean she'd surprised me and my cock in the way that I mentioned. I don't mean that she'd given any hint whatever of seeing me as anything but a friend of her family, but I felt the danger of harming her again. Jarret had given me a work phone number, and he seemed the likeliest person to tell my new plans to, but he'd left work when I called, and neither the directory nor Information had any record of a home number for him.

So I risked calling Hesta. As you've heard, I thought I'd sworn off her for now; but who else had known me, or my whole background, as long and well as she? I've mentioned my deep-grained liking for black people. Nothing in my childhood had shaken that liking; and the thousand black men I'd known in the Army had deepened it further, give or take the odd loser. Who in America has been through more, and come up shining a lot of the time, than those strong people?—and Yes I know all about bad black folks and how we've built a jillion prisons to pen them apart.

Hesta actually let me bring a carload of take-out food, and we sat down and ate a big portion of it. She was hungrier than I'd ever seen her in her life, though she seemed even thinner than she'd been last time. I'd determined in advance to stay off hot subjects—my mother mainly—so we managed to oar ourselves through an evening that lasted three hours and was generally civil. Maybe the big glass of good white wine helped Hesta forgive me for my long host of wrongs. In any case she slowly untied some knot that had held her memories in, and she told me a good deal more than I'd known about my father and mother's life before he left us.

Hesta thought he had sufficient reason to leave when he did. She said my mother was "hell on men" because Mother's own dad was a "knee-walking" drunkard. My maternal grandfather had died before I really knew him, but Mother had always described him to me as an angel of light. I'd learned years before that anything Hesta said about any woman had to be diluted by the fact that Hesta, like the Bible itself, *knew* that women were the root of all the world's wrongs—barring plagues from God like cyclones and smallpox—and she wasn't convinced that the Hand of Woman might not be detected in some of those disasters, on a case-by-case basis. That of course had in no way prevented Hesta's regular visits to Mother and the bulldog devotion she had for her, the mixture of horror and pity she felt for Mother's sin and her present plight that was surely somehow way too hard on a person "not in her right mind." In Hesta's opinion—and Hesta didn't really have *opinions*, just utter *convictions*—they should have just gone on and sent Mother to the Chair for all the good they were doing her now in the "moron penitentiary" where she was.

Late in the evening, as Hesta grew dozy, I finally told her my recent plan. She asked no questions as I spelled out the details; and when I'd finished she didn't say a word but stood up, a little shakily, and cleared the whole table—wouldn't let me lift a dish. When she'd swept off the last crumb and sponged down the surface, she stood beside me and touched the back of my right hand which was lying on the table.

I don't think Hesta had touched me five times since my childhood, and the word "Thanks" slipped out of me in a whisper.

She removed the hand and laid it on my mouth. "Don't thank me yet, Nobie. Too early for that."

As always I accepted the order.

Then she said "I've got two houses over by the high school on Cherry Street, right nice clean houses. You want to rent one? I'll rent it to you cheap."

Hesta *owned* two houses in a good part of town? Would wonders never cease, as Mother always said? It slowly appeared that Hesta was correct and not hallucinating. She'd bought the houses on her lawyer's advice, as good investments, only six weeks ago and hadn't got around to hiring men for the painting and a few necessary repairs. As I'd had occasion to be in the past, at first I was mainly bowled over by being reminded of how much interest this poorly-paid woman had earned on her savings through her stripped-down life. Then I gathered my wits and asked enough questions to establish her meaning. Turned out one house was in good shape and ready for me or anybody else but the most demanding tenant.

As I sat there at last, in calm amazement, this old woman said "You can live there the first twelve months free, Nobie, if you paint every room. I'll pay for the paint."

I finally said "Hesta, I've thanked you so many times before, what can I say now?"

She faced me with her blankest look. That instant she might have been either the queen of ancient Egypt, awarding me a prize of hammered pure gold, or a giant mantis preparing to eat me in sizable pieces. Then she said "Well, try saying *thank you* just one more time."

I grinned and said "Thank you, grand noble lady."

Hesta said "Careful now. I'm not *Noble's* lady."

I said "*Noble* is the word I *meant*—you're a noble soul."

"I am," Hesta said. "Glad you finally recognized it."

I nodded agreement and said "How's this? I'll accept the free rent with deep thanks, lady; but I'll buy the paint."

Hesta thought it through slowly, then also nodded. "Don't go buying those cheap brands of paint. Get the best stuff they got. I want it to last."

I promised I would and so I did, and the paint held up—every wall dove gray with off-white trim—as long as I lived in Hesta's new house.

That got me through the first two years of nursing school, but two years of courses took me three years to finish. At that point I became a Registered Nurse. All through school I had to work in the same hospital, sometimes full-tilt on day and night shifts, to pay the incidental expenses that Uncle Sam's monthly checks didn't cover. He covered tuition and books, which left me with food, gas, household expenses and modest additions to my wardrobe which was, let's say, subdued but cool—bell bottoms, vests, mildly arresting belt buckles (it *was* the seventies) and occasional trips to the satisfactory massage salon that had opened right there on Grandee Street while I was abroad.

I say *satisfactory* and it always proved to be, thank God. In those three years I managed to keep my hopes from settling on any one woman, not to mention leaning on anybody the way I had on Farren. It may be hard to credit in an able-bodied hetero Army vet—age twenty-one to twenty-four in the free-love years of the early seventies—but Yes I had fairly regular dinner and movie dates with my fellow students and even an occasional recovered woman-patient who'd contact me once she'd been released; and I never once went all the way with one. Looking back I realize how cautious I was of one more failure on the sizable order of me and Anita or me and Fare. So as I had in Nam, I leaned for relief on the old reliable—my ever-ready "home entertainment center"—and in the absence of legal whorehouses (are there any in the States outside Nevada?), I availed myself two or three times a month of the friendly salon right on Grandee.

Way back up above here, I gave a full account of my first such visit, when I was seventeen, to the All Girl Staff near Charlotte, N.C.—the time I met Antoinette, the woman whose face and kindness may very well have tripped some switch in my peculiar mind and left me hoping to worship women from that day on, maybe as a way of thanking Antoinette. So again I won't add more than necessary about my later adventures in the world of "sensual massage" as it was publicly called by the time I was home, but I thought it was interesting to note the changes that had gone down since my first experience of the old-type parlors.

First, there was no Hell's Angel at the door or anywhere in sight—no man at all for that matter, not in any position but prone or supine. The person in charge was a tall woman, maybe twenty-eight years old. She had what was plainly natural black hair down below her shoulders and gently wavy (at a time when girls were *ironing* their long hair on *ironing* boards to make it as straight as railroad rails; and her face was strong in an almost American Indian way).

She also looked like she should have been a star in the country-music world of those days, when the stars were real veterans of Kentucky coal-valleys or West Virginia cabins on rocky ridges with lustful uncles and brothers all around. She always wore good-looking snug dresses, never slacks or jeans, and always in the dead-right flattering color for the way her face and body looked on any given day—almost always colors like peach and apricot and pale shades of violet. Her dark eyes told you, the minute you met her, there was no chance whatsoever you could—in your grandest dream—lay so much as your little finger on her (tacked up behind her head, with red thumbtacks, was her permit to carry a concealed pistol; and I'm fairly sure she did so).

Yet with all her goddess traits and manners, she also turned out to be one of my really helpful friends, though I never spoke a word to her anywhere outside the dim-lit salon. I saw her a time or two in the grocery store with a darling daughter, but she wouldn't meet my eyes there. She never gave me a whiff of a sense that I was weird to be in her place. I might have been there to get my dry cleaning. And she always remembered which masseuse I inclined to at any given time (her personnel understandably changed fairly often). If they told her much about who I was, once I shut the door of my cubicle and stripped for the hands of the woman in charge of my body for half an hour, she never brought it up with me (sometimes more than her hands were involved; more than times had changed in the sensual business—you could get pretty much what you could afford).

But there was one big time when I stopped to thank the imposing manager on my way out one night in the sad backwash of Christmas Day; and she said as I started out the door "Mr. Norfleet, let me pour you a beer." Not having a license, they couldn't sell beer; but nothing stopped her from giving one to any good customer. Of course I accepted and sat in the small reception room. For a few minutes she went on filling out some papers, and I figured she had nothing special to say and that I'd leave as soon as I finished the beer.

Then when only two swallows were left, she looked and smiled for maybe the first time. As you've no doubt detected, I'm no great consumer of smiles or tears; but this was one of those smiles that comes a lot nearer to breaking your heart than the average picture of a famine victim. I could tell she was honestly trying to demonstrate holiday cheer; but bless her heart, it failed on all cylinders.

I said "Ain't Christmas a whole big suburb of Hell itself?"

She said "*Amen*" and the smile underwent two seconds of change that almost looked pleased. Then she said "You been as alone as me?"

I understood that was a fairly safe observation to make in this place. But I said "Well, I don't know your life story; but since my only kin is in prison, Yes I've been alone as I ever was in Vietnam."

She said "My husband was in Vietnam."

For an instant I went cold all down my spine. *Jesus Lord, is this Nita Acheson?* With her dark hair and eyes, I suddenly believed it. But of course I was wrong. I said "Is he doing all right, back home?"

She looked down at the forms she'd been filling out. "He's in prison too," she said.

Since she hadn't asked details on my mother, I accorded her the same courtesy.

But she looked up. "Armed robbery—twenty years."

So I said "Murder—of my brother and sister. But she's hopelessly crazy. She'll die in prison."

The woman said "Pray God."

And only then did I realize I didn't know her name (she had to know mine from my credit card). I stood up and formally introduced myself by my full name.

She held out her hand. "I'm Mallory but please don't call me Mally—everybody calls me that and it sounds too young."

"Well, you're not exactly decrepit yet; but sure, I think Mallory's a beautiful name."

Mallory said "Thank you."

And with that I somehow felt freed up to ask her a question I'd just come across in a paperback life of Doctor Freud I'd read in Nam (in Nam I read every minute I wasn't on active duty or deep asleep). I said "Since we're here by ourselves for a minute, can you help me with one big question I've got?"

She said "I'll try."

So I said "Dear God, what do women *want*?"

She actually laughed—I'd never known she could. Then she thought a good while and finally said "Whoever claimed there was any such thing as *women*?"

I said "An old psychiatrist I know."

Mallory said "Next time you see him, send him in here to me—I'll set him straight on that much at least."

I told her I would.

But she wasn't finished. She lowered her voice and pointed all around us. "I employ four to five women in here on busy weekends—final-exam time, Commencement, Fourth of July—and let me tell you, I've never met any two of them yet who agree about any two major questions. So I couldn't tell you what *women* want, but I could sit here for months to come and list what each and every *woman* wants, and each one is different as feathers on a peahen. Most of my women are cracker-jack pros and never complain; but every now and then, I'll hire a girl that thinks the world owes her more than air. She won't last long under these conditions here. I estimate you can well understand that these girls are called on, as often as not, to be unofficial psychiatrists. But anyhow with the ones that come with a chip on their shoulders about life in general—if I don't fire them in very short order, I'll guarantee you this: they'll leave here to marry a customer in no time."

"A customer of yours?"

"Absolutely. I can set my watch by the fact. Let a girl complain to me for three weeks running—wanting this and that from her job and her life—and she'll be married by the end of the month to a paying client of this very *place*." It made her smile again.

"Tell me why," I said.

She already knew and told me at once. "Because every man on Earth's had a mother, and that's what *men* want."

I opened my mouth to ask her to clear up the mysteries of her claim, but another post-Christmas melancholy victim walked in off the street—a boy as young as I'd been when I first came in to such a place some years ago—so I kept my silence, finished my beer, thanked Mallory and walked on home. But even now, all these years later, I occasionally think about Mallory's statement. I've never doubted it's a serious truth you couldn't change with a hammer and chisel or acid or any kind of human firepower, but I'm still not sure I understand her meaning.

Is it just an obvious conclusion from what evolution says about the history of our kind?—men have to leave their mothers, yet most men want their mothers back ever-after all their lives (just look at who their wives are, ten years after marriage). Or did Mallory mean that men in general, with our fuel-injected drive to sow our seed in as many vaginas as the Earth affords, are also driven to shipwreck ourselves in rocky coves past the hope of rescue—and all in the dream of worshiping one or more of the bodies we've entered in pure blind biologic need? (Clear as mud, right?) In any case you can already guess it's been my story, or a huge part of it, on down through the years. And whether my story is a comedy, farce or tragedy is a decision I'll leave to you if you care enough to make it, though I'm not finished yet. I have my own suspicions of course.

What I think matters more now is saying a little about the job I worked myself into, professional nursing. I've hinted at the main things in my early life that seemed to be aiming me toward some job that was meant to help out—Tom Landingham's urging me, the visions that came to me back then and later, the year in Nam that went much better than I'd expected and surely because I was getting outside my own self-pitying skin and working on other boys' troubles, the day I'd seen Fare Langston calmly disarm a man who might have otherwise have wound up killing numerous people in a basement, my visits to Mother that reminded me how bad off so many souls are in *facilities* with resident doctors who've sworn to be healers but wind up as little more than semi-brutal traffic cops on a swift track to the morgue if not Hell.

So I gradually got my nursing degree, near my twenty-fourth birthday, and have ever after nursed in the big University hospital not six blocks from the house where I was raised. I won't say it's been the easiest job I might have chosen, even with the modest gifts I possess. On Uncle Sam's money I could almost surely have been an architect—I'm good at math, I've always loved drawing; and one of the main things I've always drawn are detailed buildings (residences mostly, low rambling houses with numerous porches, all of them screened). I could have switched tracks late in the seventies, gone to the local technical college, learned computer programming and made more money while dying of boredom. I could even—and I *thought* about it a good many nights—have taken serious physical-therapy training, then bought a good book on heavy-duty massage and published ads in the local press as an all-purpose therapist with *tolerant* hands (I've got a male friend who does just that; he hauls in the money by the ten-pound sackful and furthermore has a steady stream of personal thrills, all of them legal).

But every time I was tempted to take a fresh fork in the road, some patient would offer a moving word or send me a card once they got home or I'd watch a child roll out of the ward with a grin on its face and at least a slim chance of years more of life when all of us knew how grim the options had looked only days or weeks before. It's easy enough to think I've stayed with the nursing as some sort of recompense to my brother and sister whom I couldn't save—or didn't, if I was asleep in the house when their hearts stopped. I have no serious trouble with the thought. Who wouldn't want to find a substantial way to plug a hole in the air as big as the murder of two good children? And if, as I do, you still have a hope that my brother and sister may catch an occasional glimpse of my work from wherever they are, then so much the better.

I think this is closer to the real truth, though. What I've mainly been doing in my nursing years is calming a sizable eddy inside me or a vortex like the one at Nags Head that maybe tried to kill me. And I don't mainly mean what you might guess—the harm done to me by Mother's acts and the terrible life she had after that. No, I believe I've been treating what—for three decades—I thought was my big personal failing, fate or tragedy. For whatever reason I have more love to give certain women than any man I know (and in the Army and in three hospitals, I've heard several thousand men describe the way they love women—frankly the big majority of it is *hair-raising*, but that'll come as no surprise to women). Whatever I claim, though, no woman I've really got to know agrees with me—not once they've truly been with me a substantial stretch of time.

You've read my accounts of the time with Antoinette at the All Girl Staff in Charlotte, with Kealy in San Antonio, with Farren in Virginia, and the several women at Mallory's place in my hometown. There's very little by way of news to add to those memories. I try to love women in ways they turn out not to want—or be able to live with very long. I've claimed I've never done one iota of physical harm to a female body (or any intentional harm to a female mind or soul); and I don't think you could find a witness who would flat deny me, not the first part anyhow. But they can't take my adoring worship.

A billion times, I've wondered *why?* Tell me why I insist on offering it to them, and why do they eventually fend me off? One advantage of nursing on the night shift, as I've mostly done, is that you generally have quiet stretches of time when you can sit and read. One of my main interests, especially after Nam and the D.C. hospital, has been psychology and also true crime. The psychology probably speaks for itself. The interest in true crime may need a word of explanation. The fact is I don't have a criminal bone in my body, in spite of my background.

But many times when I've read about the great serial killers, from Jack the Ripper on to the present, I've wondered if there wasn't a trace of similarity between whatever wild engine drove them and the drive that's possessed me right along. I mean, it gave me a considerable bout of raised hair on my neck when I read how the Ripper very skillfully removed the private parts of one of his victims and draped them around the room she died in—and did it so skillfully that many detectives still think he had to be a trained surgeon.

Now the nearest thing to a surgical instrument in my entire home is a normal kitchen knife, and it's never cut more than common groceries; but there have been times—with truly magnificent women—when I've felt the powerful wish to keep their private zone, isolated from their body (and especially their *mind*) when they finally turned and left me. I mean keep it safe in a *box* nearby for my private use. And if any woman finds that too awful to credit, they better believe it when I add that there are very few straight men in the world who won't say the same if forced to confess.

The main difference between me and them is that I've *acted* on the feeling, all my adult life, in what you might call a symbolic way, a way I've never been able to change, though I've made real efforts with more than one counselor. I need a certain part of a woman in a way that's very personal to me, and the truest way to say it at this advanced point is this—my mouth deeply craves to caress their cunts. If a single bearable woman on Earth could accept my need as a central feature of a life together, maybe more than once in a day and night, I'd set her up in the house she wanted and be as good a partner as the nation can provide. And even then I'd lack the words to tell her all that her patient physical presence, her loyalty and laughter, meant to me.

An extra roadblock between me and marriage has been my stubbornness about bringing children into this world. You could easily say, and I'd agree, that my past is a powerful part of that feeling. But if it still seems strange or, as some have said, *pathetic* or *unnatural*, I might just offer the mild suggestion that a level gaze at the state of children in America today, not to mention the world, might be called for. Who else on the globe at any given moment is in deeper danger—or is more perpetually starved, shaken, beat, cut, burnt, confined to dark closets or subjected to non-stop cruelty of mind and word—than children of every age and place?

The answer of course is *nobody else*, and anyone who doubts it is criminally wrong or dumber than a sane adult should be and still be running loose. So a childless life has more and more seemed the right course for me. I'm fairly sure I'd be a good father, but I know a fair number of first-rate parents, and I've just decided to leave it to them. Furthermore, though I know they're increasingly frequent, I personally have never met a woman who would live with that decision. Maybe I could still put feelers out for a renegade nun. Meanwhile I've wondered more than once if I ought not to be the sole head of a committee that issues licenses to couples intending to have a natural child. Does the simple possession by any human couple of a penis and a uterus, joined together however briefly, qualify for the vast and very scary privilege? To be sure, I understand as well as anybody how wild such a licensing board might become, with the wrong guidelines and psycho members; but still I wonder.

In case all that makes me seem even weirder than I am, let me say a little more about my daily life in those middle years—the seventies through the nineties. Once I'd finished my nursing degree and had some hours to call my own, in the night and the day, I began to be a more normal person. One of the first things I had to learn, when I started living alone in a whole house with no roommates and slender funds, was how to cook and keep the place clean. I've always hated living in mess. I can step around dirty socks on the floor and old magazines for just so many days, and then they begin to creep into my brain and clog up the circuits I badly need for other activities; so I sank four dollars in an ancient but sturdy vacuum cleaner at the Salvation Army Store and made a vow I'd suck up the dust, swab down the bathroom and clean the kitchen stove every Sunday morning. Every Wednesday evening I'd go to the Laundromat, wash my clothes, come back, fold them neatly and stash them in order in drawers and closets. Those routines alone have kept me saner than I might have been otherwise, and I commend them to other troubled souls.

The cooking took longer, though to my surprise the first meal I cooked turned out pretty much as I hoped (I'd invited another nursing student and his wife to supper). The man was one of the funniest people I've known, but I knew the wife was some kind of deep-dyed Christian, so I figured I'd better approach the menu with caution. The first thing I did right—I went to the bookstore and bought, on the manager's recommendation, *The Joy of Cooking* by Irma Rombauer and her daughter Marion, two remarkable women who could teach a half-blind donkey to cook in under an hour (if the donkey could read and follow clear directions to the absolute letter).

I decided on something more ambitious than I should have tried—chicken cacciatore, a favorite in our Arlington house when Michael cooked, our Italian roommate from Rhode Island. And I started cooking at four P.M. on the day in question, a Saturday. My company arrived at 6 P.M., I offered them cold wine (the great American wine boom had only just reached the East coast); and to my amazement the Baptist wife accepted. Well, to make a lengthy evening brief, by the time I served the chicken at nine (with noodles on the side), the wife was peacefully asleep on my couch, the husband was barely able to speak in words of more than one syllable; but the chicken was grand beyond a doubt.

And I never looked back. Since then I've cooked for hundreds of friends—Jarret James and his wife on many occasions, the director of our whole world-famed Medical Center, the chairman of the neurosurgery department (a Venusian surgeon of staggering skills), a few dozen picnics for children in our leukemia division—and of course a fair number of women in whom I'd invested much hope. Even when they can hardly boil eggs, certain women are made extremely uneasy in the presence of a man who can navigate the kitchen. Many times I've foreseen the need to conceal my cooking skills from this or that truly first-rate woman. I'll only take us out to restaurants until I can see she knows me better, and even then I'm likely to find she'll barely be able to eat a hundred calories of some fine table I spread before her. And all that despite the uncontested fact that tasty food is one of the very few guaranteed ways to bring joy to all the human race with the rare exception of anorexics and moribund patients.

I even struggled to get permission to bring some edible food in for my mother at her facility when she gradually lost the pounds she'd gained on her anti-hallucinatory drugs and began to look drawn. I well understood the warden-doctor's reluctance to let me bring in a morsel. He patiently explained the obvious. His metal detectors could scan any dishes for knives or files, but then I might have been importing beef stew with cyanide to ease her on out, and he didn't have human tasters on his staff whom he could sacrifice if I proved to be a poisoner (he already had three of them on his wards).

That was back in the fairly early days of my being settled into home life. Sad to say, before I could get well launched on my serious studies and a harmless routine of daily chores, Mother seemed to know me less and less at every visit. In the meetings I've described above, you can tell how unpredictable she was—how she'd sometimes have me confused with my dad, how she'd sometimes lash out in ways she never showed before she was confined (not to me at least) and how she'd invariably know the way to end every visit with a sentence or even a word or two that would press in on me for days to come. Whoever she thought I was at any time, something deep inside her always knew I was Noble Norfleet, her oldest child. And she knew every button and knob in Noble's mind—the ones that could grind him to almost a halt and leave him certain he'd somehow caused all the pain that had gone down in our long past.

So I saw her less and less. It seemed not only a kindness to myself but also to her. Clearly my visits didn't give her any pleasure, and at times I could see they'd riled her up for no good reason. Once I could call myself a real nurse then, I'd phone the warden-doctor—they changed too fast—and get a report on her current status. He'd always say something more or less like "No, Mr. Norfleet, Edith doesn't ask for anyone or anything so far as we know. She seems at ease, pretty much of the time, with where she is."

The possibilities that lay concealed behind *so far as we know* and *pretty much of the time* didn't bear a great deal of thinking about. But of course I thought about them a lot, both awake and asleep. Nobody with more than a third-grade education needs to hear about my dreams of Mother, of Arch and Adelle and still my old father, far-gone as he's been for so many years. Invent them for yourselves if you care at all. Even now, my nights can still get busy with the stories my mind makes out of old rags and pieces it's unknowingly kept in storage.

There finally came a time in the early summer of 1978, almost the tenth anniversary of her confinement, when I made what I thought would be the final visit, unless she seemed to know who I was or gave the least sign of relief in my presence. I'd written ahead to the warden-doctor and asked if Darwin could possibly be the guard who brought her out, and sure enough it was Darwin who followed her into the meeting room. For the first time ever, he showed some pleasure in seeing me there. Once he'd seated Mother at the usual table, he even came forward, shook my hand and asked how "the nursing business" was treating me. I'd never told him a word about my business, and I had to assume Mother had somehow filled him in. That seemed to prove she retained some knowledge of me, and I felt more hopeful than usual at the start of any visit for a very long time.

So once I'd asked her how she was—if she was speaking at all on a particular day, she always said she was "Kicking but not high," an old expression of her mother's—I went on and told her about my new position. A few days earlier my supervisor had called me in and offered me a nice raise if I'd take on what he called "the hardest job we've got."

Without even pausing to think, Mother said "That'll be something to do with hurt children."

I told her she was right, but I didn't specify and she didn't ask.

What she did say next was a far bigger shock than I'd expected from this strange woman (she looked very different from her old self now—so lean in the face and not really older, just turning fast into somebody else). She said "Have you moved back in at home?"

I didn't remember ever saying I'd kept her house but was renting it out. Was she maybe just wandering in her mind and asking questions anybody might ask? I said "No ma'm, I've got good renters. I'm staying in a nice house that Hesta owns." It dawned on me then that Hesta might have told her where I was living, but Hesta was too lame to visit Mother now. Was she writing her letters? "Hasn't Hesta told you about her two houses?"

Mother said "I don't let Hesta come here. She gets me *down*."

I gave a short laugh and that was some kind of wrong signal.

Mother stood up, quick as a shot, and grabbed Darwin's shoulder (Darwin seemed to be dozing). "Get me out of here."

He shook himself. "Mrs. Norfleet, we're safe. Your son's come all this way to see you."

Mother said "My son is *way* out of place."

I'd stood by then but I had no idea what she meant.

As she left the room, though, she stopped and looked back. Her face had never turned hard against me in this brief visit, and now she nearly smiled. "You rescue that good house of ours, Noble. It's your birthright."

If she'd started at once to break up into soft shards of light and drift through the ceiling, I couldn't have been more deeply amazed. *Birthright* was a word she'd never said to me before that moment. I doubt anybody had ever said it in the same room with me. And I surely never thought I had such a right, least of all to that terrible house. So I packed the memory down as far as my mind could thrust it; and I drove on back to Hesta's rental house, an excellent abode.

I lived on there, did my work as best I could. That's not entirely true of course; but I was generally conscientious—sometimes better than that—and I got considerable personal returns, though very little money. I also had as much private life as I could manage (I'll say more about that below). And as it seems to do in the lives of everybody that lives past thirty, time gradually took off like a silent rocket and plunged on ahead as I ran my various thrilling routines—about as thrilling as soaking your feet after working a double shift or making yourself a Spanish omelet at two in the morning after taking the tubes out of three dead patients and calling the morgue. Anyhow the rocket got me on forward to the midst of the nineties before anything truly new rose to meet me.

At that point, for reasons known only to Fate, my old supervisor called me (as you know I told Mother) and offered me "the hardest job in the building." I knew right off exactly what he meant—the pediatric burn ward. I'll have to admit I swallowed hard. Every nurse and orderly, every food-service worker, the very last employee with a gram of human feeling knew what a hard assignment burned children were. I thanked the supervisor and, since it was time for my afternoon break, I asked if I could let him know in an hour.

He told me to take overnight.

In fairness he might well have said "Take a year," but I understood how precious time is in such departments; so I said No, I'd tell him in an hour. I knew if I waited any longer, I'd just torment myself every minute of the time—thinking through the prospect from ten billion angles.

I went outside to the small clump of pines that were all that was left of the woods that used to come up on two sides of the hospital, and there was a woman sitting at the table in a patient's bathrobe—they were gray-and-white striped seersucker. I say a *woman.* She was really a girl; turned out she was seventeen. I asked if I could sit at the same table. It was made out of concrete, maybe eight feet long.

She said "Help yourself" but didn't smile or show any interest in a small conversation.

I knew better than to ask her the nature of her hospital stay, but finally I just asked her if she could help me answer a serious question.

She took what felt like half an hour to think through the proposition. Then she said, very slowly, "I'm no expert on *anything,* chief. But sure—fire away." She'd still barely met my eyes.

So I laid out the question in the simplest terms. I'd been asked to work, day and night, with children who'd suffered third-degree burns over more than half their body surface (not to mention less dire situations). A big part of burn treatment, once you've got past the initial danger of severe infection, involves the peeling or cutting away of the dead scorched tissue. That's a process that causes the child, or whomever you're tending, terrible pain; but it's got to be done. And however braced we caregivers are to the sight of hurt flesh—blood, pus, pierced guts and stink, bones jutting through skin—there's nothing in the reach of any healer's hand that's harder to bear and smile at and be gentle to than a child's charred face. Not unless you're farther down the road to practical sainthood than I've ever been or am likely to be.

When I'd got that much out, the girl looked round to see if we were alone. Then she loosened the knot in the belt of her robe, opened her pajama shirt and peeled back a sizable bandage on her right side just below the breast. Beneath it was a jagged wound, five inches long, parallel to the ribs. It had been stitched carefully—those were still the days of stitches—but had barely started healing.

Right off, I thought she'd tried to kill herself. Women tend to use knives or pills; men use guns of course, nine times out of ten. But I said "You fall against something sharp?"

With a slow finger, she traced the puckered edges of the wound and then the purple flesh around it as if it all belonged to someone else. Then she nodded. "My dad. You could say I fell against my father."

So I went on and said something nurses are recommended not to say. "Your dad tried to cut you?"

She laughed like a well-struck silver bell. "I'd say he managed it, wouldn't you?"

I told her I agreed. And then I said "Where is he today?"

She said "Oh he'll be up here this evening with Mama and Tim"—whoever Tim was.

I guessed she was just old enough to be married. She had a little wire-thin silver-colored ring on her left hand, but I figured I wouldn't go further into her private relations. Still I couldn't resist what was only half a joke. "You want me to stand by in case your dad needs a nice hypodermic of CO_2 straight into his heart?"

Her eyes decided to consider my offer. "That would stop him in his tracks?"

I nodded and found I was no longer smiling. "Kill him dead on the floor."

She sat still long enough to think the scene through. "Well, it *is* an idea. And thank you very kindly, but I figure Tim can rassle him down if the need arises." Then she chose to laugh hard.

It kind of relieved me. I'd begun to think I was serious.

We swapped a few more laughs—she was smart and sharp, for seventeen or any age. But then she fished out a brand-new pack of unfiltered Camels, lit one as if it had just been personally delivered by God Himself to cure all problems on Earth and elsewhere and sucked down a first enormous drag.

Ever since I got home from Vietnam, I couldn't stand being near cigarette smoke; so I wished her good luck and headed on back to finish my shift. I wasn't more than halfway toward the building before I knew I'd maybe had the near-equivalent of one of my visions. I'd seen I was meant to take on the burn-ward job, and the money was a fairly small part of my choice.

I did it for four years and fourteen weeks. It went, more or less every minute of it, pretty much the way I'd laid it out to that cut girl in the hospital yard the afternoon I got the offer. My supervisor must have gambled on me having the guts and endurance for the job—I'd never squirreled out on him before, and I'd seen some decidedly grim situations involving humans of all ages who'd never volunteered for the pain they were in. People often think that duty in an emergency room is the hardest of all. I won't say ER time is easy, but frankly (and this'll be hard to hear) a fair proportion of the people you see in the ER have brought the trouble on themselves—in shoot-outs, drug overdoses, drunk wrecks and other acts of folly. No, I'll take any form of oath you're offering that the pediatric burn ward of any hospital is the main form of Hell on the entire premises.

Not that you don't help numerous children. You save the lives of kids who've come in as black all over as a sausage you'd throw to the nearest dog on July Fourth when the grill flames up. In the immensely slow process of saving them, though—as I told the cut girl—you have to subject them (for weeks, sometimes months) to forms of treatment that are indistinguishable from cruelty of the sort only practiced by Gestapo geniuses or monster parents from your worst nightmare. And even when you save them, the chances are that you finally send them back to the world with faces and bodies so gruesomely scarred as to be unlovable by all but the world's best mother or, again, a saint.

The strangest and hardest thing of all in any such ward is discovering something you may not have learned anywhere else in life unless you maybe are, or have been, a professional torturer. And I can state it, without fear of contradiction from anyone who's ever done any such duty, as an absolute law—*The more you hurt any one of your charges, the likelier they are to love you in time.* I worked with one white boy named Larry

LeGrand who had caused a can of gasoline to explode in his face. He was fourteen years old, unusually tall; and from the base of his neck on down, he had perfect skin that covered a naturally well-built body. Only his neck and face were ruined.

And oh they were ruined on a scale that the average horror movie would refuse to portray. I was on duty when they brought him in, a Saturday night; so I worked on him from the start and pretty steadily thereafter. One of the merciful peculiarities of our burn ward was that mirrors were forbidden. Whatever the children asked you about their looks, you didn't offer them the least chance to see what had happened—and what could, frankly, not ever be fixed in their whole lives to come.

But within an hour of getting to the ward, Larry craned up and outright asked me. "Sir, how do I look?"

I told him he looked like he'd make it out of here in record time.

He knew that was a put-off, yet he took it and never asked me again through the two rough months he spent on the ward. I personally peeled his face and neck more times than I could count—he wound up having no eyelids at all—and while he flinched and shuddered some, he never once screamed as so many others did, even boys his age. But the night before he was due to head home, he buzzed for me at three in the morning.

He had long since been up and walking around the ward and outdoors whenever I could go with him, so I knew he couldn't need help in the bathroom. Still I didn't foresee what he hit me with.

He was sitting upright in his bed with the small deck of color photos he had of his girlfriend. She'd never paid him a hospital visit, but he'd thumbed those pictures a thousand times and sometimes played them out on his sheet like a hand of cards. This last night he had them tight in his grip with a rubber band around them; and when I came in, he laid them carefully between his covered knees and said "Noble, you're bound to have some kind of mirror. You got to help me, son."

For some weird reason, from almost the first night I got to know him, he'd called me *son*. Maybe that's what reached me that late in the night (have you noticed how people tend to call me *son* when I least expect it?). I told him "You know a mirror won't be easy on either one of us."

And young as he was, he said "I'm sitting here waiting for the worst. Bring it on."

So I reached into my hip pocket, found my wallet, pulled out the small hand-mirror I kept for combing my hair and passed it to Larry.

He held it a long time, tilting it numerous ways to catch the light and see all there was to see of his face and neck.

Finally he leaned forward into the mirror and kissed his reflection, awful as it was, and passed the mirror back to me. Then he reached down and gave me his deck of pictures.

I of course said "What must I do with these?"

And he laughed for the first time in those four walls. "Oh, thumbtack em up all round your bedroom and greet her every morning. She's sweet to look at."

Being who I was, especially now standing there by him, I thought I understood. Turned out I did. I said "Many thanks. I'll do just that."

Then he asked me to leave him.

No patient had ever done that before, not in all my memory in whatever ward nor on any battlefield. I went in the Men's room down the way, locked myself in and let sobs wrack up through my ribs for the first real time in many long years.

That happened on almost the fourth anniversary of my going to work in the burn ward. Up till then I'd thought I was doing all right. I knew I was keeping my hours without fail and doing my duties and some extra to spare. Hesta had died some years before and left me the house I'd been living in since returning to town. By then I'd saved a nest-egg of money, and I'd recently started fixing the place up—adding a room for some modest gym equipment (I'm no exercise addict but I did need the workouts and couldn't run now with any regularity because of my varying work schedules), painting the gray walls a lighter color, installing a new roof and new venetian blinds.

The blinds were likely a middle-aged man's hopeful gesture toward my new love life. For too long I'd got by with some flimsy curtains Hesta gave me; so now that I was upgrading the place, I figured I might have a thing or two to hide—nothing criminal of course, unless you think fornicators still ought to be flogged in the marketplace. In the love and fornication department, you can imagine that the years had gone by fairly much as the past had gone, though time's silent rocket seemed to move a lot slower when it came to love and women.

As usual I'd meet a woman whose mind and body attracted me and who seemed to find me bearable to look at and be around on at least a casual basis. We'd see some movies, eat some good food, maybe take a road trip to an interesting place like Monticello up in Virginia or Biltmore near Asheville or the Outer Banks or even Charleston. She'd generally seem to enjoy the difference between weird me and most men she'd known. She'd almost always be younger than me, sometimes by as much as ten years. Then eventually I'd begin my characteristic *bearing down* in our sexual connections. In its plain emotional and physical details, it remained very much the same old hope that still has never felt strange to me but has pretty much turned out to be the same mistake that just won't die in my peculiar mind. If the woman had lasted longer than six weeks or so in my company, the bearing down might intrigue her for a while. Then she'd either gradually, or *fast,* decide to vanish.

By the time my hopes of female companionship were fading faster and faster on me, I'd got down to the late 1970s; and I was staring the oncoming age of thirty dead in the eye. It brought me, as it does with a lot of American men, a kind of premature mental menopause. A lot of women are still busy with their children at thirty, but an equal lot of men seem to have the spare hours to pause and notice that the road is taking its first very steep downward plunge. Just as I was spending a fair amount of time wondering if solitary life would prove to be my fate, the great porno boom hit America broadside. Throughout the nation, except for a few counties in Alabama and the Dakotas maybe, for the first time you could go to a movie theater in your hometown and see reasonably attractive women and rodentlike men enthusiastically engaged in acts you'd dreamed of watching since you were, say, eleven (if you were a boy anyhow).

For a year or so, I dived face-downward into the boom. There was a porno drive-in theater a couple of miles out in the country, and I often went there late on a good many nights when I didn't have to work and had no female company. Even in the dark you could see that the other cars contained mostly single men like me, upright glumly behind their steering wheels and bathed in the tinted glow off the bodies of women involved in amazing feats involving their once-secret parts. The other main audience component was young couples, which I could never quite figure out. When I was their age, I wouldn't have needed any such stimulus. Maybe these young men were just trying to educate both themselves and their girls for future joy or were hoping to get their partners warmed up for later in the night.

When the drive-in was bulldozed down in the eighties for an upscale shopping mall, I bought my first videocassette player; and I spent the first few weeks renting all the films I'd loved, or regretted missing, in my childhood. Soon enough I came to the sad conclusion that I'd been wrong about so many of them, and then I switched to watching what I'd silently vowed not to give in to—home porn. And yes I enjoyed it mightily for months. A decade had gone by in the porn business, and a good many of the eighties movies featured even better-looking performers than you'd seen before. The women didn't all look like potential survivors of gravely abused childhoods; and the men didn't all look like swarthy veterans of careers in pimping and drug-pushing.

My own favorite, and apparently in this I was a typical American male, was lesbian porn. There, for some reason, you were likely to see better-looking women still, and best of all you didn't have to contend with some other guy groaning away between you and your target. But after a year of maybe two such bouts per week, I confessed to myself that the practice was driving me deeper and deeper into a dim tunnel of loneliness which was hardly where I needed to be. So I didn't entirely swear off again; but through the eighties and nineties, porn has played a slim part in my home entertainment hours (and for what it's worth, I've never shared any such viewing with another human being). It's consoling at times to be reminded that nothing you've desired is remotely as weird as what any number of people will do on the screen for ready cash, and it's also fun—in short doses—to see the occasional beauty caught up in genuine ecstasy or a first-class imitation.

* * *

Which brings me on to the turn of the century, the dreaded millennium that proved so tame in the nation and the world, despite dire predictions, but that may well have ruined or made my life. I'd got to the year 2000 anyhow when young Larry LeGrand with the melted face gave me the deck of pictures of his ninth-grade girlfriend, I was six weeks into loving a woman who was nearly my age, and I was near fifty. She'd recently come to work in the hospital, interviewing the endless line of people who came in with no medical insurance, no money to speak of but either a serious illness of their own or some family member's, most often a child or an aged parent with diminished mental assets. Her name was Kinloch Britten. Her first name was a Scottish family name, pronounced *Kinlaw.*

She'd moved to town from deep in the Sandhills of southeast North Carolina where the Scots are still thick as ticks on the ground from the seventeen-hundreds when they flocked over here after Bonnie Prince Charlie got defeated in battle by the English crown. Kinloch's move was caused by divorce, one of the usual titanic Scots divorces. *Godzilla Meets Frankenstein* is child's play by comparison. Her husband, a lawyer, had won sole custody of their only child—a seven-year-old girl—and I never did have the nerve to ask Kinloch the story of that, though it had to have been a permanent hurt.

Some of that hurtful mystery may have stood behind her taking to me so plainly from the time we met at a coffee station in a hallway when I was nursing Larry. Can't you generally tell when some other person comes to life in your presence? I can *absolutely* know when I light up as somebody else enters space near me, and I noticed Kinloch's eyes growing deeper the second time I saw her—again in that hallway. I'd reached the age where lit-up eyes were a rarity for me, so I could feel the whole notion of her steal up my legs and through my loins and upper body every time thereafter when I happened to see her (I love the word *loins* and would like to bring it back).

Still I tried to resist the mutual attraction since I was involved, way over my head, in the restoration work on my house, not to mention my mental involvement in all young Larry's troubles. But after maybe two weeks, I asked her to dinner; and I cooked it myself. I'd established, as you did by now in my state-university town, that she had no major dietary restrictions. I can truthfully say I like every food I've ever tasted except calf's liver; and I ate monsters in Vietnam that every other known American had run from in terror, like their notorious fermented fish sauce that they make by setting kegs of fish out in the broiling sun for days on end till a dark brown paste oozes through the keg slats, and then they scrape it off for their rice. I thought it was swell. Anyhow Kinloch's only taboo was okra, which made life simpler. I cooked her my chicken stuffed with country ham and cheese, wild rice and Mother's cold buttermilk pie.

It proved a real hit, so Kinloch and I were off and running—*loping* may be a better word. In another ten days I began to think, very much to myself, that I was in more Heaven than I'd been in for maybe twenty years; and Kinloch seemed a lot lighter on her pins, a lot less melancholy in the eyes. Even her natural chestnut hair didn't look like someone had run it through a mangle the previous night. Neither of us went off at crazy angles, though. We weren't buying each other chocolates and flowers several times a week or mailing scented greeting cards every hour or two. But I thought I was more at home in her company than I'd ever been in my previous life (and you know what a tough word *home*'s been for me).

Once we'd gotten truly intimate in gradual fashion, she touched my chin as I lay beside her one Sunday afternoon, lifted my head very slightly and said "Noble Norfleet, without a doubt you're the first man I've actually *seen* and I thank you."

Understandably, I think, I asked what she meant.

She thought about it and wondered if she could postpone her answer till she really knew.

I said "Sure" but I don't recall she ever told me.

The silence wasn't really her fault either. Or even mine, I still believe.

The trouble in a nutshell was that, fourteen weeks after my fourth anniversary in the pediatric burn ward—after Larry surrendered his girlfriend's pictures while Kinloch and I seemed to be progressing beyond his view—I broke again. Nothing could have surprised me more, at the time it happened anyhow. I thought I was getting on better than usual—a remodeled house, an elegant lady who seemed prepared to take everything I had to give and a job that (beyond a shadow of doubt) was more than worth doing—yet down I came like the best sandcastle, with flags and cannon, in a child's worst dream.

The first sign of the trouble was that I was walking home from work one morning at six; and as I passed my old grammar-school playground, another rough sob cut up through my chest and throat. At first it felt like some kind of blunder, like a big fist of bad food or gas that had to escape; and I had the kind of scare I had sometimes as a child at the school—that I'd shit my pants or piss down my leg or vomit on some other kid's foot. So I speeded up to get to my house and my own bathroom that had new tile on the walls and a new commode lid.

But that was no help. By the time I was inside the door and had locked it behind me, I was sobbing the way I never could afford to, even as a boy. I shucked my pants and sat on the toilet and waited a long time. And then I prayed, something I'd hardly done three times since Vietnam. No answer of course. And no other help came. Even the sound of a garbage truck on the street outside might have told me the world was still out there and had a job for me, occasional stores where the clerks could swear I paid my bills. There was even a woman named Kinloch Britten two miles away who'd be beside me in under half an hour from the instant I called her, ready to give me all she possessed.

I didn't call her that morning—she was at work. I stripped and tried to get a little sleep, but the dreams were tougher than I could stand, so I got up and painted the last of the kitchen ceiling and cleaned out the pantry's truly archeological deposits of ancient cans and bottles and boxes of supplies that I'd been given or had laid by in my weaker moments of half-suspecting a return of Noah's flood or a nuclear winter. I even found jars of apple butter that my own mother had managed to cook long decades ago and seal against time—Hesta had saved them. They were neatly labeled and dated in her hand, the summer of 1967, when Arch and Adelle were still up and running. Arch was in camp in the Smoky Mountains and Adelle was in Bible school down the street, making paperdolls of the major women in Jesus' life (I think she invented some; the gospels name so few). I didn't open one but the apple butter looked safe in the jars, old as it was. In any case I put it in with the overflow I meant to take to the Salvation

Army Store. If it killed a few souls, well, they couldn't claim they didn't die warned—I left on the labels with the clear old date.

I got through all that in fairly calm shape, but I didn't walk out for my usual lunch at the downtown drugstore. They still made—all these decades later—the world's best pimento cheese sandwiches, lightly toasted and far more soothing than any more recent pharmaceutical drug. I pictured a sandwich in my mind, and it did seem almost alluring enough to draw me outside; but then I figured I'd better stay in and test myself, behind walls in private, for a few more hours before committing to a regular graveyard shift in the ward. I painted some more and then, by midafternoon, I felt tired enough to fling myself down and sleep like a drowned man. Not a single dream, bad or good. But I scared myself when I finally woke up—the clock said nine-thirty and the windows were dark. I'd damned nearly overslept and raced to clean up and dress for my shift. I didn't even have time to phone Kinloch. I'd do it during break (she was from that last generation of women who'd never phone a man, even if the planet was splitting apart beneath her feet).

But I never made it to my late-night break. When I reached the ward, we'd just admitted a girl whose father had set her on fire with dry-cleaning fluid (he was a professional cleaner) as a way to punish his mother-in-law who was keeping the child in the midst of a bitter child-custody dispute. The child's name was Connie. She was eight years old, and I'll spare you any serious description of how she looked when I got to Intensive Care in my protective gear—gear to protect her from outside infection (a cap that entirely covered my head, a nose-and-mouth mask and long rubber gloves). Of course I'd read her name on her chart. Years ago I'd learned how important it is with almost every patient to call him or her by name from the first time you see them. So I walked up to this child's side and said "Hey Connie, I'm your new friend Noble."

What was left of her lips said "I'm glad you told me. You sound a lot more like Darth Vader." I couldn't guarantee she was smiling, not with what remained of a face. Her eyes were clearly working though.

I'd had a deep voice from the age of fourteen, but I'd never guessed it might scare a child. I raised my pitch a little and said "Isn't Darth Vader Luke Skywalker's dad?"

Connie shook her head No; but then she said "He's Luke's *father,* Noble." She turned her head to look at a toy mobile I'd made out of disinfected seashells and strung up just a week before, and then she died without another word. Her heart simply gave out. We'd known she was in shock and badly dehydrated, but this was surely something *I'd* caused. I thought that the instant we knew she was gone.

Again I managed to get through the final hours of my shift, and I made the walk home without further incident, but then I did the old thing I hadn't done for a very long time. I slept through a whole day and through the next night, a steady nightmare (it was the start of my three-day weekend). I'd unplugged the phone before I lay down, so nobody bothered me with noise or knocks. And when I went into the second day of sleep—no drugs at all—I revived just long enough to know I was in deep trouble. Up till then I'd peed in a urinal I kept under the bed. It was full up now, my bladder was bursting, so I rolled back onto my belly, soaked the bed like any month-old baby and slept again. Sometime later, still in the bed, I also shat myself.

When I finally woke I'd ruined the whole mattress; but I lay on in my stench long enough to think "Son, you're in dire straits here." I'd nursed on the psychiatric ward long enough to know how clinical depression can swoop in on you, with no warning at all, as sudden as a hundred-pound hawk from the sky and bowl you right *down*—no warning at all and no trace of mercy. But like the average man my age, I denied any such thing had happened to me.

I rolled up the mattress and tied rope around it—nothing to do but haul it to the dump. I showered for a long time, then tried to eat breakfast but could only swallow coffee. I thought about phoning Kinloch but didn't. I couldn't imagine enough words to say. While I sat in the kitchen, though, I thought of my mother and how I hadn't seen her for six months. She'd long since ceased to recognize me, though she'd lost her mean edge. But I knew I ought to visit every few months at least to let her know an outside world was in existence, and one human being had taken the pains to pay her a visit. Was this new weird spell a symptom of some buried guilt about my failure to see an old lady who'd destroyed my family and claimed not to know me now? My mind said *Yes.*

I still had the warden-doctor's home phone number. By then it was Sunday afternoon.

But he answered anyhow. He'd known for years that I was a nurse; so he cut me some slack and said that Yes, I could come on short notice. He'd tell the guard to "welcome" me. He truly said *welcome*.

Just that one word had my eyes stinging with the threat of tears the whole way there; but maybe I was short on tears by then, in light of the weeping in recent days. Anyhow when I checked in the rearview mirror as I got to the facility, I recognized myself more or less—the old reliable man and boy who'd got himself to early middle age upright and moving at least, for this late afternoon anyhow, in the parking lot of a madhouse prison containing his mother.

Edith Norfleet was seventy years old when she came out to see me with no apparent hesitation. Since my last visit they'd spruced up the visitor's room—some lighter paint, new chairs (but still metal chairs with no upholstery, nowhere to hide any contraband imports)—and most of the guards on duty seemed new. Old Darwin had long since retired or vanished, and since then I could never anticipate who'd turn up with Mother in tow. One new thing over the past twenty years was that gradually women had taken over most of the guard jobs, women as heavyset as TV wrestlers which of course they needed to be should an inmate turn violent on them.

In the six months since I'd seen her last, Mother's appearance had hardly changed. She'd put on a few pounds, but losing and gaining weight had been normal with all the combinations of drugs they'd poured through her veins in nearly four decades. Her hair had long since gone snow white, and her eyes had got even bigger than ever (old people's eyes either shut right down as their lids slowly droop, or they yawn wider still while they grow more amazed with all they're still asked to watch in the world). When they saw me this time, there seemed to be an instant of—not so much recognition as slight relief—and her first words seemed to confirm it. She said "I wondered when they'd finally catch you."

That seemed a promising tack anyhow; so I said "They did, didn't they? Well, maybe that's just as well."

She considered that carefully and even turned, as if for advice, to the guard who was glaring at everything around us. No response from the guard, so Mother took it upon herself to look almost pleasant and say "I think the public will be pleased."

That did more than anything in recent days to lift my spirits, and I said "Yes ma'm, I've had a good many nice cards to that effect."

She said "I haven't had a greeting card since I came to this place. I was told they're forbidden. They must have made an exception for you."

I was trapped in my unwise little joke. But before I could think of a way to back out, the guard said "Edith, no exceptions are made."

Mother plainly didn't believe the claim. She told the woman "He's been an exception all his life."

What was I meant to do with that? Could it mean she had some sense of who I was? Had her mind swum around to knowing me again—or knowing me today for however many seconds? Or was she just speaking from the whole dim floating country of psychotropic drugs that I'd glimpsed so often in the psychiatric wards or in my own hours on marijuana in my Army years? In any case what did she mean by *exception*? Or did she mean a damned thing I could use in my present state?

Anyhow I heard myself say more than I'd ever risked in this weird room. "Mother, I'm in terrible shape here now."

Mother looked to the guard again. Her nametag said *Deena*.

There was such a long silence that I thought Deena was either about to pull her stun gun in case I charged or she'd lurch to her feet and hurl me out.

I'd never pushed the facility's limits this far, so maybe there was some kind of undeclared rule that forbade a visitor from making confessions to the inmates. But hell, Edith Norfleet was the only mother I'd ever had—or would ever get at this point—so why not try for a little home comfort?

And Mother said "Please remind me of your name, son."

Had she said the word *son* in all these prison years? At the moment I couldn't recall but I said "Nobie."

She shook her head. "Noble."

I said "All right" and gave a slight laugh.

And then the years seemed to pour off her body like pond water off a good retriever's broad back when she scrambles ashore. In five or six seconds of silence between us, she seemed to rush back to the days before my brother Arch was born and she and I were alone in the house, the start of a family. She looked to Deena again and said "There's no legal betting in this nation, right?"

Deena said "That depends."

There'd been no legal betting in our state anyhow for long decades, so where on Earth could she be headed now? I took hold of myself—*Don't forget this old woman's crazy, Noble. This is really not your mother.*

Then she looked back to me and slowly said "I'd place a small bet on you lasting awhile. You used to be tough as a hightop shoe." She leaned down and touched her own bare ankle (she was wearing plastic flip-flops I'd brought her last year).

In my childhood she still kept a pair of her grandfather's shoes in a closet at home. They were handsome black leather, still well cared for, with tops that reached way up the ankles and with shiny brass grommets and strong leather laces; and whenever I'd ask to put them on and clomp through the house, playing grown-man, she'd let me but always warn me to be gentle. She'd say she meant to have them bronzed as souvenirs of "a better day." She never got around to the bronzing, and I'd discarded the shoes when I cleared out the old house.

But here and now, at her facility, I thought I understood what she meant by *hightop shoe.* And I managed to thank her, say goodbye, get myself outside and into the car before I lost hold of myself again. A lot worse lay ahead for me, and I didn't see my mother again for a long time, but more than once in all that time her final sentence would occasionally surface in my sick mind and feel for an instant like a raft or a floating timber that might yet save me, and maybe those instants were part of the help that brought me back. At least they didn't hurt; and though I couldn't bear the thought of seeing her again while I was so low, I remember that every time I said her sentence in my mind, I'd also say *Let her live till I'm well.* I had no special plan for seeing her later or doing anything about her, but just the fact of hoping she'd live seemed to prove I half-believed in her small bet on me.

* * *

It was Kinloch Britten, from the human race anyhow, who did the most to bring me out of the slow nightmare. The diagnosis could have been delivered in a New York minute by anybody who's read a magazine in the past twenty years—clinical depression, no doubt about it, with all guns blazing. Or the *silence* machine, the death ray that's beamed from the center of your skull all through your body without a moment's pause. You can literally feel your cells dying off one by one—and sometimes in masses the size of your fist—till you finally fall to your knees in the kitchen, or next to the toilet when you've been heaving for half an hour and nothing's come up but strings of blood, and you beg that the next cell to die will be the last one you can't live without: that you'll finally die on the spot and stop hurting.

Why I never took up my father's straight razor, that lived in my medicine cabinet like a copperhead, I'll likely never know. Why I took out my grandfather's shotgun, that hadn't been shot in sixty years, and polished it carefully without any serious thought of quick death, I still can't guess (though I have my suspicions and I hope you will when you know the whole story). And why I never actually took my depression to anybody's clinic for even a single overnight stay is also a mystery—except that maybe, as a registered nurse, I felt invincible in the quiet unassuming way of the people who run the world at the nuts-and-bolts level, the men and women who get up at dawn or midnight and take their miserable backs and lungs and migraine-skulls to some windowless room for an eight-hour shift that's urgent to the life of their village or city or just to a field of tomatoes or corn on the outskirts of Akron.

After seeing Mother, I managed to work for three more days, doing strictly paperwork at the ward desk—I begged for that and got it—but then I knew I could take sick leave. I had several thousand sick days coming to me (not really of course but I'd been a loyal worker). I'd contacted Kinloch and told her frankly that I was in trouble. She came to the house when she got off work on my first sick-leave afternoon. I was up and dressed at the kitchen table, but I hadn't eaten solid food in a week—oh a few tablespoons of peanut butter straight out of the jar and six or eight rancid almonds left over from a tipsy cake I'd made at Christmas but nothing any other creature would have touched.

Kinloch didn't ask whether I could eat a meal, or what it should be. She went to the pantry, found a box of rice and in under an hour had baked a dish of rice and cheddar cheese and canned mushrooms that was bland as baby food. She wet a dishtowel and came over silently and wiped my face and hands. Then she sat in the nearest chair at the table; and still not asking for my wishes in the matter, she fed me a sizable portion of the dish with a big soup spoon. I never said No but by then I couldn't, or wouldn't, speak at all.

Looking back, I guess the main question is *Why?* First, why did I so suddenly get so sick? And second, why did Kinloch—who hadn't known me all that long and had no elaborate reasons for loyalty—stick by so closely and help me so much when I was, at times, not much more than a broken dog on a foul wet mat? As a person with considerable medical training and experience, I knew of course that unpredictable biochemical storms inside a particular skull are as real as Texas tornadoes and nearly as harmful to all concerned. But since so very little is known about why they swoop into any one household or what precisely will end them, I'm still at a loss for an explanation.

To be sure, when I could manage to think at all—as opposed to staring out the window with all the thoughts or dreams that a loaf of supermarket bread might have—I'd try to dig back through my years and find a cause. I haven't had all that busy a life; and if you watch your local daily news, you'll understand that even a life including a mother who killed your harmless brother and sister—followed by your own stint in a war so evil it makes other wars feel like church picnics—even such a life is fairly normal in America now. Oddly it never occurred to me to wonder if I was going down Mother's sad path to permanent madness. I knew that what I had was a gruesome bout of deep depression—in theory—that would sooner or later end itself, no matter what kind of therapy I got.

The trick of course is getting *through* the minutes till you recover. Maybe some genius can picture it, but I could never imagine being well again. I'd lie on my back and study the ceiling and try to picture myself returning to work on a different ward (I'd had the sense to ask my new supervisor for a transfer before I caved in and she said Yes). I'd try to see myself cooking suppers for a few friends and Kinloch, making satisfactory love to that fine woman, taking care of my house, going to movies and visiting Mother more often than I had. I'd even long for the kinds of visions I had as a boy, and I almost prayed for a true one to save me.

But nothing sustained or helpful would come; and as for prayer, I'd been so bad about God all my life that I didn't have the nerve to call on Him now. I've never much doubted He's out there somewhere, in some form that no human being can imagine, though whether He's watching me at any point or giving a damn if I thrive or fail, I've no idea—probably not. Can the Lord of the Outer Ten Billion Galaxies mind if I steal from a gumball machine or strangle my old landlady's pet poodle or, for that matter, copulate with a menstruating woman (which the Hebrew scriptures specify as a crime)? I admit I'm to blame for giving no serious time to thinking about God's life or His interest in the world. I sometimes hope I'll get around to reading and cogitating those problems; but nothing I've ever heard about in the churches of my town, or any church that's advertised from here to Asia, makes me have the least suspicion that I'll find God in any one of those buildings or learn the least hint of His wishes or traits in any such well-dressed huddle of humans, liberally seasoned as all of them are with spiritual quacks, mirror-gazers, frauds and Pharisees—the worst of whom are often in the pulpit.

Anyhow I lived. And after ten weeks Kinloch finally convinced me to take an evening walk with her. I hadn't been out of the house, no farther than to pick up the daily paper off the stoop, in all that time. My doctor, who was a good old friend, had literally paid me a few house visits to assure himself I was sane and progressing. I'd also had a few telephone talks with my fellow nurses, though I'm the kind of person who can't stand to talk about his physical troubles with anybody. It just brings me down even further to hear their cheery voices saying "Noble, how are you?" If you tell them the truth—and if they're women, bless em—they'll be at the door in under twenty minutes with a first-aid kit and fresh gingerbread; and if you lie and say you're improving, they'll say "Noble, *really*? I know it's hell. You can trust me with the truth."

So that dry evening in early summer we waited for dusk, and then Kinloch and I walked three blocks before I had to take her by the elbow and stop her. She thought I was weak from inactivity, and so I was but the weakness was fear. I'd cooped myself up so long that the open sky above me and the weird recesses of space on all sides had me partially panicked. I told her that.

And she said "All right. How about this? Let's walk another two blocks. That'll make five. Then we'll have taken a ten-block walk, a block for each week you've been indoors."

I was scared but also eager to stretch my endurance. Still Kinloch's logic seemed truly corny. On the spot I decided to go with her, though; and when we'd accomplished the two extra blocks, I felt a little calmer. When Kinloch stopped and said "Shall we head back?" I said "Let's duck through this short alley. I know a better way." By then the alley was almost dark and Kinloch looked uncertain, but I took her hand finally and guided her on. It was the first real incentive I'd taken in so long, and it felt like a butt shot of pure adrenaline.

In another five minutes we were at Mother's house. While I'd been at my worst, the rental agent had called and said she couldn't find a tenant—did I have any candidates? I told her I'd call her back, but I still hadn't done so. In the darkness now it looked so much like the house I'd lived in for eighteen years that I almost bolted, but Kinloch's nearness and my gratitude to her somehow held me in place on the pavement. So I told her where we were and what the house meant. She'd never known till now. In fact she'd never been down this street. Before I'd talked for even a minute, I could see she was edgy and wanted to move ahead; so I took her lead, though with some reluctance that, at the time, I didn't understand.

Back at home I finally made a kind of love to Kinloch for the first time in months. I don't mean to say I was suddenly pounding on all my cylinders on such short notice, but I managed to show her some long-delayed attention. And I think it pleased her. I surely meant it as a partial reward. And it helped me sleep. Then at three o'clock in the morning, I woke up beside Kinloch in my bed and began to see what my whole body had truly intended when I lagged behind her as she pulled me away from Mother's old house. *I had to live there.* I was wide awake at that hour anyhow—through all these weeks I'd slept little more than two or three hours—so I got up quietly and sat in the kitchen, trying to write down what I felt in some detail. Kinloch looked in on me fairly soon. I sent her back to sleep (it was Saturday anyhow and she needed the rest). By the time she was rested, I had a few sentences—it was really just a list—that seemed to explain the thing I must do.

The steady pain I'd hunkered through these past ten weeks was the direct outcome of all the wrong that lay behind me, the wrong I'd caused or had anyhow stood by and watched take place in rooms or spaces where I was a watcher. My list included the following items—my father who'd left us when I was eight, my killing mother and the ways I'd failed her lately in prison, hungry Tom Landingham that I couldn't save, everything I'd done and witnessed in Nam, the women I'd harmed or disappointed, the ways I'd cheated myself of more life. Once I'd admitted that much to myself, what was left to do but find a way to repair or recompense as much of that damage in whatever ways remained open to me at my present age?

It had come over me, starting from the moment I stopped at Mother's house a few hours before, that I was meant to move back into that place—by myself or with Kinloch Britten—and live the rest of my life on the spot where all the wrong started and to do what I could from there on outward. I wouldn't change my job. I'd do what I knew and had done for years. That would be scope enough. So when Kinloch came back in at daybreak, wearing my bathrobe, I poured her coffee and read her the list. Then I asked her to move into Mother's house with me and help me onward, a stronger man than I'd been here lately or ever before. When I said the words to her, I felt a happiness pour up in me like nothing I'd felt since the day I'd driven back home from Maryland in Mother's old Buick and thought I was shown my useful future in a vision from God or just from my own hopeful mind.

First, Kinloch listened as carefully as I'd ever been listened to. I well understood, with every word, how crazy I might sound. I even told her I wondered if what I had to do was demented—truly insane. She gave no opinion, though she stayed there beside me, entirely calm, with no signs of fleeing. At last when I got up and started assembling the first real breakfast I'd made in months, she said "Noble, where did you get this plan?"

I actually laughed. It sounded as if she thought I'd sent off for it in the mail. But when she looked rejected, I slowly told her from how deep in me this present plan had come or from how far away. I still don't know where that much certainty could have come from, and Kinloch didn't ask me. But after that I cooked French toast and bacon (she'd kept my refrigerator stocked with essentials all through my illness, though I seldom ate a morsel); and the two of us ate it like a normal small family or the core of one.

When she'd finished her last strip of bacon, she faced me and gave her finest smile (and I've still not seen the match to her smile). Then she said "I wish to God I could join you, but I know I can't."

I'd reached the point where I could say "Tell me why not please."

And she'd got to where she could finally mention a subject I'd never had the gall to raise. She said "I'm struggling with a demon of my own. I couldn't stand to share it with you or risk sharing yours."

So I pushed her forward. "Name the demon please." I thought I knew the answer.

She said "I'm trying to comprehend why my vicious husband has got sole custody of my only child and why I'm up here, a hundred miles away, doing nothing whatever to further her life."

I'd known her daughter was in the Sandhills and had never visited Kinloch here, but I'd carefully never asked her why. Still we were in one of those dangerous slots that sometimes slice themselves open in time—you can ask any question and get a true answer. I said "Why's he got exclusive rights to her?"

I'll grant this to Kinloch. She met my eyes squarely, though her face seemed paralyzed for a long instant in an agonized flinch; and she said "I beat her unmercifully once."

Kinloch had been as gentle with me as the mother of your dreams. "You want to say why?"

She nodded. "I'm a drunk."

If she'd said she sold cocaine on the grounds of my old grade-school, she couldn't have surprised me more. I'd noticed she never drank wine with our meals. In the South, though, that's no big shock from anybody. So I said "But you've quit?"

She said "I'm in a twelve-step program. My meetings are at dawn in the hospital basement. I guess I never told you."

I said "Kinloch, no problem at all. Haven't I just told you how I truly mean to pay my own and my family's debts? Come on with me. We can try to help each other."

She said it very quietly, as if she still thought I might shatter before her like glass. "Noble, I can't even *enter* that house, much less live there."

And she stuck to her guns. I spent another two weeks, mostly at the house Hesta left me, gradually moving back into the world—short trips to the grocery store and the car wash, a try at the movies (that didn't go well) and even a meal at a small quiet café. Kinloch was with me for a lot of the time, and you'd have thought she might have changed her mind. She showed real interest in my main concern, which was getting things ready for the move to Mother's. Through my illness I'd mostly lived on worker's compensation. But as I planned the big move, I went into my considerable savings and brought in an old track-team friend—now an honest contractor—to rebuild the house.

I sketched the plans myself; and though my friend warned me I could make it unsaleable, I went with my instinct. I kept the walls of my own room intact at one far end and enlarged the bath which would still have four walls and a door, but I tore out the other walls and opened those five small rooms—with all they'd harbored—into one bright space (the windows were old-style and went all the way down to the floor). We'd paint it all white like one of those whitewashed houses on an island in a picture of Greece, the ones that look like something the Earth thrust up while the human race was asleep. I planned to live there the rest of my life; and if anybody else couldn't stand that openness, then I'd beg their pardon and live alone. And if whoever I left the house to at my death couldn't find a buyer, they'd be welcome to tear it down, board by board.

Up till two days before I moved in, Kinloch and I went on spending a lot of time together. I got stronger and stronger in my abilities to make real love or what I've always called love and still do, and Kinloch seemed to have no trouble in accepting the pleasure I needed to give and the ways I gave it. I certainly intended it for her and me both but also still as my form of honor to something I'd long since given up hoping to see or comprehend (though maybe I'd seen it in bits and pieces at Kitty Hawk so long ago). I'd silently test myself at calmer times to check if I truly wanted her with me for however much longer she'd commit to. The answer was Yes I did, and I told her so more than once. But what I didn't say was that, just from living to the age of fifty and with the hard truths I'd learned in this long ditch of depression, I understood now that I possessed one piece of scary knowledge—I could live alone the rest of my life if I had to. Completely alone except for jokes with friends and patients at work—all of course until I either collapsed from a heart attack or stroke or died in the hospital of something overwhelming or in an old-age home, no longer even knowing my name or what I'd seen in so many long years. I suspect that once a person gains that knowledge, other watchful souls can read it in his eyes; and a lot of them run for cover at that point.

Anyhow two nights before the weekend when I'd scheduled my move (I'd rented a truck and Jarret James had volunteered to help me move the stuff), it was Kinloch's turn to cook supper. She got off work a little early and produced, in her always spotless and effortless-looking way, a wonderful meal consisting of cold cucumber soup, amazing crab cakes and a lemon pie of the perfect kind I hadn't run across since my early childhood when Mother's mother, Tall Agnes Redden, would make them any night as if the feat were merely the finals in solo figure-skating at the height of the Olympics. Since my recovery it was the first dish I'd tried that truly *struck*, a word I remember my father using for perfect food at the height of its flavor. Bite by bite, from meringue to filling to buttery crust, it went down deep and fully reminded me of what a miracle fine cooking is and how it doesn't just come from the sky, ready-made for consumption but is mostly the handiwork of one careful woman who intends to reward a particular person or a small group of kinsmen.

Kinloch and I hadn't mentioned her drinking since the time she first broached it, and I'd noted with interest that she brought in a bottle of wine for tonight and had drunk two swallows to toast us at the start. So once we finished the meal and the dishes, drying each one and wrapping them in old newspaper for the move, I suggested we take a short walk before dark. I figured we'd do that to settle our meal and then return and sleep together since that was now possible in excellent ways.

But Kinloch said "Noble, I'd better not."

I asked if she was feeling all right. I didn't ask if the wine had upset her or caused her some guilt. As I understood the twelve-step programs for alcoholism, they didn't believe you could give yourself one single drop of drink, but who on Earth was I to judge?

She said "I've decided this is when I should leave." And she actually stood up—but calmly, with a smile and no sign of panic.

I asked if she could do me the favor of sitting down long enough to tell me what was happening.

She said "I think you know." When I must have shown the puzzlement and hurt that I still felt, from her refusal to join me, she sat back on the near-edge of her chair. "Noble, I could stay here another day and help you pack those dishes and glasses; but I know one thing after my divorce—the cleanest possible cut is the kindest to all concerned. It'll hurt me badly. It may hurt you—it's selfish to say so, but I hope it will. I love you that much. But nothing I've thought, all through these nights, has changed my mind. I can't go with you into that dead house."

Of course I knew she might be right. I'd cleared out, after all, three decades ago; and here I was, moving back in at what I hoped was the end of a bad breakdown of my own. How ill-advised was that? And could I stand it? Well, I had no answers to any such questions; but the whole of my life I'd lived from minute to minute on visions. And while I'd had no visions of the kind I had in my boyhood for many long years, I was more than half sure that I was still being *led*.

So I went on. And in one long weekend, hot as Hell, Jarret and I moved all I owned—which was not a great deal (I've never been a pack rat)—back into that house. On the Sunday night, he and I took the first two showers in the bright new john; and then we went out, bought a carload of take-out food, collected his fine wife Irene and all came back to the house for supper. I hadn't swallowed a crumb under that roof since I was eighteen—and I was still twenty pounds underweight from my bad weeks—but the two of us men ate like water buffaloes, and Irene herself ate more than a little. By the time they left at ten P.M., I was flat worn out. I went to my boyhood room and slept a dreamless nine-hour night which was maybe a ten-year record for me.

Then I got myself back to work. At first they kindly kept me writing up charts in several ward offices and stocking the various medication closets in every one of my old ward specialties except the burn ward. Then after a month of satisfactory work, the supervisor called me in; and we talked about my future. Being a woman, she tended toward thoughtfulness about such matters; and I knew I could tell her my own line of thinking without any risk of misunderstanding. I told her my age. I said I hoped to nurse right on till I toppled over or could no longer count the candles on my birthday cake.

She nodded after every sentence I said, and when I was finished with my own thoughts, she said "All right then, pick your next ward. It's yours unless it's got a full component," which both she and I knew was a highly unlikely conflict in any known earthly hospital.

Honest to God, I'd planned everything but the answer to her question. Yet I didn't ask her for extra time to consider. I opened my mouth and said "The old people." A few years ago we'd opened a geriatric ward for people with problems related to age, not mainly those with memory loss (I can still barely make myself say "senile dementia") but things like brittle-bone fractures and the losses from strokes. I'd only wandered over there a few times to deliver a message or see a friend, but the idea to go there had come to me suddenly, and again I went with it.

Once my supervisor heard it, she took about a nanosecond to say "Fantastic, Noble."

That's not a word I use to mean *fine*, but still I was glad that she welcomed my choice. I didn't know why she seemed so relieved. Turned out, to my surprise, that very few others of the younger nurses wished to work with old-timers—too depressing, they felt, to work with people so "limited in outlook," as one young male nurse whispered to me. To the contrary—fast—I discovered I much enjoyed their wisecracks, occasional wisdom and even those moments when their minds slipped a cog and produced some funny or weirdly impressive slant on life. The first day I worked there, a lady who'd had her third stroke and was dragging both feet in a standup walker looked me up and down and said "Lad, your penis is longer than your leg." Then she broke out laughing and slogged on past me. I was fully dressed, my zipper was zipped, and if I may say so—and I say it in sorrow—her observation was a little inaccurate, but I took it as an excellent entry to the ward, and enough of my work there in subsequent years has been so rewarding as to keep me content in the sense that I matter a small amount at least.

And it's lasted me right up till now. A whole lot remains to be seen, as you'll notice; but during the early time I was there in the family house, I know I got stronger in my mind and body. I took up running again and did it four days a week, with no excuses for anything but flu (which I never had). I kept up a steady line of work on the house. Like any old place it required fairly constant attention to its woes—small cracks and leaks, a termite invasion in one of the floor sills, a colony of black bats in the attic that had the flesh all but crawling *off* my neck when I went up there with a rented smoke machine to shoo them out and plug up their way in, nothing worse than that.

I tried to keep myself in repair in the usual ways. Kinloch stayed on at her hospital job, and we'd have coffee or lunch there occasionally. I even took her out to a restaurant for dinner now and then, always explaining clearly in advance that I had no intention of taking her to my place. They were always nice dinners—good talk about work and movies we'd seen, cases we'd observed from our various angles and world events. By then we were able to laugh a lot at the same kinds of things (our backgrounds were so similar), but we never spoke of my private life nor certainly hers, above all her drinking.

Then finally, after all our time together, she all but bowled me over by asking me to come to dinner at her apartment; her daughter was in town. I'd never met the daughter, never heard her mentioned in recent years, so I dressed up for the evening, and I think it went well. The girl was eleven now, and you'd have never guessed—unless you're a psychic—that she and her mother had gone through rough times. Calm and friendly as the dinner was, though, it somehow concluded something between Kinloch and me. I thought I could see she'd turned a big bend in her bent life; and while I knew the daughter wouldn't stay up here with her, I felt the visit was a natural time for me to bow out of the whole situation. Kinloch and I would still pass pleasantly in the hospital and exchange friendly questions about small things, but I never asked her out again; and of course she'd never have invited me to anything on her own if a meteorite the size of a ballpark was scheduled to hit the Earth at midnight and wipe us all out, including the mosquitoes.

I saw other women, mostly younger than me but nobody anywhere near the statutory-rape zone. As I aged I began to realize that the women whose looks and manner reached toward me were women of almost the exact age of the first woman I'd ever loved. That of course was Anita, my beautiful teacher, who as you may remember was twenty-six years old when she and I had whatever we had. I even think I've noticed how many other men—of my generation anyhow, married or not—are most attracted to women (or other men) the age of the first person they ever loved or had good sex with.

The women I spent any serious time with, once I changed houses, were people I met outside the hospital. I'd decided that relations connected with my workplace were just too likely to prove a hindrance to all concerned, maybe because we share too much heartache from the people we nurse. It may have been because of the age gap—I was often nearly old enough to be their fathers—and surely it had a lot to do with the long-term fallout from the sexual revolution of the recent past. Whatever the causes, the younger women generally found it a good deal easier to take and enjoy my personal brand of physical attention. That brand had never been able to stop being various forms of admiration on the order of worship of the sexual zones of their bodies—the sight and taste, the odor, the hair, the willingness to give. It's adoration anyhow, entirely sincere. The women I've known since, say, 1990 have been—as a rule—much more at ease with their bodies, much more ready to extend their range and glide along the edge of their limits (if they have any limits, this side of real harm).

Each woman I cared about decided, though, that I was too old for them to count on a life with. Most all of them either politely drifted away on their own or let me sincerely thank them for their patience and do my own slow disappearance. Of course I'm sure you could interview them all and find opinions very different from mine. A few of them even left phone messages or sent me letters declaring their anger or regret they'd known me or wishing I'd never meet another woman I could disappoint so thoroughly. I never tried to answer such complaints, and in my mind I seldom disputed them.

For several years I even kept my favorite complaint tacked up on the kitchen pantry door where I could see it often and remind myself to weigh its meaning. The woman in question, whose name was Marla, had gone to the local greeting-card store, found the tackiest get-well card ever printed (it was even perfumed with an odor guaranteed to kill any convalescent at the first deep sniff) and sent it to me with no further comment than just the words "*Deep sympathy, sir, in your advanced condition,* (signed) *Spoiled love from Marla.*" By the time it arrived, such revelations had pretty much ceased to cause real pain. I'd all but granted, in my realistic hours, that a single life was my Tragic Destiny.

I capitalize both words to indicate how the idea actually hurt and amused me at the same time. If my health hadn't been so robust since the breakdown ended, I very well might have reflected more often on what would happen when old age crept in and left me helpless to live alone. But in the scarce moments when such a thought surfaced, I'd think *Oh well, let's hope I've earned the best reward a human can get—a quiet death in your own bed while you're deep asleep.* It happens all the time, to occasional saints and countless villains. The neighbors notice the newspapers piling up at your door. The one that has a key calls the Law or your most trusted friend, they knock, then walk in and find you over-ripe but at actual peace.

Meanwhile I was making a gradual retreat to the land so many older men inhabit, a version of boyhood. You surely don't have the same unpredictable testosterone floods to power you through your solitary bouts; and as I've mentioned, pornography pretty much played out with me years ago. One of the very last things I want now is winding up alone in my dark house with the TV flickering across my right hand still holding my cock and clots of my trusty but useless cum cooling on my belly (which is flat at least). No, except for very occasional porn what I rerun, when I need good pictures, are long excerpts from my big file of excellent internal homemovies—actual memories I've carefully harbored from my best loves. So I'm by no means dead below the waist, but I do get sporadic glimpses of how good life might be if I reach the age when all that sleepless machinery *sleeps*, and I can throw its huge load of voltage down other wires. Hell, I might wind up as an ancient Anglo virtuoso on the Spanish guitar or (far more likely) a peaceful home-grower of truly fine corn and heirloom tomatoes.

You may be surprised to hear that through these years I've still had trusted normal law-abiding friends but truly I have. I've mentioned that Jarret helped me move. He and his wife Irene have stayed close to me. I haven't noted that they joined Kinloch in helping me through the worst of my illness, but they did in all the ways they could think of. The main way was bringing me cooked food steadily. Jarret brought it every other day and stocked the refrigerator, and that was despite all Kinloch's provisions. I never had the heart to say I seldom ate a bite but would creep out at night and leave it by the back steps for Kingdom, my neighbor's new black bitch mastiff. Then on Sundays both Jarret and Irene would drop by after church with flowers that they'd either grown or picked somewhere (they were prone to take long drives in the country). Again I'd let the flowers sit where I wouldn't see them more than once a day, and Kinloch would throw them out when they faded. Once I was back in Mother's house, though, I could go back to cooking my own food for them; and they'd come over to reminisce or just watch TV. Jarret thought it was a fine idea I'd returned to what he always called "my place." I've neglected to mention the fact that, when I decided to leave the house Hesta gave me, I deeded it to Jarret and Irene. By every kind of right, it was theirs—and their daughter's when they died. And I liked the simplified feeling it gave me.

I even got a dog of my own. I hadn't had one since well before Easter 1968—they complicated Mother's mind too much—but since I thought I was on my own till Judgment Day now, I searched a good while and couldn't find what I'd always wanted. So I put an ad in several nearby country papers—"*Wanted. Laid-back short-haired yellow dog with straight legs that stand him about two feet tall at the shoulder. No barking or biting.*" I'd hardly noticed putting a masculine pronoun in my specifications. It wasn't that important. But after a few days, I got a collect telephone call from deep in the country. I hadn't had such a call since Mother's earliest days in prison, and I knew it wasn't her, but I accepted the charges anyhow.

You wouldn't have guessed such a voice and accent could have survived the decades of TV-homogenized America. It seemed to be a woman. The pitch was way up past the hearing range of radar, and even no aged veteran of "Grand Ol' Opry" could have easily deciphered the entire message, yet it seemed to say the person had a dog that had "served its time but was a girl," would soon "need a home bad," so "come on and get her." Directions followed that well might have stumped any Spanish conquistador breathless for gold, but two days later I managed to track the voice to its hideout up a dirt track that would surely have gutted any automobile more recent than mine (mine is twelve years old and sits high off the ground).

Turned out the voice belonged to a man; but the dog was indeed a girl, yes, and answered the door. When I knocked, a very long wait ensued. Then I called out loudly "I'm here to get your dog," and at once something inside jumped hard against the door and it sprang open. Inside the house was pitch dark, but standing just in sight was the yellow dog I'd long waited for—the precise right dog. All my mind could think to say, and I spoke it out loud, was "Why on Earth have I waited so long?"

The dog didn't bark or come forward to me. She was standing up and she waited in place with a lot more dignity than most human beings.

The same voice that had left me the message spoke from somewhere in the dark. "Her name is Tarn."

I laughed and said "Is that short for *Tarnation*?"

The voice said "No, it's an old English word meaning *mountain lake with no significant tributaries*."

I still haven't figured the significance of that, but I stood on the narrow porch and waited for the voice to materialize. When it didn't after a minute or so, I hunkered down and extended both my palms to Tarn.

She considered them judiciously and finally came forward, accepting my strokes but never once licking or nuzzling my hands or face.

Eventually, when I'd all but given up and was close to fitting Tarn up with the collar and leash I'd brought, I heard shuffling footsteps.

Tarn calmly turned to face them, no sign of fear.

I read that as a good sign. She hadn't been abused.

And the voice turned out to belong to a man far older than anyone I'd seen in the geriatric ward, Vietnam or elsewhere. He wore a pair of high-water black pants that almost came up under his armpits. His shirt was the ancient collarless kind, and his feet were bare and thin as bone rakes.

He told me he was "somewhere near a hundred," and I'm sure he was right. All he'd say otherwise was "Take her quick and get out of here." All his other responses were tiny nods or shakes of his head. He wanted no money, no—none whatever. She'd had all her shots but had never been spayed.

Only when I put the collar on Tarn and saw nothing else to do but leave, I at last said "Thank you, sir. She's my dream dog."

That made him speak again. He said "You get two last things straight. My name's Trader Gates. Remind her of that when it comes to your mind. Then—" Here he took a long pause to get it right. "Then believe this is true because it is—she's no dog or human or anybody's pet. I *suspect* she's a certified angel of light. Don't have the papers to prove it, though, since she just walked in here one day maybe three years ago." Mr. Gates never took one last look down at her nor she at him. He turned, faster than I thought he could manage, and shuffled away.

He'd left the door standing open, so I gave a weak tug on Tarn's collar, and she followed me out. I waited five seconds, then shut the door; and Tarn and I headed off on a trip that's not finished yet, thank whatever gods.

Don't cringe. I'm not about to subject you, or me, to another dog rhapsody; but I'll say this much to be true to the story. Tarn went into Mother's house with clear reluctance. She took three weeks to decide she trusted me enough to sleep in my room on the cushion I'd bought her (at first she slept very near the door she'd first come in through). Then once she chose to inspect the new cushion and deign to sleep on it, I slowly realized she was also occupying a small narrow vertical—but truly authentic—slice of the hole near the core of my chest. My longing for a female human partner died off a little more, and any temptations I'd felt to wander in my spare time all but totally vanished in a few weeks. I well understood that Tarn was a dog and that dogs are really not human beings (they are sometimes finer), but before she'd been in the house two months, I understood I loved her. And I hadn't loved a living thing that loved me back, not since I was seventeen. Maybe this was a start.

It may seem like I abandoned Mother after my hard time. It's true I didn't go to see her in the awful weeks. First of all—and I've seen it in far more patients than me—when you're that low down, you don't spend two minutes a day thinking of anything but your own pain and how to end it. In the brief instants when the sight of Mother flashed through my mind, I'd think that a visit from low-down me would be more harmful to her own stability than any sign of care from Noble. Of course I might have phoned the warden, told him the condition I was in and asked him to do whatever he thought best with the news—either to tell Edith Norfleet or, if she should by any chance ask about me, just find some harmless excuse for my absence. Maybe I'd been sent on some sort of nursing mission that wouldn't involve me in serious bodily danger (Vietnam had clearly worried her a good deal). But that was the kind of gesture I never thought of making. In depression all you think of is *self self self.*

Then as I began to surface, I had my chances with Kinloch to think about; then the work on the old house and the move and then, hard as it may be to credit, I had Tarn on hand to occupy a lot of my time and my feelings. I also put a fair amount of thought into rebuilding myself, as soon as possible, into a reliable and responsive nurse. When I was so nearly desperate, one of the things that haunted me most was realizing how rotten I'd been so much of the time in my career—being lazy and working strictly "by the book" so much of the time (just going through the motions I'd learned down the years, wearing pasted-on grins for my patients who are mostly trapped on a graph that runs from mild unease to outright terror).

Some of those haunted guilt feelings were overdone; but like a lot of people who do the same job year after year, I'd begun to slide and coast way too often. And of course that last sentence is a shameful one to write.

I ought not to take the least gram of comfort from comparing my slackness to a lot of other people's. Anyhow I set out to haul myself back to my early days, to think about what good nursing truly meant and required and how I was going to do better at it on a daily basis, starting now.

If you've ever spent serious time in a big hospital, you've probably found that the medical doctors are chilly as dawn in February, though some of them wear their own lacquered smiles. If anybody ever challenges them about their coldness, and I've heard occasional fearless senior nurses do it, the doctors will invariably say that they have to keep their distance; or they'll be swamped by the sadness of what they see and have to deal with daily. Well, I've known a few callous nurses—*very* few and most of them were white males—but in general nurses, however long they've served, somehow don't feel the need to grow such calluses on their minds and souls; and nurses spend a hell of a lot more time seeing and *touching* misery, including more blood and shit than you might imagine, than any medical doctor does unless he's in a war zone.

Anyhow as I surfaced I began to try harder to give my patients more than I'd previously managed, even the ones in the burn ward. Maybe it was easier to do in my new job with the old-timers. Of course there are bastards and whiners among them, but a good proportion of them are surprisingly cheerful and ready to accept their pain and whatever shackles time has clamped on them. They're just glad to wake up one extra morning and to make it through the day till sundown. The women are more susceptible to sadness than the men, mostly because their children always fail them—absolutely always. The men in general don't give a damn.

I had one fellow who was eighty-six and whispered to me that he'd "screwed" his wife every day of their marriage (*screwed* was his word, not one I favor)—sixty-four years of marriage—till she died in her sleep three months ago.

When I said "You ever think you loved her to death?" he almost fell off his wheelchair laughing.

At last he got his breath again and managed to say, at normal volume, "Son, it was her idea *way* more often than mine. But honest to Christ, I believe I never failed her. She was kind enough not to complain anyhow."

I said "I'm sure you miss her badly."

He nodded solemnly, then thought, then beckoned me to bend down next to his face, then whispered "I thank God minute by minute that she's gone."

I wasn't quite shocked but I was fairly curious, and I whispered "Why's that?"

"Lord God!" he said, "Now I've got the strength of a matched team of tigers." And he rolled away from me with considerable vigor, though I've seen stronger tigers. He died that evening, right after his supper. The orderly told me he ate every morsel, "even his Jell-O," which he'd mostly refused.

And I've personally witnessed, by accident, one actual geriatric copulation (funny as it looked, it seemed satisfactory to both the parties); and of course I've seen more than several episodes of fumbling in each other's pajamas. Such moments have done a steady lot to help me. But though I was seeing a great many oldsters, I didn't entirely forget my own mother. It had been four months since my last visit. Since I'd never written her letters or cards, there'd been none of that and of course no phone calls ever to her; but I still hadn't phoned the warden-doctor, and he hadn't phoned me. Not that any one of the wardens had initiated any contact in all the years.

You may recall that I'd gone to see her at the very start of my breakdown and that she'd given the faintest clue, the first in years, that she might recognize me. She'd even "bet" I was going to last. Well, whether she'd known me—or had the least sense of my prognosis—she'd turned out right apparently. So every time I thought about her now, I could smell that scorched-hair stench I always smell when I know I've failed somebody; and I told myself I needed to get my butt in gear, my butt and my *mind*, and go to see her. I kept telling myself I was strong enough by now.

Try to guess then how hard it struck me—on all my blind and criminal sides—when I got home from work one late fall evening, collected the mail, threw it on the kitchen table, did a few small chores and only got around to checking the letters as I ate my supper past nine o'clock. (It was left-over chili and rice with some pitiful water-logged frozen broccoli—

why does any live human ever buy frozen vegetables, I ask myself every time I eat a mouthful: why not eat wet newspaper instead?) Like most of my fellow countrymen now, I chuck out more than half of my mail entirely unopened—it's so clearly junk mail—but the return address of a single envelope caught my attention like a cold bear trap.

It came from the state mental prison where Mother had been for thirty-two years. I studied it carefully before even thinking of cutting it open. The first strange thing was, it had been sent to this present address—Mother's old house. Who at the hospital knew I was here? Or had this old address somehow been on file all these years? My second thought was *This means Mother's dead.* Surely they'd have phoned, though, if that was the case. But then, when I moved, I unlisted my number. Nurses sometimes get unwelcome calls from former patients. I'd halfway meant to get unlisted a long time ago, and now I felt old enough to do it. Anyhow I needed a pause before truly knowing what this envelope held; so I went to the bathroom, peed, washed my face and hands and even brushed my teeth before coming back. I took my best paring knife from the drawer and very carefully slit the letter open. Nothing I'd done in all my years as a medical professional had ever been accomplished more precisely or in so much truly frightened hope.

I'll just quote the beginning—

> *Dear Noble R. Norfleet or Next of Kin: Edith R. Norfleet will be released from the William Upton State Hospital on Saturday, December 9, at 9 A.M. Please contact the number indicated above and confirm your intention of collecting her at that hour and location or make other arrangements. Releases will not be postponed for more than twenty-four hours.*

It was signed by a new director, Dr. Jonathan Daniel. Two things surprised me—that he'd lasted this long in a punishing job and that the man who'd seemed unusually patient and kind, the one time I met him, had now sent out such a shocking and incomprehensible letter.

Was he truly prepared to let a demented woman who'd killed two human beings just wander off free from the gate of his grim facility if Mr.

Norfleet—or his next of kin (who the hell was that?)—failed to show up to get her? Well, the subway gratings of all big cities and the broken-glass alleys and undersides of bridges in smaller towns are populated with just such abandoned women and men; so maybe he was truly prepared for just that possible failure by Noble R. Norfleet.

I needed to talk to this man right away, and I had his phone number at work, but it was nearly ten P.M. Since I had an unlisted home number, you could bet your ass the brand-new psychiatrist in charge of a state asylum for the criminally-inclined had a home in deep hiding; so I'd have to wait till morning at least. And that meant a miserable sleepless night. By the time I'd lathered my face and arms in slimy self-pity, I managed to think how many thousand sleepless nights my mother had had in three decades—in a cell surrounded by a good deal of howling, some of it her own—and I threw up my chili and rice in the sink, a modest payment on the shame I felt.

Even so, I slept maybe half an hour throughout the night. What I harped on, strangely, for the first few hours was a list of the things I'd missed in life, the things I'd wanted and never got. The hardest to think of, in dark or daylight, is the fact that to this point nobody I've loved has ever said that they love me back and want me near them as long as they live; but then I'm aware that a huge lot of humans stand with me in the lack. I'd also never spent enough quiet time in trying to situate my thoughts around the life of God. If my early visions, and some of the acts that had fallen my way in later years, really did come down on me as guidance from a higher power, then wasn't I meant to have given more thought than I had to Him, Her, It or Them? I hadn't, though. I'd put one foot in front of the other, or stepped or fallen back on my ass, with no more care than the average well-intentioned dog. And here I'd put five decades behind me, which was surely way over half the span of time I'd get.

All the rest of my thinking, through that long night, in the old dark room of my boyhood came down to this—*What can I do with this old woman when she comes back to me?* In the first hour or so, I'd slogged past my first wild hopes that I could somehow sidestep her entirely—either fail to meet her at the gate or take her straight to the cheapest nursing home I could find and enroll her before the manager discovered her record. To the best of my knowledge, she'd shown no trace of violence since Easter weekend thirty-two years ago. There might be a chance then of finding a place that, with help from her State and Federal insurance, I could maybe afford.

In my work on the geriatric ward, I'd learned a lot about the nursing homes in my vicinity. As usual everywhere, they ranged from facilities that barely offered the amenities of a slave ship to the ones with country-club assets. I'd need to start that search right away—and pray depression didn't bowl me back over in the first few days. Men with wives or grown children might have had some partners in any such crisis, but this was going to be *me me me* all the way from here till the day Edith Norfleet died—or me. And not a damned thing could be done before morning. At three A.M. I actually picked up the telephone to call Kinloch and beg for her help—in her job she dealt with such apparent deadends every day—but I hung up, shamed again and lay on my back, thinking the meanest word on Earth which is surely *Wait wait wait*.

The single best thing you can say about doctors is, they come to work early; and the rest of us medical personnel tend to follow suit. So I was up and dressed by dawn myself, and promptly at eight I phoned the asylum and reached Dr. Daniel. It took thirty seconds to tell him who I was, a registered nurse and the son and only kin of Edith R. Norfleet. I also mentioned that previous directors had been kind to me. When that much registered on him—and he said "How may I help you?"—I'm afraid I fired a harder salvo than I'd planned (though it was true enough to my feelings). I said "Sir, please tell me what the hell this means"; and I read him the letter.

After I paused, right away he said "Mr. Norfleet, that letter's gone out in error over my signature."

I said "I sure hope so. I guess I'm a little more careful with *my* signature. Please explain what you mean."

He went on, remarkably calmly, to say that—given the budget cuts they'd been hit with by the state legislature—they were forced to release as many patients as possible soon. Apparently his staff had concluded my mother was more than ready for release.

I said "But you're saying you disagree with them?"

Dr. Daniel took his longest wait yet. "How recently have you seen your mother, Mr. Norfleet?"

At first I heard it as a reprimand, and I said "Your staff wants to set this woman scot-free just to punish her son who's himself been clinically depressed for nearly four months?"

Another long wait, then Dr. Daniel said "Noble, I'm sorry to hear that news—and it *is* news to me—No, that's not what we want. But are you saying you couldn't receive her if she should be released?"

Doctors, if you'll notice, mostly call themselves *Doctor*. They'll walk in a room where a scared patient's waiting; and instead of saying "Hey, I'm Jonathan Daniel," they'll almost invariably say "I'm Doctor Daniel"—just in case the white coat isn't magic-badge enough. So since Dr. Daniel had just called me *Noble*, I took him up on it. I said "No, Jonathan, I'll collect my mother and try to find a place that can care for her needs. But I'd sure have appreciated some notification a lot less brutal than this vicious letter. Hell, a seventy-one-year-old killer of two, with a forty-odd-year-long history of dementia, might well not be ready to reenter public life. Not to mention whether the public's ready to welcome her back."

That finally seemed to grab his full attention—I thought I'd even heard him flinch when I said his first name. He said "Give me forty-eight hours please. I'll review her file and talk with my staff. Then I'll let you know what the best plan is."

I gave my own flinch at his claim that he'd know what the "best plan" was within two days, but I downed my objection and said "Shall I phone you day after tomorrow at this same time?"

He said he'd "await" me. And then he said "Noble, this was cruel, I see. Such a letter will never leave this office again, not without my personal approval—you've got my word for what it's worth."

I could hear that his use of the one word *cruel* had left him open to a suit from me or, at the least, a powerful complaint through state-agency channels; and I knew he was smart enough to know he'd yielded me that chance. So I said "Dr. Daniel, your word's worth a good deal—thank you, sir. I'll await our next talk."

He said "Please call me Jonathan hereafter."

I said "I will." And then I laughed.

He said "Something funny?"

I said "Oh no, I was only thinking, if I call you *Jonathan*, then I should be *David*."

He said "My dead brother's name was David. He died before I was born."

I told him I was sorry to hear that.

And he said "Thanks. It completely changed my life."

I didn't ask why or how—I thought I knew—but I said "I'm entirely sure it did, Jon."

For the next two days, of course I spent every waking moment and most of the night harping on the whole new problem—*What would I do if she came out now?* I talked to some of my more alert patients about the nursing homes they knew of. I talked with my supervisor about her sense of whether my mother's criminal record would be a reason for homes to refuse her (she thought it well might, and I had to agree). And I had lunch with Kinloch, who expressed her sympathy but plainly retreated a whole mile farther from any real friendship as I sat there before her, with a chicken salad sandwich in my helpless-feeling hands. Just before we finished I tried to bring her a little way back by saying "Tell me what you'd do if you were in my boat."

Kinloch actually took the time to fold her paper napkin as carefully as linen, then she got to her feet. She finally said "I'm not in it, thank God; and if I were I'd dive out and swim for the South Pole, fast."

What could I do but laugh?

And she had the grace to join me. Or is *grace* the word?

Anyhow before she turned and left, Kinloch seemed to want to come back slightly. She lowered her voice and said "I've passed my six-month anniversary without a single drink."

I figured she could use a word of praise, so I told her I was glad for her and her family.

She smiled but she said "I lack a family, Noble. Just like you."

It may not have been intended to harm me, but I took it hard.

* * *

Most of that night I stayed awake and worked on my new computer at home, tracking down mainly sad information on the local status of nursing homes and trying to answer my legal question. Could they refuse to take an elderly woman with a criminal history but a calm thirty years since her last sign of trouble? There didn't seem to be any law on the subject, so I had to assume it would strictly be up to the facility in question. And how would they find out if I didn't tell them—and if Mother didn't (how proud was she of her history now, or did she even recall it)?

By four A.M. I'd pretty much decided there was little point in me pounding on with my investigations till I talked to Dr. Daniel again and had the reality back in my hands. I managed to sleep a couple of hours and even managed a fairly normal day at work. It was not till the end of my shift that something struck me. One of our patients was a very courtly black man from deep in the mountains, which you almost never hear of (much less meet). He'd had his second stroke but could still get around upright in a walker. I'd enjoyed his good humor ever since he came to us. He always had some keen remark on the day's news—he claimed he was the only black Republican he knew of—so as I left the ward that evening, I saw him in the hall and paused in the hope of a little mental uplift. I said "Mr. Jamison, tell me something funny." I didn't say why.

He looked me up and down as if he'd never seen me. Then at last he seemed to half-recognize me, and he said "The funniest thing I know is, I'm crazy as any serial killer, and not one goddamned person on Earth knows it's true but me. If you ever lay any one of your lily-white hands on me, you're one dead motherfucker—don't forget it for a *second*."

I laughed but I also figured I should do at least a light check on his condition. I asked him his name, a standard procedure.

He said "You called me Jamison just now. You're wronger than bird shit. I'm Boaz Bartley and nobody knows it."

There was truly no question that his legal name was Jamison. It was on his chart, and the son that had visited him several times was also named Jamison. On the spot I wondered if the old man might just have had a third stroke, even a slight one. His speech was normal, though; and his face showed no signs of sudden paralysis, so I chose to consider that my workday was over.

And Mr. Jamison took another four or five steps in his walker, then turned back and faced me and laughed a little dry laugh that I couldn't read.

Still I headed home and again I had a fairly normal evening. I'd purposely not arranged any meeting with friends or planned any phone calls. I wanted to be quiet and think of the various things Dr. Daniel might say in the morning and what my responses might, or ought to, be. I'd already concluded that he wasn't very likely to change the decision stated in the letter. In long years of nursing in a hospital yoked to a state university, I'd learned what "budget constraints" could do to the best or most merciful or laziest programs. No ice-cold axe could come down more suddenly. Edith Norfleet was coming out of her confinement, and my life was bound for drastic change. Considering my life—and what you know about it to this point is as honest as I could make it—a drastic turn might well be the main thing called for.

But every time I tried to think what I'd do if imminent release was the verdict, my mind would throw me back to the moment when old Mr. Jamison had his peculiar spell this afternoon. No matter what relations you think you've built with a senior citizen, they can turn on you faster than a mongoose on a cobra. And Mr. Jamison had nothing on his record remotely like my mother's long trail. In an hour of trying to think my way past him, and all he implied, I got nowhere except scared badly; so for once I decided not to sit down alone and try to tough it out.

I didn't call ahead. I just got in my car and drove straight over to Jarret and Irene's house, the one I'd passed on to them from Hesta. They were there, gave me a generous serving of crème caramel that Jarret had made from *The Alice B. Toklas Cook Book* (he'd switched his loyalties from Britain to France and was now a really good French cook). A big dish of blackberry cobbler might have gone even further toward taking me back to mine and Jarret's more peaceful days, but the Toklas crème had a smooth simple taste that calmed me down however briefly.

We stayed on at their broad kitchen table, and I laid out the recent developments slowly. I tried not to show my own fears yet or to indicate my desperate hope that there'd be more than one way for me to leap, come tomorrow morning on the phone with Dr. Daniel.

When I got to the end of my description, Jarret spoke up at once, though quietly and in the natural tones of our childhood when we'd be tired at the end of a long match of horseshoes or damming the creek. "Noble, who's going to keep her while you do your job?"

Being a natural man, I guess, I looked to Irene.

Fine as her head was, she was not facing me. She looked to Jarret and nodded clearly to what he'd just said.

What he'd said then was truly not a question. It hadn't crossed either one of their minds that I would think of any other course than taking my mother, whoever she was now, into my home until she died. Still I decided to answer Jarret as if he'd asked me something genuine. I said "I honest to God don't know. If she comes, I'll just have to start looking fast for some good person."

Irene said "Try me."

That set me free to get a night's sleep at least. Of course I dreamed like a hobbled runner pursued in the dark, but when my eyes came open two minutes before the alarm, I knew I'd rested. I surely won't claim I felt no dread, but I ate a real breakfast and called the doctor at eight precisely. This time it was he who picked up directly and on the second ring—not even a secretary's voice to ease me into his presence. I could tell right off he was waiting for me and was fully prepared.

What he basically said was, he'd studied Mother's file and pretty much agreed with the staff's opinion. So long as she kept to her present medications, she was ready to leave and "likely had been for over a year." There was no cause whatever to think she presented any risk of harm to "the public or herself." He didn't explain what made her so ready, and he took one of his characteristic waits at that point.

So I said "Jonathan, am I the public?"

He asked me to "clarify."

I said "Am I included in the *public*? You recall she killed all my family but me the last time she was free."

"Noble, I'm deeply aware of that. This elderly woman who has the same name is no danger to you."

I said "I'm not the world's strongest psyche, if you really want to know."

Dr. Daniel said "You've mentioned clinical depression in your past. Is there any other problem I should know about now?"

I took a considerable pause of my own. "Well, I'm Edith Norfleet's son. I guess you could say that's an ongoing problem." I'd never said that to another soul before. I'm not sure I'd ever felt it so strongly.

He said "I think I can sympathize with that, so let me finish what I'm meaning to tell you. I'm prepared to certify to the state that Ms. Norfleet should stay on with us for at least another year. Would that be helpful?"

That bowled me over flat—the last thing I expected—and right off it felt like I'd been offered another year on death row before the next round of my appeal to the courts. If I could have reached down the telephone line and seized both Jonathan Daniel's hands, I'd have all but kissed them, but then I heard Irene James's voice again saying "Try me." So I said "Dr. Daniel, is there any chance I could drive up and talk to you, and then maybe we could bring my mother to your office and talk together?"

He said "Absolutely" with a lot more vigor than I'd heard from him up till now, so we made an appointment.

Two days later I got a friend to take my shift, and for the first time I met Dr. Daniel. He'd given me detailed directions for finding him—a different entrance from the way to see Mother—so I half-expected one of those airless wall-to-wall carpeted executive suites. But if anything, his quarters were even more stripped-down than the visitor's room where I'd always been before. That alone made me feel more hopeful, and my first sight of Daniel also helped. Maybe it's because my father was tall; but I always tend to expect that men with any kind of power will be well over six feet tall (which very seldom proves to be the case—in the Army, for instance, the taller an officer is, the dumber).

Jonathan Daniel was maybe five ten, and he couldn't have been more than forty years old. He had a good face—Jewish enough to look a little like King David at the start of what he expected to be a hard day. The face also had some real thought behind it—so many doctors look like brand-new Sheetrock walls with no rooms behind them. His eyes were so dark they looked the way several friends of mine looked in Vietnam as I watched them die right under my hands when I was helpless to bring them back. And he didn't ask me to sit, facing him across his crowded desk. He sat me on an old maple bench, and he took a hard chair right beside me. The first thing he said was "What's best for you, Noble?"

That was also a help. I knew my options here were by no means unlimited. He was a psychiatrist after all and couldn't help checking my psyche out. Still his interest in my opinion bolstered me to say "Jon, maybe what's best for *me* is not the question." I think I expected at least mild applause.

But he said "All right. You ask me one." Then he gave his first smile, very slight but a smile.

So this was going to be a game. All right then—a very sober game. I'd played them before, all my year in the war. I hadn't planned to ask this—I hadn't really known it was still a question anywhere in my mind; but I heard myself say "Have you people ever come to any understanding, in all these years, of why she killed my brother and sister?"

Dr. Daniel waited at least ten seconds, a long time for a man as burdened as he. Then he touched my mother's enormous file on the desk before him. It was more dog-eared than the saddest dog in the saddest pound. "I guess I'm the only man alive who might even risk an answer for you—I've read through this like I told you I would. But no, nobody's ever reached a conclusion. If the truth be told, nobody's really asked her; and that represents no failure, I think. In the various forms of paranoid schizophrenia—and hers is way the least treatable of all—such answers are harder to track than young birds. I think I can swear your mother never knew, no doctor who's left any notes on her knew; and Noble, Jon Daniel will never know now. This is what I think matters—she's a calm old woman, we're prepared to trust her, any harm left in her is too cold to burn."

The last thing I'd expected here was these bleak scraps of—what? maybe poetry—from this young doctor, warden, gatekeeper of the Pit. Whether my mother was calm now or not, I at least felt easier in my own skin. So I took a serious pause of my own, and then I said "Please keep her here another ten days. See, I'm back in the old house where we lived when she lost it. I've made a lot of structural changes and brightened things up—I hope it won't spook her—but I do need to fix a thing or two. After that I guess I'll be ready as I can be, and I'll come get her."

Dr. Daniel said "Ten days or two weeks, no problem at all." Then he looked at me longer than I needed him to at such a tough moment, and at last he said "But you said we ought to bring Edith in here with us now. Do you still want that?"

Somehow in the last five minutes with him, I'd mislaid my plan. And now I even said "You think that's advisable?"

He said "*Advisable* may not be the word, but I think it would be a good idea. I've already checked with her nurse this morning. She's awake and calm. I can send for her now."

I suddenly realized a thing that amazed me. I hadn't been in a room this small with Edith Norfleet since the time she materialized so weirdly in Hesta's kitchen after all her mysterious weeks on the road. In an instant I went as cold as I'd been since the Easter morning, and I actually stood up where I was.

Dr. Daniel waited to see what I'd do—no words, no look of approval or otherwise.

Finally I sat down and said "Let's see her."

He picked up the phone to call her ward, then set it back down. "I'll go get her. She seems to like me. I can get her prepared."

When she came in the door and saw me, she smiled—a slightly overweight woman with clean white hair in a dress that wasn't standard-issue—a blue-and-white seersucker dress that seemed a little light for winter, but then she hadn't been outdoors in God knew when. And pale as she was, she—or some kind person—had put a little rouge on her face and trimmed her eyebrows. It took me five seconds to realize I was still sitting down; I got up quickly and smiled back at her.

She spoke before I could. "I told you you'd last."

"Yes ma'am, you did." For the first time in years, I tried to remember when we'd last exchanged even a routine family cheek-kiss. Nothing came to mind and I didn't feel any honest need to step forward now and offer such a gesture. When had I last touched her, come to think of it?

Dr. Daniel got us seated—Mother was watching him entirely, not me—and then he said "Noble, Edith and I have talked a little recently about the possibility of her moving on from here."

Mother never dropped her eyes from his good face, and now she nodded agreement to something—just the fact that they'd talked?

I said "Miss Edith, how does that sound to you?"

Finally she looked across toward me, a slow kind of roam over my face and down my chest to my hands. Then she looked back to Dr. Daniel and said "He's always had my father's hands." She pointed quickly at my hands.

Dr. Daniel said "He's a strong man, I'm sure."

Mother said "I very much hope that's true," and she faced me at last. "You ready now?"

Slowly I had to say "Tell me *ready* for what, ma'm?"

And she actually laughed. "I haven't heard the word *ma'm* since I was a girl."

We all three laughed awhile, and then I told her I worked with a number of "seniors" in my job, and I still used *ma'm* and *sir* a good deal.

To the room in general, she said "I've been looking forward to seniorhood." And then she asked me "When does it start?"

I said "Senior status?" and balked for a moment.

Dr. Daniel said "Edith, it starts when you want it to. How about if it starts two weeks from now?"

You could literally watch the question bore its way into her mind—the drugs had slowed her that much. When the challenge got to whatever core was in her, she paused and let it settle. Then she pointed slightly in my direction and said to the doctor "With this gentleman here? You mean, *starting* with him?" Her voice was dead-level, but she hadn't met my eyes again.

Dr. Daniel said "I mean starting with your family, Edith—your good son Noble here. He's living back in your old home now. He's fixed it up. He's got a fine dependable job. You've done so well on your new medication."

Mother said "I'm big as the fattest pig on anybody's farm."

Dr. Daniel nodded. "People do gain weight on your medications; but when you leave here and have real control of your own daily diet, plus your exercise program, I bet you'll *lose* weight."

Mother said "My exercise program will just be sleeping round the clock when nobody else is screaming nearby" but she almost smiled. Then she looked to me. "I know what I did to your brother and sister. Do you know I was totally out of my mind?"

I nodded Yes.

"Do you hold it against me?"

I said "No, ma'm. That's *way* behind us."

"If I come to you now, must you punish me for it?"

I thought of how right she was to say *must*. However I might now think I should help her, would hate or something worse overtake me? I was thinking faster than I'd thought since working under fire in Nam. Finally I managed to speak the words plainly. "I doubt I could punish anybody but Hitler, and I know you were *troubled* when you made your mistakes."

Again she seemed to let that go far down into whatever mind she'd kept. Then she finally spoke. It was the most I'd heard her say since I was a boy; and the sentences came out, one by one, very slowly and almost like they were surfacing up from a deep thick ocean. "Hitler, Lord God—when have I thought of him? Well, I got a mustache when I had the change of life; but I shave it off every three or four days. I use those little disposable razors that couldn't harm a gnat. If I ever look too much like Hitler, you tell me." By the end she was almost smiling again.

Dr. Daniel laughed hard.

I told Edith Norfleet I'd inform her if she did.

The three of us talked—mostly Jon and I—for another five minutes. Then I could see Mother slipping off from us. Her eyes dropped down as if she were dozing; and when they'd reopen, she'd look to her doctor as if on the verge of begging to get back to something a lot more predictable than what we were weaving here between us. Jon Daniel didn't seem to notice it.

So finally I said "I've got to head on back to work now."

And Mother stood up, quick as any strong school girl.

I didn't want to say too much—the doctor and I still had to talk between us and make the long choices that were pending—but I did offer her my hand to shake again.

She gave no sign of refusing to touch me—no frown at all—but she didn't raise her hand. And while Jon Daniel was on the phone, asking a nurse to come and get Edith Norfleet, she looked me full in the face and said "I don't see any way on Earth I could stay with you, sir." Her head was shaking a slow but firm No.

The nurse was on us before I could rally and risk an answer.

But the doctor said "Edith, don't you worry now. You and I can talk through it."

My mother turned the same hard eyes on him. "There's no room for one single word on this subject. This man you've brought in here has caused every pain I've suffered." In case there was any uncertainty at all, she aimed a finger in my direction. I was the man.

After the nurse came and Mother departed, Jon Daniel sat me back down again and explained what I knew, in principle anyhow—that such quick changes of response are normal in a person with my mother's history.

I'd of course seen the same lightning change in old Mr. Jamison at work the day before. But in his case—an elderly black man with no doubt a bottomless warehouse of reasons to loathe white males—I well understood that any such "change" was in fact an escapee from his truest fears and hatreds. What did Edith Norfleet's last words to me mean? I had no serious fears she'd constitute a physical threat. I'd get all my sharp-edged kitchen equipment stashed far out of reach, but could my mind stand the long succession of hurtful changes that might well mark our time together, however long or short? I didn't bring up that fear with Jon Daniel. I figured I could phone him to talk about many things before we made a final decision.

When I left this time, though, he took my hand and said "I know it's rough."

I had to say "Yes sir, rough as a *cob*"—an old country saying from the days of outdoor privies and corn-cob butt-wipes.

Jon said "But if you can ride out the first hard weeks, you *may* be glad you did." He turned my hand loose and took a real pause. "Maybe *glad*'s not the word, but then I'm a doctor not a poet, right?"

I said "Me either, though I may need to be—a lot sooner than I planned."

Turned out the drive back home was also rough. By now I'd pretty much tucked my chin and taken the bit deep into my mouth. A few hours before I turned her in to the Law long ago, she said a thing I'd never quite shook—that now I was our family's whole story and could tell it my way. All right then, I'd *tell* it as far as she'd let me, till she or I went to our graves at least. My mother was coming out of her prison and moving in with me, at least till I found out that either she or I couldn't live in such an arrangement. I knew I'd have to be braced for hard times; no doubt she would too. Jarret's Irene would kindly sub for me for at least a few days till I could either find somebody permanent by way of a sitter, or until I realized Mother would need more care than a sitter or I could provide in the family home. So now I'd go home, call Dr. Daniel and tell him that Yes I'd be most grateful if he could keep Mother another two weeks; and then I'd come get her.

Meanwhile I'd need to do a number of things, some of them physical and some of them not. You recall that when I remodeled Mother's house, I tore out all the old interior walls except for the ones around my bedroom and the original bath. That meant there was now no private space for Mother. Should I beg my carpenters to come back in and throw up temporary walls so Mother could have a little privacy before we decided what the long-range future looked like? Or maybe I could just buy a few temporary panel screens and give her at least a chance to dress and undress on her own. And the whole of our family had always got by with the one bathroom. That should be no problem.

The problem I could *see* pouring toward me down the road was the mental part; and the part that concerned me right now was the state of my own mind, way more than my mother's. If she moved in with me, and wound up staying, not only would I worry about being triggered back into depression, I'd also truly have to concede to myself that—in strong middle age—I'd likely be surrendering any last chance at companionship with a normal woman, till Edith Norfleet died anyhow (and by *normal woman* I just mean one that would take me for love and fun and not for pity). Hell, I knew a lot about tending old people; so if I took informed good care of my mother, she could easily live another twenty years.

When I got home, I spent the rest of a very long day just sitting alone in the kitchen and sketching out possible ways to build a private room for Edith—I was trying to begin to think of her as Edith. I figured right off that I shouldn't try to rebuild her old bedroom. If she had any memory of the house at all, that space might well be too hard for her. Not to mention the space where Arch and Adelle's bunk beds had been. By midafternoon I'd come up with three conceivable plans—the one bathroom would have to serve us both. And by five-thirty I decided to call up Jarret and Irene and ask them over for a pizza supper and some practical advice. Irene answered. I could hear Jarret tell her he had a basketball game on TV, but Irene called out "Jarret, you and I are needed." She said if I'd phone in the pizza order, they'd pick it up in half an hour. I'd long since known it, but I had to sit there and remind myself that nobody on Earth had truer friends.

By the time they got to me, Jarret had calmed down about the missed game; and we just sat among rejected pizza crusts and remnants of salad, looked at the sketches and made a few more. By nine P.M., as Jarret began to draw his fifth or sixth idea—they were getting grander and grander as time passed—I had to gently call a halt and ask them to tell me what to do now. I'd reached the point where I knew I must take some sane outside advice and simply go with it.

As always at any such moment, Irene waited for Jarret to speak first, and he wandered on with dreamlike contingencies for two or three minutes; but he finally said "Your mother's a woman, Noble. Let the woman here tell us."

So we both turned to watch the two near-perfect sides of Irene's face. She leafed back through the drawings slowly, then shut her eyes and laid her hands on them. I didn't know whether she was praying or somehow consulting my mother by supernatural means—I'd never seen her go spooky before—or maybe she was simply resting and thinking. And then she looked down the length of the house, the long empty space, and said "This poor lady's slept in wards for years. A private room might scare her. Noble, I say let's get a nice single bed and a set of new sheets that are some pale color, not hospital white. We'll set the bed up right by the door to your room, at the start anyhow, where she can hear you breathing and turning over at night. The bathroom is big enough for her to shut the door and have some privacy. She can dress in there, if that's what she wants. Surely this woman has been scared enough since she left here."

Jarret just nodded. "She's done her time."

And that's what we did, the two of them helping me every evening when I got home from work till Irene had fixed it the way she thought right. Jarret and I barely offered a syllable to alter her instincts for the job we were facing, and of course Irene stuck by her offer to be with Mother in the hours I was gone. She said she had a very slight memory of seeing Mother back when she and Jarret were courting in 1967, and Jarret introduced them in the supermarket produce department—"She was wearing a bright green dress, her hair was glossy dark, and she told me I looked like the queen of the Congo" (Irene still looked a good deal like such a person). Then she also said, without my asking, that she had no qualms at all about Edith Norfleet proving too much for her. Jarret and I stole a glance at each other, and we both blinked hard; but neither one of us tried to deny her.

Two weeks later, half an hour short of home, Mother and I were riding along in the gathering dusk. Leaving the prison had been a little easier than I expected. Dr. Daniel was having a family emergency of his own, so he didn't come out to say goodbye to one of the facility's longest-lasting inmates. But a pair of the guards—African-American men so dark that the whites of their eyes were actually gray—followed us right out the door to my car. They looked fairly young, neither one over forty; but one of them told me he'd known my mother for twenty years, and the other one told me "Ms. Norfleet has always been a lady." That younger one carried her very few belongings in a black plastic bag, the kind you rake leaves in; and once we actually got to the car, both men asked Mother if they "could hug her neck." I hadn't heard that expression since Hesta James died.

Mother didn't say a word, but she stood in place and let both men embrace her lightly. Just before I helped her sit down, she faced each guard. I figured she'd say "So long" or "Thanks," but she said "Remember how good you are."

After that, in our whole trip, she hardly spoke again; and she took several naps. Of all things, a little way into our distance, we had a flat tire. It deflated slowly so I got to one of the last surviving service stations that possessed a live mechanic. He said he'd fix us if we waited awhile. I offered Mother the chance to get out and take a walk with me—a little mall was nearby—but she shook her head No and kept her place. She did accept my offer of a Pepsi which she drank with a new slow dignity, new to me anyhow. When the fellow was ready to fix the tire, I asked Mother if she didn't want to step out while he raised the car on his lift. Again she shook her head, and the fellow didn't mind—he went on and jacked her up with the car, five feet off the ground. She sat up there, again as if that unexpected elevation were merely her due. Even when I could see her nodding off, she stayed upright and self-composed.

And once we were back on the road, she went on sleeping most of the way, neither of us saying anything. Then just before night really set in, her eyes came open; and she looked all around her. Where we were at that point was deep pinewoods and occasional fields with dry cornstalks or wild dead grass. It had to be more natural life than she'd seen in three decades, but she didn't greet it with any words or any strong expression on her face. Whenever I'd catch a glimpse of her profile, she'd be nearly blank, though there did seem to be hints that someday now she might be able to frown or smile.

I was looking to my left at the used-car museum that had been there forever but was quietly rusting away in the open. It seemed like something the Martians had left here a billion years ago—some sort of instructional device for their heirs, which had to be us, but what was their lesson? It was gone now surely.

Then Mother laughed suddenly.

When I looked over she was pointing out her window, not especially pointing for me to see but really for herself. What she'd seen was a place I'd also noticed on my last few trips—a franchise biscuit café, supremely

Southern, called Biscuitville but under the Biscuitville logo, new owners had draped a hand-lettered sign saying "Now a Chino-Hispanico Enterprise!" Her finger kept pointing, long after we'd passed that peculiar promise.

Then I realized she couldn't have had any real idea of how the population around her had changed in her absence—the great many Asians who'd arrived since Vietnam and, in far greater numbers, the Mexicans who now were doing every mean stoop-labor job that blacks had done when Mother departed. In fact I suddenly saw the world around us as a truly alien creation. She'd had a hard enough time with her last two worlds (our family and her prison); what on Earth could she do with this one? Well, it was too complicated a tale to tell now—assuming I had a true and usable tale to tell—so I just said "It's a new world, Mother."

I thought she nodded but she didn't turn toward me. She stayed hunched over against the passenger door. Then at maybe ten seconds before full dark, she leaned forward and rummaged awhile in her bag of belongings. Eventually she came up with a long envelope that had once been white. It was so old and used and had plainly been folded a thousand times, it looked like some communication from Caesar. First she pressed it up to her lips, an apparent dry kiss. Then she held it out to me.

Of course I kept driving, but I took the envelope. "You want me to open this?" (it wasn't sealed, just closed with a rubber band so old it had almost turned to gum).

She nodded Yes, firmly.

So I set it on my right thigh and fished through the contents—several dozen small slips of paper of various colors, all seeming old. I couldn't take my eyes from the road; but slim as the light was, I managed to see that each slip bore the name and address of another person, mostly women. They were all in different handwritings from Mother's. A few addresses were from other states, but mostly they specified North Carolina. I set the envelope on the seat between us. "Are these some old friends?"

She nodded Yes again.

And we drove onward.

Then at almost the moment it was full night, she looked square at me and said very clearly "You notify every one of them that Edith is out now."

I told her I would.

The side-porch light was on when we pulled up in the drive; but with the new paint and all the other work I'd done, I'd figured she might not recognize it—at first anyhow. I killed the engine and meant to sit a moment. I wasn't especially overwhelmed, I didn't expect any revelations on either side, but it had been a long important day, and I guess I needed a peaceful deep breath.

Mother opened her door, though, and moved to step out. Was she truly eager to see the old place?

But I took her elbow. "Wait just a second and I'll come help you."

She swung both her legs out but stayed in her seat. I'd left the headlights on to guide us; and when I came around to offer my help, she calmly took four steps away from the car, then reached up under her dress, pulled her pants down and squatted to pee. It had been a long wait.

I almost said a quick word to delay her till we were indoors, but I knew no neighbors were watching. And if they were, then they could just learn to get over it fast.

After a lengthy outpour of water—the poor soul must have been very near bursting—she got to her feet and headed to the porch.

I came on behind her with the keys in one hand and her leaf bag in the other.

When I got up onto the porch, she said "My envelope—" It was still in the car. I said I'd get it in a minute.

She said "No, now."

Then once I had it safe back in her hand, I unlocked the door, switched the inside light on and guided her in. (I'd left Tarn, the dog, with a friend from work. I figured a dog, even one as good as Tarn, might confuse her at first.)

She let me lead her two or three yards inward, and then she halted.

I didn't want to make a big production number of it, so I didn't say anything at first—except to point to the bathroom and mention that it was in good working order. But I stood quiet behind her and wondered what she could be making, if anything, of such a sight, so old and so new. Did she recognize anything here at all?

She stayed on in place, looking slowly around her—the far end, the length of the space where I'd cleared out so many walls, the chairs I'd put by the TV set, the kitchen in its former place but with all-new fixtures. At last she didn't turn to face me, but she said "You've done a real job, I can see."

I couldn't tell whether that was praise or blame or, even, whether that showed she recognized the place at all; but anyhow I told a slight lie. I said "I meant to honor the occasion."

She thought about that and decided to nod. Then she said "It's way past suppertime," and she took off her coat.

By half past eight we'd eaten the macaroni and cheese I'd made from scratch last night and kept ready for us. I figured she'd been served a bland diet, to say the least, for all these years and that I shouldn't try to change it too soon. Any trained nurse knows you can actually kill people with the wrong food too fast, however fine it tastes. She ate an encouraging portion of the macaroni, the boiled green peas and the peach cobbler with vanilla ice cream (which the Jameses had left while I was on the road). When she was finished I quietly reminded her to fold her cloth napkin and put it in the napkin ring by her plate. We'd always done that throughout my childhood, and I kept up the habit.

She remembered the exact old way she used to fold it.

I couldn't have described it in advance, but I knew it when she did it.

And then she stood up. She hadn't spoken again since her first remark on entering the new space, but now she said "I'm very much afraid I need to lie down, but I don't see where."

So I led her to the far end and showed her the new bed behind the new screens that Irene and I had bought. I waited to see if she'd show an objection, but she simply started to pull off the sweatshirt she'd worn all day. I'd suggested to Irene that she and Mother could go out and buy clothes whenever they were ready, but now I realized she might not have any clothes at all in her leaf bag. She'd dropped it at her feet as if it were useless now. What would she wear for sleeping? While she went on with her undressing then, I went to my room, found a big old shirt, came back and held it through the screens toward her. She took it and, when I glimpsed her next, she was headed for the bathroom with a tiny hand-towel and a prison-issue toothbrush. In another five minutes, she'd come back out, climbed into bed and turned to face the wall—not another word between us.

I had to figure we'd had a lucky first day. I dimmed the lights and waited for firm sounds of sleep from Mother before I phoned the Jameses with the news. Both of them shared my relief of course; and since tomorrow was Sunday, I suggested they drop by after church (they were loyal churchgoers) and let Mother get acquainted with them both before Irene turned up on Monday morning to sit with her while I went to work. Then when I hung up, I suddenly knew I was tired as Mother. It was only nine-thirty, but I quietly got my own teeth brushed and went to bed in my old room with the door half open.

I generally sleep on my right side, turned away from the door and facing the window; and for whatever reason I seldom do much turning in the night. So at four in the morning, when I was somewhere near the pit of the Planet Earth in a deep and badly-needed sleep cycle—where my heart had very nearly stopped beating and my limbs were almost paralyzed—a person (or a sizable fumbling creature) moved into my bed and lay close beside me. I don't recall that it touched me at first. I don't think it made any noise at all, not beyond the noise of a body on sheets. When my eyes came open, I was still facing away from the door; but I'd left a dim light on in the main room in case Mother woke in the night, disoriented.

The first thing I felt seemed to be cold terror. My body was cold from head to foot, and the air above me seemed bitterly cold. Slowly I put out a hand behind me and felt around—another human body, colder than me but just warm enough to be still alive. In the confusion of sudden waking, I literally didn't think of my mother. *Who in hell could this be?* A person who lives alone in America, even an able-bodied male, can find himself in strange troubles in the night. I was just about to roll to my back and face my visitor.

Mother spoke out then. "I think I've frozen."

And so it seemed. I rolled to face her and laid my knowledgeable palm on her forehead—truly cold. I sat upright and Yes the air around us was cold. I normally turned the thermostat down to sixty-five on winter nights (the winter solstice was not a week off), but something was wrong. The heat pump had failed. I said "Let me go check on the furnace, Mother. You stay warm here." As I left I took a quilt I kept at the foot of the bed and laid it across her.

The lights still worked but, as I looked in the breaker box, I could see that the breaker for the heat pump had tripped. I wondered how safe it would be to trip it on again and see what happened, but I couldn't get a maintenance man at this hour, and I couldn't let Mother die of exposure on her first night here. I tripped the breaker and at first nothing happened, good or bad; but in thirty seconds the splendid sound of the heat pump started. On my way back to bed, I checked the thermometer over the thermostat—forty-two degrees, our first cold night and these walls had no real insulation. When would I have waked up if Mother hadn't joined me?

When I got to my room, she was where I'd left her—turned to her own left side, away from where I normally slept. No humane way I could lead her back to her own chilly sheets and ask her to trust me that the air would improve in another half hour. I sat on the edge of the bed near her feet and explained what had happened.

I could see her head nodding, though she didn't speak again.

Now I need to be truthful about what I did next. I made it seem like I was a good nurse, adjusting her cover; but in fact I pulled all the cover down below her waist and gave a quick look at both her hands—was there any sharp object anywhere near her, even a kitchen fork?

Nothing, no.

I went around to my usual place, climbed in and tried to sleep again. By then, across the space between us, her body seemed maybe five degrees warmer. And somehow within the next half hour, I managed to ease on into sleep—nothing like as deep as my earlier dive but rest all the same.

For the first time in easy memory, my alarm clock woke me. It was seven o'clock, Sunday morning. I'd forgot to turn it off the night before. The light at the window was so clear you could tell it was piercing cold outside, but the air in the room was almost warm again, and again I reached behind me—nobody there. I'd worn pajamas which I almost never do, so I got up quickly and looked for Mother. Her own bed was carefully made in a tight style she'd clearly learned in prison, and her clothes from yesterday were folded at the foot. I almost failed to notice the major surprise. Somehow—somewhere in this house since bedtime last night—she'd found the magnificent knife Jarret gave me long ago, the one that belonged to Hesta's ancestor who came here from Africa on a slave boat. It was lying in full sight on top of Mother's folded clothes. I told myself she meant me to see it and hide it away like the rest of the dangerous tools. That may have been too easy an assumption, but of course I put it in my pocket at once and meant to keep it in my hospital locker.

Meanwhile there was no sign of Mother down at the kitchen end, but the bathroom door was shut, so I paused there to listen. At first I heard nothing, so I said "Miss Edith, are you in there?"

No answer, no sound.

This time I knocked and was on the verge of trying the handle.

But she said "I'm taking an old-timey tub bath."

How long since she could have had a real soaking? I said "Are you happy?" At first I thought how sappy that sounded, but then I thought *I'm sure nobody's asked her that in a million years.* I said "You need anything from me?"

A very long wait, then she said "You're supposed to just call me Edith."

I said "Yes ma'm."

"Don't *ma'm* me. I told you that's out of style."

She had indeed—and I was relishing the thought of Mother as an up-to-date fashion guru—so I laughed and said "Well, breakfast is still in style at this house. I'll go cook breakfast."

She just said "Breakfast is mighty late."

I waited at the door long enough to hope she didn't slip getting out of the deep tub (I hadn't replaced the fine ancient tub), and I silently reminded myself to ask for her medication bottles so I could be sure she took them as prescribed. Then I went to the kitchen. I started the coffee, then laid the bacon strips in a cold pan and turned the burner to medium low—I cook bacon *slow* and it comes out first-rate. Then I mixed the batter for buckwheat cakes and laid out the brown eggs to fry, over easy. I'd also laid in real maple syrup. It would be the same breakfast she'd had the last time she and I ate together, at the café before I turned her in. I doubted she'd recall, and of course I wouldn't have minded if she hadn't, but I took a small pleasure in assembling the feast. As soon as she dressed, I'd move into final gear.

Meanwhile I set the table—just the cutlery and napkins, no flowers or cheerful placecards and mats, though a girl at work had urged me to get some "bright welcome-home stuff." I started to switch on the small TV beside the stove (I have one of those for watching games or the news while I'm cooking). But then I thought *She's probably seen enough TV in prison to last her forever,* so I stood at the window over the sink and just looked out past the porch to the side yard. I hadn't thought of my old vision in the dogwood tree for maybe twenty years—the hands which had seemed to beckon at me from among white blossoms that Easter morning—but the tree was still there, stripped bare for winter and as crooked as dogwoods mostly are. No hands waving me onward today. I heard the sound of the bathroom door coming open behind me. I didn't turn—*Give her plenty of room.*

Little quiet clicks and shuffles from behind the screens round her bed, then finally the shuffling footsteps down the length of the house in my direction—toward the kitchen at least.

When I finally turned she was pulling out her chair at the table. I don't know why I expected a change, but she looked very much as she had last night. She was wearing her N.C. State basketball sweatshirt over her seersucker dress and her same white sneakers. She'd washed her hair and combed it carefully; and when I finally made myself look closely at her face, Yes it was changed—rested and younger by maybe three years. I came up behind her and offered to push her chair when she sat.

If she understood my gesture at all, she entirely ignored it.

So I didn't ask but poured her black coffee with enough caffeine to sober up a platoon of Marines on any Sunday morning.

No words whatever and she still didn't sit, but she took up her mug and tasted the coffee. Then she said a word. "Strong."

"Is that a complaint?"

She said "No sir."

"Call me Noble please—*sir* is also out of style."

She nodded to that, then sat on her own and waited in what seemed a genuine calm while the winter light took the whole table, flooding her face.

Though I had both hands busy at the stove, I offered to tilt the blinds and shade her.

She shook her head No and went on giving a fairly convincing likeness of an older woman having a peaceful morning in her home or maybe at the home of a host she trusted to work behind her.

So I cooked on and in time I served two bountiful plates and sat down at the head of the table, my place ever since my mother disappeared. I wish I could tell you it somehow felt natural; but for maybe the first five minutes of the meal, I thought the lid of my skull might lift off, and I'd see my brain spew out in all directions—the pressure of all this strangeness was so enormous and scary. I couldn't really face her, and she didn't ask for any attention, but it wasn't as if I wanted her *gone* or felt the least need or desire to harm her. And yet my mind kept repeating the question she'd asked me in Dr. Daniel's office—"*If I come to you now, must you punish me for it?*" The word *must* had seemed almost unbearable when she said it, but I couldn't stop dreading the fact that she'd planted that one word in me.

All through my silence she ate along steadily, polite as always in her table manners. If she realized this had been the menu at our last meal together, she gave no sign; but there did seem to be some hint she was relishing the various items, especially the bacon. When she finished the three strips I'd supplied, I silently got up and brought her two more.

Finally she said "A surprise."

I was seated by then. "What's surprising?" I smiled and, in a quick glance, she seemed to field it like an excellent catch.

She pointed to the perfect bacon on her plate. When she'd left this house, I could hardly cook toast much less good bacon (good bacon cooks are rarer than fine French chefs). Then she ate both strips, continued till she'd absolutely cleaned her plate; and then she went back to sitting patiently while I finished up beside her.

My left hand was no more than twenty inches from her right hand as it lay on the top of her folded napkin. Did either one of us truly want to touch hands, for even a moment? There's way too much of my brain that's secret for me to answer that, from my point of view anyhow. And who knows what Edith Norfleet thinks at any moment of the day or night, any month or year? Anyhow I had to move us onward, so I said "Is there anything else I can get you?" I was thinking of course of any more food or another harmless beverage.

Edith said "Nail clippers."

I looked to her hands—both were flat on the table now. The nails were fairly closely trimmed, and I wondered if they did that to her in prison as a guard against scratching herself or others. But I had clippers, sure. They were not far behind me on the window ledge above the sink. Before I cleared a single dish, I went to get them; and when I handed them to her, I said "Careful now. Those nails are already short."

But she'd pushed her chair well back from the table and pulled her right foot from the canvas shoe. Her toenails were long and earnest as blades. Who the hell had left her in this condition—but then nobody ever used their toenails as weapons, right? Slowly she brought the foot up and laid it on her left knee. Then she held out her hand for the clippers.

I held them out to her, but then I thought different. I said "Just a moment."

That finally got her full attention. Her eyes fixed on me, and her face seemed to clear in a real new way. I could have been wrong, but maybe she was seeing me for the first time in a good many years.

So I stepped back to the sink and quickly rinsed my hands. Then I moved toward her slowly—nothing scary now. I got down on one knee beside her and said the word "Permission?" It was something I'd learned to say in the Army with wounded men if they were still conscious enough to care—could you touch them in some truly private injured place?

She seemed to nod Yes.

Lightly I took the foot she'd set on her knee and set it on my thigh. The nails were the kind old people get, thick as rhino horn and gnarled; but her long tub bath had softened them some. I took the big clippers and started to work, and within five seconds I suddenly dreaded that Arch and

Adelle would pour back in here as vengeful ghosts and devastate us both. Nothing happened of course, not from those two long-gone children. So I clipped on as gently as I could. Mother flinched a time or two at first, but there was no blood. I hadn't nicked her. I'd done this before, several hundred times if not thousands in the course of my job. Never to this one woman to be sure. But this time I moved unusually slowly to be entirely right. She watched every move as if it were some kind of distant event, not simple home business; and the whole task took us maybe eight minutes. By the end it almost didn't seem a task.

When I put the last foot back in its shoe, she said the words "Thank you."

I said "You bet."

She asked what we were betting on.

I told her I didn't have the slightest idea.

That seemed to ease her. She extended both feet in the warm air and sent a short laugh in their new trimmed direction.

Since I started working on her, she hadn't faced me. That was a temporary relief. Still I thought she seemed ready to pause here awhile. On my part, I felt at least half ready for whatever came next in this old place that was hers after all. So in my mind from that same minute, we started over; and God knows where we'll ever wind up.

REYNOLDS PRICE

Reynolds Price was born in Macon, North Carolina in 1933. Educated at Duke University and, as a Rhodes Scholar, at Merton College, Oxford University, he has taught at Duke since 1958 and is James B. Duke Professor of English. His first novel, *A Long and Happy Life,* was published in 1962 and won the William Faulkner Award. His sixth novel, *Kate Vaiden,* was published in 1986 and won the National Book Critics Circle Award. *Noble Norfleet* is his twelfth novel. He has published thirty-four volumes of fiction, poetry, plays, essays and translations. He is a member of the American Academy of Arts and Letters, and his work has been translated into sixteen languages.